THIS UNITED STATE

COLIN FORBES

THIS
UNITED STATE

MACMILLAN

First published 1999 by Macmillan

an imprint of Macmillan Publishers Ltd
25 Eccleston Place, London SW1W 9NF
and Basingstoke

Associated companies throughout the world

ISBN 0 333 74441 1

1 3 5 7 9 8 6 4 2

A CIP catalogue record for this book is available from
the British Library.

Typeset by SetSystems Ltd, Saffron Walden, Essex
Printed and bound in Great Britain by
Mackays of Chatham plc, Chatham, Kent

Author's Note

All the characters portrayed are creatures of the author's imagination and bear no relationship to any living person.

The same principle of pure invention applies to all residences or apartments whether located in Britain or Europe.

For

JANET

Prologue

Paula Grey's nightmare began at exactly 10 p.m. on a cold February night in Albemarle Street, the heart of Mayfair, London.

She walked out of Brown's Hotel, left hand clutching the collar of her coat, shoulder bag slung over her right arm. A taxi pulled in to the kerb, the door was flung open, a man dived out. Cord Dillon, Deputy Director of the CIA. The last person in the world she'd expected to see. He stopped abruptly, close to her.

'Paula, get away from me. You'll get killed.'

'Cord, what the devil—'

'That white Cadillac coming up the street. Full of men trying to shoot me—'

'Come this way. My town. Don't argue!'

She grabbed the right arm of the large American, guided him swiftly up the street, away from the approaching car. The rear window on their side lowered as she hustled Dillon. She had a glimpse of a bald man holding a handgun.

A taxi cut in front of the Cadillac, delaying it. They were already beyond the façade of Brown's Hotel. She hauled Dillon into the partial shelter of a setback, in front of a large plate-glass window. *Crack!* She had heard no sound of a shot fired. Glancing behind them she saw the bullet hole in the window. A huge triangular section of plate glass toppled. Inwards, away from them.

'Keep moving,' she ordered. 'A truck has swerved in front of the Cadillac.'

'You'd better leave me—'

'Shut up! Keep moving,' she repeated. 'I didn't hear a shot.'

'They use silencers on their weapons.'

Arriving at a T-junction, she urged him across the road, turned right along Grafton Street. This was crazy – trying to murder someone in Mayfair. At that time of night Albemarle Street was usually a haven of peace. Just a few parked cars. No one on foot – not in this cold. All the buildings without lights – except for the hotel. Out of sight of Albemarle Street she heard a vehicle coming up behind them. A taxi with its lights on. She flagged it down.

'Victoria Station,' she told the driver.

'Hop in, then.'

They were already inside, the door closed. The taxi drove off. Paula glanced through the rear window. The Cadillac had turned the corner. The driver had seen them board the taxi. Paula extracted a ten-pound note from her wallet. Leaning forward, she passed it through a gap in the glass partition separating them from the driver.

'This is your tip. There's a white Cadillac behind us. Please lose it well before we reach Victoria. My husband's behind the wheel.'

'Righty-ho, lady. Will do.'

The cockney cabbie tucked the banknote inside a pocket, closed the partition, pressed his foot down. Paula lost track of the devious route the cabbie took, racing down side streets, turning at speed round corners. When she looked back there was no sign of the Cadillac. She heaved a sigh of relief.

'Why Victoria Station?' Dillon asked.

'Don't want to lead them to Park Crescent.'

'They know about Tweed's HQ . . .'

2

'Leave it to me.'

'Have you got a gun?' he whispered.

'Yes.'

Her right hand was inside the special compartment of her shoulder bag, holding the butt of her Browning .32. She glanced at Dillon. His craggy, clean-shaven face was so familiar. She noticed a touch of grey in his hair, his haggard drawn look.

'Better let me have the gun,' he suggested.

'No. Leave it to me. You're short of sleep, aren't you?'

'I came straight off a flight from Montreal at Heathrow. Didn't sleep a wink during the whole flight. Never stopped checking the other passengers.'

'Why from Montreal?'

'I guessed they'd be watching flights from Washington to London. So I flew to Montreal first.'

'Who is after you?'

'A small army. Let's keep that for Tweed . . .'

Arriving at Victoria Station, she paid the driver, led Dillon inside the cavernous terminus. Very few people about. An old man in shabby clothes sat on a seat, drinking from a bottle of beer. She scanned the concourse, then led the American back the way they had come.

'What are we doing now?' he asked.

'I wanted that cab we took to go away. I saw a passenger get inside while we were walking in. There's another taxi. We'll take that to Park Crescent.'

Dillon wore a camelhair coat, carried a large executive case. In his late forties, he had a pugnacious jaw, a strong nose and a determined mouth. In many ways he was a typical American – tall, wide-shouldered, the build of a quarterback. He lapsed into silence during the drive. Paula sensed he was near the end of his tether and kept quiet. She checked the rear window several times. No Cadillac.

3

She was paying the driver generously as he turned into Park Crescent. They left the cab and she pushed open the heavy door with a plate alongside it on the wall. General & Cumbria Assurance. George, the guard, was standing behind his desk as they entered the hall.

'Tweed's in, I hope?' she queried.

'Yes. He has Bob Newman with him.'

'Ask Monica to tell Tweed we're on our way up. This is Cord Dillon.'

'I remember Mr Dillon.'

'And I remember you, sharpie,' the American growled.

'The strain's telling on you,' Paula rebuked him as they mounted the staircase.

When she opened the door on the first floor Tweed was seated in his swivel chair behind his desk, hands clasped behind the back of his neck. Of medium height, clean-shaven, of a certain age, he wore horn-rimmed glasses. The Deputy Director of the SIS was a man you could pass in the street without noticing, something which had proved invaluable in his work. He stood up to shake hands, his penetrating eyes studying his visitor as he ushered him to a chair facing the desk.

'You look washed out, Cord.'

'You could say that. Tell you about it when I get my heard screwed on again.'

'You've met Monica.'

Dillon twisted round to look at the small middle-aged woman who kept her grey hair tied up in a bun. Tweed's close assistant for many years, she sat behind her desk which supported several telephones, a fax, a word processor.

'Guess I should remember you, Monica, by now. Can't understand why you go on working for this monster.'

'Coffee?' Monica suggested, standing up. 'How do you like it these days?'

'Black as sin.' Dillon grunted. 'And there's plenty of that comin' into town here from the States.'

'What kind of sin is that?' queried Bob Newman.

The world-famous foreign correspondent, in his forties, had fair hair, a wry smile on his strong face. Also clean-shaven, five feet ten tall, he was well built and women found him engaging – an advantage he exploited only spasmodically. Fully vetted, he had worked with Tweed in a number of dangerous situations.

'Hi, Bob. Been a long time.' Dillon paused. 'The sin is a wolf pack of professional thugs infiltrating this country by devious routes. Top guns.'

'Give me a devious route.'

'The one they like is fly to Paris from Washington. Then come in here by Eurostar by rail.'

'Why that route?'

'I guess they figure there's less of a check arriving by train. They dress as Brits – the contemporary businessman's uniform. A suit as black as night, a flash tie. They really worked this one out. Suits in different sizes bought here, flown to the States. They carry American diplomatic passports.'

'Here's your coffee,' said Monica, who had returned with a tray.

'Thanks. This I really need.'

'While you're drinking it maybe I could tell Tweed and Bob how we came to meet this evening,' Paula suggested.

She did, after Dillon had nodded his agreement. Paula had a gift for describing complex events tersely. Tweed watched her as she sat behind her desk, hands clasped in her lap. She was very calm, matter-of-fact.

'It was a million-to-one chance that I came out of

5

Brown's when I did,' she concluded. 'I'd met my informant, then waited ten minutes to give the informant time to get clear without risk of our being seen together.'

'I think, Cord, we'd better get you out of London,' suggested Tweed. 'Right away. Bob, could you drive Cord down to the Bunker in Kent? You left your luggage downstairs, I presume, Cord?'

'Left it on the carousel at Heathrow. Decided I'd better get a cab out to Brown's fast. I remembered you use the hotel a lot. I was going to phone you from there. Didn't want to risk leading the people after me here. To hell with my case back at the airport.'

'Any personal identification on the case – or inside it?' Tweed persisted.

'No. The label only gives the flight number and destination. Not a thing inside.'

'Then we'd better get moving down to Kent,' Newman said, standing up. 'We'll go in my Merc.'

'Not so fast. Wait.' Tweed took a pair of powerful night glasses out of a drawer, went towards the large window masked by drawn curtains. 'Monica, switch out the lights, please.'

With the room in darkness he opened a gap in the curtains, focused the glasses. His action had created an air of tension. No one moved but Paula was close enough to peer over his shoulder. The large office overlooking Regent's Park in the distance was full of an ominous silence.

'Did you get the registration number of that Cadillac?' Tweed asked.

'Of course.'

She recited it from memory. Tweed called over Newman, handed him the glasses. Then he quietly walked back and sat behind his desk before he spoke.

'The same Cadillac is parked on the main road at the

right-hand entrance to Park Crescent. Four men inside. Obviously watching this building.

'I'll go out and move them. They're illegally parked,' Newman announced after checking through the glasses.

'You can't,' Tweed informed him. 'Paula, have you checked the car too?'

'Yes, it's the same one.'

She handed the glasses back to Tweed, having first carefully closed the curtains. Monica put on the lights again. Everyone stared at each other and Dillon then spoke.

'We're trapped.'

'I'm going out to move the bastards,' Newman insisted.

'You can't,' Tweed repeated. 'That Cadillac has diplomatic plates.'

'And the rats inside will all have diplomatic passports,' Dillon told them. 'Before I left Washington I heard the staff at the Grosvenor Square Embassy had been increased by two hundred. All with diplomatic passports.'

'You still want Cord taken to the Bunker?' Newman demanded.

'Yes. As soon as possible.'

'Then we'll leave now. We'll alter your appearance.' Standing up, Newman studied the American. 'We're about the same build – you can wear my trench coat. That camelhair is a giveaway.'

'And Marler's beret is in the cupboard,' chimed in Paula as she fetched it. 'The fit may be a bit tight but it will do the trick.'

'And,' Tweed suggested, 'walk more slowly, Cord. Not your usual stride. Take shorter steps. Body language identifies anyone.'

'I'll put your executive case inside a canvas holder,' Monica decided.

7

'And I'll carry it,' said Newman.

'Harry,' instructed Tweed over his phone. 'A small immediate problem. We're smuggling someone out of the building into Newman's car. A white Cadillac with gunmen is parked on the main road. I don't think they'll risk opening fire on our visitor – although they did just that in Albemarle Street.'

'I'll wait outside with a smoke bomb.'

'Only use it if you have to. They're on their way down.'

'They'll shoot me if they can,' Dillon said over his shoulder at the doorway. 'And I have things to tell you . . .'

'Tell Bob on your way to the Bunker. He'll relay what you say to me. If necessary, I can call you down there on a safe phone. Go!'

The beret was a tight fit but it concealed the American's hair. The trench coat Newman had given him fitted better. The camelhair coat was left on a chair. The horn-rimmed glasses, provided by Paula, perched comfortably on his broken nose. George, the guard, waited by the door after taking a brief call from Tweed.

'Where's Harry Butler?' Newman asked, the executive case tucked under his arm inside its canvas covering.

'Went outside,' George reported. 'Said he was going for a quick stroll . . .'

Butler, a burly man, armed with a Walther 9mm automatic pistol inside his hip holster, had his right hand holding the smoke bomb concealed under his windcheater. He was halfway to where the Cadillac was parked when Newman emerged, unlocked his Merc, ushered Dillon into the front passenger seat. Unfortunately, the exhausted American forgot to disguise his normal way of walking.

As Newman started the engine Butler was in two minds about hurling the smoke bomb at the Cadillac.

Remembering Tweed's explicit order he resisted the temptation until trouble started. Newman drove at speed out of the Crescent, turned along the main road in the opposite direction to where the enemy was parked. As he did so the driver of the Cadillac, who had kept the engine running, purred after him.

'They're coming,' said Dillon, twisted round in his seat.

'Let them,' Newman replied. 'Plenty of time to lose them on the way south . . .'

'This sounds to be getting more dangerous,' Paula said to Tweed when the two men had left.

'It's certainly getting interesting,' Tweed responded, seated casually in his chair, hands again clasped behind his head.

'Interesting? Two hundred men sent to the American Embassy. A brazen attempt to murder the Deputy Director of the CIA in the middle of London in an American car carrying diplomatic plates. Another horde of thugs flying to Paris, then coming in here via Eurostar. And you call it interesting?'

'I need more data to work out what is happening. Cord Dillon may provide that when he talks to Newman.'

'Why did you take all that trouble creating the Bunker down in Kent? It's almost like a stand-by headquarters.'

'That's exactly what it is. In case we have to move out of here quickly.'

'This is getting scary. You only got back from Washington three days ago. But you didn't seem surprised when Dillon turned up.'

'I heard a rumour from a source that Cord was on his way out – that he was being replaced by a man called Ed Osborne. A very tough ruthless gentleman.'

'I meant to ask you,' Paula went on, 'where is Marler?'

'He's in Paris, meeting some of his informants. He'll be back any day now.'

'And you'll go all cryptic on me if I ask you what Marler is trying to find out.'

'Incidentally,' Tweed mused, 'I found Washington in a state of feverish activity. No one knew why – or they wouldn't tell me. Like a volcano about to explode.'

'You didn't answer my question about Marler.'

'Marler?' Tweed suppressed a yawn. 'He's attempting to discover who assassinated our Prime Minister in Manchester last week.'

1

'This traffic is as bad as I've seen in LA,' Dillon commented. 'And the Cadillac has picked us up again – it's three cars behind us.'

Newman was driving his Merc among an armada of speeding cars in the dark moonless night. He chose his moment carefully for the manoeuvre when a huge truck masked the Cadillac, then turned in to the left-hand lane. They climbed a hill via a slip road and the traffic had disappeared.

'We were on the M20 motorway driving south,' Newman explained. 'So much traffic at this late hour was due to the accident which held us up further back. Now the poor devils back on the motorway are ramming their feet down to get home hours late.' He checked his rear-view mirror again. 'We've lost the Cadillac.'

'So where are we headed for?'

'Canterbury, eventually. Which is where we don't want to go. So at the next roundabout we'll turn back and rejoin the M20. I want to turn off it at Junction Eight. Are you too tired to talk?'

'Guess not. Strange things are happening in Washington. A heavy delegation is heading for Britain – some have arrived.'

'Give me some names.'

'Sharon Mandeville, for one. Taking up some position at the Grosvenor Square Embassy.'

'She's made the papers a lot. A girl friend of the President?'

'Never. She's too smart to risk upsetting the President's wife. She carries a lot of clout. Then Jefferson Morgenstern himself is coming over,' Dillon said.

'The Secretary of State. Very big gun. Went to the States from Europe as a young man. They say he would have been the President one day if he'd been born an American. Clever as Kissinger and similar background. Here's the roundabout – we can turn back, rejoin the motorway . . .'

Scores of headlights glared like marauding tigers. Side by side, almost touching, a torrent of cars roared south at dangerous speeds. Risks were taken. Everyone seemed to sacrifice safety in their urge to get home, knowing they were very late.

'Never seen anything like this,' Dillon commented, glancing back. 'Like an enemy attack.'

'Were you looking for the enemy?'

'No. I guess you lost him for good.'

'Don't be too sure . . .'

They reached Junction Eight, left the motorway for a country lane. The sudden quiet and solitude in the night was startling. Dillon sagged with relief. Newman turned off the lane down another empty hedge-lined country road, switched his beams full on as they approached a series of bends.

'Anyone else important coming in from Washington?' Newman asked.

'Yes. Ed Osborne, the roughneck who has got my job. A tough guy. Dangerous. You never know what he's thinking.'

'Any ideas why they tried to gun you down in Albermarle Street?'

'I knew too much. I'd ferreted around checking on

12

people. A huge operation is planned but I couldn't get the hang of it.'

Newman sensed that his companion was making an effort to think. The American was close to a state of total exhaustion. They had driven some distance along the lonely country lane without meeting another car when the headlights illuminated a road sign. PARHAM.

'This is an old village,' Newman commented. 'There's another one of the same name in Suffolk, I think. And a good three miles north of us is a very good hotel, Chilston Park. Tweed has stayed there—' He broke off as they swung round a bend, dipped his headlights, slowed down. 'Well, well – look what's ahead of us. The white Cadillac.'

'Have you got a gun I could have?' Dillon growled, jerking himself into his normal alertness.

'I'm carrying my usual Smith & Wesson .38 – and you can't have it. We don't want to start a shooting war out here.'

'Those guys in the Cadillac will see us.'

'I don't think so. I've experienced this before. One car tails another, loses it. From then on the occupants are looking in front of them. They rarely look back. Might be interesting to see where they're headed for.'

Parham was a working village. Even at this late hour lights were on in pubs and restaurants. The Cadillac drove slowly along a narrow street lined on both sides with white clapboard houses. Newman was familiar with the place laid out in a series of chessboard-like squares, one leading into another, an old village typical of the area. A cutting icy wind had been blowing in the countryside but the village was sheltered by the layout of its buildings.

'Looks like they've arrived somewhere,' Dillon commented.

13

'Let's find out where . . .'

Everyone was indoors. There was not a soul on the deserted narrow streets, lit at intervals by ancient lanterns. They followed the Cadillac into one small square and then it turned into another even smaller square. Newman parked his Merc by the kerb.

'That's a dead end. Let's follow on foot.'

'Bloody cold night,' Dillon observed, standing on the cobbled pavement.

'You'll feel it – you're very tired. Now where have they gone?'

Leading the way, he peered round a corner into the smaller square. The Cadillac had stopped at one side in front of tall gates which gave no view of what lay beyond them. On either side the property was further concealed by old twelve-foot-high brick walls. A hand protruded from the driver's window. Both huge gates slowly moved inwards automatically.

'That's weird,' Newman whispered as Dillon stared over his left shoulder. 'They're electronically controlled and the driver has the gadget which opens them.'

They watched as the Cadillac drove slowly forward up a curving drive. At the end they had a glimpse of a large grim-looking mansion built of stone with turrets at the corners. All the windows were masked by closed shutters and there was no sign that the place was inhabited – until the front door opened and light streamed on to the drive. Then the gates closed and the mansion was gone.

'Let's take a closer look,' Newman suggested.

They crept into the square and on the three other sides were more high brick walls almost hiding the large houses behind them. Newman handed Dillon a pair of gloves, told him to put them on. The American was shivering with cold and fatigue. Newman had a torch in his left hand as they reached the outside of the mansion

14

where the Cadillac had disappeared. The gates were constructed of tall iron rails and attached to them on the inside were sheets of metal, obstructing any view. On the right-hand brick pillar was a metal plate which gave the name when Newman switched on his torch. *Irongates.*

'Let's get back to the car,' Newman whispered.

Once inside the Merc they savoured the warmth of the heaters. Newman had left the engine running in case they had to make a quick getaway. He drove back into the large square, took another exit and suddenly Parham vanished and they were out in lonely countryside, moving along another deserted country lane.

'Irongates,' Newman said half to himself. 'I know who lives there. Sir Guy Strangeways. Spent over twenty years in the States building up a property empire. Never met him.'

'I have,' Dillon told him. 'A mogul. Had the right contacts with certain senators in Washington. Money changes hands and he always got permission to buy an old building to erect a high rise after demolition. He was over there a long time but stayed very British.'

'Never went native?'

'I guess that's what you think we Yanks are – just a bunch of natives.'

'I always respect other people's opinion of themselves,' Newman joked back.

Dillon must have woken up to be capable of a wisecrack. Probably the brief excursion into the cold night air, Newman decided. They drove on through the night, each smoking a cigarette. Dillon looked to his left. The moon had risen, illuminating a range of low hills which fanned away into the distance.

'Thought this part of the world was flat,' he remarked.

'It is. Wait till we get beyond Ashford. A very ordinary town but difficult to drive through if you don't know it. Have to get into the right lane – otherwise you're going miles out of your way.'

Newman had turned onto a wide highway which stretched south as far as the eye could see. No traffic now. Hardly a village. They passed through a deserted Ashford and continued along a highway. Dillon saw what Newman had meant. The world was flat as a billiard table. On both sides fields stretched away to nowhere. Newman slowed down as they approached a signpost. Ivychurch. He turned left off the highway, drove slowly along a twisting narrow lane. Ivychurch was an isolated church, a handful of cottages, then nothing.

'What is the Bunker?' Dillon asked.

'You'll see when we get there.'

'Where are we now?'

'A place where you'll be safe,' Newman said.

'Tells me everything.'

'Gunmen in Cadillacs will never track us here.'

'You don't know those boys.'

'Maybe I do,' Newman retorted. 'Let's stop for a minute. We could get out for a moment.'

Putting on Newman's gloves again, Dillon stepped out of the car. The wind had dropped, the night air was still. There was a heavy silence which seemed to press down on him. Bare hedges, networks of bleak twigs, lined the narrow road. Beyond them flat fields sprawled away for ever. Here and there was dotted the silhouette of a leafless tree, its extremities like skeletal hands clawing upwards towards the sky. No sign of any kind of habitation or life anywhere.

'Too damned quiet for my liking,' Dillon commented. 'Reminds me of certain parts of the Midwest back home. Where the hell are we?'

'We're inside Romney Marsh,' said Newman who

had joined him. 'This side of that hedge is a wide gulley, a drainage ditch – they're all over the place.'

'Think I'd like to get back in the car. Where to next?'

'Deeper inside the marsh . . .'

Dillon lost track of the number of lonely forks and crossroads they came across. Newman seemed to know the way even with his headlights dimmed. They met no traffic, passed through two tiny villages with no lights in the huddled cottages. Dillon thought this was the most desolate area he'd ever encountered. Would they ever reach the mysterious Bunker?

'Will I be out here long?' he eventually asked without enthusiasm.

'You'll be safe. That's the object of the exercise.'

'Anyone to talk to?'

'Yes. We're close now.'

Ahead of them, just off the road, a strange shape loomed in the night. A large round windmill, its four huge sails motionless. Dillon stared at this first sign of civilization.

'What's that thing?'

'A windmill. The only one on Romney Marsh, so far as I know. It's five storeys high and they say the view from the top is awesome.'

'There was a light in the top window. It's gone out. Any idea who lives there?'

'A hermit, I gather. No one ever sees him. We're close to the Bunker – and not so far from the sea. At times a mist, even a fog, comes rolling in. The atmosphere is pretty ghostly when that happens.'

'Goddam ghostly now . . .'

Newman had slowed to a crawl. They turned yet another curving bend and what appeared to be an old farm gate closed off a track leading through a gap in the hedge. Stopping as the car faced the gate, Newman flashed his lights in an irregular series. The gate slowly swung inwards, Newman drove through on to the track, the gate closed behind them.

'While I remember,' Dillon remarked, 'Washington has also sent a team of top communication experts to the Embassy. No idea why.'

'Useful to know.'

A large old tumbledown farmhouse stood at the end of the track. Laid out on three sides it enclosed a cobbled yard Newman drove onto. They got out of the Merc as an old wooden door opened and a small plump woman in her fifties was framed in the light behind her. She wore a flowered print dress with an apron over it. Dillon's idea of a typical Brit's farmer's wife.

She had red apple cheeks and a warm smile. Her grey hair was tied back in a bun, reminding the American of Monica's hairstyle. She ushered her guests inside and Newman patted her affectionately on the rump.

'Meet your hostess, Cord. This is Mrs Carson. She runs the Bunker and we take orders from her. This is Cord Dillon – just arrived from the States,' he introduced. 'No sleep for days and hungry as a hunter, I'm sure.'

'That door has a solid steel plate on the inside,' observed Dillon as Mrs Carson closed and attended to three sophisticated locks.

'Behind the closed shutters of every window is armour-plated glass,' Newman told him.

'Place looks like a series of shacks and turns out to be a fortress. Who protects it if we come under attack?'

'I do,' said Mrs Carson. 'Not that anyone will find us.'

Dillon stared at her in disbelief. His expression became more pronounced as she slipped her hand inside a large canvas shopping bag perched on a shelf and took out a Heckler & Koch MP5 9mm sub-machine-gun.

Effortlessly she inserted a magazine, then, still smiling, looked at Newman.

'Is he trustworthy?'

'Totally. And he may be staying here for a while. He's on the run from gunmen.'

'You'd better have this, then,' she said, handing the weapon to Dillon. 'You do know how to use it?' she asked.

'Cord is very familiar with it,' Newman assured her.

'I have another one ready hanging in a cupboard,' she assured her guest. 'And down in the cellars we have an armoury. Handguns, machine-guns, smoke bombs, grenades. I'll show you, then you can have supper. Tweed phoned me, said he thought you'd need a good hot home-cooked meal . . .'

They were standing in a large kitchen-breakfast room with a wooden table laid for three people to eat. The atmosphere was warm, cosy and Dillon detected a slight humming sound.

'You've even got air-conditioning, for Pete's sake.'

'We have,' Newman told him. 'Powered by our own generator. We have a spare as back-up in case of a breakdown.'

'Are you a drinking man?' Mrs Carson enquired. 'I haven't Bourbon but I could supply a double Scotch. You look as though you could do with it.'

'I sure could. Thank you.'

'Nothing for me,' Newman chimed in. 'I may have to drive back tonight. I'll know when I've phoned Tweed.'

Their hostess had walked quickly to check what was happening on her Aga cooker, lifting lids of several pans, stirring one gently. She then opened a cupboard, brought out a bottle of very expensive whisky, poured a generous double Scotch, handed it to her guest.

'Get that inside you. Supper's not quite ready. I'll show you your sleeping quarters underground.'

19

'This is what I need.' Dillon took a large swallow. 'The weakness of this place is that a mob of gunmen could ignore that gate, scramble through the hedge. They'd be all round this farmhouse before you knew what was happening.'

'No, they couldn't,' Mrs Carson said sharply. 'Look at this.' She opened a large white metal panel on the wall. Behind it was a series of small porthole windows, each with a number above it. 'There's an electric tripwire all round all the hedges. If there are intruders a buzzer goes off. I only have to check this and whichever number is flashing tells me which sectors they're coming in through. Three teenage boys did try to break in. I knew where, saw them coming through my binoculars, went out to meet them with my miniature water cannon. The pressure on the jet is very powerful. It is so strong I knocked them over when I aimed it at them. And it was in winter so they were soaked in icy water. They ran for it, I can tell you.'

'I'm dazed,' reacted Dillon.

'Must be the drink,' Mrs Carson suggested, pulling his leg. 'Now follow me . . .'

Crossing to the opposite panelled wall, she pressed a button. A section of the panel slid back, revealing a doorway. Telling Dillon to mind the steps, she switched on a light and led the way down a flight of concrete steps with a handrail on either side.

The underground complex was vast, one cellar leading to another. The floors, walls and tunnel-like ceiling were painted white. There was nothing primitive about the complex. Opening one door, she ushered her visitor into a comfortably furnished bedroom with a modern bathroom leading off it. Dillon could hardly believe it as she escorted him to more rooms. Taking out two keys she unlocked a steel door and a light came on inside automatically.

'The armoury.'

Dillon stared in amazement as he wandered slowly round, looking at the racks holding a vast majority of guns amd grenades. Below each rack holding weapons was another rack stacked with the correct ammunition. As he turned round Mrs Carson was checking her watch.

'Must have taken you ages to excavate all this,' he said.

'No, it didn't,' Newman explained. 'This place has a history of being used by smugglers in the old days. The cellars were here so they just had to be modernized. Marler supervised the development.'

'Difficult to keep it secret. Workers talk.'

'Not the workers who created this. Marler recruited them in Eastern Europe. Brought them in secretly aboard small launches by night. They never knew where they were. Marler could talk to them in their own lingo. A lot were miners – used to working underground. They never left the place until it was done. Then they were transported secretly back to where they'd come from – with a load of dollars, their favourite currency. For the sophisticated technical work we used boffins from Park Crescent and the training mansion down in Surrey.'

'You two will be gabbling all night and the meal is ready,' Mrs Carson said severely.

'What do they think about the assassination of our Prime Minister in the States?' Newman asked as they followed her upstairs.

'The rumour they spread was it was the work of a splinter group of the IRA.'

'Who might "they" be?'

'Top-flight spin doctors. Incidentally, a team of them have also arrived at the Embassy. Experts in TV, radio and the Internet. Why, I don't know. Something very big is being planned.' Dillon drank the rest of his Scotch.

21

'When I said top-flight I meant it – recruited from private industry.'

'What do these spin doctors do in America?' Newman asked as they entered the kitchen-breakfast room.

'Brainwash people. Which is why the President is still in the White House.'

'Stop chattering, you two,' Mrs Carson ordered. 'Supper is ready. I hope you like roast beef and Yorkshire pudding, Mr Dillon?'

'Lead me to it. And call me Cord.'

'I must call Tweed from the office here,' Newman told her. 'I may not have time to eat anything. Back in a minute.'

Opening another door, he went into a small room after switching on the light. Closing the door, he sat in a swivel chair behind a desk. Its surface contained a phone, the machine Mrs Carson typed her reports on, but no fax. Security was very tight at the Bunker. When Monica answered he asked for Tweed.

'I'm on the line . . .' Tweed's voice.

'Be careful. I'm not sure this is any longer a safe phone.' Newman was recalling Dillon's reference to a team of communication experts arriving at Grosvenor Square. 'I've arrived here with the parcel.'

'Any important data?'

'Yes, but I don't think I should give you it on the phone. I propose to drive straight back. I can give it to you in the morning.'

'I'd like it tonight. I'll wait for you.'

'I'm on my way . . .'

Going back into the other room, he found Dillon ravenously devouring Mrs Carson's meal. She had refilled his whisky glass and was eating a small portion herself. The aroma made Newman suddenly feel hungry. Mrs Carson was an excellent cook, besides being a crack shot with a variety of weapons.

'Sorry,' he said, 'but I have to drive straight back to London. Cord, I have a full outfit of clothes down here, including pyjamas and shaving kit. You'll find everything you need.'

'Thank you, friend, for bringing me here.' Dillon had stood up, left hand holding his napkin, shaking Newman's with the other. 'How long will I be in the Bunker?'

'Until it's safe to come out. There are fifteen acres round the farmhouse. Mrs Carson will show you outside. She'll give you some old farmer's clothes in case anyone sees you. They'll think you're a yokel.'

'Better practise my yokel accent.'

Mrs Carson was putting the plates of food in a warming drawer. She produced her keys, ready to let Newman out.

'One more thing, Cord, before I go. All the things you have seen recently, what has happened to you. Any idea what it's all about?'

'The whole grim business is a mystery.'

Mrs Carson dimmed the lights before unlocking the main door. Newman hugged her, went out into the breathtaking cold air to his car. He drove slowly back up the track and Mrs Carson timed the opening of the gate perfectly.

Leaving the farmhouse behind, he turned his lights on full beam. As he navigated the maze of lanes half his mind was on driving the car, half on what Dillon had told him. Why did he have a sense of imminent doom?

2

When Newman walked into Tweed's office in the middle of the night there was a tense atmosphere. Paula and Monica sat silently behind their desks. Tweed was leaning forward in his chair chatting to a man in his thirties who Newman detested. Basil Windermere.

Leaning against a wall, smoking a king-size, stood Marler, a key member of Tweed's team, reputed to be the best marksman in the whole of Western Europe. Shorter than Newman – he was five feet seven tall – Marler was slim and, as usual, smartly dressed. Wearing a grey suit with a Prince of Wales check, his trouser creases were knife-edged, his white shirt fresh from the dry-cleaner, his blue silk tie decorated with a subtle chain link design. His dark hair was neatly trimmed and his clean-shaven face had an expression suggesting he was miles away in thought.

'I think you know Basil,' Tweed said.

'We've met,' Newman replied without enthusiasm.

'Good to see you, old chap.' Windermere extended a hand which Newman ignored. 'What a bunch of night birds we are,' he went on in the soft voice which made many women fall over backwards. 'I'm here to put Tweed on to a good thing. Heard on the grapevine Sharon Mandeville is up for insurance to the tune of thirty million dollars.'

'Thought she was in America,' Newman lied.

'My dear chap, you're the world's greatest foreign correspondent. Thought you kept up to date. The delectable Sharon is in town here. Some big job with the American Embassy. Thought of Tweed at once. His insurance company handles protective cover against eminent souls being kidnapped.'

Which confirmed to Newman that Windermere had no idea the General & Cumbria Assurance plate on the door at the entrance was a cover for the secret HQ of the SIS. He simply nodded. Windermere turned back to Tweed.

'I'm a bit short of the readies.' He flicked index finger and thumb. 'Some of the folding stuff for the tip would most certainly not come amiss.'

'Who is proposing to pay this enormous premium?' Tweed asked.

'Presumably her latest billionaire boy friend back in the US of A.'

'Presumably? The boy friend has a name?'

'Sorry, I haven't got that far.'

'Maybe this anonymous boy friend hasn't got that far either. He could just hope to.'

'Mind if I smoke?'

Windermere extracted a gold cigarette case from his pocket and selected a Turkish cigarette with a flourish. On the outside was engraved a royal-looking crown. Undoubtedly a fake, Newman decided. Just like the owner.

Windermere was known to live off rich women. Once a male model, he was six feet tall, and took care to keep his weight down at a health club. This was one place where he encountered female prospects. He was wearing a white linen suit, which was ridiculous for the time of the year. He hardly ever stopped smiling, which Newman described as a smirk. He had a head of thick hair and too-perfect features.

'How did you come by this information?' Tweed probed.

'Met her at a party, didn't I? She's something else

25

again – a real knock-out. Intelligent with it. Told me during the course of our long conversation. Think she rather liked me. I took the liberty of mentioning your organization.'

'Who mentioned my name?'

'She did, as a matter of fact. Hope you don't mind.'

'Don't do it again,' Tweed said. 'I don't tout for any of my business.'

'Any chance of a small advance for the tip?'

'None at all. Too vague.'

'A couple of hundred pounds would make me happy.'

'Try your luck with the lottery.'

'Suppose I'd better love you and leave you.' Windermere stood up. The hostile reception has at last penetrated his thick skull, Newman said to himself. 'I had a coat.'

Monica was already taking down his white coat from a hook. She simply handed it to him without making any effort to help him on with it. Windermere stood very still, glancing round the spartan office. Newman could see why he would be attractive to a certain type of woman.

'Don't think I know you,' Windermere remarked, addressing Marler.

'You don't.'

'And what a charming lady,' Windermere went on, gazing at Paula.

She had her head down, studying some papers. She appeared not to have heard him.

'Newman will accompany you to the door,' Tweed told him.

'Let's keep in touch, you beautiful people . . .'

Newman had the door open. As he closed it and followed their visitor down the stairs Windermere began talking over his shoulder.

'I say, Bob, maybe we could have a drink together one evening.'

'Maybe.'

'I frequent Bentleys in Swallow Street. You'd find me there about eight in the evening. In their sumptuous bar downstairs.'

'George,' Newman called out, 'our visitor is leaving if you'd unlock the door . . .'

Windermere paused just outside the exit to button up his coat. Newman stayed inside after glancing outside across the Crescent. As George was closing the door Newman ran back upstairs into Tweed's office. He looked annoyed.

'Why on earth did you let that gigolo get inside here?' he asked.

'To see if he'd provide me with any information. He did,' Tweed replied.

'You mean about someone insuring Sharon Mandeville for thirty million dollars?'

'No. That was nonsense. His excuse for coming here to check up on my staff, to identify as many as he could. Marler caught on and so did Paula. So who could be anxious to penetrate our organization?'

'Sharon Mandeville,' Newman suggested.

'Not necessarily. Windermere babbles on but is a stranger to the truth. He may not have even met the delectable Sharon, as he described her.'

'Well,' Newman retorted as he sat down, 'you might be interested to know that everyone who leaves this building is being photographed. This time a Lincoln Continental is parked out on the main road. I caught a glimpse of a man aiming a camera at Windermere as he was leaving.'

'Get a picture of you?' Tweed enquired.

'No, I kept well back.'

'I don't understand it,' protested Paula. 'First a Cadillac, now a Lincoln Continental. If it is an American gang you'd think they'd use British cars. Why American?'

'To intimidate us,' Tweed told her. 'I expect their campaign to get a lot worse, even more aggressive. But enough of that. Bob, you arrived back just in time. Marler has discovered who assassinated the Prime Minister.'

'Up to a point,' Marler drawled in his upper-crust accent. 'I'm just back from Paris,' he explained to Newman. 'While over in Gay Paree, as the Yanks used to call it, I met three of my informants in various seedy parts of the city. The first two couldn't give me the time of day.'

'They didn't know?' Newman queried.

'The question scared them stiff. Then I met the Ear in another low-down bar.'

'The Ear?' asked Paula, puzzled.

'That's his nickname in the French underworld. He has guts. He plays both sides. For money, of course. By both sides I'm referring to the police and the underworld. And what I have just said is utterly confidential.'

'He's playing a dangerous game,' Newman commented.

'With great skill,' Marler told him. 'He's helped the Prefect of Paris to put some very lethal saboteurs – especially from Algeria – behind bars. Bit of a patriot, the Ear.'

'And was he also scared stiff when you put the question to him?' Newman suggested.

'Not a bit of it. He just doubled his normal fee, which I was happy to pay. This assassin is pretty damned good. He killed that French Minister a few weeks ago, the one who made a powerful speech attacking the Americans, accusing them of trying to take over the world. A month before that he took out Heinz Keller, the German politician who is anti-American and might have one day become Chancellor of Germany.'

'Sounds as though the assassin is American,' Paula speculated.

'That's one thing he isn't,' Marler corrected her. 'It makes sense when you come to think of it. If he was ever caught Washington would take worldwide flak. Our friends across the Atlantic appear to have become more sophisticated. Diabolical might be the word.'

'Do we get a name?' Newman prodded impatiently.

'Why not?' Marler said offhandedly. 'He's called the Phantom.'

'He sounds very sinister,' Paula commented.

'Sinister,' Marler agreed, 'highly skilled and professional. He assassinated the heavily guarded Prime Minister. Afterwards Special Branch never found the rifle he used. Imagine smuggling that away with a horde of security men checking everyone they could find. And the devil's firing point was the rooftop of a warehouse used for storing books. A repeat of Dallas all those years ago.'

'Has the Ear any clue as to his nationality?' pressed Newman.

'He's European, could even be an Englishman. The Ear stressed that was a rumour. He didn't know whether it was true.'

'So his identity is completely unknown?' Newman asked.

'Completely. Rumoured he has a number of girl friends. Again the Ear emphasized that also was no more than a rumour.'

'So we have no name.'

'None at all. As yet. The Ear is going on digging. Speaks good English. He'll contact me here if he finds out more. Monica, he'll give the name of Maurice and leave a message. Maybe just an address and a time and day.'

'Any other clue?'

'Only one, which could be misleading. The Ear says it's known he's paid in dollars. That could be a smoke-screen. Could be some other nation is his paymaster.'

'You've done well,' said Tweed. 'Now I think we should all hear what Bob has to tell us.' He looked at Marler. 'He has just returned from escorting Cord Dillon to the Bunker. Come to think of it, maybe Paula had better put you in the picture first. She had a bit of an adventure late yesterday evening.'

'A bit of an adventure,' Paula repeated ironically. 'That's one way of describing it. Here goes . . .'

Newman and Marler watched her as she gave a terse account of her experience with Cord Dillon. She started with her leaving the hotel in Albermarle Street. Yet again Newman thought that Paula was a very attractive woman. In her thirties, slim with a very good pair of legs, her black hair had a glossy sheen, falling just short of her collar. She had a face with strong bone structure and a determined chin. Her voice was soft but he could hear clearly every word she said. Smartly dressed in a two-piece navy blue suit she was a woman men in the street turned to look at. Above all else she was enor-mously capable and had great stamina.

'That's it,' she ended. 'And that's enough, I'd say.'

'Tough cookie,' said Marler, squeezing her shoulder.

'If you say so.'

'Now it's Bob's turn to bring us up to date,' Tweed suggested.

He made occasional notes as Newman outlined everything that had happened when he'd escorted Dillon to the Bunker. Monica was recording the entire story, as she had with Paula.

'That's it,' Newman concluded, 'to quote Paula.'

'It's a lot,' Tweed said. 'Some of it very disturbing. Now we have quite an array of players in this grim game. Monica, in the morning I'd like you to start building profiles on these people. Jefferson Morgenstern, esteemed Secretary of State, whom I know. Ed Osborne, the new Deputy Director of the CIA. Both now in London. Sir Guy Strangeways, who lives at the mansion called Irongates at Parham. And . . .' He paused. 'Sharon Mandeville. Her whole history, which could be interesting.' He stared at the ceiling. 'Add Basil Windermere to that list if you would, please.'

'I'll start tonight,' Monica announced. 'New York is five hours behind us and some of my contacts work late. Then San Francisco – they're eight hours behind us so I'll catch my contacts there. Don't look at me like that. I'm fresh as a daisy.'

The phone rang. Monica picked it up, frowned, put her hand over the mouthpiece, looked at Marler.

'It's for you. Maurice on the line . . .'

'Marler speaking. Where are you?'

'On a public phone at Heathrow. Need to see you urgently.'

'Hang on a moment.'

Marler put his own hand over the mouthpiece. He spoke to Tweed, spoke quickly.

'The Ear has turned up at Heathrow. Needs to speak to me. Can he come here? He thinks I work for an insurance outfit.'

'Yes. Tell him to take a cab. You can see him in the waiting room.'

The moment Marler ended the brief call, giving the Ear the address, Tweed reacted. He gestured towards the curtained windows.

'We have to shift that Lincoln Continental fast. If it's still there they'll photograph the Ear.'

'I'll handle that,' Newman said, standing up. 'There's

going to be an accident. I'll take the four-wheel drive. Could you get the police here yesterday?'

'I'll call my old sparring partner, Roy Buchanan at the Yard. I've already reported the attack in Albemarle Street. He's not best pleased with the Americans.'

Newman snatched a scarf and his trench coat off a hook. As he hurried downstairs he was wrapping the scarf round the lower part of his face, covering his nose. He pulled up the military-style lapels, darted out of the front door and round a corner to where the vehicle with a ram was parked.

He drove a roundabout route which brought him back on to the main road. A plane was flying very low overhead as he saw the Lincoln parked at the edge of the Crescent. He pressed his foot down, slammed into the back of the American car, smashing up its rear badly. He then reversed, dragged metal off the damaged car.

'Made of tin,' he said under his breath.

Turning off his engine, he got out as a tough-looking passenger jumped out of the back of the Lincoln. He had a boxer's nose and the face of a moron. His head was bald. He swaggered up to Newman, now standing in the road as a car pulled up alongside him. Chief Inspector Roy Buchanan was at the wheel with Sergeant Warden, a heavily built man, beside him.

'Buddy, I'm going to put all your teeth down your throat,' the thug said with a rough American accent.

'You could try it,' Newman replied.

'Here it comes then. Kiss your mouth goodbye.'

Newman timed it carefully. As a huge bunched fist slammed towards his mouth he jerked his head sideways, took the punch on the side of his jaw. The fist slid off him. Newman made no attempt to retaliate as Buchanan appeared with Sergeant Warden on his heels.

'This car was illegally parked,' Newman told him. 'A

plane flew very low and distracted me. You don't expect a car parked here at any time.'

'And I saw you assault this man,' Buchanan said grimly.

'Who the friggin' hell are you?' the thug snarled.

'Chief Inspector Buchanan of the CID . . .'

'I've got a diplomatic passport, so frig off.'

The thug raised one finger almost in Buchanan's face. Then he swore foully.

'I wish you hadn't done that. Diplomatic passport? And the moon is blue.'

'Look at the licence plates, buddy,' the thug ranted on. 'It has diplomatic plates.'

In the distance Newman heard police sirens coming closer. Buchanan folded his arms and studied the thug. Then three police cars with uniformed officers aboard appeared and pulled up, forming a laager round the Lincoln. Buchanan was a tall lanky man in his forties, wearing a dark suit, an ironic smile on his lean intelligent face. Villains found something disturbing about his casual manner.

'I think I recognize you,' he said, addressing the thug. 'A bank raid in the City a month ago. No money taken – just security documents about a number of prominent British citizens. One of the raiders was caught on video. Looked just like you. I'd appreciate you giving me your name.'

'See for yourself,' snapped the American. 'Hank Waltz.' He shoved a diplomatic passport at Buchanan.

'Sometimes known as Diamond Waltz,' Newman remarked. 'Look at all the flashy rings on his stubby fingers. Fakes, I imagine.'

'Fakes?' Waltz clenched his fist. 'You want another one?'

'Cool it, chum.'

One of the uniformed police who had spilled out of the cars stood very close to the American. While Buchanan was examining the passport the driver of the Lincoln stepped out and came up to them.

Tall, with the appearance of a quarterback, his manner was very different from Waltz's. Wearing a Savile Row suit, he was smiling, conciliatory, his American accent soft.

'Good evening. I'm sorry if we've caused any problems. And Hank has a short fuse. He's fond of the Lincoln – normally he drives the car.'

'I do?'

'Hank, now the Chief Inspector has given you back your passport I suggest you get back to your seat. Every time you open that mouth of yours you shove your big foot in it.'

'Could I have your name?' Buchanan asked stiffly.

'Sure. Why not? I'm Chuck Venacki. Attaché at the Embassy.'

'What are your duties, sir?' Buchanan demanded.

'Public relations.'

'Diamond Waltz isn't going to help you much in that direction.'

'Hank Waltz. He's a bodyguard. The new American Ambassador has received threatening warnings. You'd like to see my passport?'

'I don't think that will be necessary.'

As Buchanan replied there was a heavy rumbling noise behind them. Newman glanced back to see a large vehicle transporter pulling in behind them. Men in working clothes got out, started walking round the Lincoln.

'May I ask what is happening?' Venacki enquired smoothly.

'You may. That Lincoln is blocking the road. The transporter will take it on board and move it. I'll get you a taxi.'

'Taxi coming,' said Newman, flagging it down.

'Good.' Buchanan stared coldly at Venacki. 'That will take you wherever you were going.'

'And the Lincoln?'

'Will be dumped outside your Embassy. Alternatively it could be taken to a maintenance garage to see if repair is possible.'

'No, thank you,' Venacki said hastily. 'Grosvenor Square will do nicely.'

'Then I suggest all four of you are on your way in the cab. I may add that if he hadn't had a diplomatic passport Diamond Waltz would have been arrested on a criminal charge. An incident here a month ago.'

'Thank you for your help, Chief Inspector.'

'I suggest you leave at once. Meter's ticking up on the cab.'

Buchanan had offered to drive Tweed home. He was talking as the Lincoln was swiftly manoeuvred aboard the transporter. Newman had earlier used gloves to wrench off the wreckage he had hauled off the Lincoln. The four-wheel drive was in perfect driving condition.

'I saw the light was still on in his office,' Buchanan said as they mounted the stairs together. 'Time he went home.'

'I suppose you're right,' Tweed agreed when Buchanan made his offer. 'Monica is staying on, checking the names I gave her. And Roy can tell me what happened outside – plus I have a few things to tell him.'

'What about Paula?' Newman asked as they went back down the stairs with Buchanan.

'She's staying on too . . .'

This had been Marler's suggestion.

'The Ear will be more comfortable if I have Paula with me in the waiting room,' he explained to Tweed.

'He relaxes more in women's company – that is, the few he can trust.'

'He may not trust me,' Paula pointed out.

'He will. His ability to weigh up people is remarkable. He has an uncanny knowledge of human nature. But only if you feel up to it.'

'I can't wait to meet the Ear,' she replied.

3

When Newman had left the building with Tweed and Buchanan, Marler set the stage for the arrival of the Ear. He raided the drinks cupboard of Howard, the Director. Holding three glasses and a bottle of white wine he took them downstairs and laid them on the bare wooden table in the waiting room. He then upset George.

'I'll guard the front door. You go upstairs and make yourself at home in one of the offices. Not Tweed's.'

'I'm supposed to be the guard,' the red-faced ex-army sergeant protested.

'I know. We have someone coming who won't want to be recognized.'

'Have it your own way.'

'I'm going to . . .'

With Paula seated at one of the three chairs round the table, Marler waited behind George's desk, listening for the sound of a taxi pulling up. Instead, after half an hour someone rang the bell. Peering through the spy-hole in the heavy front door Marler stared in surprise, then opened it. He ushered the Ear into the waiting room, closed the door.

'This is Paula. I hope you don't mind her being with us.'

Paula looked at their visitor. She hadn't expected such a small man. No more than five feet tall, he had shuffled in and now he gazed at her through thick pebble glasses, perched on the bridge of a hooked nose. He took off the glasses, glanced at Marler before reverting his gaze to Paula.

'Disguise,' he explained. 'Nice name, Paula,' he went on, still staring at her in a way she did not find offensive.

Without the glasses he became a different person. His nose seemed even more hooked, his thin mouth was firm, his jaw pointed. Penetrating blue eyes surveyed her. His cheekbones were prominent and his thick dark eyebrows curled upwards. He reminded her of a Dickensian character.

'I shall be very happy for the lady to be present,' he decided. 'I like your clothes,' he told Paula. 'Smart but not a mantrap.'

'He does speak his mind,' Marler said quickly.

'I think he has a wonderful sense of humour.' Paula laughed. 'His description of me is perfect.'

'And very practical shoes. For moving silently or running.'

He doesn't miss a thing, thought Paula, who had her legs crossed, exposing the rubber sole of one shoe. The explanation he had given was precisely the reason she wore them. Marler pulled out a chair for their visitor to sit down. He extended a hand to Paula. His grip was firm.

'I am Kurt Schwarz.'

'I don't think Kurt will mind my telling you his base is in Switzerland. In Basle.'

Marler sat down in a chair facing them. The Ear put down on the floor an old trilby hat he had been carrying. He wore a shabby windcheater with patches on the sleeves and a pair of denims which had seen better days.

Below the sharp nose his Adam's apple was also prominent, heightening the Dickensian impression. He picked up the bottle of wine, glanced at it, put the bottle down.

'Not bad, could be better,' he told Marler.

'You don't have to drink it.'

'That would be impolite. And I wish to toast the health of this charming lady.'

'Flattery will get you somewhere. How did you find those old clothes? You look like a tramp.'

'I saw a junk shop still open on the way from the airport. I told the cab driver to drop me there. They had a selection of second-hand clothes. There was a public lavatory nearby. I went into it after leaving the shop and changed in a cubicle.'

'Kurt,' commented Paula, 'your English is very good.'

'I once spent two years in Hammersmith. Is it still there?'

'Unfortunately, yes.'

'Well, Hammersmith is like Hampstead compared to half of Paris. Tourists don't see the slums I know so well.' He watched Marler struggling with a gadget to extract the cork from the wine bottle. 'I could get that cork out now with my teeth. Maybe yours are false.'

'That's enough of that.'

Marler poured the wine. The Ear raised his glass. 'To Paula, a long and happy life.'

'Thank you,' she said as they clinked glasses.

'What did you do with the clothes you came across in?' Marler asked.

'Put them inside the canvas hold-all by the side of my chair.' He reached down, pulled out a black beret, fitted it on to his thick grey hair. He still reminded Paula of a Dickensian character. Even his voice fitted – it was hoarse but warm. 'Now, shall we be serious?'

'That's why you're here,' Marler replied.

'The Americans have transmitted electronically one

hundred million dollars to an account at the Zürcher Kredit Bank on Bankverein.'

'That's in Basle?'

'Yes.'

'You're sure of your information?'

'Of course. I shouldn't let you know but I have a teller in that bank who is a contact. For a fee.'

'That's staggering,' said Paula.

'They also have some kind of base in the area. Not in the city.' He turned to Paula. 'You probably know the city is unique. Three countries meet there. Switzerland, Germany and France. You can slip across the border easily. They have a unit somewhere, but not in the city,' he repeated. 'So my next mission is to locate their base.' He sipped more wine. 'I will inform you when I discover it. This wine is not bad.'

'Which means he'd like more,' said Marler, refilling his glass. 'And you'd better be careful. There are some pretty nasty types floating about.'

'There always are.'

'You were very late phoning me from Heathrow,' Marler remarked casually. 'The last flight from Paris had arrived ages before.'

'I was tailed. I had to lose him before I came here. I headed for the multi-storey car park. As you know, it has many levels. Eventually I hid behind a car and he lost me. But I was cautious – I waited a long time before I left the place. Then I called you.'

'How did the tail spot you?'

'He happened to be on my flight. I made a bad mistake. I had been talking to the stewardess in French. Then she dropped a tray and I said, "Don't worry. I'll help you to pick them up." In English. I think the tail heard me. That's what always gets you in the end. Random chance.'

'Any more dope on the Phantom?'

'I was coming to that. The rumours that he's English are now stronger. But they are still rumours. No name. And he's very cautious.'

'I'll say he is,' agreed Marler. 'He assassinated the Prime Minister over here. The security people only think they found his firing point on the rooftop of a warehouse. If they did, he left behind no spent cartridge, nothing.'

'The same as when he killed the German, Heinz Keller – and the French Minister. Bear in mind he could be a Frenchman, a German – or an Uzbek.'

'How are we going to get you away from here? It's late.'

'That is easy,' Kurt explained. 'There are many areas not far from here with cheap hotels. You get a room for the night – providing you pay in advance.'

'You've been here – I mean in London – recently, haven't you?' Paula suggested intuitively.

'Clever lady.' Kurt smiled, his lips twisting in a crooked way, but the smile was very human. 'Yes, I have. On several occasions.'

'You didn't tell me that in Paris,' Marler said sharply.

'Why should I? When I am not certain what I have found out? I only pass on information when what I say is positive. I take your fees. To do otherwise would be dishonest. I will tell you that something very strange and dangerous is happening here. England is facing the greatest enemy since it fought Hitler.'

'What we'll do,' Paula said decisively, 'is the three of us will drive to my flat in the Fulham Road. It won't take me long to prepare a meal, and I'm hungry. I think you are, Kurt.'

'And I'm starving,' Marler lied. 'Afterwards I can drive Kurt to my place for the night. I have a spare bedroom. It's not far from Paula's flat.'

'Don't argue,' Paula said severely as Kurt opened his mouth.

'I surrender.' Kurt threw up both hands. 'I am grateful . . .'

He travelled alongside Paula in her Ford while Marler followed in his station wagon. On the way Paula found Kurt's phrase repeating itself time and again in her mind. *'. . . something very strange and dangerous is happening here. England is facing the greatest enemy since it fought Hitler.'*

4

'Sharon Mandeville,' Monica announced. 'Let's start with the profile I've built up on her – so far as it goes . . .'

It was the morning of the same day that Paula had provided a meal for her two guests. Newman sat in an armchair, his long legs casually crossed. Paula, hiding a yawn, was behind her desk, and Tweed was leaning forward in his swivel chair.

'Sharon is forty-two years old, looks younger,' Monica began. 'I obtained a recent photo of her from the editor of a fashion magazine, a friend of mine. Here it is.'

Newman took it from her. Sitting down again, he studied the glossy print. Then he whistled before passing it to Tweed.

'She's a blonde stunner.'

'She's enigmatic,' commented Tweed. 'I met her at a party in Washington. Not the most recent visit. When I was there three weeks ago.' He passed it to Paula. 'What do you think?'

'Hard to say,' she said eventually. 'A photo can mislead.'

'If I could proceed,' Monica said impatiently. 'Sharon was born in Washington, DC. So she's an American citizen. Her mother was English, her father an American industrialist with money. Sharon was partly educated in

41

England, partly in the US. When Sharon was fifteen the three of them moved here. Apparently her father thought he could make more money in Britain. Result? He lost everything on the stock market and they all returned to the States. Soon after they got back the parents were both killed in a car crash. Sharon was eighteen. A year later she married a Texan oil millionaire. There was a prenuptial agreement. Twenty months later she divorced him and was a rich woman.'

'Because of the prenuptial arrangement?' Tweed suggested.

'Exactly,' Monica confirmed. 'There's a pattern. To cut it short, she remarried three times, always to millionaires or, in one case, to a billionaire. Always there was a prenuptial agreement with a generous settlement for her. Now she may be the richest woman in America.'

'Gold-digger,' said Newman.

'Not necessarily,' Tweed objected. 'Didn't strike me like that when I met her. You have to remember it's a jungle in the US. Rich men treat their wives like trophies, but they can be mean and unreliable. Maybe Sharon spotted that – hence the prenuptial agreements.'

'If I may go on,' snapped Monica. 'So now she's single with four husbands behind her. After the fourth fiasco – if you can call it that – she bought an apartment in luxurious Chevvy Chase and mixed with high society in Washington. She became a friend of the President's wife and was given various jobs.'

'I'd say Newman was right. Gold-digger,' said Marler. He had come into the office a few minutes earlier, nodded and now had taken up his usual stance, leaning against a wall. 'And very attractive,' he concluded, handing back the print.

'You can't always tell from the photo what someone is like,' Paula protested.

'Jefferson Morgenstern, Secretary of State,' Monica

continued, 'is difficult. I'll get there but I concentrated on Sharon. Morgenstern, as I'm sure you know, originated in Europe. Not sure where yet. His real name is Gerhard Morgenstern. He's now at the American Embassy here, like Sharon.'

'You've done very well,' said Tweed.

'Haven't finished yet. Sir Guy Strangeways, who lives now at Irongates in the village of Parham, made his pile as a property developer in the States. An ex-Guards officer, I gather he's still very British. He was in America for twenty years and for some time he lived in Washington. Travels a lot all over the world. There are mysterious gaps in his whereabouts at certain periods. More later.'

'When did he come back here?' Tweed asked. 'He was still in Washington when I was there three weeks ago.'

'Came back two weeks ago. A sudden departure.'

'That's interesting,' Tweed remarked.

'Now, Ed Osborne,' Monica went on. 'The most mysterious of the lot. He also had an English mother and an American father. He was born in New York, in Hoboken. Not the most salubrious part of that place. His father was an unsuccessful locksmith. His childhood was poverty-stricken. Then, Heaven knows how, he's at Harvard. Afterwards there are huge gaps in his life. No knowledge as to whether he was somewhere in the States or somewhere abroad. Then he joins the CIA and rockets up. I'm still digging.'

'Keep on digging,' Tweed suggested.

'Finally, Basil Windermere. Chucked out of Tonbridge when he was discovered with an under-age girl. I've only just started to build up his file. That's it for now.'

'So, Tweed,' Marler enquired, 'what's your reaction?'

'Menace.'

'How do you make that out?' Paula asked.

43

'Sixth sense.'

'Now you're going cryptic again.'

As soon as she had spoken it struck her that Kurt Schwarz and Tweed had one thing in common. They never revealed their thinking until they were sure. She guessed why this was. Tweed was careful not to point his team in any direction until he was sure he had worked out what was happening. This made his team think for themselves, come to their own conclusions.

'I simply don't have enough to go on,' said Tweed, answering Paula's comment. 'Incidentally, you'll find several key people here have disappeared. In the night I sent them down to the Bunker. A skeleton team, if you like.'

'You said that casually,' Newman told him. 'When you talk like that it usually means there's a major emergency.'

'There is.'

'I've had an idea,' Newman remarked. 'Basil Windermere came up with the suggestion that I meet him in a bar during the evening. I wasn't encouraging, but I think I'll have a chat with him. Might help Monica to build up her file on him.'

'Good idea,' agreed Tweed.

'If that's all, think I'll mosey off,' said Marler.

'Another good idea. I know you're all short of sleep. So go home and catch up on some rest.'

'Half a mo,' Marler replied. 'Your camp bed is pushed against that wall behind Paula's desk.'

'I noticed that too,' Paula agreed. 'Decided not to ask any questions.'

'Well, I've just asked one,' Marler insisted. 'Tweed, Bob told me you went home soon after midnight.'

'I did.'

'So why is your camp bed out of the cupboard?'

'My fault,' Monica piped up. 'I managed to get the

44

linen to the laundry, then you all came storming in before I could put the bed away.'

'I'll confess,' Tweed said with mock humility. 'I came back from my flat by cab in the middle of the night. I wanted to supervise those members of the team who were going down to the Bunker. They'd been warned in advance.'

'So we wouldn't know,' Marler accused.

'So I didn't have a lot of questions asked in the middle of the move. Then I slept here instead of another trip back to my flat. Off you go, all of you.'

The phone rang before anyone had time to leave the room. Monica answered it, frowned before she looked across at Tweed.

'George says there is an Ed Osborne downstairs. The gentleman wants to see you.'

'Wheel him up, then. The rest of you stay for a while.'

'How the hell did he find out this address?' demanded Newman.

'Maybe Cord had no time to erase certain confidential information from the computer in Langley, Virginia.'

A restless, guarded atmosphere had spread through the office. Only Tweed seemed unaffected, undisturbed. He looked up as George opened the door and a six-foot aggressive American burst inside. It was as though a hurricane had entered. The new arrival was big in every way, radiating dynamic energy. His thick hair was grey-white, his expression dominant, and ice-cold blue eyes swept round the room. Above them were shaggy white brows, below them a straight wide nose and below that a broad thick-lipped mouth. His gaze homed on Paula.

'Hi, baby, you're lookin' good. You and I could make music.'

'I don't think so, Mr Osborne,' she replied coldly.

'You must be Tweed.' He swung round, extended a large hand, looked surprised as he gripped Tweed's hand and squeezed it with the force of a powershovel. Tweed's grip was equally strong.

'You'd better sit down,' he invited his visitor. 'I do prefer people to phone me for an appointment.'

'Waste of time. I just crash the barrier.'

Osborne lowered his bulk into an armchair. Newman had already resumed his seat in his own chair close to the American's. The American lifted his legs, planted his feet encased in very large shoes on the edge of Tweed's desk. Newman leaned forward, grasped both feet by the crossed ankles, dropped them on the floor.

'We don't do that sort of thing over here,' he explained. 'We like good manners.'

'Get you nowhere. World's movin' on. Move with it or get left behind.'

'Britain has been around for quite a time. Your lot has been on the planet only two hundred years.'

'You're Bob Newman, the foreign correspondent. Hoped we'd get on together. Any time you want to interview me, I'm available. Might give you something to write about. They've set up an outfit at the Embassy called the Executive Action Department. Don't know what it does – if anything. You might enquire about it – just for laughs. EAD, they call it. I'm the new Deputy Director of the CIA. They handed me the job on a plate when Cord Dillon went. Don't forget. EAD.'

'You Americans love initials,' Newman commented.

'Saves time. We like to move fast. I'm at the Embassy.'

'Maybe, Mr Osborne, you could enlighten us as to why you have come here?' Tweed suggested.

'Sure. Why not? And who's the thin streak of a guy holding up the wall?'

'He just called in for a cup of coffee,' said Newman.

'That I could do with myself.'

Monica rose slowly from her chair. Tweed had nodded his agreement. Osborne swung round in his chair,
stared at her.

'Black, honey. Don't ruin it with milk or sugar.'

Her lips pursed, Monica left the room. I hope she
doesn't put poison in it, Marler thought. Although it
might not be a bad idea.

'Why am I here?' Osborne rumbled on in his deep,
aggressive voice. 'We have this special relationship with
you Brits. We think it ought to be strengthened. A lot
more close cooperation. A lot more exchange of information about what's really goin' on in the world. The
way I see it we're natural partners. We have to sit on the
same bench. Be buddies.'

'Why?' asked Tweed.

'We have the same problems. A lot of dangerous
characters have been flooding in to your country . . .'

'We have noticed,' Newman informed him.

'Mafia men from Eastern Europe. Saboteurs from
fanatic Muslim outfits. Same in the States. Sneaking in
over the Canadian and Mexican borders. Take the bomb
at the World Trade Center in New York. We need tough
controls before both our countries go down in chaos.'

Osborne took a gulp of the coffee Monica had put
down on the desk close to him. His face screwed up and
he choked briefly.

'This is like tar.'

'It's the strong coffee you asked for,' Monica said and
sat down behind her computer.

'Fell a friggin' ox.'

'Watch the language,' Tweed said. 'Ladies present.'

'And they probably use worse language than I do.'

'I doubt that's possible,' Newman interjected.

'Screw yourself.'

'If you can't control your language I suggest you get
up and go,' Newman snapped.

47

'Mr Osborne—' Tweed began.

'Ed.'

'If there are issues we should discuss I suggest we set up a proper meeting in advance.'

'At the Embassy,' Osborne growled. 'When?'

'When an opportunity comes up I will get in touch. Thank you for calling in to see me.'

'Guess it's time to leave you folks.' Osborne, wearing a loose windcheater, the zip half open, exposing a wild sweater of many colours, and corduroy slacks, stood up. He was calm, stared all round, looking longest at Marler. 'I'll know you when we meet again.'

'I'll know you,' Marler responded offhandedly.

'At least we've got to know each other,' Osborne said, looking at Tweed. 'We'll get to know each other much better, I'm sure.'

'Thank you again for calling in,' Tweed replied.

'I can let myself out.' Osborne paused as he opened the door, his gaze again sweeping the room. 'Have a nice day.'

'My God, what a bloody boor,' Paula exclaimed.

'American,' Marler drawled. 'All brawn, no brain.'

'I'd say,' Tweed disagreed, 'that he's highly dangerous and it would be a great mistake to underestimate him.'

'In that case,' Newman said after a pause, 'maybe he's the man in charge of all the thugs flooding into London. He could handle that job.'

'You may be right. That strange organization they've set up. EAD. Executive Action Department. I don't too much like the sound of it.'

'As long as the first word doesn't mean Execution,' Paula ruminated.

'I'm really going to check that man out,' Monica announced venomously.

'Do that,' Tweed urged her. 'Try to fill in some of those large gaps in his life. Now, I think all of you really should go home and get some rest. I'll stay here awhile. I have a lot to think about.'

'Could I stay on for a few minutes?' Paula requested. 'I want to ask you about something.'

'Of course you may . . .'

As they left the office Marler followed Newman downstairs and walked alongside him to his Merc. They were both wearing sheepskins and the wind was bitter, the temperature way down. Along the main road beyond the Crescent people hurried, shoulders hunched, heads down. Girls walked with their arms folded to give extra protection.

'You mentioned when you phoned me this morning before leaving your flat that you'd decided to take Basil Windermere up on his invitation to meet you at Bentleys this evening,' Marler said.

'That's right. At eight o'clock. Downstairs bar. Why?'

'I'd rather like to be there. Not with you,' Marler added as Newman frowned.

'Windermere will recognize you.'

'No, he won't. You may not either. You don't mind?'

'Why this interest in Windermere?' Newman questioned.

'For one thing I happen to know he's made a number of extended trips to the Continent recently. And prior to that he was seen in Paris frequently.'

'Join the party, then,' Newman said reluctantly. 'But you'd better not be seen.'

'I'll be the Invisible Man.'

*

'You wanted to ask me questions,' Tweed said to Paula. 'Fire away.'

'This Bunker down on Romney Marsh – which, of course, I've seen. It must have taken months to build. What triggered off the idea? You've made three trips to Washington, which is unusual for you. One several months ago, two more recently.'

'First, the Bunker was completed in thirty days.'

'I can't believe it.'

'Marler kept his imported workers going hard at it. The main reason it was put together so quickly was the maze of cellars which already existed under that old farmhouse. I heard about it from a historian. I'm sure it was once used by smugglers ages ago. One distant tunnel comes up underneath an abandoned old bell tower not far from the sea.'

'I didn't see that.'

'Because I didn't show it to you. The door at the end of the tunnel is concealed. You'll see it the next time I take you down there. Satisfied?'

'No. You're evading the second part of my question. I also asked what triggered off the idea. Your trips to Washington?'

'You've forgotten.' Tweed smiled. 'I've also made trips to Paris recently.'

'There he goes again,' Paula said to Monica. 'As cryptic as Marler's friend,' she commented, switching her gaze to Tweed.

'What happened to him? When I called you after getting back to my flat last night you said the three of you were having a marvellous time – that your guest had a great sense of humour.'

'He has. He said he was flying back this morning. Now, time for me to go.'

'She's probably off to her health club,' Monica informed Tweed.

'Health club?'

'I haven't bothered to mention it,' said Paula as she put on her coat. 'For the past six months I've attended this health club.'

'Aerobics and all that.' Monica snorted. 'She's on a health kick. Fit as the proverbial fiddle and strong as a horse.'

'I approve,' said Tweed. Paula was just leaving when he called out to her. 'Did Marler's friend say where he was flying to?'

'Paris.'

Tweed remained behind his desk when Paula had gone. Monica was using her computer to record certain aspects of a profile she was working on. None of it was on the network. Tweed had warned her earlier to work in this way. He was writing groups of names on a large pad, then circling groups and drawing lines from one to another, trying to work out whether they linked up. The phone rang.

'American Embassy on the line,' Monica called out.

'Not that pest, Osborne?'

'No. Sharon Mandeville. Said she'd met you at a party once in Washington.'

'Tweed speaking.'

'This is Sharon Mandeville. I don't know whether you'll remember me. We had a long chat at a Washington cocktail party.'

The voice was soft, tentative, appealing. Tweed detected a note of hesitancy.

'Remember you well, Ms Mandeville. What can I do for you?'

'I need to talk to you privately. Would it be too much to ask you to come over to the Embassy to see me?'

'Of course not. When do you suggest?'

51

'It's probably inconvenient for you, but I was wondering whether you could come over this morning – at your convenience?'

'I could come now.'

'I'll be waiting for you. Just ask for me at reception. Till then . . .'

'I'm off to the American Embassy to meet her,' he told Monica as he put on his overcoat.

'Don't fall for her.'

'Hardly likely. And it fits in nicely with my driving down to Parham this afternoon. I want to have a long talk with Sir Guy Strangeways. See if I can find out what *he* is up to.'

5

Tweed asked his cab driver to drop him just outside Grosvenor Square. March had come in like a lion and a biting wind was battering at him. Above the elegant square an armada of low dark clouds scudded across the sky, threatening a cloudburst.

Tweed paused at a corner, gazing at the huge white modern building facing the central garden. It reared up, solid as a steel wall with windows. A monument to the immense world power it represented. Tweed grunted, mounted the deserted flight of wide steps, pushed his way through a new revolving door. A short walk took him to the reception desk. Behind it an attractive brunette watched him coming warily.

'Ms Mandeville is expecting me. Tweed is the name.'

'You have identification, sir?'

She spoke in a broad American accent. Her voice was nasal, harsh. Tweed took out his wallet, extracted a card

which showed him as Chief Investigator, General &
Cumbria Assurance. She studied it as though it might be
forged, which it was.

'I'll let you know when she can see you. Take a seat
over there.'

'I'll stay here. I have an appointment now.'

The receptionist made a moue of displeasure. She
expected people to do what she said. After speaking on
the phone she gestured towards the lift. No attempt to
escort him.

'Take the elevator. Floor One. Room Twenty-one. To
your left as you get out.'

'Thank you.'

He glanced at an obvious guard in plain clothes. A
weapon bulged under his left armpit. Eyes like stones
stared at Tweed, who gave him a little wave on his way
to the lift. Cosy atmosphere these days at the American
Embassy – almost as though they were expecting an
attack.

Tweed strolled over to the lift, pressed the button for
Floor One. The door opened silently. He stepped inside.
The door closed silently, the lift began to ascend. He was
struck by the silence of the building. Like a stage setting
prepared for his arrival.

The door slid open, again making no sound. He
stepped out into a wide corridor, his rubber-soled shoes
as soundless as the lift door, then stopped. To his left,
further along the corridor, he saw the back of Jefferson
Morgenstern, Secretary of State, America's Foreign Minister. Tweed recognized the small man because he had
met him at a party in Washington. Morgenstern was
carrying a thick black file.

He was accompanied by two tall men, one on either
side of the most powerful man in the American adminis-
tration. Expecting that at any moment one of the three

men would see him, Tweed remained perfectly still. They didn't see him. They appeared too intent on where they were going.

Pausing before a closed door on the right, one of the aides took out a key, unlocked the door and Morgenstern hurried inside. Since they hadn't closed the door Tweed guessed they would be coming out again when they had finished whatever task they were engaged on. He began to walk along the corridor.

Slowing down as he reached the open door, Tweed glanced into the room. A safe like a bank vault set into one wall was open. Morgenstern bent down, slipped the file inside. Tweed walked on. He had already observed the odd numbers were on his left side. He had also noticed the number of the room Morgenstern had entered. Number 16. In addition he had seen the metal plate on the half-open door engraved with one word: SECURITY.

He quickened his pace. Arriving at Room 21 he raised his hand to knock. Before his knuckles could reach the surface the door opened in his face. The woman he had come to see ushered him inside, closed her door. Tweed was under cover before anyone emerged from Security.

It was as though he had met Sharon Mandeville the day before. Her manner was restrained but easy. Tweed reflected that she looked more like a mature thirty-five than her real age, forty-two. She escorted him to two leather-covered swivel chairs by the side of her massive desk. Behind the desk was another chair but as soon as he was seated she occupied the chair next to him.

'Thank you for coming to see me so quickly,' she said in her soft voice. No trace of an American accent. 'I'm sure you would like some coffee. It's a bitter day.'

'That would be very acceptable.'

'Black, if I remember rightly. No sugar. No milk.'

'You have a remarkable memory.'

'And you're wearing the same suit you wore in Washington. I like a man to look smart.'

'Again, your memory.'

'A woman notices small things . . .'

As she conversed she was pouring two cups of coffee from a silver pot perched on a silver tray on a side table. Tweed studied her. She had beautiful blonde hair, very thick, arranged in waves and falling so it just touched her shoulders. As in Washington, it was her large greenish eyes which held him. She had a strong chin without spoiling the striking appearance of her pale face. Her forehead was high. Her mouth was wide but the lips were not full.

Five foot six tall, she was slim and was wearing a pale green dress which went well with her intense eyes. It was high at the neck. She crossed her elegant legs, sipped at her coffee, put the cup down and turned to face her visitor.

'What are you doing over here, if I may ask?' said Tweed.

'It's rather confidential. No, don't worry. I will tell you. The first time we met I decided you could be trusted.'

She paused. Her hypnotic eyes held his. She was a very unusual woman, Tweed was thinking. It was not just a matter of beauty, her graceful movements. Any time she walked into a room full of people all the men would stop talking while they gazed at her. She had *impact*.

'I'm not even sure what my job here is,' she went on. 'I don't know why, but I get on well with the President's wife. She's given me various assignments in the past. I do know that over here I'm supposed to keep an eye on a man called Ed Osborne, the new Deputy Director of the CIA. He's a rough diamond and my main task is to smooth the path for him. Don't let him upset the Brits, is what I was told by the President's wife. I hate that word Brit. Typically American. Osborne will probably try to get in touch with you,' she warned.

'Why would he do that?' Tweed asked innocently.

'He told me you were a friend of his predecessor, Cord Dillon.'

'That's true. What has happened to Dillon?'

'I suppose he's retired. I asked Ed that question myself and all he said was, "He's gone fishin'" – which told me a lot.' She paused, took a cigarette from a silver box. Tweed produced a lighter, lit her cigarette.

'Thank you,' she said.

The typical American woman would have said, 'I can do that for myself,' Tweed thought.

'I'm not offering you one because you don't smoke,' she went on.

'You could produce a file on me,' Tweed joked.

She frowned, then half-smiled. 'I told you I remember trivial things.' She used her other hand to push back a wave of hair.

Tweed knew she was a natural blonde. In Washington she had produced two colour photos of herself from her evening bag. One of herself at twelve and the other when she was eighteen. In both photos her thick blonde hair had jumped out at him. She had apologized for showing them to him.

'I don't carry these about with me,' she had explained. 'I want to give them to a man here who is good at framing photos. To remind me I'm getting old.'

'Hardly.'

'Thank you.'

'Why did you ask me over here?' Tweed now asked. 'Is there something I can help you with?'

'Yes, there might be.' Her eyes still gazed at him.

56

'Dillon apparently told the President's wife you were a key figure over here, that you know a lot of people. Washington is trying to strengthen the bonds between the two countries. I was hoping you'd introduce me to people who matter from time to time.'

Tweed's expression was neutral. He took his time finishing off his coffee, then refused more. He stared round the room. On a side desk was a pile of folders, some with a red tab attached. The furniture was expensive. The windows looked out on to a side street.

'They should give you an office overlooking the square,' he suggested.

'I prefer it back here – on my own. Osborne has an office the size of a tennis court looking out on the square. How is the insurance business? I suppose you are rich?'

'Not really. I certainly couldn't compete with you. Four husbands must have been a roller-coaster ride.'

'Something like that,' she said after a long pause. 'When I first went – was taken – to the States, I realized my English accent was a passport to successful men. When you're young you're easily flattered. I suppose I did exploit my accent. Does that sound awful?'

'No.'

'Money isn't everything.'

'How is it you still speak perfect English, after all that time spent over there?'

'I came back over here frequently. I have a small mansion in Dorset. Sometimes I think I'd like to live here for good. I find America raw. You glanced at your watch.'

'I've enjoyed our conversation. I hope you'll excuse me – I have an important appointment this afternoon.'

'Of course.'

A light had been flashing on her phone for several minutes. It had been reflected in a mirror close to the door. Tweed collected his coat from the hanger she had put it on while Sharon sat behind her desk. Picking up her phone she listened, then answered.

'Yes. Yes. Yes. Now don't bother me again.'

She got up and walked slowly towards him. Again it occurred to Tweed that she was an incredibly elegant woman. She shook hands with him.

'When you have the time perhaps we could meet again for lunch or dinner to chat some more.'

'It will be my pleasure . . .'

He walked into the corridor, she closed the door and he felt very alone.

There was something about the atmosphere of the building which Tweed found disturbing. No sign of anyone. No sound. He'd have expected the Embassy to be a hive of activity. He had paused, was about to turn to his right when the door across the corridor opened.

A tall American with a smooth face and a blank expression stood facing him. Tweed had the impression of a man conscious of his position in the pecking order. When the American spoke he wondered how he had known Tweed would be in the corridor. Sharon Mandeville had finished speaking before she opened the door, which had not made a hint of noise.

'Tweed?' the American enquired.

'Yes. Who are you?'

'Chuck Venacki.'

The penny dropped. Tweed recalled Chief Inspector Buchanan's story of the encounter when Newman had rammed the Lincoln Continental on the edge of Park Crescent. This physically impressive man had said he was an attaché at the Embassy.

'Main elevator you came up in is out of order,' Venacki said tersely. 'Turn left, end of corridor turn left again. Take the elevator there. There's a door to the side street.'

'Thank you.'

Venacki didn't hear his reaction. He had closed the door in Tweed's face. A certain lack of warmth, Tweed said to himself. As though Venacki resented his presence. And there had been an air of hostility. Tweed turned right, heading for the elevator which had brought him up.

There was a notice hanging from the elevator's closed door. *Out of order*. He pressed a button. Nothing happened. Next to the elevator was a wide staircase which, presumably, led to the exit floor below. He was just descending the first step when he looked back along the corridor. Chuck Venacki was outside his office, watching him. He disappeared instantly, as though he had dashed back into his quarters. Tweed frowned.

He descended the several short flights of stairs slowly, listening. Still not a sound. Peculiar. The atmosphere now seemed menacing. He reached the bottom and the spacious hall was empty – except for the receptionist behind her desk. Her phone rang. She answered it, slammed down the receiver, got up, vanished through a door behind her. Tweed walked quickly to the door. When he tried to open it the door wouldn't move.

He turned round, headed for the revolving door leading out to the square. Close to it was a small desk with a phone. He was about to pass the desk when the phone buzzed faintly. Carefully, Tweed lifted the receiver. A man's voice he didn't recognize was speaking.

'The operation's under way. Double-check with Charlie . . .'

What operation? And who the heck was Charlie? Tweed moved swiftly, pressed a hand on the revolving door. It remained stationary. He couldn't get out the way he had come in. He was trapped. Calmly he surveyed the reception hall. There was no one he could contact. No doubt about it – he was imprisoned inside the building.

He peered out beyond the immobile revolving door. A stretch limo had pulled in behind a blue Chrysler parked at the kerb. Without waiting for his uniformed chauffeur to alight, a passenger jumped out of the rear seat, slammed the door shut, ran up the steps. On his arrival Tweed had noticed two video cameras aimed down the flight of steps. He recognized – from pictures in the papers – the lean energetic man running up the steps. The recently appointed American Ambassador.

Taking no notice of the man inside, the Ambassador pushed at the doors and they began revolving. Tweed walked out as the Ambassador walked in. The keen cold air hit him after the warmth of the air-conditioned building. Tweed paused at the top of the steps, scanning the street. Then he ran one hand over the top of his head, smoothing down his hair.

He had almost reached the bottom step when three tough-looking men emerged from the Chrysler. One opened the rear door. Another addressed him in a harsh American accent.

'Mr Tweed?'

'Yes . . .'

'We'll drive you back to where you're going. Get in.'

'No, thank you . . .'

'I said get in, Buddy.'

Something hard and circular was rammed into his back. Two men took him by the arms, began to hustle him inside the rear of the car. On the far rear seat a small bald man was playing with a Colt automatic pistol, grinning unpleasantly at Tweed.

Tweed became aware of a commotion, a scuffle

behind him. He was released from the hand grips. Newman hit one thug over the head with the barrel of his gun. Marler hit another of them with the stiffened side of his hand, the blow connecting with the side of his neck. Harry Butler pointed a wide-barrelled gun, aimed inside the car, pulled the trigger. The interior was sprayed with Mace gas. The bald man and the driver behind the wheel collapsed, choking, unable to see. Newman heaved one unconscious thug into the rear of the car, Marler bundled the second unconscious bundle inside. Butler, who had earlier broken the jaw of the third assailant, shoved him in, fired one more blast of Mace gas, slammed the door shut.

'Let's go,' Newman said to Tweed. 'Merc's parked over there.'

'I know. I saw it.'

'What brought you here?' Tweed asked as Butler drove the Merc back to Park Crescent.

'Monica,' Newman replied, for once seated beside Tweed in the rear. 'When she told us you'd gone to the Embassy we decided you might need back-up. Too many not-nice people floating around our city these days.'

'Well, thank you all. I don't know what they had in mind for me if they'd pulled off the kidnap. Maybe interrogation, maybe murder . . .'

He then explained concisely his experiences inside the Embassy. When he'd finished he looked out of the window where a drizzle of rain was smearing London.

'One key is to find out who Charlie is. I think he may be the real leader behind their Executive Action Department.'

6

At four in the afternoon Tweed was driving his Ford Sierra along a narrow twisting lane approaching Parham. By his side Paula sat keeping quiet. She sensed Tweed was thinking as he drove.

It was almost dark and his headlights shone through the gloom. Overhead dark clouds massed as though preparing for a cloudburst. She noticed he kept glancing in his rear-view mirror. He slowed down at an isolated spot where he could see the lane ahead for some distance, pulled over onto the grass verge, put one hand out of the window he had lowered, gestured for a car behind to stop.

'We have company.'

'Hostile?'

She reached into her shoulder bag and gripped the .32 Browning. When she looked back as Tweed climbed out she saw Newman's Merc pull in behind them. She got out to join Tweed. In the rear seat behind Newman sat Harry Butler and his partner, Pete Nield.

'Just what is the meaning of this?' Tweed demanded.

'Simple,' replied Newman, still seated behind the wheel. 'We think you need protection.'

'I thought I emphasized before I left Park Crescent that I was coming down here by myself.'

'You've got Paula with you.'

'Paula met Sir Guy Strangeways awhile ago at a dinner in London. They got on well. I think he'll be more relaxed with Paula present. He won't be if he sees you three. He's a bit of a martinet.'

'May I remind you,' Newman told him, 'that when I was bringing Cord Dillon this way we saw the Cadillac with four American thugs drive inside Irongates? Those gentlemen may still be there. Have you forgotten your experience at the Embassy?'

'I have not. Strangeways is English. Now that you're here find a place open in Parham. Go in and have afternoon tea.'

'I don't think you can get afternoon tea in this country these days,' Nield remarked amiably.

Harry Butler and Pete Nield worked well as a team. There was a great contrast between the two men. Butler was short, burly, with broad shoulders, his dark hair roughly brushed, a man who used words as though he regarded them as money. Pete Nield was slim, had fairish hair and a thin moustache. Unlike Butler, wearing a shabby windcheater and a pair of well-worn slacks, Nield took trouble with his appearance. He was clad in a smart grey suit, a pair of shoes from Aquascutum, a raincoat from the same shop. He was never backward in voicing his thoughts.

'You'll find a tea shop in Parham,' Tweed told him. 'Just keep away from Irongates. This will be a quiet visit.'

'Famous last words,' Paula said under her breath.

Returning with her to his car, Tweed drove on. In his rear-view mirror he noted the Merc was still stationary. Paula was furious.

'That's no way to talk to them after what happened this morning. They rescued you from God knows what.'

'And I thanked them when we got back to Park Crescent. Here is the beginning of Parham.'

He guided the car along the old village street, turned into the first, larger square, then into the smaller square with no other exit. There was no sign of life outside the large mansion and the gates were closed. Tweed stopped the car.

'There's a speakphone in the right-hand pillar. Would you mind letting our host know we've arrived?'

63

'Of course not,' she snapped.

She got out, still steaming. Tweed was taking risks in a situation which had already proved potentially lethal. It was not only the incident at the American Embassy she had in mind. She was recalling the brutal attempt to murder Cord Dillon in the middle of London. Pressing a button by the side of the speakphone, she waited. A buzz. Then a commanding voice she recognized. Strangeways.

'Who the hell is it?'

'Paula Grey. I have Mr Tweed with me. We understood you—'

'Enter.'

'The gates are closed.'

'Use your eyes.'

She caught sight of movement. The large gates were opening inwards. She ran to the car, jumped into her seat. Tweed immediately drove forward at a slow pace. Behind them the gates closed, making no sound.

'Hinges must be well oiled,' Tweed remarked.

Their tyres crunched on the gravel surface. High banks of rhododendron bushes masked any view on both sides. Paula was experiencing a feeling of claustrophobia – shut away from the outside world like the approach to a monastery where the monks had an evil reputation. At the end of the gently curving drive crouched the house, an ancient mansion, three storeys high and dormer windows in the mansard roof, round like ports for cannons. The style of the mansion was Gothic, grim, its dark stone bleak. Gargoyles leered down at them below the turrets flanking each end of the house.

'Strangeways himself answered me,' Paula recalled. 'He sounded strange – no pun intended. Like a bear with a sore head. When I sat next to him at that dinner he was charming. Amiable and jokey.'

'Interesting.'

64

She realized Tweed was only half-listening to her. He was peering up at the right-hand turret. He parked the car at the foot of a wide flight of old stone steps leading up to a balustraded terrace. As he locked the car Tweed again looked up at the turret.

'What a ghastly place to live,' Paula whispered.

'You have to remember Strangeways spent twenty years in the army as a young man before he went into business. Prior to that he was at a public school. That sort of background does not make you aware of your surroundings. You take no interest in taste or comfort.'

A heavy front door opened as they reached it. Framed in the doorway was Strangeways. Five foot ten tall, well built, his fleshy face was red, his nose like a hawk's, the eyes dark and forbidding, his mouth tight-lipped above an aggressive jaw. Grey-haired, he sported a trim moustache, stood ramrod erect and was wearing a blue business suit.

'You're late,' he rapped out.

'We're on time. Your watch must be wrong,' Tweed said mildly.

'I pride myself on punctuality,' Strangeways barked. 'An old army habit.'

'My watch is an Accurist. Greenwich mean time. Better buy one for yourself,' Tweed rapped back. 'Are we going to stand out here all afternoon in the cold?'

'Of course not. Please do come in.' Their host's manner had mellowed. As he closed the door he lowered his voice. 'My apologies to you both, but my wretched son turned up out of the blue. I'll introduce you, then tell him to push off . . .'

They followed Strangeways across a large stark hall with woodblock flooring. The only furniture was a large ugly oak chest stood against one wall. No pictures. Strangeways opened a door into a large room, again without a carpet or rugs. Close to the left-hand wall was a plain desk supporting an outsize globe and behind it a map of the world. A heavy oak table occupied the middle of the room and the chairs which surrounded it were hard-backed and looked uncomfortable to Paula. The interior of the house reminded her of a prison.

'This is my son, Rupert,' their host said without enthusiasm.

Sprawled on a couch was a man of about thirty. He wore riding kit with jodhpurs thrust inside gleaming knee-length boots. His right hand held a riding crop which he was tapping against his thigh. His boots were resting on the end of the couch.

'Get those damned boots off the furniture,' Strangeways growled. 'This is a friend of mine with his assistant, Paula.'

Rupert took his time about planting his boots on the floor. He stood up, five feet eight inches tall, a slim man, his jet-black hair neatly trimmed. He had his father's hawkish nose, his dark eyes alert, and a foxy chin, and he surveyed Paula insolently. She bridled inwardly as he slowly took in her legs, higher up her body and then her face.

'Rather like the look of you, Paula. You're not bad.'

'I'm supposed to take that as a compliment?'

'I take my time.'

Tweed had been studying Rupert, who ignored him. Strangeways guided Tweed to a seat at the table. Standing behind him he stood erect, looking embarrassed. He coughed, glanced at Paula.

'I don't quite know how to phrase this. The last thing I want to do is to appear impolite.'

'But you'd prefer it if the two of you could talk alone,' Paula suggested with a smile.

'My dear, there's a library on your left as you go back into the hall. If you're interested in books it's quite an unusual collection I've built up over the years.'

'I'd be happy to wait there.'

'Not so fast.' He went over to the wall, pressed an old-fashioned bell. 'The housekeeper, Mrs Belloc, can provide you with tea and cakes. Indian, Darjeeling, Earl Grey? And I'd better warn you Mrs Belloc is an odd character. Goes around with a black shawl over her head. A hard worker but it's difficult keeping local servants. They don't like her. Ah, here she is.'

Paula had a shock. When the door opened a short powerfully built woman walked slowly in. The black shawl was worn so it concealed most of her features, exposing only gimlet eyes and a nose like a parrot's. A black dress reached almost to her ankles. There was something sinister about her.

'You wanted me, sir?' she asked, addressing her employer.

Strangeways gave her instructions to serve Paula tea in the library. Mrs Belloc was staring at Tweed while she listened. Then she withdrew without a word.

Rupert opened the door again, bowed in an exaggerated way. He was smiling sardonically. Without a backward glance at the two men in the room, he closed the door and caught up with Paula.

'You don't want to waste your time in the library. Let's go riding. I can give you a gentle nag.'

'I want to see the library. And Mrs Belloc is bringing me tea.'

'Never read a book in my life,' he replied jauntily, following her as she opened the door on her left.

'Might do you good if you did read a few.'

'I seem to get by without them.'

She was already inside a large room, the walls lined with bookcases. A wheeled ladder was attached to one wall so the high shelves could be reached easily. Nondescript coffee tables were scattered round the room near large leather couches which looked as though they'd

67

been there for generations. The room was chilly. She pulled out a book on Alexander the Great and perched at the end of a couch. Rupert joined her.

'You'll end up with that old horror, Mrs Belloc, for company. I'm much more fun.'

'I'm sure you are.'

'Please yourself, then,' he said acidly. 'Bury your nose in a crummy book. You don't know what you're missing. We could shoot a few birds instead of riding.'

'That idea doesn't appeal to me.'

'Playing hard to get.' He stood up. 'Have it your own way.'

It was a relief to Paula when he left the room, closing the door behind him. Something caught her eye. She looked at a side window, jumped up, ran into the mullioned bay. Outside was Harry Butler, one finger to his lips. Behind him a trim lawn stretched away to a hedge and beyond it was a field. Wrestling with the old security catch, she pushed open a casement window.

'What on earth are you doing out there?'

'Prowling. And keeping an eye on Tweed. Newman's orders. Got over the side wall with a telescopic ladder he carries in the boot of his car.'

'Get out of sight! Quick! The housekeper is bringing me tea . . .'

'I'll have a cuppa,' said Butler and was gone.

She was struggling to close the window, had just managed it, when she heard a sound. She hadn't heard the door open but now she heard the sound she had heard when Mrs Belloc entered the other room earlier. The rustle of the stiff black material she wore as a dress. Paula froze.

'Wouldn't have anything to do with him if I were you,' a harsh voice advised.

For a tense moment she thought the housekeeper was

referring to Butler. Then, in the field beyond the hedge, she saw Rupert riding a large stallion. He reined in his mount suddenly. It bucked, reared into the air. Rupert stayed in the saddle, waved his whip at her as his steed's forelegs dropped to the ground.

'Showing off, as usual,' Mrs Belloc complained.

Paula turned round and the squat hooded woman was laying on a table a sparkling silver tray containing the tea. The tray looked genuine and Paula guessed it was an heirloom. It was difficult to imagine Strangeways bothering to purchase the tray.

'Milk and sugar in your tea?'

'Just milk, please. This is very kind of you. And the cakes look scrumptious.'

Mrs Belloc showed no inclination to leave as Paula sat down.

She had closed the door when she came into the library and now she stood close to Paula as she perched on the couch and sampled the tea. Her large, ugly hands were clasped across her middle, her penetrating eyes fixed on Paula.

'This tea is perfect,' said Paula. 'Thank you.'

'Rupert goes to the Continent a lot. Takes one of his fancy ladies with him. He's had a harem of floozies. No, that's not quite right. They're a snooty type, well educated, with not a hint of a brain.'

'Really?'

'He likes the casinos over there. Gambles heavily. Must cost him a packet.'

'I expect he can afford it.'

'Don't know he can. When his mother died she left him some kind of regular allowance. Wouldn't have thought it ran to the sort of life he lives.'

'I see.'

Paula ate one of the cakes. She was being careful not

to say much. She didn't like gossip. Above all she didn't want to say anything which might be repeated to Rupert's father.

'He likes shooting. Pheasants. Boasts about it. He's always saying one bullet, one bird. I'd better leave you now. I'm going up to the turret.'

'What's up there?'

'Gives me a good view of what Rupert is up to. You mind my words. Give Rupert a clear berth.'

On this note she ambled slowly to the door, left the library, closing the door behind her. Paula selected another cake. As she consumed it her mind whirled with thoughts. She was also wondering how Tweed was getting on with his host.

'How about a double Scotch?' Strangeways had suggested as soon as they were alone.

'No, thank you. I'm driving.'

He watched Strangeways walk briskly to a cabinet against a wall. Taking out a glass and a bottle of expensive whisky, his host poured a generous drink. As the bottle touched the rim of the glass it rattled. He drank half the contents, returned to the table, sat facing Tweed.

'That's better. I needed it.'

'You're worried about something?'

'Tweed, you know I've spent a long time in the States. By now I know America. I know a lot of the top people. I know the way they're thinking. Incidentally, I'm having dinner with Jefferson Morgenstern in town this evening.'

'Is he worried?'

'I think so. Look at it from their point of view. Globally. They feel encircled. Across the Pacific they have China facing them. That's a distance, but not in these days of inter-continental ballistic missiles. They think the Russians are going to ally themselves with the Chinese.

That's looking west from where they sit. Now take Europe and the Middle East. Iran, to mention only one Muslim state, is building a nuclear arsenal. If it combined with Turkey – which could soon become a Muslim state again – they might over-run Europe. Turkey, as you know, is close to having a population of a hundred and fifty million. Bigger than any nation in Western Europe.'

'Iran is a long way from America,' Tweed pointed out, glancing at the wall map of the world facing him.

'London is roughly half the distance Beijing is from San Francisco – and they're worried about Beijing.'

'Why mention London?'

'It's much closer to the East Coast of America.'

'Why is that relevant?'

'If an enormous Muslim power took over Britain, America would be an isolated fortress, menaced on both coasts.'

'Why do they think that would happen?' Tweed enquired.

'Because they think this European Union idea is a shambles. Umpteen nations, speaking different languages, with different histories, many secretly hating each other. They quote the old Austro-Hungarian Empire – also a goulash of nationalities – which collapsed at the end of the First World War. More recently, they point to Yugoslavia. Again a mix of races with their own languages, religions. Tito dies and the whole house of cards comes tumbling down.

'So?'

'They foresee a scenario whereby an overwhelming Muslim force could conquer Western Europe. Supposing a federated Europe was attacked. Imagine the indecision in Brussels. They'd still be working out what to do when the Muslims crossed the Rhine. There'd be a large element arguing that any life would be better than death.'

'So what do the Americans propose to do about it?'

71

'They have a plan. I do know that. Morgenstern, remember, was born in Europe. Was in Europe until he was a young man and went to the States.'

'It's his plan?'

'I don't know. But he carries tremendous influence in Washington.'

'What is the plan?' Tweed asked point blank.

'I don't know. They never forget I'm English.' Strangeways finished off his drink. 'So they don't confide in me.'

'But you seem to know a lot.'

'I simply know how they're thinking. What about you? Have you a clue as to what is going on?'

'Nothing, really,' Tweed replied evasively.

'I do know they think very highly of you, Tweed,' Strangeways said casually.

Strangeways was looking at the wall as he said this. His right hand was playing with his empty glass. For a moment Tweed detected a hint of shiftiness in his host, something he had never seen before.

'Why me?' he asked.

'They respect your global outlook. Your achievements in the past. Above all, you're not a politician. Morgenstern once described you as having the brain of a statesman.'

'Nice of him. Do you agree with what is happening?'

'Damn it, I can't make up my mind. The world is changing day by day. There's no precedent for the present grim situation.'

'Why did you ask me down here, Guy? If I may call you that?'

'Of course you may. I felt a strong need for a sounding board. To get your reaction. I'm going to have another drink.'

'I hope you don't mind –' Tweed checked his watch – 'but I'll have to be going soon.'

He looked round the chilly uncomfortable room. Yes, it all came from a boarding-school upbringing. There was an atmosphere in the room he didn't like, a restlessness which he felt sure originated in his host. He also felt alarmed and couldn't put his finger on the reason for this sensation.

'Sorry, Tweed,' Strangeways said, returning with his refilled glass. 'I've been pouring out my anxieties to you. Not like me.'

'Why do you think the Prime Minister was assassinated?' Tweed asked suddenly.

Strangeways was sitting down. He froze. The liquid in his glass shook. Then he stood up, his expression grim.

'That was a nasty business.' He drank more whisky. 'But I'm detaining you.'

He accompanied Tweed into the forbidding hall, went over and opened the library door. Paula was immersed in her book. She looked up and smiled.

'I've really enjoyed the peace and quiet in here.'

'Rupert hasn't been bothering you, has he?'

'Heavens, no.'

She spoke over her shoulder as she carefully replaced the volume where she had found it. Strangeways watched her action with approval.

'You know something,' he told her, 'you're the first visitor who hasn't taken out a book and then left it on one of the couches. Tweed is leaving now . . .'

The three of them were walking across the hall when the front door was hurled open. Rupert entered, slapping his crop against his thigh. He stared hard at Tweed.

'Don't know you.'

'No, you don't,' Tweed replied abruptly.

'But I must say goodbye to the alluring Paula.'

'Go straight upstairs to your room,' Strangeways snapped.

'Your wish is my command.'

Rupert began running up a wide curving staircase to the left of the doorway Tweed and his father had just left. As he ran he twirled his riding crop in a way which reminded Paula of an American girl leading a parade before a sports match, manipulating her symbolic stick. He's athletic, she thought. Then Rupert threw the crop into the air, caught it with one hand as it fell behind his back. And quick reflexes, she said to herself.

'I'll give you a buzz,' he called down to Paula. 'We'll have dinner in London.'

She didn't reply, Strangeways tightened his mouth and then his son was gone. The doorway where Rupert had entered was still open. Paula thanked their host as they left and Tweed turned on the terrace.

'Enjoy your dinner with Morgenstern,' he said.

Strangeways said nothing, merely nodded before closing the door. At the bottom of the steps Tweed paused with Paula, glanced up at the right-hand turret before getting behind the wheel of his car.

'Someone is watching us.'

'I know. Mrs Belloc, seeing us off the premises. I'm glad we are going. Something creepy about that place.'

7

Tweed had a shock when he arrived back at Park Crescent. He had found the Merc parked outside a tea shop in Parham. Newman had emerged immediately with Butler and Nield. Paula was secretly relieved to see Butler. During the drive back Tweed had told her he would explain what had happened with Strangeways when they got back. This made Paula resolve to say nothing about her encounter with Rupert for the moment.

It was dry and bitterly cold when Tweed parked his

car and they entered the SIS building. George, who let them in, pointed to the waiting room.

'You'll never guess who is waiting to see you.'

'Then I won't try.'

Newman and Nield were heading up the stairs to Tweed's office when George called out to them, 'Marler has arrived. You'll find him up there.'

Butler paused. He made no attempt to follow the two men up to the first floor. He spoke tersely before heading for the door to the basement. 'I have to visit the boffins. They're cooking up a new gadget for Marler.'

'Well, George, what is it?' Tweed asked when he was alone with Paula.

'And you'll never guess what he said to me. Chief Inspector Roy Buchanan has been waiting for almost an hour. He told me that if anyone at the Metropolitan Police asked if he was here I was to say I hadn't see him.'

'He used the phrase Metropolitan Police?' Tweed checked in a puzzled tone.

'His very words.'

'Sorry to keep you waiting so long, Roy,' Tweed apologized as he entered the waiting room with Paula. 'You didn't phone to let me know you were coming.'

'Deliberately. My office may be bugged.'

Paula was gazing at their visitor. Normally Buchanan's manner was sardonic, deceptively offhand. Now he looked like a man under pressure, his expression grim. She recalled the bizarre change in Strangeways' appearance, how the jokey amiability had been replaced by tension. He had struck her at Irongates as being taut as a guitar string under unbearable strain. What on earth was happening to these men?

'Roy,' said Tweed briskly, 'in my office there are Newman, Nield and Marler. And, of course, Monica. Would you sooner they didn't hear what you have to say?'

'I'd sooner they did. At least *they* are trustworthy . . .'

75

When they were all settled in his office Monica suggested some coffee. Buchanan accepted the offer gratefully. Paula sensed that Monica had noticed the change in the Chief Inspector. Their guest normally lounged in his armchair. Now he was sitting bolt upright.

'Fire away, Roy,' Tweed invited.

'Something terrible is happening to this country,' Buchanan began. 'Like a monster octopus extending its tentacles round every key position. I've been told to lay off the Americans,' he said savagely.

'In what way?' Tweed enquired.

'For starters, no investigation of the outrage in Albemarle Street. No witnesses . . .'

'Oh, yes, there are!' Paula exploded. 'I'm a witness – that is, if Tweed agrees. But I can't reveal the identity of the man they tried to kill.'

'I know it was Cord Dillon, ex-Deputy Director of the CIA,' the Chief Inspector replied. 'Tweed called me at home from his flat. I gather he's in hiding and there are no other witnesses.'

'The street was empty,' Paula went on vehemently. 'It was a freezing night. And it happened just after ten o'clock. No one was about – which isn't surprising.'

'Then,' Buchanan went on, 'I've been told to destroy my report on the Lincoln Continental incident, when Newman rammed it outside here. Again, lay off the Americans.'

'Who told you this?' Tweed asked.

'The Commissioner himself. Had me in his office this morning. Just the two of us. He was apologetic, defensive. The trouble is there's a strong rumour he's going to be replaced. And he's the best man in the country to hold down the job.'

'He was adamant?' Tweed suggested.

'Not entirely. He was escorting me to the door and then said, "You must use your own judgement, Roy."'

The phone rang. Monica had just returned and served

76

Buchanan with coffee. She picked up the phone, listened, looked across at Tweed.

'Sorry to interrupt. Butler's on the line from the basement. Said it was urgent.'

'What is it, Harry?' Tweed asked on his own phone.

'Thought I'd better own up. While you were at Iron-gates I used a telescopic ladder to scale the side wall. Wanted to check you were OK. Then explored round the back, found a big garage. Padlocked shut but there was a gap in the old doors. Shone my torch inside and there was the Chrysler they tried to shove you into outside the American Embassy.'

'You're certain?'

'Same number plate.'

'You did well. I need that information.'

Putting down the phone, Tweed told Buchanan there was something he ought to know. He then described the attempt to kidnap him and Butler's Chrysler report. Buchanan's expression changed. He relaxed in his chair.

'Now I've got something I can get my teeth into. Kidnapping – or the attempt – is a major crime. And, if you agree, Tweed, I've got witnesses. Newman and Butler would do.'

'I agree,' Tweed said promptly.

'You can keep the SIS out of this?' enquired Marler, standing against a wall.

'Newman would make the perfect witness,' Buchanan pointed out. 'He's the best-known foreign correspondent on Earth. Butler works for the General & Cumbria Insurance outfit. Tweed is its chief investigator. His speciality is supposed to be the insurance of prominent men against being kidnapped. A clever counsel could link the whole thing up – someone Tweed has insured is in danger of being kidnapped.'

'Any idea why the Prime Minister was assassinated?' Tweed asked out of the blue.

'None at all.'

'I think I have. Normally we know who would have taken his place. But the Cabinet and the MPs rebelled. They chose someone else. An apparently neutral figure. Whoever paid for the assassination banked on their own man getting the job.'

'That's shrewd,' Buchanan commented. 'Incidentally, Interpol contacted me about the possible identity of the assassin.'

'Who did they come up with?' interjected Marler.

'I know why you've asked. If anybody eventually locates the bastard you will. Interpol told me it could be the Phantom. They're sure he killed that German, Keller, and the French Minister. They then told me – emphasizing it was no more than a rumour – that the Phantom could be an Englishman.'

'So what about the Chrysler?' Tweed prodded. 'You've been told to lay off the Americans.'

'Blow that. I'm getting a search warrant for Irongates so we can open up that garage. If I get the sack, then I do. I'll send a team down there. Think I'd better get moving.'

'Watch your back,' warned Tweed.

'I've been doing that for years – some of the people I've had to deal with.' Buchanan stood up, grabbed the overcoat Monica had put on a hanger in a corner near the door. 'And thanks, Monica, for the coffee. You make the best in London.'

With one hand on the door handle, he turned to look quickly at everyone. He pulled a wry face.

'Don't do anything I would. Otherwise you'll get yourselves into a proper pickle . . .'

'He's his old self,' said Paula when Buchanan had gone. 'Must be the coffee.'

'We gave him something he can get hold of,' Tweed asserted.

'Oh, I had an early morning phone call before I left my flat,' Newman announced.

'Give,' rapped out Paula. 'You look pleased with yourself.'

'Sharon Mandeville wants me to have dinner with her tomorrow evening. How she got hold of my ex-directory number I have no idea. She suggested Santorini's, the new place down by the river.'

'And you're going to oblige the lady?'

'Thought I might get some information out of her.'

'Of course. That ravishing photo of her we showed you had nothing to do with it.'

'I just wonder,' Tweed mused, 'whether she's had it up to here with America. Maybe she's decided to settle down over here. Hence her buying a house in Dorset. In which case she'll be keen to build up a circle of friends.'

'I've just found out about that,' Monica intervened. 'She's actually bought a small manor in Dorset.'

'Which backs up my theory about her,' Tweed remarked.

'I'd better get moving,' Newman said, standing up. 'I want to go home and freshen up. I'll need my wits about me. I'm meeting that slug Basil Windermere this evening.'

'Look forward to tomorrow,' Paula told him. 'Santorini's will cost you a fortune. The lady would make an expensive girl friend. Lucky you can afford it,' she continued to tease him.

'I'm getting out of here. I'm Paula's target.'

He was walking to the door when it opened. Butler walked in, carrying a cardboard box with a pink ribbon round it. He handed the box to Marler.

'It works,' he told him.

'What works,' demanded Newman.

'It does.'

'I'll come with you, Bob,' decided Marler.

He walked out, carrying the box under his arm. Newman warned him again on their way down the stairs that there would be hell to pay if Windermere recognized him.

Inside the American Embassy, in the large room over-looking the square, was a conference table. At its head sat Jake Ronstadt. Only five foot four tall, his presence nevertheless dominated the eight Americans seated on either side. Clean-shaven, he had a large head, a thin mouth, a short thick nose and a lot of jaw. His chest was like a barrel but his legs were thin, his feet small. He shuffled a pack of cards as he gazed from one man to the next, his eyes hard, intimidating.

'You guys had better work a damned sight harder for the huge pay cheques you get,' he growled. 'I'm having to do everything myself. Met a guy who gave me the data on Strangeways. He wanted five thousand bucks for what he told me. He's at the bottom of the Thames now. Get the message?'

'Sure, Jake.'

It was a chorus from the eight men assembled around the table. A fulsome chorus, motivated by fear. Jake continued to shuffle the pack of cards. No one had ever seen him play a game. It was just a weird habit he had, part of his forceful personality. His accent was New York's back streets and he spoke in a deep rumble, spacing out his words as though addressing a bunch of morons. All his subordinates wore black English business suits. Jake was clad in a leather windcheater, leather trousers.

'Charlie says the operation is moving too slowly.'

'Who is Charlie?' asked Diamond Waltz.

'Hank.' Jake paused. 'I guess you kinda asked the wrong question. How cold do you reckon it is at the bottom of the river?'

'Sorry, Jake.' The bald-headed Waltz was shivering with fright. 'I'm very sorry. I made a bad mistake.'

'Don't hire guys to make mistakes. Keep your god-damn trap shut. Maybe then you'll live longer, Baldy.'

'Are we still working with Chuck?' asked another man. 'Just want to get the score clear.'

'Chuck Venacki wasn't invited to attend our little meetin' – you check everything you find out with me. Here are your targets.'

Jake stood up, holding a sheaf of papers. He walked slowly round the table. Behind each man he paused and the man he stood behind was careful not to look round. Then he laid a sheet of paper in front of each man. The sheets were white paper, blank except for the names typed on them. There was no identification that they had originated from the Embassy. Completing the job, Jake lowered his bulk into his chair, picked up the pack of cards.

'You guys all have different names on your sheets. Your job is to dig up any dirt you can on your names. All are prominent people in this country. Baldy, the first name on your list is important.'

'Paula Grey.'

'That's great, Baldy. Really great. You can read. She's to have the full treatment – unlike all the other names on the lists. Do it quickly.'

'I make her talk first?' Baldy said eagerly. 'Then she goes overboard?'

'You've got it. Charlie says it will break the morale of her boss. When she's fished out of the river.'

'Her address in Fulham is here. Should be easy.'

'Nothing's easy.' Jake waved a warning thick finger, taking in everyone round the table. 'I've trained you all how to dig up dirt. Some guy with gambling debts, cheating on his wife, a pervert, open to a bribe. Anything that gives us a grip on them. So when we say dance, they dance. To our tune. You all have addresses of your targets. OK?'

'Very OK, Chief,' said a thin-boned man with a hard face who sat nearest to Jake.

'Not OK, Vernon,' Jake snarled. 'You need more.' He shoved a bulky envelop at him. 'Don't see why I should take another walk round this table. Inside that package is an envelope for each gentleman present. Has his name on it. Inside is a photo of each target, man or woman. Why not get on your feet and deliver the goods.'

Jake sat shuffling his cards while Vernon stood up, opened the package, walked round the table, dropping an envelope in front of each of his collegues. Baldy opened his, went through several photos, frowned.

'May I speak, Chief?' he suggested nervously.

'If you have anything to say.'

'No photo of a woman in my envelope.'

'So we didn't get a pic of the Grey twist. You've had to look before without a pic.'

'Sure, Chief. When I get her can I use the old warehouse in Eagle Street, down in the East End. Vernon showed me the place the day we arrived on Eurostar.'

'Sounds like a good idea. Wonder where that came from? Nobody will hear her screaming.'

'Paula,' Tweed suggested, getting up from his swivel chair, 'it has been a gruelling time. How would you like to join me for an evening at Goodfellows?'

'Lovely idea. Thank you. I could do with some relaxation – and Bob and Marler are off on a bar crawl with Windermere. I'll drive home to change, then come back here to join you.'

82

'I'm not changing. I put on a decent suit to see Strangeways,' Tweed told her.

He looked at Monica when Paula had left. She was talking to someone on the phone, making notes on a pad. When she put down the phone she nodded with satisfaction.

'That was a contact in Washington I was talking to. I'm still building up profiles.'

'I have an additional fact I'd like you to concentrate on. I need to know which of the profiles you're working on has a second name. Charlie. Or Charles.'

'English or American?'

'Could be either. I heard the name when I picked up a phone at the American Embassy and overheard a snatch of conversation. His identity could be the key to what is happening.'

'What is happening?'

'I'm not sure yet. I'm beginning to fear a gigantic operation is under way which bodes ill for this country. But Charlie can wait until the morning. Go home now and get some rest.'

'Not yet. The adrenalin is surging. I'm going to keep at it for a bit longer. You should enjoy Goodfellows. I hear it's a sophisticated nightclub. Expensive too. Nice for Paula.'

'I'm just hoping she won't be mad with me when she sees the clientele after we've arrived.'

'Why should she be?'

'Because it happens to be the in-place patronized by top Americans at the moment.'

Paula parked her car in the cul-de-sac off the Fulham Road. She was lucky – she had a permanent slot which went with her flat. She lived in the top half of a small elegant house divided into two flats.

She was standing under a wall lamp when she dropped her car keys on the cobbles. Swearing, she stooped to pick them up, then straightening up, she paused to smooth down her glossy dark hair. Then she ran up the outside staircase, paused again under another wall lamp to get out her two sets of keys to open the door.

Across on the other side of the Fulham Road, a man stood hidden in the shadows of a doorway. Baldy was dressed in an almost comic fashion. He wore a Borsalino hat, its wide brim well pulled down. It was partly a disguise and partly to shield his head from the intense cold.

'Got you, Paula Grey,' he said to himself. 'I guess you're not going to enjoy the last few hours of your life with me. Not one friggin' bit.'

8

'Cheers, my dear chap,' Basil Windermere called out.

Newman had just entered the ground-floor bar. He acknowledged the greeting with a wave of his hand. Windermere was perched on a bar stool. Walking slowly towards him Newman glanced at the couples dining at tables by the wall. No Marler. Quickly he averted his sweeping gaze. Marler was there, with a girl.

He's practically unrecognizable even to me, Newman thought. Marler was wearing a smoking jacket with a velvet collar. He also had a pair of large horn-rimmed glasses perched on his nose. It was the glasses which did the trick, Newman decided – he'd never seen Marler wear them before. For some reason his raincoat was folded over the empty chair next to him.

'Just finished a drink,' Windermere said as Newman sat on the stool next to him.

He wore his usual polka-dot bow tie, a pink shirt, a Prince of Wales check suit. It should have looked wrong but instead it looked smart. Windermere always took a lot of trouble over his appearance.

'Can you hold out a few more minutes?' Windermere said.

'Hold out?'

'Before you have a drink. This place is quiet tonight. I vote we go up the street to Goodfellows. Where the action is.'

'Where the rich ladies are?'

'Got it in one, chum.'

'Then we're leaving,' Newman agreed, raising his voice.

'At the double, as Rupert would say. Mockingly.'

Marler leaned across his table, spoke quietly to his companion, his wallet in his hand. He extracted a fifty-pound note, left it on the table as he spoke.

'Sorry. Warned you I might only have time for a drink. Have to rush back to the office. My pager just beeped.'

'I didn't hear anything . . .'

'You weren't supposed to. I'll call you.'

'Don't bother. You haven't even finished your food—'

She was talking to a blank space. Newman, trying to catch what Marler said, left his stool. Windermere was already on his way out. Marler slipped past Newman as though he didn't know him. He peered out while putting on his own coat, stiffened.

Looking down the narrow street he saw a small man wearing an old trilby hat, a shabby windcheater and denims, peering inside a dustbin. The Ear. As he watched, standing well back, Marler saw the small man start shuffling up the street at surprising speed. The little man passed him, Marler looked to his left. Basil Windermere was striding up the street, his long legs moving at an athletic pace. Marler was startled. The Ear was following Basil Windermere.

'I think this place is full of Americans,' Paula whispered.

They had just entered the luxurious interior of Goodfellows. Chandeliers were suspended from the ceilings. Each table was illuminated by a rose-coloured shade supported above an expensive, tasteful vase. Most of the tables were occupied and there was the sound of buoyant chatter mingling with the clinking of glasses.

'We have a table reserved. Name is Tweed,' her escort said to the head waiter.

'By a window, sir. I'm sure you will find it satisfactory.'

Paula sat in a chair facing in the distance the mahogany bar. She glanced round the restaurant, glad she'd taken the trouble to change. A lot of the men wore evening suits with black ties. Others were in smart business clothes. The women had all dressed up. She felt comfortable in her blue dress with its high collar and long sleeves. Round her slim waist she wore a thin gold belt. She looked at the bar again.

'I thought you were taking us out for an evening's relaxation.'

'That was the idea,' said Tweed, glancing up from the menu.

'The place is packed with Americans. That nice Ed Osborne is holding up one end of the bar. You brought us here to check up on who is in town.'

'Should I apologize?'

'Of course not.' Her tone softened. 'I'm sorry I talked like that. We have a job to do.'

'And there may not be much time left.'

Tweed returned to examining the menu, glancing down the wine list, turning pages of the leather folder. The waiter appeared quickly and Paula ordered a dry Martini. Tweed said he'd like a glass of dry white French wine. Paula stared again at the bar.

'When you can, look at the far end of the bar. Osborne is talking to a weird man, and gestured towards our table.'

'Wonder who he is? Not sure I like the look of him.'

The individual she had drawn his attention to was short, had wide shoulders, a large head and a barrel of a chest. His brown hair was cut short and he wore an evening suit. He left the bar, sidled his way between the tables and headed straight for them.

'Hi, folks. Ed Osborne suggested I came over to give you both a big hello. I'm Jake Ronstadt.'

'Paula Grey,' said Tweed. 'And to finish the introductions I'm Tweed.'

'You have a real good taste in beautiful ladies. I sure do envy you.'

He bent down, wrapped a bearlike hand and arm round Paula's shoulders. Inwardly she thanked Heaven she was not wearing an off-the-shoulder dress. Tweed was staring at Ronstadt. When he mentioned Paula's name the small, heavy-lidded eyes had flickered. Just for a millisecond, but the reaction had been strange.

'You sound to be from New York,' Tweed commented. 'What are you doing over here? You're a long way from home.'

'Right on the button. New York.' Ronstadt released Paula from his grip, stood up. 'I'm with the Embassy.'

'Really?' Tweed persisted. 'In what capacity? What job?'

'I guess you could say I'm in public relations.'

'And what does that involve, Mr Ronstadt?'

'Jake, please,' his voice rumbled. 'I smooth the way for making friends with people the Ambassador wants to meet.'

'Well, I don't see any reason why he'd want to meet me.'

'He sure does. That's why Ed sent me over to get to know you both. And I'll tell you something else.' He lowered his voice. 'Jefferson Morgenstern, our Secretary of State, is anxious to see you.' He placed a thick finger beside his stubby nose. 'That's off the record. Know what I mean? Guess I'd better leave you folk to get on with your dinner. Enjoy.'

'I don't like that man,' Paula said when Ronstadt had left. 'He radiates physical vitality and power – but he has the smile of a crocodile.'

'Someone else for Monica to profile,' Tweed said quietly. 'I see you've spotted someone at the bar, from your expression.'

'You're not going to believe it. Bob has just walked in with Basil Windermere. They're sitting at the other end of the bar from Osborne.'

'Guess I'll start with a Scotch,' Basil said as he settled on his stool.

'Do you ever sit on anything other than a bar stool?' Newman enquired.

'Not if I can help it. You'd be surprised at how many ancient dowagers think it's fun to perch on one with me. Makes them feel young again.'

'If you say so. I'll have a Scotch too,' he told the barman. 'Basil, you mentioned a Rupert who used the phrase "at the double". Rupert Who?'

'Rupert Strangeways, of course. There's only one

Rupert, son of *the* Strangeways. The old boy is loaded. Rupert's a drinking pal of mine.'

'On the Continent as well?'

'No.' A pause. 'Not on the Continent. Down the hatch!'

'Cheers. Do you still go to that shooting club down by the Thames?'

'Haven't been for ages. Got bored. No business there. No ladies dripping diamonds. Rupert used to come with me. He's stopped going.'

'Was he a good shot?'

'You must be joking. He hit everything except the target. I scored the occasional bull. Pure fluke. Talk of the devil – look what the tide washed up.'

A man in his thirties with a sneering expression had sat on the stool next to Basil. He wore a very expensive dinner suit, a jacket with silk-covered lapels. The barman came and stared at him.

'I'll have a double Scotch. At the double. While you're at it build me another as a reserve.'

The barman gave Rupert a look which was not friendly. Newman was trying to think of a way to get Basil out of Goodfellows. When they had come in Newman spotted Tweed and Paula at their window table. He was sure Basil, with the bar as his magnet, hadn't seen them. There had to be a ploy to persuade Basil to come with him elsewhere. Newman had also observed that Ed Osborne was occupying the far end of the bar. He wondered who the short, grim-looking individual with Osborne might be. He kept staring at Newman with his hard eyes. Newman thought it was a long time since he'd seen such a ruthless-looking man. His opportunity to shift Basil came unexpectedly.

'You shouldn't talk to the barman the way you do, Rupert,' Basil told him. 'He doesn't like it.'

'Who gives a frig for a barman?'

'Not the lord of the manor, the king of creation, God's gift to the casinos in Europe.'

'How would you like this drink poured over your crummy suit?' Rupert snarled.

'Time to go, find fresh fields,' Newman said firmly, gripping Basil's arm.

'I think you're right,' Basil agreed. He glanced at Rupert. 'You don't get the best type of person in here.'

Rupert was lifting his glass when Newman hauled Basil off the stool. Just in time. Rupert's double Scotch flooded the stool Basil had just vacated. Newman hustled Basil away from the bar, between tables and out of the entrance. The cold air hit Basil, who stumbled, swayed.

'Time to go home,' Newman insisted. 'We can have another drink there . . .'

An hour and a half later Tweed paid the bill and left the club with Paula. They had come by taxi and Tweed was looking for another cab. Of course, there was no sign of one.

'We'll find a cab and I'll see you safely home,' he said.

'That isn't necessary. It's out of your way. You can see me into a taxi and it will take me straight home.'

'Are you sure?'

'I'm certain.'

Tweed was in two minds. His instinct was to drop her off at her flat in the Fulham Road. On the other hand he wanted to go back to his office. He felt sure Monica would be working on her profiles into the early hours. He was impatient to see what she had come up with – and to add to her list the name of Jake Ronstadt. He had sensed something disturbing about the American's personality.

'That was odd,' Paula remarked, pulling her coat

more tightly round her against the chilly night, 'Rupert, of all people, turning up at the bar.'

'He probably haunts places like that at night. Especially a new one like Goodfellows, only opened two months ago. On the lookout for new girl friends. You told me Mrs Belloc, down at Irongates, made a reference to his harem.'

'He's a typical rich man's son. An idler and a wastrel. He seemed to know Windermere.'

'Like attracting like. Both of them are worthless.'

'At one moment it looked like turning ugly,' Paula reflected. 'Bob certainly moved fast, getting Windermere out of the club.'

'Here's a cab.'

Tweed flagged it down. He opened the rear door and Paula dived inside, glad to get into some warmth. Tweed gave the driver a banknote to cover the fare and the tip.

'It's your job to see my friend gets back safely to the address I've given you.'

'With a tip like that, mate, I'd take her safely to Singapore,' the driver assured Tweed.

'I must be tired,' Paula called out to Tweed after she had lowered the window. 'I forgot to thank you for a marvellous dinner. I feel so relaxed.' She leaned out, kissed him on the cheek. 'Thank you again.' She looked down at the pavement. 'And don't get wet – it must have rained when we were inside.'

'Good night. See you in the morning.'

Newman had two surprises when he steered Basil outside Goodfellows. His companion suddenly straightened up, walked a few very steady paces before he turned back.

'Aren't you coming? You know my flat is just off Regent Street. Takes only a few minutes to hoof it there.'

Newman's second surprise was when he looked across the street at another restaurant. Sitting at the window table by himself, still wearing the horn-rims, was Marler. What on earth was he up to?

'I said, aren't you coming?' Basil called out again. 'Bloody cold hanging around out here.'

'That flat of yours must be damned expensive,' Newman commented as he hurried to walk alongside his companion.

Basil, striding along, showed no sign that he was affected in any way by the amount of alcohol he had consumed. He was even humming a tune.

'Awfully damned expensive,' he agreed in a lordly way. 'What does it matter? I've borrowed it from a wealthy lady who has gone abroad.'

'Do you ever buy anything yourself?' Newman wanted to know.

'Not if I can help it. Here we are. Down this side street.'

Newman had the uncanny feeling they were being followed. He glanced back once. Couldn't see any sign of another human being. Odd. His instinct in that direction had always been right before. They walked rapidly down the narrow street. It was deserted. Basil stopped by his front door, felt for his keys. Newman turned to see if he could fit key into lock first time. He did without hesitation.

'Bob,' he said, turning on his heel. 'Now we've got here I'm feeling a bit tired.'

'Go straight up to bed,' Newman urged, relieved he wouldn't have to spend any more time with him. 'You look fresh but . . .'

'I was up till 4 a.m. last night – that is, this morning. Do you mind? And thanks for coming with me.'

'Off to beddy-byes.'

Basil disappeared inside, closed the door. Newman

felt spots of rain on his face. He swung round and Marler was only a few paces away. Newman grinned, punched Marler on his shoulder.

'Thought I had a tail.'

'You did. But it wasn't me.'

'Who the hell was it, then?'

'The Ear. He's been tracking Windermere all evening. I just wonder why.'

'Where is the Ear?'

'Ahead of us. He slipped past you when you watched Windermere opening his door. You never hear him. You rarely see him. And we're going to get soaked. Let's walk on, find a cab.'

They turned up the collars of their raincoats. It was very quiet. Only the patter of the rain and the squelch of their shoes on the pavement. Newman stopped suddenly, staring ahead. A small figure wearing a trilby hat appeared out of nowhere, shuffling away from them.

'I wonder who that is,' Newman mused.

'That is the Ear. Maybe he wants to talk to me. Now he is slowing down. Why?'

He looked up as he spoke and thunderclouds seemed almost to touch the top of the flat roofs of the terrace houses, most turned into flats, one of which was occupied by Basil Windermere. A brilliant flash of lightning was followed instantly by a deafening clap of thunder.

'Under cover,' said Marler. 'The Ear has darted into the shelter of a doorway.'

They had just reached their own shelter, close to a front door and under an overhang of a stone beam, when the cloudburst enveloped the street. Rain sluiced down at a slanting angle like a curtain of fine wires. Rivers of water ran down the street's gutters, the top of drainpipes overflowed, sending cascades of water down.

'That's why the Ear paused,' said Marler. 'He knew what was coming.'

Frequently he glanced out to make sure the Ear hadn't moved out of his shelter. The cloudburst ceased as quickly as it had erupted. They heard the storm drifting away to the east. Marler peered out again, stood stock-still.

'What's the matter?' Newman asked.

'The Ear is coming this way. I see now why he really paused.'

'Why?'

'Four men coming up the street this way. The Ear may be the target.'

It was the first time Newman had heard alarm in Marler's voice. He followed him, looked along the street. The small man was shuffling swiftly towards them. He must have recognized Marler, who had removed his glasses. He gestured over his shoulder, dived into another doorway.

Beyond him was a sinister cluster of four black opened umbrellas, feet walking under them. It wasn't possible when Newman first saw them to identify who was approaching – the cluster had the large umbrellas lowered, the feet steadily advancing beneath the shallow black cones. Then the front two umbrellas were elevated.

Each of the two visible men held handguns. Newman saw their weapons clearly as they passed under a street lamp. Soon they would reach the doorway where the Ear was hiding. He grabbed for his Smith & Wesson.

'Not wanted,' Marler snapped. 'Leave this to me.'

He took something out of his raincoat pocket. Newman saw it was a grenade. Marler waved a hand sideways at the Ear, who responded instantly, diving inside another doorway. Crouching down, Marler thrust his right hand, holding the grenade, behind him. Pressing a button, he rolled the object at high speed along the pavement.

It shot forward and the four umbrellas stopped moving. The object reached them, arriving in the middle of the group. There was a loud crack and the four men panicked, running along the pavement until they disappeared round a corner, their umbrellas waving madly.

'It was a dud,' Newman said. 'It should have killed them all.'

'Hardly.'

Marler was grinning as he stood up. He pulled his rain-covered coat away from his knees and waited for the Ear to reappear.

'What the hell was it?' Newman demanded.

'One of the new devices cooked up by the boffins in the basement back at Park Crescent. Looks like a grenade, it sounds like a grenade when it goes off. It explodes into tiny fragments you'd have trouble finding. It also contains a glue-like liquid which sprays all over the targets. They won't know what it is – probably be sure it's some kind of poison, which it isn't. I don't think we wanted dead bodies sprawled all over the pavement. We would have had a problem.'

'Well, it worked. The thugs appear to have gone for good. They're probably rushing back to the Embassy to get checked by a doctor.'

'Here comes the Ear,' Marler observed. 'I'll introduce him as a friend.'

The little man was shuffling towards them. He glanced over his shoulder twice. A cautious chap, Newman thought – which was probably why he had survived so long. He was close to them when he crossed the street and looked back again to see round the corner where the attackers had vanished. A shot rang out. One single shot.

The Ear staggered, stumbled against the wall of a house, slid down the wall, his legs extended in front of him. He lay slumped there, very still, as Marler ran to him with Newman at his heels, the Smith & Wesson in his hand. Marler bent over the prone form. A red patch was blossoming on the forehead. He opened his mouth, staring at Marler. Blood gurgled.

'Basil . . .' Another grim gurgle. 'Schwarz . . .'

Then nothing. Marler checked his neck pulse. He stood up slowly, gazed at Newman. There was sorrow in his eyes – something Newman had never seen before.

'He's dead,' Marler said slowly. 'Not one of the thugs – he looked back towards us a fraction of a second before the bullet hit him. From the angle he was facing, the shot came from the roof of those houses. The Phantom.'

'I'll kill that bastard when the moment comes,' Newman said.

'No, you won't.' Marler placed a hand on Newman's arm. 'He's my meat.'

9

The taxi taking Paula home arrived close to the entrance to her flat. The driver had overshot the mark by a few yards. She got out into the quiet street, paid the driver, thanked him. She turned and walked the short distance back to the cul-de-sac.

Several cars were parked illegally by the kerb. It happened often at this late hour – wardens were rarely on duty at this time of night. An old lady approached her with a wrinkled hand held out.

'A fiver to save a soul,' she whined. 'I ain't eaten in two days. I'm droppin' with 'unger.'

The old woman had matted grey hair which hadn't been washed for Heaven knew how long. Her clothes were rags, held together in places with safety pins. Her beady eyes were pleading, at the end of their tether. Her thin lips trembled and her extended hand shook with the cold.

Paula tried to do two things at once. She pulled her shoulder bag in front of her, then used both hands to extract a five-pound note from her purse. Tired as she was she saw her shadow thrown by a street light on the damp pavement. Then she stiffened. There were *two* shadows.

With both hands holding her purse, she couldn't reach for her Browning in the special pocket. A rough hand grasped her throat. She lifted one foot to scrape it down the shin of her assailant. Then a pad was pressed against her face, covering her nose. She smelt chloroform. She tried to breathe out but the cold air had forced her to breathe in.

The old lady, bad teeth bared in an evil grin, blurred. Paula, as in a dream, was aware of the sound of a car door opening. Then she sagged, lost consciousness, knew nothing.

She was woozy, her eyes closed, her stomach threatening to erupt. She forced it to behave. She appeared to be sitting against some sort of couch. She kept her eyes closed. The fabric of the couch was well worn. She felt the hard edge of a wooden strut pressing against her back. It was icy cold. She forced herself to keep still.

She could hear the clump of hard shoes on a wooden floor. She opened one eye, then both eyes. A few yards away she could see who was making the clumping noise: The back of a short, thickset man with a bald head. The room was huge, like an old warehouse. She closed her eyes quickly as her captor began to turn round.

During her quick survey of her prison she had seen a large beam spanning the width of the warehouse, about ten feet above the floor. She felt sleepy, willed herself to keep awake. Something had been slung over the beam. She heard the clank of a chain.

That was what she had seen, a gleaming new chain with links about three inches wide. He was clumping about again, further away. Without moving her feet, she wriggled her toes. Anything to bring herself back to normal. The bald man had been holding something in his hand. A Colt automatic.

She became aware she no longer had her shoulder bag. He had her Browning somewhere. The feet came towards her. She knew when he stopped he was standing, gazing down at her. She kept her eyes closed, her body limp. He began to talk. Then she knew he was American, a coarse voice.

'Wake up, lady. You and I are going to have a fun time. You've got things to tell me. Questions to answer. What the hell is the matter with you? Wake up!'

He began to slap both sides of her face with his rough hand. She let her head flop from side to side with each blow. I have to get back to normal before he knows I'm conscious, she kept telling herself. The slapping stopped. He swore foully.

He was walking away from her again. She took in deeper breaths of the cold air without moving. Got to clear my head, get my strength back. I need more time. The clumping came back in her direction. She wasn't going to get more time. There was a musty smell which suggested a building that hadn't been opened for a long time. The heavy footsteps stopped in front of her.

'Wake up, you friggin' twist,' the coarse voice ordered. 'If you don't you'll get a bucket of cold water over you. You're going to be sodden wet soon, whatever you do or don't tell me.'

Inwardly she cringed. What was he talking about?

There had been something very sinister in those last words.

Then his hands grasped her shoulders and he was shaking her from side to side. She kept her eyes tightly shut. His grip was strong and painful. She kept her body loose, let him go on shaking her. She was breathing in and out slowly, clearing her mind.

'OK. You get the bucket of water . . .'

She moaned, moved shakily, opened both eyes. He was very ugly. His bald head gleamed in the light from the naked bulbs suspended from the rafters high above them. His eyes glittered with anticipation at some pleasurable experience. He hauled out the Colt from a wide leather belt under his windcheater.

'Try any funny tricks with me and you get a bullet in the head. Can you hear me?'

'Where am I? Who are you?'

'My bloody pals call me Baldy. Guess why?'

'I can't move.' She slurred the words. 'Can't see you. Where am I?'

'In a place where we won't be disturbed. You and I are going to have fun and games.'

'My head's swimming.'

She closed her eyes again. He administered several more hard slaps to both sides of her face. The pain was helping her to become more alert. She heard his feet clump a short distance, realized he was behind the couch. Then something cold and weighty was dropped round her neck. A chain. She fought down the terror which was threatening to overwhelm her. Now she was able to think, she realized her desperate situation. She was going to end up dead. Kidnappers who intended to release their victims were careful never to show their faces. Baldy hadn't even attempted to cover his face. She felt even more helpless with the chain round her neck.

'OK. You can get up now. Or I'll drag you up like a dog.' He giggled. 'Dawg on a chain. That's what you are.'

She opened her eyes. He was holding a length of chain in one hand. It must be attached to the collar of chain round her throat. She placed both hands on the couch as though for support.

'I don't think I can stand up.'

'So I'll drag you.'

'Give me a minute.'

'Get on your friggin' feet!' he screamed at her.

She stood up slowly, more slowly than she needed to. She stood still, bracing her legs to strengthen them. Now she could see far more. She appeared to be in an ancient warehouse used to dump unwanted furniture. There were a number of couches scattered round the planked floor. She saw her coat thrown carelessly over the back of a battered old wooden chair. Her shoulder bag dangled beside it. The clasp was still fastened. She felt sure he hadn't even bothered to rummage inside it. Which meant her Browning was still in the secret pocket. It could have been a mile away for all the hope she had of getting her hands on it.

'We are going for a little walk,' Baldy said, grinning.

'I may fall down . . .'

'Fall down, then!' he screamed. 'Then I'll drag you.'

'I'll try and make it.'

Baldy was holding a long length of chain. The end was attached to the part at the back of her neck. The links rested loosely on her skin, looped below her chin. She kept stopping as he approached the beam above them. During these brief pauses she stretched her legs without moving them, testing her strength.

'Keep going, little dawg,' he sneered. 'Haven't got all night.'

'My legs are going to give way,' she lied.

'So I drag you along the hard floor. Your choice, honey.'

She wished she could punch his leering face. She was feeling utterly humiliated. Then suddenly a cold fury took hold of her mind. *This wretched little thug from the back streets of God knows where!* She lowered her eyes so he couldn't see her change of expression. Which meant she was looking at the floor.

Stretching towards them from below the beam a section of the floor appeared to be a huge elongated panel, a closed trapdoor. At the far end, inset into the wood, was a small depression, and inside it, fitted level with the floor surface, was a wide metal lever. Terror returned again as she imagined what this might be. She suppressed the terror, concentrated on slowing him down.

'Come on, honey. Make with the legs.'

He jerked the chain and she nearly fell forward. Recovering her balance, she padded deliberately forward, her shoes clacking on the planks. She was almost under the beam when he moved behind her, still holding his long length of chain. Before she knew what was happening he had lifted the chain collar round her neck and inserted an extensive length under it.

'I'm not talking tied up like this,' she snapped.

'Shut your stupid female mouth. You'll talk your head off.'

Still holding the chain, he clumped over to a table. It supported a bucket of water and a glass. Dipping the glass into the water, he drank some, ran his thick lips slowly round the rim of the glass, then hurled the contents in her face. She had a double shock. The cold water dripped down inside the top of her dress. She shivered. The second shock was to have liquid in her face after he had run his foul tongue round the rim. He was behind her now. He was doing something with her ankles. She looked down. He had looped a section of chain round each one, with a gap between them of over a foot long.

She felt like a fugitive from a chain gang. It intensified her fury. I'd like to strangle him with my bare hands, she thought. Slowly. He appeared in front of her, holding a double length of chain. He grinned, touched her cheek.

'Cosy now, ain't it, my lovely?'

'I can do without the compliments,' she rapped back.

'Temper. Mustn't give way to temper,' he taunted her.

'I'm not talking trussed up like this,' she blazed.

'Let's work out how things are.' He was almost drooling with enjoyment. 'Chain round your neck is looped like a noose. Bit by bit it pulls tighter – till you choke to death. Better start using that spitting mouth of yours to answer my questions. That gives me an idea.'

He worked his mouth, then spat at her, hitting her on the chest. She just managed to stop herself recoiling with revulsion. *Don't give the little swine any satisfaction.* Standing back, he gripped the long length of chain, hurled it upwards. It swept over the beam, a length fell and he grasped the end. With horror, she knew what he was going to do. She gritted her teeth, clenched her hands.

'Let's start now,' he said. 'Quiz show. Like you get on television. Question, then answer. Get it? Question, then answer.'

'Put me back on the couch. Then we'll talk.'

'Listen to the lady! Giving me orders. Haven't you been listening, twist?'

He punched her in the ribs. Teeth still gritted, she didn't react. He'd used the hand holding the chain to deliver the punch so it had lacked a lot of his strength. Now he stood back from her and she tensed. While standing she had continued bracing her legs.

102

'Who's your boss?' he asked suddenly.

'Benson.'

'Wicked. Real wicked. Lying to Baldy.'

He hauled on the chain and she was elevated off the floor. Expecting this, her hands dived to her neck inside the chain, keeping it away from her throat. He went on hauling her higher until the top of her head was close to the beam. She found herself swaying, back and forth. She looked down and saw the top of his bald head.

'Swing 'igh, swing low,' he sang in his tuneless voice.

The strain on her hands was enormous. She knew she couldn't keep this up for long. Then he did something else which she had expected. He released the chain and she dived to the floor. She landed as she had been taught at the training mansion in Surrey, bending her knees to cushion the impact. She straightened up as his hated face peered round at her.

'You can't hold out for long. Who is your boss? Just the first question.'

'Benson.'

'Up you go . . .'

Again she was hauled upwards, held there, head almost touching the beam, but not quite as high as before. Again her body started swaying. She looked down. He was standing back a few feet from the beam. She forced herself to sway harder, hands protecting her throat against the chain. She was swaying back and forth through a greater arc, her knees lifted. She could never have done it without the aerobics and the exercises she had practised at the health club. She was beginning to sway back quite quickly when suddenly she dropped her legs to the fullest extent, opening them as wide as possible. She was staring at Baldy who gazed up at her in surprise. The chain round her ankles caught him under the jaw, round his thick neck.

He let go of the end he was holding, which she had

known he would if she could bring it off. Probably break my bloody back, she thought. The chain slithered over the beam, she plunged down behind Baldy, landed on one of the many old couches lying round the warehouse floor.

Positions reversed. Now she had him in a stranglehold, the chain tight round his neck as she clamped her feet together. He was on his back, hands clawing futilely at the chain cutting off his air supply. His heels hammered at the floor. One heeltip caught on the lever inset into the floor. The trapdoor he was sprawled along opened away from Paula. She whipped her feet apart. The ankle chain slipped up over his jaw. He was free. The trap slid downwards. Baldy let out a croaking scream. His body rushed forward, vanished into the gaping hole. Paula heard a distant splash, then silence.

Because she forced herself not to hurry, she released herself from the chain more quickly than she'd expected. She stood up off the couch, legs trembling. Cautiously she crept forward to the edge, looked down. Seeing nothing, she forced her aching limbs to take her across to the chair, took out her Browning, her torch. When she returned to the rim of the gaping hole she turned on her powerful torch. The tip of the beam just reached down to show her fast-moving water. The River Thames, she guessed. That was where she had ultimately been destined to go.

Forcing her arms into her coat, she picked up the chain, threw it down into the river. Behind her on the far wall was a closed door. She made herself walk quickly. An old key was in the lock. She had to use both bruised hands to turn it, to pull back a wooden bar. She had the Browning in her hand as she opened it and peered out. If any of Baldy's chums were waiting she was going to kill them.

She was gazing out into a deserted cobbled street, the

buildings looking fit only for demolition. A wall lamp cast an eerie glow over a street sign. Eagle Street.

To her left the street ended. Beyond it flowed the Thames, with wriggling lights reflected in its dark flow. She turned right after closing the door behind her. She emerged into a wider street which reminded her of the East End. Nobody about. A taxi came crawling along the street, its For Hire light on.

She flagged it down madly. The driver slowed, peered out to examine her. He looked surprised at her good coat and shoes, illuminated by another street light. He leaned forward.

'What's a lady like you doin' in a place like this?'

'A row with my boy friend. I just got out of his car and he drove off.'

'Better get yourself another boy friend. Where to?'

'Park Crescent, please. Facing Regent's Park.'

10

Paula was so relieved when she saw the lights in Tweed's office windows. She had guessed he might be working late. Entering his room, she found not only Monica but also Newman and Marler. Tweed took one look at her, jumped up, went to her.

'What happened?'

'I must look the most awful mess . . .'

She sank down behind her desk and told them about her experience. Reaction had set in. Her voice was shaky. Hidden beneath the desk, her knees trembled. She pressed them together, forced herself to go on talking. At an early stage Tweed asked Monica to fetch plenty of sweetened tea – he recognized that Paula was in shock. Later, while Paula continued, Monica checked her hands

– bruised where she had fought to hold the chain away from her neck. She brought the first aid kit, gently rubbed soothing salve on her hands, then on her neck.

Glancing at Tweed, Newman realized he was almost in a state of shock himself. Sagged in his chair, Tweed was appalled that he had let Paula go home by herself. He cursed himself for not insisting on accompanying her. At one moment, when Paula's head was turned away, he frowned at Newman and Marler, warning them not to mention the killing of the Ear. That could come later, when Paula had recovered.

'So that's it,' Paula concluded when she had described her ordeal. 'I think I'd like to go home now.'

'We'll come with you,' Tweed said instantly. 'Butler and Nield are still in the building. They will stay the night with you. I recall you have a couple of couches in the living room. Back in a minute . . .'

Paula was protesting it wasn't necessary as he disappeared. He came back a few minutes later, accompanied by Nield and Butler. Nield went over to Paula.

'Sorry you've had such a dreadful time. We have a plan. Harry and I drive ahead of the rest of you. Could you give me the key to your flat? We'd like to go through it with a fine-tooth comb before you arrive. You don't sound too good.'

'I haven't said anything. You used that phrase instead of saying you don't look too good. Which is the case. Thank you, Pete. Here is my key.

'I think I'd like to go to the washroom. I'm filthy,' Paula said when the two men had left.

'I'll come with you,' Monica told her.

'Jake Ronstadt is behind this,' Tweed said grimly when he was alone with Newman and Marler. 'I saw a peculiar, savage expression flicker in his eyes when I was dining with Paula and she told him her name.'

106

'When the opportunity arises I'll break every bone in his body,' said Newman.

'For starters,' Marler suggested.

There was silence in the room until, ten minutes after Butler and Nield had left, Tweed led the way downstairs with Paula. When she had returned with Monica, Newman noticed she had used a modicum of make-up and brushed her hair. Her complexion was still pallid.

They travelled back to the flat in the Fulham Road in the Merc with Newman behind the wheel. Marler sat beside him while Tweed occupied the back next to Paula. He put his arm round her, a gesture for which she was grateful. They were driving through deserted dark streets when Newman kept glancing in his rear-view mirror.

'We're being followed,' he remarked. 'A taxi cab. I'm pulling up here. Back in a minute.'

He walked back until the cab approached him. Only the driver behind the wheel. Newman flagged him down. The driver nearly didn't stop, then changed his mind. He stared unpleasantly as Newman opened his door.

'Been in this country long?' Newman enquired, smiling.

'Sure. What's it to you?'

The accent was coarse American. To talk to the driver Newman had run round the front of the stationary cab so he could open the door on the street side. He grabbed hold of the collar of the leather jacket the driver wore, hauled him out into the street. The American jerked away from Newman, his right hand slipping inside the jacket.

'Buddy, you sure shouldn've done that . . .'

He never completed his sentence. Newman's right fist collided with the American's jaw. A knockout punch.

As he was sagging to the ground Newman grabbed him again, heaved his unconscious body back into his seat. Unzipping the jacket all the way, he found a gun butt protruding from a shoulder holster. Searching in the other pocket he found an American diplomatic passport. Switching off the engine, he extracted the key, threw it into a garden, walked back to the Merc.

'We can now proceed,' he announced, seated behind the wheel.

'So we were being followed,' Tweed commented. 'They must have bribed a cab driver.'

'No.' Newman was still checking his mirror. 'The driver was an American.' He tossed the passport over his shoulder. 'See for yourself.'

'I wonder what happened to the real driver,' Tweed mused as he examined the passport.

'Probably at the bottom of the Thames,' Paula said vehemently. 'Where they dump all their victims.'

'Lew Willis is the name on the passport,' Tweed informed them. 'I think I'll phone Buchanan from Paula's flat, let him know there's a suspicious character in the cab back there. Without his passport he'll be in a real stew . . .'

Butler met them at the entrance leading to the flat. Nield arrived in their car, parked it, got out. Tweed told Paula to wait in the car until he'd spoken to them. Nield was jaunty, waving a hand.

'While Harry was checking the flat I patrolled the area in search of thugs. None about anywhere. All clear. What about the flat, Harry?'

'Clean as a whistle. The flat on the ground floor seems empty. No one inside. I've closed all the curtains in Paula's flat, switched on a few lights to welcome her.'

'Thank you, Harry,' Paula said with feeling. 'The woman downstairs is away. How did you get inside? I forgot to give you the key to the second lock.'

108

'Used one of my skeleton keys to get inside. You can't be too careful the way things are now.'

'Breaking and entering,' Paula teased him.

'That's right. One of my main occupations. It's cold out here. Better get inside. I turned up the heating.'

Once inside, Paula insisted on making coffee for everyone. Tweed made his phone call to Buchanan. When he put down the receiver he looked at Paula, who had just poured coffee.

'Do you feel like talking for a few minutes?'

'Of course I do. I'm tired but the brain is ticking over.'

'What happened at Eagle Street never happened. We've never even heard of the place. If we reported this to Buchanan we'd get bogged down in his investigation. We can't afford the time. The body of Hank Whoever . . .'

'Hank Waltz,' Newman said. 'Known as Diamond Waltz. I had a run-in with him months ago in New York when I was trying to interview Sir Guy Strangeways.'

'You mean a thug like that was protecting Strangeways?' Tweed asked in a tone of disbelief.

'So it seemed.'

'Before I force myself to take a shower,' Paula said, 'I'll get two pairs of blankets to make Pete and Harry more comfortable on the couches.'

'One pair,' said Nield. 'We'll take it in turns to stay awake while the other sleeps. God help anyone who tries to sneak in here.'

'Then I'll say goodnight.' Paula went to Tweed, hugged him.

'Now, don't brood over the fact that I came back to the flat from Goodfellows alone. I can look after myself. I did . . .'

'Earlier,' Tweed began after she had gone, 'I was going to say the body of Hank Whoever is likely to be washed up further down the Thames. Which is why we

109

don't know anything about it. And how, Bob, did you know he was Diamond Waltz?'

'Two things. First from Paula's description of the thug. Also he happened to be in Goodfellows the night you were there with Paula and I was up at the bar with Basil and Rupert. Where to now?'

'Back to Park Crescent. It's going to be a long night . . .'

'I had sinister news when I talked to Buchanan on the phone,' Tweed told Newman and Marler when they were settled in his office. 'An American syndicate is bidding for control of two leading London daily newspapers. Plus bidding for one of the top TV stations and three key radio stations. They're offering so much money they're bound to succeed.'

'What's going on?' asked Monica, who had finished one phone call prior to making another.

'It's serious. The syndicate – when it gets control – will be in a position to start brainwashing the British public. There are shades of Dr Goebbels here.'

'Creepy,' Monica replied.

'The size of this gigantic operation is growing by the hour,' Tweed warned.

'How do we counter this?' Newman wondered.

'We need more men as tough as – or tougher than – the opposition,' Marler interjected. 'As you know, I've spent quite a bit of time in the East End. Just in case we ever needed reinforcements I've trained a team of cockneys. They're known as Alf's Mob. They're gut fighters.'

'They will never be a match for men with guns,' Tweed objected.

'Really?' Marler's expression was sardonic. 'They are lethal with their fists. In addition, in a remote spot in the countryside, I've trained them to use grenades – stun,

110

smoke, the deadly variety. They're now familiar with automatic rifles and handguns. They're masters of stealth – they can creep up on me and have their hands round my neck before I know anyone is near me.'

'I'm impressed.'

'Don't forget,' Marler reminded him, 'if you read the history of the Burma fighting in World War Two it was cockneys who out-fought the enemy. Cockneys! In jungle warfare.'

'So we have a reserve. We may well need it. I'm working on a plan to go on to the offensive. We're not going to let these thugs have it all their own way. More details later.'

'About time,' Marler drawled.

'Tweed.' Monica leaned over her desk. 'I ought to alert you. Howard is back from his overseas visit. So he could be up here any moment.'

'We'll all go home and leave you to it,' Newman suggested.

'Hear, hear,' agreed Marler.

Howard, the Director, was not popular. A pompous man, he was always complaining that Tweed didn't keep him fully informed about what was going on. His complaint was not without foundation – Tweed had a habit of keeping progress to himself until he was certain he knew what was happening. The phone rang, Monica answered it, looked surprised, put her hand over the mouthpiece as she spoke to Tweed.

'There's a Denise Chatel on the phone. Says she's Sharon Mandeville's assistant. Asked if you were still here – she's speaking from a car phone. She could be here in five minutes.'

'At this hour? Oh, well, we need to find out all we can. What does she sound like?'

'She has a lovely voice. Enchanting.'

Tweed stared at Monica. He had never before heard

her refer to a woman with such words. Nodding, he indicated that the woman calling could come to Park Crescent.

'Now,' he began as Monica put down her phone, 'before Paula returned from her ordeal in Eagle Street we were talking about the Ear. You were telling me what happened to him.'

'I still feel rotten,' Marler said, 'leaving him there propped up against the steps, then making an anonymous call to Buchanan, telling him where there was a body.'

'Don't feel guilty,' Tweed assured him. 'The last thing we can cope with is getting caught up in an involved police investigation. Are you sure those men with umbrellas didn't kill him? You said they had guns.'

'Handguns,' Marler corrected. 'I should know enough now to recognize when a rifle bullet has hit someone. It has to be the Phantom.'

'And,' Newman pointed out, 'Basil Windermere had disappeared inside his flat a few minutes earlier. Plus the fact that the last words Kurt Schwarz grasped out were *Basil . . . Schwarz.*'

'Funny that he used his own name. Incidentally, I told you that when I was inside the American Embassy I saw Jefferson Morgenstern, accompanied by guards, putting a file in a safe. I'd like to get hold of that file. I think it's a job for Pete and Harry. They'll need a diversion. Heaven knows how they can manage it.'

'Set fire to the ruddy building,' Monica burst out.

'You know, that could be a good idea.'

'I was only joking,' Monica protested.

'I wasn't.' He paused while Monica answered the phone. She told him their visitor from the Embassy had arrived. 'Ask her to come up,' Tweed told her.

*

George opened the door, stood back, closed it when Denise Chatel had entered and stood quite still. Newman stared, then stood up. Marler leant against a wall, straightened up. He gazed at their visitor. Tweed was amused at their reaction.

Denise Chatel, thirty-something, was about five feet eight tall. She had a good figure, without being voluptuous. A brunette, her hair fell below her shoulders. She had a longish face, excellent features and the hint of a warm smile lingered on her mouth. Wearing a figure-hugging two-piece blue suit, she was enticing. Tweed stood up, held out his hand.

'Do sit down, Ms Chatel. I'm intrigued to know why you have called to see me in the middle of the night.'

She crossed her legs elegantly as she sat down. Neither Newman nor Marler could take their eyes off her.

'I'm an owl, like yourself, Mr Tweed. Which suits Miss Mandeville, who likes to work when most people have left the Embassy.'

'Would you like some coffee?' Newman suggested.

'I'll make it,' Monica said in a brittle tone.

'That would be most acceptable. And a glass of cold water – if that's not too much trouble.'

She had a cool American voice. Underneath it Tweed detected a very different accent.

'Denise Chatel,' he mused, scrutinizing her through his horn-rims. 'That sounds like a French name.'

'My father was French, my mother American. When I was almost thirty they moved to Washington – my father was offered a good job. I went with them.'

'Do you ever return to France?' Tweed persisted gently.

'Oh, frequently. My job takes me to the American Embassy in Paris. Sharon likes to keep herself well

113

informed about what is going on in Europe.' She smiled. 'Are you interrogating me?'

'Just interested in your unusual international background. An American mother, a French father. What job does he have?'

'He was a diplomat.'

Tweed had not been looking at her as he talked. He was doodling circles on a pad, intertwining one with another. Something in her change of voice made him look up.

'Was?'

'He died a year ago. So did my mother. They were killed in a road crash outside Washington.'

He could have sworn there was a film of moisture in her eyes. She suddenly picked up her cup of coffee, drank some, put it down, stared round the room like someone hunted.

'My condolences. Not that words mean a thing when something like that happens. What happened to the other car – or cars? I hope you don't mind my asking.'

'Of course not.' She swallowed more coffee. 'The police said there had only been one other car involved so far as they could tell. It vanished. They never found the driver.'

'I say,' Marler interjected, 'would you care to join me for dinner tomorrow evening?'

'May I think it over?' She had twisted round in her chair to address him, to look at him more carefully. 'Thank you for the offer.' She turned back to Tweed, leaned forward and whispered, 'Can you trust the people with us here? I know the woman who brought me coffee doesn't like me.'

'I could trust all three with my life,' he answered quietly. 'I have done in the past.'

'I'm frightened. Scared out of my wits.'

She was speaking again in a normal voice. But a transformation had taken place. When she had arrived she had been full of life, buoyant. Now her blue eyes appealed for help as she gazed at him. On the surface, she was indeed a very frightened lady. Newman refilled her cup.

'Is that the real reason you came to see me?' Tweed asked.

'Yes. I had an excuse to come – I can tell you that later.'

'Why me?'

'Cord Dillon said if ever I was in trouble you were the one man in London I could trust.'

Nothing in Tweed's expression changed. But she had shaken him. His mind was moving round at top speed – considering a variety of possibilities. All of them menacing.

'How did you come to meet this man, Cord Dillon?' he enquired carefully.

'Sharon used to ask him to come to her Washington office from Langley. I was always sent out of her office. Dillon struck me as a reliable soul. Once he arrived early and we were alone together in my office. I knew then that Sharon was due to come to London, that I'd be coming with her.'

'What is scaring you?'

'Well . . .' She paused. 'I saw some of the men who were to come to London. I've seen them since at the Embassy. They watch every move I make. I found my phone had been bugged. My apartment over here in Belgravia – close to Sharon's – was searched while I was at the Embassy. It was a highly professional job. Only a woman would notice that certain things were not quite as I'd left them.'

'What do you suggest I do to help you?'

'I want us to keep in close touch.' She turned to look at Marler. 'I'll be happy to have dinner with you tomorrow night. What is your name?'

'Alec,' Marler said instantly, using the first name to come into his head. 'We'll go to the Lanesborough. Can I collect you at your apartment?'

'No! Don't do that.' She was alarmed. 'They have someone watching my apartment whenever I'm there. I'll come to the hotel.'

'Eight o'clock suit you?' Marler suggested. 'I'll be waiting in the bar. I'll arrive early.'

'Thank you.'

'Maybe you'd better tell us why you were supposed to come here,' Tweed reminded her.

'My God, I nearly forgot that.' She turned to look at Newman. 'You're having dinner with Sharon tomorrow evening at Santorini's. She sent me over in a limo to say she'll be there at eight thirty.'

'She could have phoned,' Tweed pointed out.

'She told me she'd tried to get you but the line was always engaged.'

Tweed glanced across at Monica, who nodded agreement. She had tied up the lines, making calls to her contacts inside America. She was still building up her profiles.

'I'd better go now,' their visitor said, 'they may wonder why it took so long. And please call me Denise.'

'I'll see you safely into your limo, Denise,' Marler suggested.

'No! Don't do that. They may have followed the limo and then they'll see you. But thank you for the offer.'

'Keep in touch,' Tweed told her, standing up to shake hands. Her grip was firm. 'If you want to tell Marler more tomorrow evening he'll report it to me . . .'

Monica waited until she had gone. Then she began tapping her fingers on her desk to get their attention.

'You're all hooked on her.'

'I don't think so,' Tweed contradicted.

'Well, I do. I grant you she's a real looker.'

'Monica, maybe yes, maybe no. You've overlooked something.'

'What's that?'

'Your profile on Sharon Mandeville showed *her* parents died in a car smash in the States. Now we hear Denise's parents were also wiped out in another car accident, so called. That's too much of a coincidence – you know I don't believe in coincidences.'

'What are you suggesting?' she asked.

'One theory is the parents – in both cases – were killed so there was no risk of the daughters telling them something Washington didn't want spread around. I emphasize that is no more than my first thought. Have you identified Charlie?'

'Not yet. It's difficult,' Monica explained. 'I have to get copies of birth certificates faxed to me. A lot of people are given several names by their parents, then use only the one they like. I'll get there.'

'I know you will.'

Tweed began to doodle again. After a short time he looked at Marler.

'Basil . . . Schwarz . . .' he said half to himself. 'What nationality was Kurt Schwarz?'

'Swiss,' Marler said promptly.

'Which part of Switzerland?'

'The German-speaking part. His natural language was German.'

'Got it!' Tweed threw his pen down. 'Soon we'll all fly to Switzerland. Better get some warm clothes packed. There's heavy snow on the Continent.'

11

Jake Ronstadt sat at the head of the long table in the large room at the American Embassy. The blinds were closed over the windows. He was shuffling a pack of cards. Eight Americans sat beyond him, four on either side of the table. The Executive Action Department was in session in the middle of the night.

'Two of my guys went missin' last night,' Jake growled. 'I don't like two of my people to disappear. Which is why Brad and Leo have joined us.'

'What happened to them?' asked Vernon, the thin-boned man with the hard face.

'Shut your stupid trap. I was comin' to that. Hank Waltz was sent to deal with Paula Grey. Don't know whether he made it. Don't like what I don't know. Remember that. Lew Willis has also gone missin' – I heard from him on his mobile that after he hijacked a London cab he followed two men from Park Crescent. They drove like hell round all the friggin' side streets here. He loses them, drives back to Park Crescent. Next I hear he's following four people in a Merc. Then nothin' – friggin' nothin', so I try to call him on my mobile. No answer. You boys had better understand I'm good and mad.'

'We understand,' said Brad, a squat individual with large teeth.

'What you understand would fit into a pearl – but there'd be no value in it. Kinda shut your trap.'

Jake made them wait while he shuffled his pack of cards some more. It was important to make them know who was running this outfit.

'I figure it's time now we organize a reign of terror

for London. Show them our muscle. Show the people in this town their police are a bunch of kids. Get it?'

'Sure, Jake,' eight voices echoed in chorus. 'We got it.'

'No, you ain't. So I'll tell you. It's called destabiliza-tion. For you who don't know what it means – which means all of you – I'll explain. We'll leave bombs – big bombs with timers – in markets. Over here they call them supermarkets. We'll plant them in bars, restaurants – everywhere a lot of people gather. The Brits will get so they daren't leave their homes. Until bombs start explod-ing inside houses. Terror is a powerful weapon. Got it now? Great idea.'

'Terrific!'

'A winner!'

'A blaster!'

Every man tried to compete with his colleagues in thinking up a better superlative. Jake glowered at them, his mouth a thin tight line. He shook his large head, shuffled his pack a few times.

'You still ain't got it. When a load of bombs have gone off – with heavy casualties – the Brits will start shoutin' their heads off at their police. "Why can't you do something?" That's when we offer to send in an FBI unit. About a week after the FBI have supposedly gone for the tails of the bombers the explosions stop. Result? The Americans are much better at the job than the Metropolitan Police jerks. "Give the job to the FBI," the Brits will beg. We're in control. No more yapping. You had a trial run in Philadelphia when you planted dummy bombs all over the city. None were discovered.'

'When do we start?' asked Brad, daring to open his mouth.

'Soon. First I have to check with Charlie. Timin' is so goddamn important . . .'

*

119

Tweed had fallen asleep on the camp bed Monica had hauled out of a cupboard then made up with pillow, sheets and blankets. The phone began to ring at 4 a.m. and he was instantly awake as Monica answered it.

'Are you awake?' she called out softly.

'Yes.'

'I have Ed Osborne on the line. Wants to speak to you . . .'

'I'll take the call.'

Slipping on a dressing gown over his pyjamas, he sat behind his desk, picked up the phone.

'Tweed here, Ed. What can I do for you?'

'Hope you weren't asleep.'

'I was. What is it?'

'Think it's time you and I had a talk. Just the two of us. Do you know a pub called the Raging Stag in Piccadilly?'

'I do.'

'Can we meet there today? Say noon?'

'Can you give me a hint as to what this is about?'

'Sooner not, over the phone . . .'

'Noon at the Raging Stag, then.'

He told Monica the brief gist of his conversation. She raised her thick eyebrows, frowned.

'After his performance here I wouldn't have thought you would want another session.'

'The Americans can be a bit brash. Doesn't worry me. And the more I can find out what they're up to the better. We're very short of time, I sense.'

'You realize they are taking a great interest in us? Tonight Bob is dining with Sharon Mandeville at Santorini's. Then Marler is taking out Denise Chatel.'

'The same thought had occurred to me. Incidentally, I want you to book seats on the early morning Swissair flight to Basle for six people. Me, Paula, Newman, Marler, Harry Butler and Pete Nield. Not sure when we'll be going but it will be suddenly. So, each day book, then cancel, and immediately book for the next day. Keith Kent, the money tracer, called me to say millions of dollars have been deposited with the Zürcher Kredit Bank – confirming what Schwarz said. I wonder why.'

'Who knows? Millions of dollars. That's a vast sum. Going back to Osborne, I doubt he'll tell you much.'

'He might let something slip. Oh, at a civilized hour, get me Renée Lasalle, chief of the *Direction de la Surveillance du Territoire* – French counter-espionage in Paris – on the phone.'

'Will do.'

'Any luck with identifying Charlie?'

'No. As I told you earlier it's difficult, but I'll go on digging.'

The phone rang again. Monica pulled a sour face, took the call. She looked even more sour.

'Now we have Roy Buchanan on the line. Says it's urgent – at this time of night.'

'I'll speak to him.'

'I know you work all night,' Buchanan began.

'Sometimes I try to get a bit of kip.'

'Sorry, and all that. Something's happened. Can I come and see you now? I think you'd want to know about it,' Buchanan suggested.

'Can't it wait till morning?'

'It could, I suppose. When would suit you?'

'Eight o'clock. You sound worried. It's too early to worry. Wait a bit longer and then you'll have something to fret about. That is, if my present reading of the situation is correct.'

'I've got enough on my plate,' Buchanan snapped.

'Get a bigger plate. Goodbye . . .'

'And you'd better go to the office next door and get some sleep yourself,' Tweed told Monica.

'I think I will. You talk as though you're expecting a storm.'

'A gale. Force Ten.'

Tweed had two hours' sleep. He woke up, alert, hearing the door to his office open. His right hand slid under the pillow, gripped the 7.65mm Walther automatic under it. It was a measure of his estimate of the gravity of the situation that he had taken this precaution. He hardly ever carried a gun.

The light came on. Tweed, twisted on his right side, aimed the weapon at the door. Howard, the Director, stood framed in the doorway, looking startled. Tweed sighed, shoved the gun back under the pillow, got up, put on his dressing gown.

'Sorry if I wakened you,' Howard burbled. 'But George told me you were still here.'

'As you see, I am.' Tweed glanced at his wristwatch. 'I've had two hours' sleep and that will have to do. What are you doing, prowling about the place? I heard you'd returned from a holiday.'

He sat behind his desk while the Director flopped into the largest armchair. Howard was six feet tall with a plump, clean-shaven, pink face, and touches of grey in his neatly brushed hair. A large man in his fifties, he was immaculately garbed in a blue Chester Barrie suit from Harrods, a snow-white shirt and a Hermès tie. He rested one long leg over the arm of the chair, his usual posture. His voice was plummy.

'Hardly a holiday. I've just returned from Washington. I caught up on sleep by going to a hotel after the flight had landed. Had early breakfast, then came straight on here.'

'What's happening in Washington? Why go there?'

Tweed poured water from a carafe into a glass, left

122

for him by Monica. He sipped as Howard ran a hand over the dome of his head, a characteristic gesture when he was worried.

'I went there at the invitation of the august and influential Jefferson Morgenstern – only to find he had suddenly dashed off over here. He'd left some of his top staff to look after me. I was wined and dined at all the best places. Everyone I met made a big fuss over me as though I was the most important man in the world. Not the usual reception by a long chalk. All of which worried me. They wanted something – but never got round to saying what it was. Under their glowing greetings I detected tension. Something's rotten in the woodshed.'

Tweed was surprised. The pompous Howard often didn't grasp what was going on. But sometimes he had flashes of insight. Tweed drank more water before he began.

'The woodshed where there's something rotten is over here. I've got a lot to tell you . . .'

It was unusual for Tweed to tell Howard everything that had taken place. He did so now. If I don't survive, he thought to himself, someone had better be in the picture. Howard listened with great attention. He even removed his leg from over the arm of the chair, leaning closer to Tweed.

'So now you have the full story up to date,' Tweed concluded. 'Didn't they tell you anything in Washington?'

'They kept going on about the importance of the special relationship between Britain and America, the way things are in the world today. Each time I asked them to be more specific they changed the subject.'

'Interesting. Anything else?'

'They also kept asking if I knew where Cord Dillon might be. Told me he'd been sacked for embezzling funds.'

'Poppycock.'

'That's what I thought. I wouldn't have told them he was over here even if I had known. You said all the key personnel are down at the Bunker. I see why you had the place created now.'

'Not *all* the key personnel – but enough to make it an effective operational headquarters in a secret location.'

'What's this Ed Osborne you're having lunch with like?' Howard asked.

'What a lot of Americans would proudly call a tough guy.'

'Don't like the sound of him. Thank you, Tweed, for being so frank. You'll be wanting to take a shower and get dressed.'

'I will. One more thing before you go. I slipped over to see the new PM at Downing Street. Luckily I knew him when he was a Cabinet minister. He's playing the present situation softly, softly.'

'That wouldn't be your idea?' Howard enquired.

'I did make a few suggestions. Apparently Morgenstern keeps asking to see him urgently. The PM has fended him off, saying he'll see him as soon as he can but at the moment he's grappling with his new job.'

'Interesting, as you said a minute ago. Think I'll leave you to it for now. Anything I can do to help, you know where I am. Take great care.'

Which was another surprise for Tweed. He had never before known Howard to be so cooperative. When he returned to his office, fully dressed, Monica was already behind her desk, using the phone. When she had finished the call she looked at Tweed.

'I could get René Lasalle in Paris now. He gets in early to work, I remember.'

'Try him . . .'

'René, you old ruffian, how is life?'

124

'Life, Tweed, is pure hell. I was going to call you. What is on your mind?' the Frenchman asked in perfect English.

'I'm trying to get information on a Frenchman called Chatel. I haven't got his Christian name. He was married to an American, has a daughter called Denise. Your people sent him across to Washington as some sort of diplomat. He was killed in a car crash – along with his wife – about a year ago.'

'Is this line safe?'

'I met Harry Butler when I was coming into my office recently. He had just flashed the place. It's clean.'

'Good. Because this is highly confidential. Jean Chatel was posted to Washington as an attaché to the French Embassy. He was actually a member of the Secret Service. We'd heard rumours that Washington was considering mounting a major operation somewhere in Europe. Jean went to try to find out what it was. Before he could report he died, as you've just told me.'

'Probably murdered.'

'We were suspicious.'

'Any data you could collect on his daughter, Denise, would be helpful. When you can. Now, why were you going to call me?' Tweed asked.

'A small army of Americans has been passing through Paris from Washington, on their way to London. Not normal tourists – although they pretend to be. All carry diplomatic passports, look like tough professionals. Some fly on to Heathrow but more are coming to you via Eurostar. When I caught on I sent men to the airport. Passport officers signalled when a man showed a diplomatic passport and my people photographed him secretly. I have a collection of pics.'

'Could I see them? Urgently. I'd appreciate your sending them by courier to me.'

'Consider it done. What is going on? We don't like Americans too much.'

'I'm trying to find out. Let's keep in touch.'

'The courier will reach you today. Take care, my friend . . .'

Tweed sat staring into the distance. In his absence Monica had removed blankets, sheets, pillow and camp bed. She had also opened the curtains. In the distance trees in Regent's Park cringed under the onslaught of a bitter wind. Men hurried along the street, heads down. Women walked clutching their collars tighter, trying to keep in some warmth.

'Monica, could you please add Denise Chatel to your profile list? Sorry to burden you with more work. I gave you the gist of her life story so far last night before I went to sleep. Check it out.'

'I put her on the list myself.'

'Roy Buchanan is late. Not like him.'

'No, it isn't.'

'Thank you for the breakfast. I hope nothing's happened to Roy.'

At precisely 9 a.m. a long queue of people crowded into a large department store in Oxford Street. SALE EXTENDED. LAST-MINUTE BARGAINS. GREAT REDUCTIONS. Soon the ground floor was crammed. Shoppers sidled past each other, grabbed hold of goods, queued again to pay. They then had trouble leaving, so many people filled the place. There were several arguments as two women grasped the same bargain together.

The huge bomb detonated at precisely 9.15 a.m. There was a brilliant flash, a deafening explosion. Counters were lifted into the air. Shattered glass flew in all directions. Bodies slumped to the floor. Shoppers streaming

126

with blood staggered about, their expressions dazed. Then the screaming started.

There was a powerful aroma of perfume on many people. The crowd surged towards the exits, stepping over bodies. Ambulance sirens in the distance came closer. It was a scene of havoc. Like a picture on TV of a foreign war.

12

'I think I should summarize what's happened so far. It might help us to get events into sequence – at the moment we're in a fog,' Tweed began.

In his office were Newman and Marler, with Monica and Paula behind their desks. Roy Buchanan had still not arrived and there had been no word from him. Monica had served everyone with strong coffee to increase their alertness.

'It began with the arrival of Cord Dillon, and Paula spiriting him out of a murder attempt. Cord, sacked from his job on the grounds of so-called embezzlement, is at the Bunker. Recently I hired Keith Kent, the money tracer, to check on American movements of money. He called me from Basle in Switzerland, suggested I went there. Then he tells me that huge sums in dollars have been sent from Washington to the Zürcher Kredit Bank – in Basle. Paula, give us your impressions of the characters we've encountered so far.'

'You're having lunch with Ed Osborne at the bar in Piccadilly today. At his suggestion. You went to see Sharon Mandeville. At her suggestion. Bob is dining with Sharon this evening. At her suggestion. Marler is taking out Denise Chatel, also this evening. It was at Marler's

127

invitation, but she agreed immediately. All these people are key Americans. I get the idea they're trying to smoke us out.'

'You could be right,' Tweed agreed. 'Now give us portrait snaps of the characters involved.'

'Ed Osborne is tough, clever and dangerous. I'd say he's pretty high up in the opposition. Sharon I haven't met so far. Denise Chatel *appears* to be the nicest, but she's a mystery, so an unknown quantity who should be watched. Sir Guy Strangeways is also clever, but he's playing a peculiar game. Big question mark. Basil Windermere is a piece of social rubbish. Ditto for Rupert Strangeways, a worthless idler. Don't you agree?'

'Not entirely, but please go on,' Tweed urged her.

'Jake Ronstadt. I only saw him for a short time at Goodfellows but I feel he's very dangerous. He exudes dynamic energy. He was suave when he talked to us – I wonder how he talks to his staff. Hank Waltz tried to torture me to get information – he would have killed me later. I won't dwell on that episode. But it demonstrates the lengths to which they'll go. Then we have a horde of professional thugs entering the country via Paris. Why Paris? Because they hoped to get here secretly.'

'I spoke to René Lasalle of the DST this morning,' Tweed told her. 'He's very worried about the Americans – he's sending me by courier some photos discreetly taken of a lot of them. I'd like you to look at them when they arrive. What is really happening, then?'

'They're trying to increase their influence over Britain. At the least.' She paused. 'They could be planning to occupy Britain. You'll think I'm mad—'

She stopped speaking as the phone rang. Monica answered, told them Chief Inspector Roy Buchanan had arrived. Tweed told her to ask him to come up immediately.

When Buchanan entered they were all struck by how grim he looked. At Tweed's invitation he sat down, accepted Monica's offer of a cup of coffee.

'I need it.' He looked round the room. 'I trust everyone here, so I can talk freely. You've heard the news?'

'What news is that?' Tweed enquired. 'You look haggard.'

'A huge bomb went off this morning at a big department store in Oxford Street, when it was crowded with shoppers because of a sale. The bomb was planted under a perfume counter with a lot of boxes of stock. Casualties so far thirty dead and many injured. I've come from there – I closed off Oxford Street, which is why I'm late. It was horrific.'

'A rebellious IRA splinter group?' Marler asked.

'Absolutely not. The Bomb Squad arrived quickly. They found a second huge bomb which hadn't detonated. They locked the timer, dismantled it quickly. They told me it was such a sophisticated electronic device it couldn't be the IRA. Electronics suggests Silicon Valley in the States. Guess where the second bomb was planted.'

'Where?' asked Tweed.

'In the baby clothes and children's toys section. And there are dead children among the casualties.'

'Bastards,' snapped Newman.

'How did the bombers get in?' Tweed probed.

'No idea. The staff who opened the doors saw no signs of forced entry. In addition they had neutralized the alarm system, then re-set it so the staff wouldn't be alerted when they came in first thing.'

'Someone trying to cause panic?' Tweed mused.

'If it was, it worked. Oxford Street was deserted before I had it closed off. The news spread like wildfire. Thank you,' he said to Monica, who had brought him a second cup of coffee. 'It was an atrocity,' he concluded.

'Any idea who was responsible, then?' Tweed asked.

'None at all. It's early days.'

'Roy, you were coming to see me anyway. What was that about?'

'First, a body was washed up on a mudbank just south of the East End. A small, thickset man with a bald head. A Hank Waltz.'

'How do you know that?'

'Had a soggy American diplomatic passport in his pocket.'

'You're informing the American Embassy?'

'No, I'm not,' Buchanan said vehemently. 'And, would you believe it – I've lost the passport. Let the Yanks ask me – if they do. Then there was a second body.'

'Also dragged out of the Thames?' Tweed suggested.

'No. Had an anonymous call. For some reason I decided to go myself. Probably to see if it was another American. Found the deceased on some steps off Regent Street. This one had a rifle bullet through his head.'

'Any identification?'

'Yes. A Swiss passport with the name Kurt Schwarz.'

'He was murdered, then?'

'No doubt about it. Just one rifle shot. Why did I think of the Phantom?'

'Maybe because the PM, Keller in Germany and the Minister in France were also shot through the head with one rifle bullet. Any witnesses?'

'I had the team with me call at every house, waking people up. One of them was Basil Windermere. We know he lives off playing up to rich women.'

'And what did Basil have to say?'

130

'Said he'd been woken up by a faint crack! Thought it was a car backfiring, so he went back to sleep. He had no idea of the time when he heard the noise.'

'Was he sleeping alone?' Marler interjected.

'Yes.'

'Was he in his pyjamas?' Marler persisted.

'Yes. Why this interest in Windermere?'

'Suppose I just have the natural instincts of a detective.'

'I see.' Buchanan drank more coffee. 'You're not usually so vocal.'

'One more question, Roy,' Tweed said to divert the policeman from the subject of Windermere. 'The Chrysler in Strangeways' garage at Parham. Did you manage to check the vehicle?'

'Yes. I sent a team down to Irongates. They had a search warrant but they were careful. The entrance gates were closed. There were no lights on in the house – even though it was almost dark as night. They scaled the side wall. A locksmith released the padlock on the garage doors. There was nothing inside. No sign of a Chrysler.'

'They'd got out in time.'

'Seems so.' Buchanan took a folded sheet of paper from his pocket, handed it to Tweed. 'That is for your eyes only. Do you recognize any of the names?'

'Yes. Two Cabinet ministers. Several prominent MPs. And a number of well-known businessmen.'

'All of them have been bribed by the Americans. Given large sums in dollar bills inside executive cases. Special Branch officers have been watching the Embassy in Grosvenor Square. They have followed Americans coming out carrying executive cases. They meet the recipient of the bribe in out-of-the-way places. Obscure bars and pubs. They have a drink with the target, then leave alone, having propped the executive case against a bar or table leg. After they've gone one of the men on that list leaves, after picking up the executive case. Three of them opened the case before they went off – produced several stacks of one-hundred-dollar bills and dropped them back inside the case. It's bribery of key British figures on a massive scale.'

'This is getting even more dangerous.'

'What I've told you all in this room is strictly confidential.'

'And will remain that way,' Tweed assured him.

Howard burst into the room at that moment. Seeing Buchanan he apologized. He spoke very quickly immediately afterwards.

'I think all of you ought to come to my office. There's a TV report on the bomb left in an Oxford Street department store. Have you heard?'

Paula led the way out of the room and upstairs to Howard's office. Newman and Marler followed her. Tweed turned to Buchanan, not sure whether he would spare the time.

'I think I'll come with you,' the policeman said. 'Sometimes whoever has committed a crime has an irresistible urge to revisit the scene of what he did . . .'

Inside Howard's room his secretary had arranged chairs and the TV was on. No one sat down. They stood in silence, waiting.

'How did the TV people get through?' Tweed whispered to Buchanan.

'I left instructions for them to be allowed in. The people who did this thing may rub their hands with glee, thinking it will terrify the population. I take a different view. I think it will cause universal outrage and fury. Here it comes . . .'

Unusually, there was no commentary, which made what followed more horrifying. The cameras panned round inside the store. The floor was covered with lethal shreds of glass. Paramedics were helping injured women and some men to leave. The counters and checkout points were shattered. No item of furniture remained undamaged. Bloodstained shoppers were still lying on the floor, attended by paramedics and doctors. One man had an arm missing. A prone woman's skirt was dripping with blood, her face slashed by flying glass. A number of bodies were lying very still, sprawled on the ground. The camera panned to the exit.

A woman, lying flat, her neck bandaged, blood seeping through it, was being carried out on a stretcher by two paramedics. She raised herself up, staring at the camera as though unaware of its presence.

'My husband. Where is my husband?'

Behind her, where she couldn't see, the paramedic carrying the rear end of the stretcher, shook his head. Paula gasped.

'Oh, my God,' she said half under her breath.

'It's like a battlefield,' Newman said to Tweed.

Paula stood up to leave. In the open doorway Monica stood staring as though she couldn't believe her eyes. She went down back to Tweed's office, followed by Newman, Marler, Tweed and Buchanan. The policeman tapped Tweed on the shoulder before they were about to enter the room.

'I'll have to go now. There was no one shown who wasn't with the ambulance men or paramedics. My men did their job. Try and keep in touch with me.'

'You do the same . . .'

There was complete silence when he went into his office, shut the door and sat down behind his desk. Monica sat stunned, her hands in her lap. Paula gazed at each of her colleagues, made no comment. Marler, leaning against a wall, was about to light a king-size, decided against it.

Tweed leaned forward across his desk. They all stared at him, knowing he was going to say something important. When he did speak his voice was calm, resolute.

'We use any devious ruthless method to defeat them.'

13

The Executive Action Department was again meeting in the large room at the American Embassy. Jake, at the head of the table, was again shuffling his cards. He made them wait before he spoke. Outside, beyond the windows, branches of the trees in the square shook under the onslaught of the late morning wind.

'Guess I ought to hand out half-congratulations to Vernon and Brad.'

'Why only half?' Vernon, the thin man with the boney face asked indignantly.

'Because the second bomb didn't go off. You must have fouled up the timer. If that bomb had detonated half the people in that store would have been killed. That would have been sensational.'

There were glum faces round the table. Jake Ronstadt was, as usual, in a bad mood. Brad, the squat man with shark-like teeth, risked opening his mouth.

'Which is the next objective? Maybe now we've started we oughta keep things movin' – scare the guts out of the Brits.'

'Maybe you ought to sit kinda quiet. I've sorta had enough of interruptions. In any case, it won't be Vernon and Brad who hit the next one. I handed out sheets of targets to you all. Raise your hands if you've now looked over those targets.'

Eight men raised their hands high in the air. They held them up until Jake made a gesture for them to lower

134

them. He was shuffling his cards again. Vernon wondered if he ever played poker. He'd have liked to ask but knew that if he did he'd probably get Jake's fist in his face.

Leo, who had a head shaped like the moon, had once shot a baby in the back of the head. Afterwards he'd slipped away to down a couple of drinks in a bar. He was less afraid of Jake than anyone round the table. 'We haven't seen Ed Osborne at any of these meetings,' he remarked.

Ronstadt contemplated standing up, walking down the table and hauling the chair from under Leo. He knew Moonhead was independent-minded, that he was after his job. He decided to wait for a better opportunity to humiliate him.

'Ed is a very busy guy. Come to that, so am I. The idea to keep things movin' is crap. London will be swarming with cops hoping to get a clue, checking out their informants in the underworld. I'm sure Charlie will agree with me.'

He stood up in his brown leather jacket, his leather trousers. A man of limited height, it was his bulk, his large head, his personality, his expression which dominated the members of his team.

'Get the hell outta here,' he said, and left.

By lunchtime everyone except Monica and Paula had departed from Park Crescent. Paula had decided to skip lunch. After seeing the scenes on the TV newscast she didn't feel she wanted to eat anything. When the phone rang Monica spoke to the caller briefly, then said to Paula:

'It's Mrs Carson down at the Bunker. She's having trouble with Cord Dillon. Want to have a word?'

'Yes . . . Paula here, Mrs Carson. What's the problem?'

'Dillon is getting restless, feeling cooped up. He's even talked of coming up to London.'

'Can you hold him until I get there?' She had taken a swift decision. 'And have you see the news on TV? Heard it on the radio?'

'No. Dillon doesn't like either TV or the radio. Neither do I. Why do you ask?'

'I think Cord needs someone to talk to. Tell him I'm driving down there today, should reach you mid-afternoon. And both of you watch the next TV news broadcast. It's important you do.'

'I'll arrange that. And look forward to seeing you. It's quiet on the Romney Marsh.'

'Monica,' Paula said as she grabbed her fur-lined coat, picked up her motoring gloves, 'contact Pete Nield. Tell him I'll be back in time to accompany him to Santorini's this evening.'

'That's where Newman is having dinner with Sharon Mandeville.'

'I know. I've had a good look at Denise Chatel – seen enough of her to form a certain opinion. But I've had no chance to see Sharon. I'm not going to barge in on Bob, but I can observe the glamorous Sharon from a distance. Tell Tweed I've rushed off to the Bunker to soothe Cord Dillon. See you . . .'

Later, as she crossed the border into Kent, Paula took another quick decision. Parham was on her way. She could drop off at Irongates – in the hope of having a chat with Sir Guy Strangeways. She'd hardly exchanged more than a few words with the property magnate when she had visited the place with Tweed.

'Do come in, my dear. I'd love to see you.'

Paula stared at the speakphone outside Irongates.

Strangeways sounded exuberant, in contrast to the previous visit, when he had barked down the instrument. He was waiting for her when she parked below the terrace. She gave one last look back at the closing gates.

On her way down from London she had felt sure she was being followed. Try as hard as she could, she had not been able to identify a vehicle on her tail. It could have been imagination, but she didn't think so.

'Come inside. Mrs Belloc has prepared tea. A little early, I know, so just eat what you feel like and leave the rest.'

As he escorted her across the large bleak hall, into the library where she had waited on her last visit, Paula studied her host. Outwardly affable, she detected signs of strain. His eyelids were puffy, as though from lack of sleep. The crackling military-style voice she had heard before had disappeared. Instead, he spoke softly. He wore a sports jacket with leather patches on the sleeves, a heavy pair of beige slacks, gleaming brown handmade shoes. She waited until Mrs Belloc had poured tea, stared at her, then left the room.

'What do you think of this bomb in Oxford Street?'

'Dreadful. Truly dreadful.' His voice trembled. 'As you can imagine, when I was a soldier I stood on battlefields amid carnage. It didn't affect me. Can't do the job if you permit it to get to you. But those scenes on TV.'

'Who do you think is responsible? A splinter group of the IRA?'

'There are so many . . .' He paused. 'So many terrorist outfits in the world today. Could be any of them.'

Paula had the impression he wasn't happy with the subject. He drank tea, helped himself to a cake. Paula ate ravenously.

'I have another problem on my mind,' he began. 'Rupert. He's a terrible disappointment. I know he runs after every pretty woman in sight. Don't mind that. He grew up late. It's his gambling.'

'With some people it's an addiction.'

'I'm not going to pay for his bloody addiction!' he stormed. 'Sorry. I raised my voice. Bad language. Not in the presence of ladies. I'm old-fashioned that way.'

'I appreciate that.'

'I've had a phone call from a casino in Campione. That's an enclave of Italy inside Switzerland.'

'I know. You get there by taking a steamer from Lugano.'

'Well, this blighter in Campione phoned me, demanding that I pay Rupert's debt. A hundred thousand pounds! I told him to go and jump in the lake. He said Rupert had referred him to me. I'm not paying a penny. I could afford it but Rupert can get out of his own messes. I told Rupert before he left the house. Called me a miser. I rang him at his London flat later to give him hell. The phone wasn't answered.'

'It must be very upsetting.'

'Sorry, I didn't ask you in to grouch about my small problems. Eat up!'

'You've got big property interests in the States. Will you be going back there?'

'I'm selling the lot, getting clear out of America.'

'You're a busy man. I think I should go now. Actually I did call in on my way elsewhere. Thank you for the tea – and your company, which I have enjoyed.'

'What a charming thing to say. I'll accompany you to your car.'

Paula reached down to adjust her right shoe. Something about it wasn't comfortable, and she used that foot for accelerator and foot brake. Strangeways helped her on with her coat and they crossed the hall. He opened the heavy front door and they stood framed in the doorway. Again Paula bent down to adjust her shoe. As she did so there was a *crack!*.

The bullet hit the side of the doorway where she had been standing. It ricocheted across the drive into the distance. Paula felt herself grabbed by Strangeways, pulled back inside as he used a foot to slam the door shut.

'Wait here,' he barked. He was taking keys from his pocket. 'I'm going to the gunroom. I saw the muzzle-flash. Came from the rooftop of the house opposite . . .'

Paula took several deep breaths. In no time Strangeways was back, holding a rifle. His eyes were blazing but his manner was controlled and calm. He was about to open the door again when Paula spoke.

'If you don't mind, I'd like to make a brief phone call.'

'Of course you can. The library. I'll wait here.'

Inside the room she took out a small notebook. She had written down certain phone numbers she had obtained from Monica. One of them was Basil Winder-mere's flat in London. She pressed numbers, listened. His cultured tones came clearly down the line on an answerphone.

'Dear caller, you have reached Basil. Ectually, I happen to be rather tied up at the moment. Sorry and all that. Do please leave your name and number. Then it will be my pleasure to return your call earliest possible. Cheerio.'

So Windermere was not at home. Paula put down the phone and went back into the hall. Strangeways gave her explicit orders in a commanding voice.

'Stay well back in the hall. I'm going out to investigate.'

Opening the door, he strode out. Reaching the drive he marched down it as though leading a division into battle. His rifle was elevated, aimed at the flat top of the mansion opposite beyond the rim of his wall. He stopped a few yards down the drive, called to her over his shoulder.

'Make a dive for your car. But first press the red button on the left-hand side of the door. Drive out fast. There's never any traffic in the square. Sorry about this. Keep moving . . .'

She obeyed him, pressing the button on the automatic security device. Throwing open the car door, she jumped inside, slammed the door shut. The gates were opening after she had pressed the red button. Strangeways moved on to the verge, his rifle still elevated as he continued to scan the rooftops. Gravel spurted up as she pressed her foot down. Then she was in the first deserted square, driving on into the second empty, larger square.

She slowed a lot to navigate her way through the village. As soon as she left it behind she rammed her foot down again. She was miles away when she reduced speed, continuing to check her rear-view mirror. No sign of any other vehicle. But she *had* been followed from London.

The heavy overcast dropped lower as she drove beyond Ashford and along a wide A-road. The massed black clouds made it almost as dark as night and she had her lights on. She was still on the almost deserted road when she first heard the distant sound of a helicopter approaching.

It was half a mile away when she glanced to the west and frowned. A Sikorsky. She couldn't see any identification signs on its fuselage. It was heading straight for her. She began to worry. If she continued straight ahead she would soon lead the machine to the secret Bunker.

To her left, a long way off across a vast field, she saw

a tractor dragging a harrow. A moment later, by the roadside, she saw an old barn, its doors yawning open; the home of the tractor, she imagined. She looked again at the helicopter. It had just disappeared inside a low cloud. She reacted quickly.

Slowing down, she swung the wheel, drove inside the large barn. An aroma of straw on the floor filled her nostrils. Switching off the engine, she looked back at the entrance. She was deep enough inside the barn to be totally concealed from the air. Then she heard the loud beat-beat of the chopper, flying much lower.

She lit one of her rare cigarettes. No chance of the smoke drifting outside the barn. She sat quite still, tense. The helicopter was now circling. At one moment it sounded to be just above the barn. Now she had no doubt that the crew on board were looking for her.

'I'm having a nice couple of days,' she said to herself. 'I had the fight at Eagle Street. Today someone tried to kill me at Irongates. There's no doubt the marksman was the Phantom – for no good reason, you idiot. Now you can just sit it out here.'

Sooner than she had expected the machine flew away, the sound of its engine fading. She still stayed where she was. Could be a trick – it might suddenly dart back. After ten minutes she decided it had gone and resumed her journey.

Turning off the road where a lane to the left was signposted Ivychurch, she followed the complex route down winding country lanes. She knew the way because Tweed had driven her to the Bunker when it was in the process of being constructed. Just before she reached the automatic gate which she knew Mrs Carson would open she stopped the car, turned off the engine.

She was listening for the helicopter. Instead, an oppressive silence she could almost hear descended on her. On all sides a flat plain of fields stretched away endlessly. Not a hill, not a tree in sight. Nor was there any sign of human habitation. The leafless hedges lining the lane on either side were grim networks of stark twigs and thorns, reminding her of barbed wire. No birdsong. She shivered. I might be in the middle of the Mongolian desert, she thought. This must be among the most desolate parts of England. Romney Marsh? You can keep it.

She turned on the engine, drove on. As she approached the automatic gate, she saw it opening. Mrs Carson must have used her binoculars, seen her coming.

'Welcome to Paradise,' Mrs Carson greeted her as she parked inside the courtyard and stepped out.

'I could think of another name for it. Don't know how you stand it down here.'

'I read a lot, dear. Come on in. Cord is a changed man . . .'

'Hi, Paula. Good to see you.'

Dillon stood up from where he had been sitting by a roaring log fire, rubbing his hands. The air outside was ice-cold, but the living room was so warm Paula slipped off her coat and gloves. Dillon looked anything but restless and his expression was grim. He wore an old polo-necked jersey and shabby corduroy trousers, obviously provided by Mrs Carson, and could have passed for a farm worker.

'How are you?' she asked as he took her right hand in both of his.

'Feeling pretty bloody-minded. Mrs Carson and I watched the TV programme. A Bomb Squad chief said the massacre had definitely nothing to do with the IRA. He mentioned a very sophisticated electronically operated timer he'd never seen before. Electronics. Silicon Valley.'

'What do you mean?' Paula asked.

'Shortly before I had to run for it I overheard a conversation between two scientists from Silicon Valley and a new man, a Jake Ronstadt. They were talking about a new device which had been perfected – an electronically operated timer for delayed-action bombs.'

'You think that links up with what you heard on TV?'

'Damned sure it does. It makes me sick to think my people could be responsible for the Oxford Street massacre. If I got hold of them I'd line them up against a wall and personally shoot them, one by one.'

'Who is this Jake Ronstadt you mentioned?' she asked cautiously.

'One of the new men brought in to the CIA. He passed all the tough training tests. Except one. I got hold of the report on him. The psychiatrist who checked him out wrote "psychologically flawed". That should have kept him out. It didn't.'

'Are you willing to stay here a bit longer? Tweed would be much happier if you did.'

'Sure I am. Guess Tweed has enough to cope with without worrying about me out in the open. He doesn't show it but he does worry about things like that. The guy is very human.'

Paula joined Dillon in drinking coffee, chatting as cheerfully as she could. She appreciated the fact that he made no attempt to extract information from her about what was happening. Then she said she must go back to London.

'This place is like a fortress,' the American commented as he accompanied her to the door. 'Tweed, and I guess Newman and Marler, really know a thing or two. The defences round the perimeter are diabolical.'

She didn't have time to ask him what he was talking about. As she drove back, her car heater turned up full blast, she found her mind jumping back and forth. She was keeping an eye open for the helicopter but the machine never reappeared. She was also thinking about the new timer device Dillon had overheard being discussed at Langley. Up to that moment she had found it difficult to believe Washington could really be behind such an attack.

She was also recalling what Dillon had told her about Ronstadt. As Tweed would have said, key pieces of the jigsaw were beginning to fit together. What she wasn't prepared for when she arrived at Park Crescent was that the last person in the world she would have expected was in a state of semi-shock.

14

'A letter from the dead.'

Entering Tweed's office Paula immediately sensed a strange atmosphere. Newman was sitting upright in a chair. Marler stood upright near a wall, no cigarette in his mouth. Monica's face had a frozen look. Tweed sat behind his desk, hands clasped on its surface, his expression neutral. Nobody said a word to her – until Marler spoke those five words.

He walked across to her slowly. His complexion was ashen. He handed her an envelope without saying another word. Then he walked back to his corner and stood very still.

Paula remained where she was, standing, her coat over her arm. She examined the outside of the envelope. It was addressed in a foreign-looking script to Mr Marler, c/o General & Cumbria Assurance, followed by the address. She noticed that it had been posted in London, carried a second-class stamp. Carefully she extracted the single folded sheet inside. It was written in the same script.

Dear Marler – Be very careful of the barges. You must locate the printing presses. Yours, Kurt Schwarz.

She looked round the room again, placed the letter, folded, inside the envelope. Then she walked across to Marler, gave it back to him. Dropping coat and gloves on her desk, she sank into her chair. She was worried about saying the wrong thing, was relieved when Newman began talking.

'The letter has naturally . . .' He had been going to say 'upset' but decided Marler wouldn't like that. '. . . disturbed Marler. As it has me. Marler had known Kurt for years. They were friends who trusted each other completely.'

'One more bullet for the Phantom,' said Marler in the same monotone he had spoken the first five words when she had entered.

'We both feel rotten,' Newman went on quickly, 'about leaving him propped up against those steps.'

'You couldn't do anything else,' Paula said quietly. 'And I'm upset . . .' She paused with a lump in her throat, forcing herself not to cry. 'He was such a nice man. I liked him from the moment he came to my flat. He joked with me, made me laugh. It's too cruel. So macabre . . .' She trailed off.

'Time for me to go,' Marler said, his voice normal. 'Must have a bath, smarten myself up. I have a date with Denise Chatel this evening. See you.'

Tweed waited until he had left. When he spoke his tone was offhand. He gave the impression that business as usual had now resumed.

'Kurt may have given us valuable information at some stage. I can understand Marler's reaction. He realizes Kurt wouldn't have sent that letter unless he thought he wouldn't survive long enough to pass on the message personally.'

145

'The barges,' Paula said, mystified. 'Does he mean barges on the Thames? And which printing presses was he referring to?'

'I have no idea,' Tweed responded. 'But we may understand in due course. You looked tense the moment you opened the door. How did you get on at the Bunker?'

'I'll have to learn to control my expression.' She paused, wondering whether to tell him about the attempt on her life, feeling sure he would go up in smoke. She decided she must give a complete report. 'On the way down to the Bunker I decided to call in . . .' she began.

Tweed sat like a Buddha, his eyes fixed on hers, listening. When she had finished he decided the last thing to do was rebuke her for taking chances on her own. She had gone through enough recently.

'You seem sure the bullet was intended for you,' he remarked.

'Why do you say that?'

'From your graphic description, Sir Guy Strangeways was standing beside you. Surely the bullet could have been meant for him?'

'I hadn't thought of that. Now you mention it, I don't know.'

'The Phantom has spoilt his record,' Newman commented. 'This time he missed his target, whoever it was.'

'Interesting that Basil Windermere wasn't at his flat when you called him. That was quick thinking,' Tweed remarked.

'As I told you, Cord Dillon seems content to stay where he is.'

'Pretty conclusive,' Newman said grimly, 'what he told you he overheard at Langley about the new timer. We know who we're up against now.'

'Up to a point,' Tweed told him.

'How did your lunch go with Ed Osborne?' Paula wondered.

'Never got there. I was leaving the building when a call came through from him. Full of apologies. Would I mind making our meeting this evening. Same rendezvous. Nine o'clock at the Raging Stag in Piccadilly.'

'Shouldn't you have a bodyguard, after everything that's happened? And they did try to kidnap you outside the American Embassy. It was a good job Newman and the others were there.'

'Tweed gave us the signal that he was in trouble,' Newman explained. 'Standing at the top of the step on his way out he ran a hand over the top of his head as though smoothing down his hair.'

'I have to love you and leave you now.' Tweed stood up. 'I want to keep Howard up to date with the latest developments. Bob, enjoy your dinner with Sharon – I don't see how you can fail to do so. Paula, I suggest you go home early, get Pete Nield to drive you home, check out the area. Then cook yourself something simple and get an early night.'

Paula nodded, said nothing. She didn't want to refer to her intention to have dinner with Pete at Santorini's in front of Newman. He might not be best pleased with her idea of her checking up on Sharon from a distance. Monica waited until Tweed and Newman had left, the latter on his way home to get ready for his night out.

'Don't worry about Tweed,' Monica told Paula. 'I've fixed it up with Harry Butler to put on his best suit and to go to the Raging Stag discreetly – to keep an eye on him.'

Santorini's, the new in-place, was decked out luxuriously. One section even projected out over the river. The

147

place bubbled with activity. Sharon, with Newman at her side, answered the maître d' when he immediately came up to them.

'Sharon Mandeville. You have a table reserved overlooking the river.'

'Good evening. We have indeed got your reservation. The best table, of course . . .'

Sharon wore a close-fitting, simply cut shift dress in purple which must have cost a fortune, with elegant court shoes. Her blonde hair fell in sweeping waves almost to her shoulders. As she preceded Newman men turned to gaze at her. Some to the amusement of their escorts, other women looking annoyed. She was undoubtedly, Newman thought, the most striking-looking woman in the place. And there was competition aplenty.

Their table was placed next to a large window looking out over the river. The water actually flowed below them. Sharon sat down and her hypnotic green eyes stared at Newman. She seemed unaware of the stir she was causing at other tables.

'I hope this suits you, Bob,' she said in her soft voice.

'Perfect. You must have clout to have secured this table.'

'Not really. I used the Ambassador's name. I don't really want to be well known. The waiter's here. Let's order our aperitifs.'

She was very calm, almost withdrawn, her movements slow and dignified. Her eyes held his, without in any way being aggressive or come-hitherish. They touched glasses when the aperitifs arrived.

'Here's to a memorable evening,' Newman said buoyantly.

'I'll drink to that,' she agreed quietly.

'How are you settling in at the Embassy? Must be a major change from Washington.'

'I prefer London. After all, my mother was English.

148

So I feel at home here. Washington is rather a bear garden. I have a nice house in Dorset.'

'And yet everything important in your life happened in America.'

'You're probably referring to my four husbands. Let's study the menu. This is my treat, by the way.'

'No, it isn't . . .'

'I hope you don't mind, but you can't do much about it. I have opened an account here.'

'Wicked of you.' He grinned. 'Next time it's my treat.'

'I'll look forward to that.'

They took time examining the large selection. Newman glanced out of the window and saw a massive barge tied up for the night. He stared. *Be very careful of the barges.* Kurt's warning in his last communication flashed into his mind.

'A penny for your thoughts,' said Sharon.

'Sorry. The reflections in the river look wonderful.'

'Dreamy . . .'

'Like the outfit you're wearing. Purple really suits you.'

'Thank you.'

He noticed there was not a trace of an American accent in her voice. She spoke as though she had lived all her life in England. He found her voice, her calmness very attractive. It was no effort to talk to her. He just felt comfortable. And her greenish eyes were remarkable, although she made no effort to use them as a weapon the way some women did. They said little as they consumed a magnificent meal. Looking round the tastefully appointed restaurant, he saw a lot of the in crowd were present, most of whom he disliked. Sharon brought up the subject when they were drinking coffee.

'I hope you don't mind but I'm also in the way of a messenger tonight. I've been asked whether you'd consider writing an article urging a closer special relationship between Britain and America.'

'May I enquire who asked you to do that?'

'I'm sorry, Bob, but I'm not supposed to say. It comes from someone very high up . . .'

Paula and Pete Nield had arrived at Santorini's a few minutes before Sharon and Bob entered. Paula had used Howard's name to ask for a secluded table. Howard, a member of several clubs, could get any table he wanted in London. Their table was in an alcove and Paula had a clear but distant view of the table over the river.

'What do you think of her?' Nield asked as they finished their main course.

'They seem to be getting on very well together. What do I think of Sharon? I'm not sure. She's beautifully dressed. Real taste in every way.'

'That's not what I asked.'

'She's poised. Quite at home in a place like this. She has an unusual technique for impressing a man.'

'Go on.'

'She's cool, very calm on the surface. A good listener – and that appeals to a man. She has control of the situation, without appearing to do so.'

'You used the phrase "on the surface".'

'I just wonder what she's really like under that appearance of unusual calm. I'm honestly not sure.'

'Not sure of what?' Nield smiled. 'Come on. Give.'

'I'm simply dist— puzzled. She's hard to read.'

'You were going to say disturbed and then altered it to puzzled. What is it about her that disturbs you?'

'Maybe a touch of envy.' Paula smiled. 'She's a very beautiful woman.'

'Be cagey, as you'd say to Tweed. And for my money you're looking like a present from Heaven.'

'Thank you, Pete.' She almost blushed. 'Do you want pudding?'

'I'm full up – this meal I've had will last me for days. But you go ahead.'

'I'm in the same state as you. Talking about Tweed, I know the Raging Stag stays open late. He may still be there. Do you mind if we have coffee there? I feel we ought to check there are no thugs in that area.'

'Good idea. I'll get the bill.'

They had chosen a moment when Sharon and Newman's table was masked by other guests also leaving. Nield drove them back towards Piccadilly, found the only empty parking slot in Mayfair and grabbed it. They made the rest of the journey on foot.

Paula clasped the collar of her coat round her neck. A wind which must have originated at the North Pole was blowing. Their natural route took them down Albemarle Street, which was deserted. It brought back to Paula the evening when she had bumped into Cord Dillon outside Brown's, the nerve-racking moment when a bullet fired from the Cadillac had smashed the glass behind them as they stood in front of it.

Nield made no comment on the incident but took Paula's arm and hurried her even more briskly. They slowed down as they approached the Raging Stag. Both their eyes were everywhere, checking for men waiting in the shadows. Piccadilly, also, was deserted.

Entering the expensively decorated pub-cum-restaurant, Paula scanned the place, saw Tweed among the crowd sitting at a table in the restaurant further in. He had his back to her and next to him sat Ed Osborne. Nield had also spotted them.

'Two stools free at the bar,' he said. 'I'll take them . . .'

He reached the stools seconds before two men, who

looked annoyed and tried to muscle their way in. Nield shook his head.

'Those are our places,' a large middle-aged man said aggressively.

'Sorry, but I have a lady with me. You wouldn't want her to have to stand, I'm sure.'

Paula backed him up by slipping past and perching herself on one of the stools. She turned, spoke to the aggressive man.

'Thank you so much. That was very kind of you.'

'You worked that well,' said Nield as the two men went away, muttering. 'What are you having to drink?'

'I'll stick to wine, I think. A glass of medium dry French.'

The place was as crowded, even at that hour, as Santorini's. Paula found she was in an ideal position to observe Tweed's table – she had a clear view of it reflected in the mirror behind the bar. She slipped off her coat, folded it in her lap as the drinks arrived, then she stiffened, held her glass motionless.

Tweed and Osborne sat on chairs close together. She had the impression they were having a friendly argument as Osborne waved his hands about and Tweed nodded. What had made her stiffen was the sight of a bulging briefcase perched against Tweed's chair.

'Something wrong?' Nield enquired.

'Nothing.'

She wrapped her scarf round her head to conceal her hair. A waiter had brought back the bill to Osborne, placing his credit card on it, which Osborne whipped up and slipped inside his wallet. Nield slumped further forward across the bar. He was wearing a new suit and he'd sensed Paula didn't want Tweed to see them. The two men who had tried to take their stools were standing behind them now, holding drinks, chatting. In the mirror

152

it seemed to Paula they were concealed from anyone leaving. She saw Butler hidden in a corner.

Osborne was standing up. He slapped Tweed on the shoulder and made his way towards the exit, pushing aside anyone who got in his way by his sheer bulk. He wasn't even wearing a coat. It must be all that flesh on his large frame which enabled him to stand the arctic weather outside, Paula thought.

'We wait?' Nield asked.

'If you don't mind. Just a bit longer. It's only the second time I've been in this place. It's lively.'

Tweed waited at his table for a few minutes after Osborne had left. When he stood he was holding the briefcase in his right hand. Unlike Osborne, he threaded his way throught the crowd politely.

'Excuse me . . . thank you . . . excuse me . . .'

Paula felt a chill down her spine as Tweed walked out into the night, still carrying the briefcase. She had never seen him own anything like it. She waited a few minutes longer, then finished her drink.

'If it's all right by you, Pete, I think I've had enough.'

Something in her voice, in the way she held herself, caught Nield's attention. He waited until they were walking back to the car before he spoke.

'Is something worrying you?'

'Nothing at all. I've had a wonderful evening. I'm grateful to you, Pete . . .'

Nield had assumed he would be driving Paula back to her flat in the Fulham Road. She surprised him when they reached the car and had jumped inside it to escape the cold. He started the engine, turned up the heater.

'Be warm in a minute. Back to your flat?'

'No, Pete. I'd appreciate it if you dropped me at Park

Crescent. I've got some work I want to deal with. I can drive myself back in my own car later.'

'No good. You need a bodyguard.'

'Pete! I'm not a puppy that has to be kept at the end of the leash,' she snapped.

'You are worried about something. A worry shared is a worry halved.'

'I'm sorry, Pete – sorry that I flared up. That was awful of me after the marvellous evening we've had together. But I do want to call in at Park Crescent.'

'Fair enough. Why don't I drive on and check out your flat and the area round it? Someone very hostile knows where you live.'

'You're right, of course. And I'm grateful. Here's the keys to my flat so you can get inside.'

'If you don't mind I'll wait until you arrive.'

'Don't mind at all . . .'

She was silent during their drive. Furious with herself for the unjustified outburst, she couldn't think of anything to say. She gave him a kiss on the cheek, squeezed his hand before she got out at the entrance to Park Crescent. There was a light on in Tweed's office.

'Evening, Paula,' George greeted her. 'Mr Tweed's gone up to have a bath. Monica's still here.'

She went quietly up the stairs and opened the door. Monica wasn't there, she had probably gone upstairs to make herself a snack. She closed the door and stared. She almost trembled with trepidation. The bulging brief-case was propped up in the kneehole under Tweed's desk, the flap fallen open. Standing very still, she tried to make up her mind. She had never been one to snoop. But she felt she had to know the truth or the uncertainty would torture her mind.

Bending down, she carefully pulled out the case. She looked inside it and felt sick. It was stuffed with stacks

154

of one-hundred-dollar bills. Each package had an elastic band round it. Taking one out, she quickly counted. One hundred US banknotes. With the number of packages there the case must contain thousands of dollars.

She replaced the case exactly where – and as – she had found it. Dazed, she stood up. She had to get out of the building before Tweed reappeared. She couldn't face him tonight. She ran down the stairs, paused to speak to George.

'Don't bother to tell anyone I was here. Tweed thought I was going to have an early night.'

'Very good, miss . . .'

She sat in her car after starting the engine, waiting to calm down. Then she drove back to her flat, thankful that there was no traffic, that the streets were empty – as empty as she felt.

15

At about the time when Paula and Nield were tackling their main courses at Santorini's, Marler was dining with Denise Chatel at the Lanesborough. The brunette, her long dark hair perfectly coiffeured, wore a silk trouser suit. He was immediately impressed by her stunning appearance and told her so when they'd sat down at their table.

'That's a nice compliment. I appreciate it,' she said with a warm smile. 'Thank you, Alec.'

Later he asked her to choose the wine and she selected a very good vintage in the medium-price range. They chatted easily and he found she was the sort of woman you quickly felt you had known for years in the nicest way. She gazed round the restaurant and her blue eyes stared into his.

'This is a wonderful place. No wonder it is full of people.'

'Used to be a big hospital before they converted it into this hotel. Have some more wine . . .'

They went into another room to have coffee and she crossed her shapely legs after sitting down on a couch. Alongside her, he thought about complimenting her on them, but decided it was a bit early in their acquaintance. It was a chance remark on his part which triggered off a development, the consequences of which he could not foresee.

'I remember you said you had a French father and an American mother. That's pretty cosmopolitan.'

'I was . . .' She hesitated. 'I was going to bring up that subject. I hope you won't regard this as trying to pump your business knowledge on the cheap.'

'Of course not.' He leaned forward. 'I'm interested in everything about you. Fire away.'

'When I was at Park Crescent I mentioned they had been killed together in a car crash. There was something mysterious about it and it still bothers me. They were killed just across the state line in Virginia at a small place I'd have to write down . . .'

'Here's a notebook,' he said, producing one from his pocket. 'I'd like all the details.'

'I called the sheriff in charge of the investigation. A man called Jim Briscoe. I'll write that down. He agreed for me to go and see him. He seemed nice enough but I sensed he was embarrassed. Which didn't make sense. He said these accidents unfortunately happened. I asked him if the accident had occurred at a black spot. He said it wasn't.'

'You didn't go out to view the location, I suppose?'

'Actually I did. Jim Briscoe took me there at my suggestion. There were no signs of skid marks near the bridge where it happened. I pointed that out. Again he seemed embarrassed, said a lot of traffic could have wiped them out. The only thing is it was a quiet road. I got the idea someone had rubbed out any skid marks.' She smiled ruefully. 'You'll think me paranoid.'

'No I won't. I believe you. What did you want me to do?'

'Well, Sharon said in passing that Tweed ran a special insurance outfit – that you insure prominent people against being kidnapped. Then, if they are, you negotiate their release unharmed. Which means you have investigators.'

'You could say that is our business.'

'Later, I tried to get in touch with Sheriff Briscoe again. A strange voice told me he'd retired early on full pension. I thought that peculiar – Jim Briscoe couldn't have been a day over forty. I said I wanted the FBI brought in – my parents had crossed a state line. The new sheriff was unpleasant – told me the investigation was closed for ever. He said I could be sued for wasting their time.'

'Odd, very odd. Can you describe the scene where this so-called accident took place?'

'Yes. A wide highway crosses a bridge over a deep gorge. Reluctantly, Jim Briscoe showed me a photo of the car my parents had died in. There was a huge dent in the side of the car – as though a heavy vehicle had driven into it. And at the exact point just before the bridge started, where they'd be sent straight down into the gorge.'

'It's a wonder their car didn't burst into flames – or did it?'

'No, it didn't. My father had quick reflexes. He'd obviously turned off the engine as they went over. I asked Briscoe about that and he confirmed the engine had been switched off.'

'Have you got Briscoe's present phone number?'

'No, I haven't. But the new man said he'd retired to a house in the same town. The unpronounceable one I've written down. I've also written down the name of the new sheriff and his phone number. Probably you can't do anything.'

'Don't be so sure about that.' Marler had had a bright idea. 'Give me the notebook and I might just find out what really happened. Something about what you've told me stinks.'

'I'm putting you to a lot of trouble,' she said, handing him back his notebook. 'I've also written down the address of my apartment in Belgravia – next to Sharon's. And a private phone number I've had installed. Ex-directory. On the quiet. I think the Embassy listens in to my calls on the phone that was there when I arrived.' She smiled again. 'Really, you must think I'm nuts.'

'I think you may have every reason to be worried. I'll see what I can do.'

'Let's talk about something else. This can't be entertaining conversation for you.'

'Actually, I'm intrigued.' She had checked her watch. 'You don't have to go yet, do you?'

'I really should. The limo driver who brought me must have been waiting outside for half an hour already . . .'

When they had put their coats on he accompanied her outside to the waiting limo. Before she got into the car she turned, kissed him gently full on the mouth. She gave him a very warm smile.

'Thank you for a really wonderful evening. I'd love it if we could keep in touch.'

'We'll do that.' He handed her a sheet from his notepad, kept his voice to a whisper. 'That's the phone number of my flat. There's an answerphone if I'm out. Just say Denise called and I'll call you back at the private number until I get you.'

'Take care of yourself, Alec. It's a dangerous world we're living in.'

16

Paula didn't sleep that night. She tried to but sleep wouldn't come. The briefcase stuffed with a fortune in dollars kept coming back into her mind. She had a long bath and that didn't help.

As she made coffee, knowing she would not get any rest that night, she kept recalling what Chief Inspector Buchanan had told them. How key figures in Britain were being bought with huge bribes. The technique used. How the Anti-Terrorist Squad officers, watching the Embassy, had seen Americans leaving, carrying executive cases, had followed them, seen them in pubs meeting their 'target'. Strictly speaking, in the episode inside the Raging Stag, it had been a briefcase Osborne must have propped against Tweed's chair leg.

Her mind moved in circles. Had Tweed decided they couldn't win? Had he gone over to the other side? It didn't seem to be possible when she recalled the years she had known him. It was far more likely there was another explanation – but she couldn't think of one.

'I'm bloody wrong. I have to be,' she said aloud.

But she was not convinced. Tweed had trained her always to deal in facts. And she had personally witnessed the 'transaction'. Edgy, she threw away half the cup of coffee, made herself some tea. Pacing round the living room, she smoked another of her rare cigarettes.

'I give up,' she said, again aloud.

*

159

She arrived very early at Park Crescent, was relieved to find she was alone. The briefcase with the dollars had disappeared. On Monica's desk a name was scribbled on a pad. *Keith Kent. Basle.*

She was seated behind her desk when they all arrived almost together. Monica came in first, settled herself behind her desk. She looked across at Paula.

'While you were down at Romney Marsh yesterday Keith Kent, the money tracer, called Tweed from Basle. Said he'd cracked the Zürcher Kredit account, wanted assistance urgently.'

'How did Tweed react?'

'Ask him yourself when he comes in.'

Paula welcomed the suggestion. It gave her something to say to Tweed. If she just sat like a dummy he'd quickly notice her silence. Newman came in. He was cheerful, positively buoyant. He grinned at Paula.

'Top of the morning. Isn't it a nice day.'

'It's a terrible day,' Paula replied. 'The temperature has gone even lower.'

'Helps to keep your wits about you,' he said with another grin, plonking himself into a chair.

Marler arrived, faultlessly dressed as always. He was wearing a new grey suit. He gave everyone a little wave. At that moment Tweed walked in, his step brisk, his manner businesslike as he settled behind his desk. He looked round the room.

'Monica has told me,' Paula began, 'that Keith Kent called you from Basle yesterday, said that he'd cracked the Zürcher Kredit account, whatever that means.'

'True. Everything is beginning to fit. Bob, how did you get on with Sharon Mandeville?'

'Fine. You know, she has no hint of an American accent. She struck me as a demure English lady.'

Paula stared at him, her lips pursed. Was Newman falling for Sharon? It certainly sounded so – from his manner and what he had just said. She lowered her eyes before he looked at her.

'Really?' Tweed paused. 'So you're getting on with her well. Any chance of a second meeting?'

'I would hope so. Yes, a good chance, I'd say.'

'Then you'll have another chance to try to extract information from her as to what is going on. If she has any, which she may not.'

'The lady asked me to write an article. Not her idea. Comes from someone higher up she couldn't name.'

'What kind of an article?'

'A plea for a much closer version of the special relationship between Britain and America.'

'Really?' A brief smile flickered across Tweed's face. 'The pattern is taking shape. Are you going to do it?'

'Haven't decided. If I do, I'll show you a draft first, of course.'

'And now we come to you, Marler,' Tweed went on. 'Did you enjoy your evening with Denise Chatel?'

'Very much. She's nice. She told me a very strange story. There's quite a bit to tell. It concerns the death of her parents . . .'

Marler had Tweed's full attention as the story began to unfold. From his excellent memory he reported every word Denise had said to him. Monica stopped using the phone and listened. Near the conclusion Marler waved a characteristic dismissive hand.

'I thought Cord Dillon was the man to make enquiries – that I could feed him the data and later he could phone America from the Bunker. Or you might think this is a diversion of energy.'

'On the contrary.' Tweed paused again. 'What I'm going to say is very confidential. René Lasalle of the DST in Paris told me recently – when I asked him – that Denise's father was officially sent out as an attaché to the

161

French Embassy in Washington. Actually he was a member of the Secret Service. He was trying to uncover details of some major operation Washington was planning. Before he could report back he was killed, with his wife, in a car crash. Sharon's mother and father were also killed in a car crash. As I said earlier, I don't believe in coincidences.'

'So I can get Cord to check this out?' Marler asked.

'You most certainly can. Tell him I want to know.' He leant back in his chair. 'Years ago, when I was at Scotland Yard . . .'

'As the youngest superintendent in Homicide up to that time,' Paula added.

'What I was going to say was – in more than one murder case I investigated I stumbled across the identity of the murderer by pure chance. But at least I recognized the significance of what I'd stumbled over. I think Marler has done the same thing. I regard what Denise told him as of great significance to what we are dealing with now.'

'Bully for me,' said Marler, mocking himself.

'Also yesterday, a courier arrived from Paris with photos of Americans passing through that city on their way here.'

He took an envelope from a locked drawer, spilled out a number of glossy prints. He spread them methodically over his desk.

'I want all of you to gather round and comment if you see anyone you recognize . . .'

They formed a half-circle behind him. Paula, glad of something else to think about, studied the prints with care. Then she pointed.

'That's Hank Waltz, the man who tried to kill me at Eagle Street.'

Tweed turned over the photo. On the back was written a date. He looked over his shoulder at her.

'He came in by Eurostar four weeks ago. Go on looking.'

'That is Chuck Venacki,' Newman told them. 'Smooth faced, smooth manner. Officially an attaché at the Embassy. A bit above people like Waltz in intellect.'

'I haven't seen him so far,' Paula commented.

'You may well. Yet.' Newman warned. 'He's intelligent, so could be dangerous.'

'Came in three weeks ago,' Tweed said, looking at the back.

'And that,' Paula pointed out, stabbing her finger at another of the prints, 'is Jake Ronstadt.'

'Came in five weeks ago,' Tweed noted. 'Which is interesting. He was in the vanguard, which suggests he came early to set up something. Maybe the Executive Action Department.'

'There are three people missing,' Paula observed. 'Denise Chatel, Ed Osborne and Sharon Mandeville. Maybe the French didn't photo them.'

'I don't think that's the explanation,' Tweed objected. 'I'd say they flew direct here from Washington to Heathrow. Just as Jefferson Morgenstern did.' He stood up. 'Which reminds me, I'm having dinner with Jefferson at the Ambassador's residence this evening. It's no more than a quick walk from here. Jefferson called me before I left my flat. I accepted immediately.'

'You need a bodyguard,' said Newman.

'I do not. Jefferson is one of the old school. A very devious man – has to be to do his job – and he has his own idea of honour. Monica, you're still booking seats for us on the Swissair flight, I imagine.'

'Day by day.'

'Since you're all here,' Tweed said, glancing round the room, 'I hope you have your bags packed with cold-weather clothing. You have? Good. Because we're leaving for Basle on the early flight tomorrow morning.'

'You're going somewhere?' Monica asked as Tweed put on his coat. 'It's much too early for your meeting with Morgenstern.'

'I know. I have somewhere else to go first.'

'I'd better warn Butler and Nield about the flight,' Monica said.

'Don't do that. They have a job to do back here. They'll come on to Basle when they're finished. So keep booking seats for them daily. I've got to go now. Everything is breaking loose.'

When he had gone Monica slammed down the pen she was holding. She sat behind her desk, arms folded, looking furious.

'What's the matter?' Newman asked.

'Tweed's always doing that to me recently. Says he'll be back as soon as he can. I ask him where I can contact him. So he simply says something like, "I have to be somewhere else in a hurry." No clue as to where he's gone.'

Back behind her desk, Paula's brain was in turmoil. She had felt better when Tweed seemed like his normal self, full of activity, carrying on as usual but with a hint of great urgency. Now Monica's grumble had made her wonder again. Why was he being so exceptionally secretive? Who was he going to see?

Marler sat behind Tweed's desk to call Cord Dillon at the Bunker. Mrs Carson answered, put Dillon swiftly on the line.

'Cord, Marler here. We have a problem which might just be up your street. If you're willing to go for it. There's a young woman, in her thirties, at the Embassy. Had dinner with her last night. She's called Denise Chatel. I'll spell that . . .'

With his notepad open in front of him, Marler

164

explained the problem, gave him all the data. He spelt out the name of the little town in Virginia where the fatal car crash had taken place over a year before and everything else Denise had told him. Dillon asked him to slow down so he could scribble on a notepad.

'Can you do anything, get some facts?' Marler ended.

'Sure thing. Glad to have a problem I can get my teeth into. This is just the sort of problem I dealt with sometimes, back at Langley – tracing a missing person or someone on the run. I'll get Jim Briscoe's number, wherever he's retired to. Virginia is on New York time, so they're five hours back. I'll wait for people to get to work, then go into action. Can I call you back at Park Crescent?'

'You can. And I'm very grateful . . .'

'Consider it done.'

In his usual abrupt way Dillon broke the connection. Marler took the envelope from Paris that Tweed had left on his desk. He spent some time examining each print, memorizing faces, recalling names that had been put to each one. Eventually he put them back inside the envelope.

'Enjoying yourself?' Paula enquired.

'It helps to know the enemy. Now I'm going back to my flat to collect a few more things for what Tweed keeps calling cold weather. I thought it was pretty nippy here . . .'

Marler did not drive straight to his flat. He had decided to look at the outside of the flat where Denise Chatel lived. Plus the fact that Sharon Mandeville lived next door. It was always useful to know the locations of people involved.

There was heavy traffic on the way to Belgrave Square. Marler knew he would have a parking problem so he drove slowly into one of the most expensive squares in London. Checking the numbers, he was close to where Denise lived when he saw a big truck pulled in at the kerb. The driver was changing a wheel. Marler played with his engine, causing it to make funny noises. He stopped near to the truck. The driver, stopping for a cigarette, saluted him.

'You got trouble too, mate?'

'Engine's playing up. It would. I'm in a hurry.'

'That's when they always let you down.'

Still seated behind his wheel, Marler was watching the entrance to the Chatel flat and hoping no police car came along. He was parked illegally. Then he sat up straighter, stopped playing about with the engine. It took a lot to startle Marler, but startled he was. The door to the flat on the ground floor had opened and Tweed walked out a few paces. He turned round and Denise appeared. They chatted for only a moment, then they shook hands and Denise closed the door.

Marler slumped down behind the wheel. An unoccupied taxi came along. Tweed flagged it down after glancing round the square. Saying something to the driver he climbed inside, pulled the door shut behind him. The taxi moved off, vanished round a corner.

Marler started his engine, backed, waved to the truck driver who gave him a thumbs-up sign. Then Marler drove back to Park Crescent in heavy traffic. For once he felt dumbfounded. What on earth could Tweed have been up to? He couldn't think of any explanation. He decided to keep quiet about what he'd seen.

'Tweed's with Howard,' Monica told Marler as he entered the office at Park Crescent. 'I expect he's telling him about your trip to Basle with the others. I've got your ticket, of course.'

'Thanks. 'Fraid I have to ask you to change that. Book me on the earliest possible flight to Geneva tomorrow.'

'What's the idea?' asked Tweed, who had just returned and heard Marler's request.

'Presumably we have to pass through all the usual checks at Heathrow before we board.'

'Actually, no.' Tweed was settled behind his desk now. 'I got in touch with Jim Corcoran, my old friend and Security Chief at Heathrow. We'll bypass Customs and Passport control so we get aboard the plane before anyone else.'

'But we'll still have to pass through the metal detectors,' Marler persisted.

'Yes, we do. Even Jim can't get us past that check.'

'So we'll arrive in Basle unarmed.'

'You have a point.'

'Which is why I'm flying to Geneva. I have a contact there who will supply me with an arsenal. For a price.'

'Then you travel the same day to Basle,' said Newman, who sat in one of the armchairs. 'By train – where there are no checks.'

'Got in one, chum,' Marler agreed.

'Don't forget my Browning automatic – and plenty of ammo,' said Paula.

'The lady will be equipped with her favourite weapon,' Marler promised.

'I should have thought of that myself,' Tweed admitted, 'but I have a lot on my mind. This evening I have dinner with Jefferson Morgenstern.'

'You'll tell him where we're going?' Newman teased.

'Of course not. Don't be so silly.'

Paula narrowed her eyes, then looked away. It was very rare for Tweed to have a flash of temper. Something must be putting him under immense pressure. Her mind flooded with doubts about him again.

'I was joking,' Newman said mildly.

'Sorry. I should have realized that,' Tweed said with feeling.

167

The phone rang. Monica answered, asked the caller to hold for a moment. She looked at Marler, her hand shutting off the mouthpiece.

'It's for you. Your girl friend, Denise Chatel.'

Tweed stood up, told Marler to take the call on his phone. As he picked it up, Marler noticed everyone else in the room was suddenly interested in what was going on outside the window, which amused him. Was this their idea of giving him privacy?

'Hello, Denise. Alec here. How is the desirable brunette?'

'All right. And thank you. I'm calling on my special line from my flat. Have you heard anything yet about Virginia?'

'Not yet. It may take a day or two. As soon as I have something you'll hear from me.'

'I'm afraid I won't. Which is why I'm phoning you. Sharon told me at lunchtime that we're flying to Basle in Switzerland today. We'll be staying at a hotel called the Three Kings. I'll call you as soon as I get back – although I don't know when that will be.'

'Did she give any reason for this sudden decision?'

'Not even a hint. But she works like that. I have to go. Take care of yourself.'

'You do the same. And don't mention the Virginia business to anyone.'

'I promise.'

Tweed returned to his desk. Marler walked over to the wall near Paula, leant against it. He took his time about lighting up a king-size. No one asked why Denise had phoned but Tweed sat looking at him.

'Denise is going abroad today,' Marler eventually announced. 'With Sharon.'

'So I can forget my date,' Newman commented.

'They are both flying to Switzerland today,' Marler

168

went on. 'Specifically, to Basle. They're staying at the Three Kings Hotel.'

'Which is where we'll be staying from tomorrow,' Tweed told everyone. 'Another coincidence? Probably. It is not only the oldest hotel in Basle, it's also the best.'

'So I may see Sharon again soon,' Newman said more cheerfully.

'Bob.' Tweed smiled. 'I foresee great activity in Basle. You won't have to much time to pursue your personal affairs.'

'You couldn't care to spell that last word?' Newman joked back.

'I wouldn't like to embarrass you.' Tweed smiled again. 'In fact, the closer you get to Sharon the more pleased I'll be. She's a beautiful lady – and men talk to lovely women. She may have heard something we need to know. If she has, sooner or later she may let something slip when you're together.'

The phone rang. After answering, Monica again looked at Marler.

'It's for you. Cord Dillon . . .'

Tweed again ushered Marler into his chair. He wandered over to the window, staring into the distance. Outside sleet was falling. Moving cars had their wipers going full blast.

'Marler here, Cord.'

'We may be on to something big, reaching right up to Washington. I found Jim Briscoe's phone number. Told him who I was, what my job was, omitting to say I don't hold the post any more. He'd had a few drinks, but his brain was ticking over. He's bitter as all hell. He has no doubt at all Chatel and his wife were murdered. A heavy truck or some other vehicle slammed them over the edge down into that gorge. He called in the FBI, wrote a report. Next thing he knows, he's been replaced by a new sheriff, retired on full pension. His report was shredded.'

'This is pretty sensational . . .'

'There's a bit more. A few weeks after his forced retirement Briscoe was drinking with a young deputy brought in at the same time as the new sheriff. The boy got talkative when Briscoe mentioned the Chatel case. His boss had told him the case was closed for ever – that if it was ever reopened someone back in Washington called Charlie would see they both disappeared for good. It stinks of a huge cover-up. Guess that's all I have to give you.'

'It's more than enough, Cord. I'm very grateful. You've been very quick.'

'You've got a job to do, damned well do it.'

The connection was broken without another word. Marler relaxed in Tweed's chair, recalled out aloud everything Dillon had said. As he went on, Tweed perched on the corner of his own desk, arms folded, his eyes fixed on Marler's. Eventually Marler spread both his hands.

'You've got the lot.'

'Charlie again,' Tweed said in a quiet voice. 'I know you're doing your best, Monica, but at the earliest possible moment we must identify Charlie.'

17

Halfway through dinner in a magnificently furnished room, full of antiques, Jefferson Morgenstern brought up the subject. Earlier he and Tweed had had drinks in a smaller room and the American Secretary of State had chatted about their previous meeting in Washington.

Morgenstern was about five feet eight tall, in his

fifties. He was clean-shaven with greying hair, plump-cheeked, had a longish face and a prominent nose and wore rimless glasses. His personality radiated self-confidence without arrogance and he spoke at speed in a deep voice. His mind moved like quicksilver and Tweed considered him one of the most intelligent men he had ever met.

He had the reputation of liking the company of beautiful women, providing they were also intelligent. His expressions were mobile – sometimes grave and on other occasions amiable. He was known internationally as a man who could charm the birds out of the trees and his diplomatic skills were awesome. Despite his long sojourn in the States he was far more European than American. His energy was legendary.

'You know, Tweed,' he began, 'today the world is changing, and to survive we must change with it.'

'Jefferson, what sort of changes had you in mind?'

Tweed finished his fourth glass of wine and out of nowhere an attentive waiter appeared and refilled his glass, then vanished. On the wine front Tweed was keeping up with his host. He had an unusual metabolism. He would drink hardly anything for months, then, when the occasion required it, could consume a large quantity without it in any way affecting his brain.

'For one thing,' Morgenstern continued, 'I believe we have to considerably strengthen the special relationship between our two countries. In every field – economically, socially and politically.'

'Why?'

'You haven't changed. You never hesitate to ask the leading question. Which is one of the many things I like about you. That and your global outlook.'

'So why?' Tweed repeated.

'From Washington's point of view – and the world's – we are the great superpower. Between us, I believe we

171

have peaked. In the Pacific we face China. China is steadily building itself up into a monster . . .'

'So why,' Tweed interjected, 'is your President supplying the Chinese with advanced technology which will help them to build up a vast war machine?'

'At times he runs away with himself. But what he has done also serves the purpose of lulling the Chinese. Between us, we now have far more advanced technology in the missile fields than what we have given them. But China has a population of over a billion people. We have only approximately two hundred and sixty million. In a clash China could lose fifty million and think nothing of it. If that happens to the States it would be devastating.'

'I take your point . . .'

'When we look east we see Europe losing all its strength with their crazy idea of merging countries – nations, Tweed, all with different languages, histories, ways of life. Madness. History shows us the Austro-Hungarian Empire, also a hotch-potch of nations with different cultures, collapsed after the First World War. Yugoslavia, another mixture of nations who detested each other, was held together by Tito for a time. Tito dies. Yugoslavia, as a similar federation to the one proposed for Europe, collapses in a bloodbath. The Soviet Empire is another example of different nationalities which broke down into chaos. You see why Washington is so worried about Europe.'

'You've made a powerful case.'

The waiter appeared to fill their glasses. Morgenstern looked up, smiled.

'Thank you, but I will attend to the wine. We want to be alone. I'll press the bell when we need help.'

'I think you're leading up to something, Jefferson,' Tweed remarked.

'Then, beyond Europe, there are more menaces. Militant Islam is on the upsurge. Turkey, which could fall to

172

Islam, will soon have a population of a hundred and fifty million. Germany, the largest nation in Europe, has eighty million. It only needs a brilliant Muslim general to do a Mohammed. To sweep across Europe. Based in an occupied Britain, their missiles could annihilate the East Coast of the States – while the Chinese did the same thing to our West Coast. You agree it is possible? This dessert isn't bad.'

'It's the best I've eaten in years,' Tweed said.

'Then Iran is building nuclear bombs, has ballistic missile systems. Allied to Turkey, with Iran's huge population, nothing could stand in their way.'

'They sound pretty worried in Washington,' Tweed observed.

'With good reason, as I'm explaining. Britain, for a thousand years the bulwark against tyranny from Europe, is enfeebled in a military sense. It wasn't necessary. You have no army to speak of, a skeleton of an air force, a ghost of a navy. Yet not so long ago you were the main factor in destroying Hitler. How are the mighty fallen.'

'I find it difficult to argue against what you have said.'

'Why don't we adjourn to the smaller room for coffee and liqueurs?'

'Good idea.'

The 'smaller' room was also large, spacious and luxuriously furnished. They sat facing each other, on two couches, with a coffee table between them. Morgenstern's blue eyes were gleaming with vitality.

'With all these terrible forces soon to be so powerful,' Morgenstern continued, 'we have to adjust, adapt, be revolutionary.'

'I sense we're approaching the reason why you invited me to have dinner,' Tweed said, then sipped his Cointreau.

173

'You are a very intuitive man. I noticed that rare quality when we met in Washington.'

'Why didn't you ask Howard to meet you?' Tweed enquired.

Tweed was making no attempt to pretend to be running an insurance outfit. Morgenstern would know he was Deputy Director of the SIS, that Howard was Director.

'Howard is a nice man.' Morgenstern paused for the first time, choosing his words carefully. 'But he hasn't a fraction of your global outlook. We regard you as a key figure in the new system.'

'What new system are you referring to, Jefferson?'

'I said earlier we have to be revolutionary.' Morgenstern leaned forward. 'Britain and America have to merge in a new and much stronger relationship. That is why we are talking tonight.'

'Merge?'

'As I said earlier, economically, socially and politically.'

'Before you go any further I'd like to ask a few questions. I imagine you saw the TV pictures of the outrage in Oxford Street after the bomb detonated?'

'I did. I was appalled. Such savagery.'

'I think some of your people planted that bomb.'

'You think *what*?' Morgenstern sat back, appeared to be visibly shaken. 'You can't mean that, Tweed. It's crazy. I find it hard to believe I heard what you just said. We don't do things like that. Why would we, for God's sake?'

Tweed had been watching his host closely. He had a lot of experience in detecting when people were lying. He could have sworn Morgenstern believed what he had just said. He pressed on.

'We have evidence that a huge number of the worst American thugs – gangsters – have arrived in this

174

country by devious routes recently.' He opened the executive case which he had brought with him, took the batch of prints from the envelope, spread them on the coffee table. 'These are the men I'm talking about.'

'They must be members of the Medellín drug cartel – or maybe the Mafia,' Morgenstern said as he looked at the prints. 'I can only assume someone has fed you with disinformation.'

'You've seen any of those men inside the Embassy at Grosvenor Square?'

'Heavens no! I most certainly haven't.'

'May I ask, do you know everyone who works at the Embassy?'

'Absolutely not. Why should I? My role is running foreign policy. I have a suite of offices on the second floor. And I always enter the Embassy by a side door – to avoid the press photographers.'

Second floor? Then Tweed remembered that in America the ground floor is called the first floor. So when he had seen the back of Morgenstern with two bodyguards at the time of his visit to Sharon Mandeville, on the first floor, the Americans would refer to that as the second floor. Which linked up with what Morgenstern was telling him. Again he had no doubt that his host was speaking the truth.

'You know Sharon Mandeville?' Tweed persisted.

'Yes I do. She has an office on the same floor as my suite. I don't know what her role is, but she has close connections with the White House. She's friends with the President's wife. You know something, Tweed? You make a good interrogator.'

'I've no intention of offending you . . .'

'That's enough.' Morgenstern smiled. 'You are someone who could never offend me. Very occasionally, you might be deceived by someone trying to make bad blood between us, but I make no claim to infallibility.'

'Would you like to explain in more detail this merger between our two countries you suggested a few minutes ago?'

'I said merge, not merger.'

'There's a difference?'

'I suppose there isn't. Have you read how when France was falling to Germany in the Second World War Churchill offered the French dual citizenship? The French would also have British nationality – and vice versa.'

'Yes, I have read about that. The French turned it down.'

'Let us suppose Washington made a similar offer to this country. All Britons would become American citizens – with all the huge advantages that would give you.'

'Is Washington going to make such an offer? Positively?'

'It has been discussed by the National Security Council. And I chaired the meeting.'

'You haven't answered my question. Positively,' Tweed goaded.

'Other aspects of the joining of our two nations have been discussed in great detail. The Joint Chiefs of Staff would welcome the establishment of further air force and naval bases in Britain. It would increase the reach of, say, missiles aimed from here at the Middle East by three thousand five hundred miles. And the East Coast of the States would be safe again – safe from the danger of an attack by Muslim powers from occupied Britain.'

'What else has been discussed behind closed doors in Washington?' Tweed demanded.

'A special Act has been drafted in secret for Congress – this would incorporate Britain into the American system.'

'What are the huge advantages to this country you mentioned a few minutes ago?'

'You have a population of about fifty million-plus. At the moment the largest state in the US is California – a population of roughly thirty million. Britain would be by far the most powerful element when it came to electing a President. You would have more electoral votes than any other state in the Union. From America's point of view it would greatly increase the Anglo-Saxon vote. You would be the powerbrokers. Who knows? In the not too distant future an Englishman, now an American citizen, might be elected President.'

'You always were very persuasive.'

'Emotionally,' Morgenstern leaned forward again, 'this merger would appeal to many Americans. They would feel they were coming home again. After all, the Republic originated in England, when the Pilgrim Fathers sailed across the Atlantic.'

Morgenstern refilled his liqueur glass with more Grand Marnier after topping up Tweed's Cointreau. He drank half of what he had poured, then continued, his energy undiminished.

'If you allowed yourselves to be dragged into the doomed federation of Europe you would be nobody, out-voted on every issue. And who would you be sitting with? Old enemies. Long ago you destroyed the Armada sent against you by Philip of Spain. One of your greatest generals, Marlborough, checkmated the power of Louis XIV of France in a series of military victories. You fought and defeated the Kaiser – and Adolf Hitler.'

'The dinner was excellent,' Tweed said suddenly. He suspected the chef was French. 'Thank you for a memorable evening.'

'You're not going? You haven't given me your reaction to all I've told you.'

'You propose to turn Britain into the fifty-first state of the United States . . .'

177

18

'They've all gone home,' said George when he opened the door at Park Crescent. He was blinking as though he'd just had a nap. 'Only Paula is still here.'

When Tweed opened the door to his office Paula was sitting behind Monica's desk. She checked her watch, looked at him as she made her comment.

'I persuaded Monica to go home, get some sleep. She's worked like a Trojan in building up her profiles. I said I'd wait to take calls. You've been a long time. It must have been a very long dinner with Morgenstern.'

'After I left Jefferson I got a taxi to take me to Downing Street. I had a chat with the PM, who is also working all hours.'

Removing his coat, he sat behind his desk. He poured water from a carafe into a glass that Monica, he felt sure, had left him.

'Roy Buchanan phoned,' Paula reported. 'When I told him I'd no idea when you'd be back he told me instead. He's heard a positive rumour that the American syndicate has bid for two leading daily newspapers, a key TV station and two important radio outfits. The money offered is so huge he's sure that a majority of shareholders will accept.'

'I know. The PM told me. It's a fact, not a rumour.'

'We're letting them get away with it?'

'The PM is still cleverly playing it softly, softly. He's allowing the bids to be made, then he'll refer them to the Monopolies and Mergers Commission. Meantime, he's going to watch how the Americans handle their new propaganda machine.'

'That is clever. How did you get on with Morgenstern
– or shouldn't I ask?'

Paula was talking as much as she could. Anything to
cover up her nagging doubts about Tweed.

'Paula,' he began, his expression grave, 'what I am
about to tell you is for your ears only. I may tell Newman
and Marler later – and anyone else if I feel they should
know. Has this room been checked for bugs recently?'

'Only an hour ago. Harry Butler came in, checked
everywhere – then he told me it was clean.'

'This is going to take awhile. I'm recalling everything
which Morgenstern said to me . . .'

Paula found her confidence in him flooding back as he
recited word for word the entire conversation over dinner.
He ended by clenching his fist, banging it on his desk.

'Now you have the lot. Except I now believe the
Americans are operating at two different levels.'

'What does that mean?'

'One is the diplomatic level. Morgenstern handles
that. I'm certain he was telling me the truth when he
vehemently would not believe any of his people could
be involved in the bomb in Oxford Street. They're concealing the other level from him – knowing such a man
would never go along with it.'

'And the other level?'

'The Charlie–Ronstadt level – the thugs and killers
whose job is to destabilize Britain. I'm convinced now
the two levels are operating in watertight compartments.
One doesn't know the other exists. Someone – probably
Charlie – is being diabolically clever. They're using every
dirty method in the book – intimidation, bribery, mass
murder, you name it. The object is to bring Britain to its
knees, then the proposal that we merge with the US will
seem attractive. We may see an FBI team arriving, "to
clear up the mess".'

'Would the PM accept them coming?'

'I just don't know. Incidentally, when I was with the PM I suggested he take action in case they use logic bombs.'

'What on earth are they?' Paula wondered.

'New American expression. It covers advanced techniques for closing down phone communications and power supplies inside a country they want to destabilize. Imagine the breakdown if we couldn't contact anyone, if we had no power for heat and for lighting in present weather conditions. They could also insert misleading information into our computers. Hence the phrase, logic bombs. Logic would vanish.'

'Can't anything be done to stop them?'

'It can, provided we prepare for such an onslaught in advance. The PM has ordered troops to guard key exchanges in London – keeping out of sight. He's shutting down vital computers, fax machines. From now on communication is by a troop of army couriers on motorcycles.'

'That wouldn't be your idea?'

'Well, the PM and I did discuss the problem.'

'And we're still going to Basle tomorrow by early flight?'

'We most certainly are.'

'It will be interesting staying at the Three Kings Hotel – we stayed there once before. Remember?'

'Of course I do. Intriguing that Sharon and Denise are also staying there. I'd like another talk with Sharon.'

'I'm looking forward to this trip,' Paula mused.

'Maybe you shouldn't. My sixth sense tells me we're walking into an inferno.'

Tweed, Paula and Newman boarded the early morning flight to Basle. They were escorted to the plane by Jim

Corcoran, a friendly man in his late thirties. Later the other passengers took their seats. The plane was three-quarters empty and Tweed gave Paula the window seat, with himself alongside her. Behind them Newman occupied one of the two seats on his own. Even though no other passengers were near them, he was protecting the privacy of Tweed and Paula so they could talk freely.

Tweed was clutching an executive case which he kept in his lap. The plane was flying over France, heading for Germany where the pilot would turn south up the invisible Rhine. They both accepted the offer of drinks and Paula teased Tweed.

'You're getting to be a regular toper. Drinking on top of all that wine you told me you consumed last night.'

'You know I can turn it on and off like a tap. Like to see what I have inside this case?'

'I did wonder.'

Glancing over his shoulder, making sure the stewardess was busy at the rear of the plane, Tweed unlocked the case, raised the lid. Paula stared. It was neatly stacked with packages of one-hundred-dollar bills. He must have transferred the bills from the old briefcase, Paula thought.

'Should be enough to pay the hotel bill,' Tweed joked.

'I'll say. At a guess there must be a hundred thousand dollars you're carrying.'

'Nearer two hundred thousand.' He closed the lid, relocked the case. 'They're for Keith Kent, who is meeting our flight at Basle.'

'The brilliant money tracer. Why does he need them?'

'To pay into a certain account at the Zürcher Kredit Bank in Basle. No idea how he's going to do it, but he's going to manipulate the transaction so the millions of dollars paid in from Washington get lost in the system. That should help to stir things up a bit for starters.'

'They'll go berserk!'

181

'And that might cause them to make a big mistake. Doesn't look very wonderful out of your window.'

Paula felt a sensation of enormous relief now she knew what the huge sum of dollars was intended for. This was followed by a feeling of guilt that she could ever have doubted the integrity of Tweed.

She looked out of the window. Ever since they had left Heathrow there had been nothing but sullen dark overcast below them. It seemed even denser, the closer they approached Basle.

'I suppose that was one reason why you got Jim Corcoran to bypass most controls – all that money.'

'It was *the* reason. The case was specially designed some time ago at my suggestion by the boffins in the basement at Park Crescent. It looks normal but it hasn't a hint of metal in its construction. Plastic to look like metal was used. You noticed I carried it through the detector and there wasn't a hint of a ping. Because Jim was with us they didn't even ask me to open it. We've begun to descend.'

Five minutes later they broke through the overcast. Paula looked down at the ground and sighed heavily.

'Something wrong?' Tweed asked.

'There's a covering of snow, of all things. I didn't think Basle ever had snow.'

'It rarely does. It looks much heavier over there in Germany. That huge uplifted hump is the Black Forest . . .'

Tweed had asked Monica to arrange for two hire cars to wait for their arrival. Basle still had a very small, cosy airport, unlike Geneva and Zurich where once-compact airports had expanded into major terminals. Keith Kent was waiting for them when they walked outside.

'Welcome to Switzerland. The locals keep saying they

never get snow and are very indignant. Is it in that executive case, Tweed?'

'It is,' Tweed assured him, handing over the case. 'So how long before millions of American dollars vanish into thin air?'

'About a couple of hours from now.'

Keith Kent was of medium height, slim, clean-shaven, with a sharp-featured face and shrewd dark eyes. He had a ready smile and was dressed in a dark suit under a smart overcoat. Anyone who met him immediately had the impression of a businessman, probably the director of a firm.

'Don't wish to seem inhospitable,' he said, 'but I want to get on with this. Monica told me you were at the Three Kings. I'll come and see you there. Have a quiet stay.'

'I suspect,' Tweed told him, 'it will be anything but quiet.'

'Better watch my back, then.'

'And your front,' warned Newman, who had joined them. 'I'll drive one of the cars if you, Tweed, will take the other with Paula. Do we officially know each other at the hotel?'

'No point in pretending we don't – not with Sharon and Denise staying there.'

It took them only about fifteen minutes to reach their hotel. The first part of the journey was through open flat countryside, coated white. Then they started to enter the ancient city.

'I love this place,' Paula said. 'It's so very old. And it has narrow winding streets and alleys. And if I re-member rightly, secret squares surrounded by massive buildings ages old.'

'You remember rightly,' Tweed agreed, behind the wheel.

Old stone buildings loomed on either side as they

drew near the Three Kings. On her left Paula caught glimpses of the Rhine at the end of short side streets. They parked in front of the hotel as Newman pulled up behind them. Tweed asked the doorman to have the cars parked as nearby as possible.

The first person he met as he entered was Sharon Mandeville.

'Are you following me?' Sharon asked with a smile.

'Hardly, since I thought you were still in London,' Tweed lied. 'I could hardly have hoped for such a pleasant surprise.'

'Wow!' said Newman. 'Great to see you again so soon.' He kissed her on the cheek. 'What brings you to Basle?'

'I have Swiss friends who invited me over. I grabbed at the chance to get away from the Embassy. I don't like some of the people there.'

'I'm forgetting my manners,' Tweed interjected. 'Sharon, this is Paula, my assistant. Paula, meet Sharon.'

'Hi there.' Sharon shook hands with Paula, smiling warmly. 'You have a wonderful boss to work for.'

'I think so,' replied Paula in a neutral tone.

'I'd better leave the three of you to register, get settled in your rooms. Maybe we could all have a drink before lunch. Oh, why did you say you were here, Tweed?'

'I didn't. I'm investigating the disappearance of one of my staff. The last I heard from him was when he called me from Basle.'

'Don't forget my offer for us to have a drink together . . .'

Newman had been studying her. As usual she was expensively and tastefully dressed. She wore a red two-piece suit with a Chanel scarf round her neck. She turned back as she was walking away.

'Isn't the weather hideous? I hear several roads in Germany are closed to traffic. Wrap up well if you go out.'

While Tweed was registering, Paula looked round the comfortable and spacious lobby, which she remembered. Towards the far end small tables were scattered and close to them were cosy armchairs and couches. The atmosphere was of quiet but not ostentatious luxury. The porter had taken their bags and they travelled up together in the small lift.

'I'm on the first floor,' Tweed said as the lift stopped.

'Bob and I have rooms on the second floor,' Paula said. 'I did hear your room number.'

'Come and see me later . . .'

Tweed had a large, well-appointed room which overlooked the Rhine. He unpacked first, using one cupboard and only a few drawers. It made repacking easier. Then he wandered over to the window. A few minutes later he heard a tapping on his door. Opening it, he let Paula into his room, returned to the window.

'Both Bob and I have rooms looking down on the river. I'd forgotten how wide it is, even at Basle, hundreds of miles from where it flows into the sea.'

She became aware he wasn't listening. Tweed was staring fixedly at an immense barge gliding upstream on his side of the river. He remembered that traffic on the Rhine had to use this side of the river when moving upstream, the far side when it was on its way downriver. The barge was so huge it seemed to take a minute to pass the window before passing under the arch of a big bridge to their right. At the stern a small car was parked.

'You're thinking about something,' she said.

'Just fascinated by the river. It's started to snow again – I suggest we stay inside the hotel, at least until Marler gets here from Geneva.'

'Suits me. I'm tired. I seem to have been on the go

nonstop recently. Do you mind if I have a bath and then take a nap?'

'I think you should. Oh, what did you think of Sharon?'

'On the surface she's elegant, reserved but amiable.'

'On the surface?'

'She struck me as being an enigma. Hard to sum up.'

The phone rang. Paula stayed by the window as Tweed went to answer it. He spoke in a very quiet voice and Paula made no attempt to listen. When he put the phone down she made for the door, deliberately not asking who had called.

'That was Arthur Beck, Chief of the Federal Police, as you know.'

'I've always liked Beck. And you call him the most able police chief in Western Europe.'

'He sounded grim. He's flying here to see me from his headquarters in Berne. He ordered me not to leave the hotel until he's arrived. He's never done that before.'

'You did say you might be walking into an inferno. I thought at the time you were exaggerating.'

'Maybe I was underestimating the danger.'

'How on earth did Beck trace us here so quickly?'

'He phoned Monica. Normally she wouldn't have told even him where I was. I'm going to ask him how he persuaded her. And it will be a few hours before he gets here.'

'Then I'm off to have my bath and some catch-up sleep.'

'Paula, under no circumstances are you to leave the hotel. That is an order.'

Newman, in cheerful mood, arrived soon after Paula had left. He followed Tweed over to the window. The first barge, which Paula had watched with Tweed, had been a bulk carrier. The new monster they stared down at was a tanker. Newman whistled.

'That's a huge job to travel as far as this up the Rhine. I asked the receptionist how far up they can go. Apparently there's a harbour where they dock on the outskirts of Basle, which *is* as far as they can go.'

'There's also another harbour further down to the left of us. That's where three countries meet – Switzerland, Germany and France. Better sit down. I've something to tell you.'

Newman listened while Tweed gave him the gist of the phone call from Beck. He whistled again. When he glanced at Tweed he thought his chief had never looked more serious. Tweed stifled a yawn, flexed his fingers.

'He didn't give you any hint as to what it was all about?' Newman asked.

'Not a dickey bird. I can't imagine what can have stirred up Beck to the extent of his flying from Berne to see me. On top of that he ordered me not to leave the hotel. Which reminds me. You're not to leave this hotel until we've heard what has so disturbed Beck. That is my order.'

'I'd better tell Paula . . .'

'I've already told her. Best to leave her alone. She's having a bath and then some sleep. I wouldn't mind some myself.'

'Oh, I have some news. Denise Chatel is staying here too. I was out of sight when I saw two people coming out of the lift.'

'Marler told us she'd be here – along with Sharon. Have you been downstairs, chatting up the cool Sharon?'

'No. I asked at the reception desk. She'd told them she was going out to meet some friends. The Swiss people she mentioned, I expect. She should be warm enough. When we dined together at Santorini's she had a sable coat.'

'Well, she can afford it, so why not?'

Newman had experienced this mood of Tweed's before, when he appeared to be taking in everything said to him and made replies which seemed to confirm this impression. But Newman sensed that Tweed's brain was racing, checking over in his mind what had happened, linking up sequences of events, forming a pattern.

This was waiting time. Waiting for Marler to appear. Waiting for Beck to arrive. And normally, the lull before the storm broke. He realized Tweed had heard every word he had said when he asked his question.

'You did say two people came out of the lift when you were out of sight and saw Denise. Yet you also said Sharon had left the hotel to visit friends. What I'm wondering is, who was the second person who came out of the lift with Denise?'

'I've been keeping that for last as a blockbuster surprise.'

'Then surprise me.'

'And he's staying at this hotel. It was Ed Osborne.'

19

Newman shook Tweed gently. Waking up instantly, Tweed sat up on the bed. He had taken off his jacket and shoes, had loosened his tie before lying down under the duvet hours earlier. Newman, who had said he didn't feel sleepy, had sat in a chair, insisting on acting as a guard. Tweed stared out of the window into the dark.

'What time is it?'

'4.30 p.m.'

'Lord, I've never slept like that before.' He hurried into the bathroom for a cold wash and to brush his hair. 'I've just never slept like that before,' he repeated.

'Showed how much you needed it. You've been on the go for ages, like Paula. She only woke a short time ago. She'll be down here any minute. Reason I woke you is Marler has just arrived. He'll be up very soon.'

'That's better. Think I can face the world now.'

He emerged from the bathroom, his tie neat, wearing his jacket and shoes. He sat in a chair and poured some of the coffee Newman had ordered after waking him. He drank two cups one after the other, the first black, the second with a helping of milk. Someone knocked on the door and Newman opened it cautiously, then let Marler in. He was carrying two large heavy-looking holdalls.

'Sorry I've been so long. Decided it was safer to hire a car at Geneva and drive here – considering what's in these bags.'

'What is in them?' Newman asked.

'Tell you later. More important information to impart.'

There was a tapping at the door and Newman let in Paula. She looked fresh and energetic. Ready to start a new day, Tweed thought. She greeted Marler who said he'd tell her about his trip later. Sitting alongside Tweed on a couch, Paula put a hand to her ear to show she was listening.

'The enemy has arrived in Basle in force,' Marler announced.

'Just what we need,' Tweed said ironically. 'Where are they?'

'Tell it to you in my way. I drove into Basle and parked near Hauptbahnhof. I was going to go into the station to stock up on cigarettes. I was still sitting in my car when who should I see coming out of the Euler Hotel, a five-star job? Jake Ronstadt and Chuck Venacki. Recognized Venacki from the Paris photos. They crossed the street, disappeared into the Victoria, a smaller hotel. I waited.'

189

'How was Ronstadt dressed?' asked Tweed.

'In an astrakhan fur coat with a hat to match. Strode across the street as though he owned Basle. Minutes later he comes out of the Victoria, with six more thugs in tow. All snapped in the pics from Paris. The whole gang walks down to the Hilton and disappears inside. To the bar, would be my guess.'

'We have a spot of trouble,' Tweed said.

'A load of it, I'd say. Missed out a vital bit. When he came out of the Euler, Ronstadt paid a quick visit to get something from his parked white Citroën. When they'd all trooped into the Hilton I darted across, fixed a little gizmo my supplier of arms had given me. Attached it underneath the chassis of the Citroën. We could follow him now.'

'How could we do that?' Paula asked.

'Good question. I've a good answer. There's a tracking device I can attach to your car, Tweed. Another for you, Bob. Range of ten miles. Incredible.'

'Where did you get this stuff?' Newman enquired.

'My chum in Geneva who gave me weapons and grenades has gone into business on another front. Tracking devices.'

'Where's my Browning?' Paula wanted to know.

'Eager, isn't she?'

Opening one of the holdalls Marler produced a .32 Browning automatic and spare ammo, handed it to Paula. Newman held out his hand and Marler placed a .38 Smith & Wesson and extra ammo in it. He also provided Newman with a hip holster.

Newman immediately took off his jacket, strapped on the holster, checked the action of the empty revolver, loaded it, slid it inside the holster, put his jacket on again and buttoned it up. He looked down at the holdalls.

'What other little treasures did you buy?'

'Besides the tracking equipment, Walthers for Harry

and Pete when they arrive, grenades, and smoke bombs. He even had the type of trick grenade I threw at those four thugs off Regent Street just before the Ear was killed. Can't keep a secret these days. I thought the Park Crescent boffins had come up with something no one else had. Oh, and a dismantled Armalite rifle with sniper-scope for myself.'

'You haven't forgotten the Phantom, then? Hence the Armalite.'

'I haven't forgotten the Phantom,' Marler agreed in a monotone.

'Better get those holdalls out of sight,' Tweed suggested. 'Arthur Beck is on his way here. With some bad news.'

'I thought Marler had brought us enough bad news,' Newman commented.

'Just information,' Marler replied, picking up the holdalls. 'And now I think I'd better get back to my room and hide these away . . .'

'Well, at least Ronstadt and Co. don't know we're in the same city,' Tweed remarked.

'Be nice to keep it that way,' Paula agreed.

Tweed answered the phone, which had started ringing. When he ended the brief call he looked at the others.

'Marler left just in time. Beck is here. On his way up.'

Arthur Beck entered the room with a smile. He went to Paula and hugged her. There had always been a warm rapport between them. The smile disappeared as he took off his snow-flecked overcoat. Refusing Tweed's offer to have fresh coffee sent up, he sat down in an armchair. Beck was in his late forties, a man of medium height, well-built, with a trim moustache, his thick hair greying. He had a strong face and a hint of humour in his penetrating grey eyes.

191

'I'll get straight to it. I've been in touch with Lasalle of the French DST. He told me a small army of American gangster types passed through Paris on their way to London. Some by Eurostar, some by plane. He sent me a number of copies of photos taken of them – sent them by courier. I distributed them to officers at three airports here – Zurich, Geneva and Basle. Just in case. A number of them flew into Basle yesterday. I have these photos of those we spotted.' He took an envelope from his pocket, handed it to Tweed, who took out the prints, glanced at them.

'These are familiar faces, Arthur. René also contacted me – or rather, I phoned him. He sent me these pics. By chance we know where they are here. Some at the Euler, others at the Victoria.'

'You do keep up with what is happening in this nasty world.'

'It's likely to get nastier.'

'The frustration is I can't do anything about it. Officers at Basle airport informed me they all carried diplomatic passports. Washington is beginning to worry me. What *is* happening?'

'Briefly,' Tweed began, 'America is the superpower on this planet. They're well aware of this. Sometimes great power increases a lust for more of it. History tells us this – Napoleon and Hitler are two prime examples.'

'Britain could be in big trouble.'

'We are. It's possible, from information received, to coin a cliché, we may be able to clip their wings here. We're certainly going to try.'

'Any help I can give, I am available. I'll be staying on in Basle. Police headquarters here is just across the street. Spiegelgasse 6. I'll make it my temporary HQ. I notice, Newman, you have a bulge under your jacket.'

'I twisted a muscle, didn't I? Had to have it bandaged.'

'Do take care of that muscle,' Beck said with a dry smile. 'I must be going now. I rely on all of you to take care of Paula,' he said standing up, putting on his overcoat.

'Thank you. Actually Paula can take care of herself,' Paula responded with a smile.

'I'm sure she can.'

'He really had a wasted journey,' Newman remarked when Beck had gone.

'I don't agree,' Tweed objected. 'He now has a hint of what is really going on. And if we need him he's close by. He's a powerful ally. I'm going out now to a public phone box to call Monica. I don't want the call going through a hotel switchboard. Plus the fact that occasionally lines get crossed and someone inside the hotel, one of the guests, might listen in.'

'You'll have company,' Newman told him. 'No argument.'

Marler returned at that moment, knocking on the door. Newman held his Smith & Wesson behind his back until he unlocked the door, saw their visitor.

'Tweed wants to make a phone call outside,' he told Marler.

'Feeling like a breath of fresh air myself. I've fixed those direction finders in your cars. The doorman showed me where they were after I'd described both of you, told him when you arrived. You can see them later.'

'We'll have a quiet walk,' said Tweed, putting on his coat. 'Lucky they don't know we're here.'

'It's bitterly cold out,' the concierge warned them as they arrived in the lobby.

'We're used to it,' Tweed joked. 'We come from England.'

The lobby was otherwise deserted. Whatever guests

193

were in the hotel would be in the dining room. Marler walked through the revolving door first, stopped in the street, his eyes scanning in all directions. As Tweed, Paula and Newman followed him out he raised a hand to hold them back.

'Thought I saw a shadow disappear behind that corner.'

'Probably your imagination,' said Paula. 'Lord, it's icy cold. And mind your footing – the pavement is slippery.'

One of Basle's small green trams came into view. They heard its rumble as it disappeared, crossing the bridge. Tweed led the way, his hands in his pockets. The air hit them like a blow in the face. Their exposed skin began to freeze as soon as they left the hotel.

'We'll walk up almost to Market-platz,' Tweed told them. 'I recall a phone box in a side street. Lucky I thought to bring plenty of Swiss coins with me.'

Once the rumble of the tram had died away a heavy silence fell. It reminded Paula of the silence of Romney Marsh when she had paused before reaching the Bunker. There was no one about anywhere. The street they were walking up was lined on both sides with old stone buildings. Paula felt hemmed in. She stopped suddenly.

'I can hear footsteps.'

'It's your imagination,' Marler said, repeating what she had said to him a few minutes before.

'Are you sure?' asked Tweed, who respected her acute hearing.

They had all stopped, between the glow of street lamps. She looked back, saw nothing. Marler shrugged impatiently.

'Can you hear them now?'

'No. They've stopped now we have.'

'I want to get to that phone,' Tweed said.

With Newman ahead of them, Paula and Tweed

walked beside each other. Marler brought up the rear on his own. They reached the beginning of the large open market square with the Town Hall, elaborately decorated with the symbols of Swiss cantons, behind the huge open space which was the Market-platz. Marler hitched up the strap of the canvas bag he was carrying higher up his shoulder. They walked a short distance and Marler glanced back again. But he was watching for shadows, not listening for footsteps.

'We turn up this side street,' Tweed told them. 'It's the start of a very ancient part of Basle. And there's my phone box.'

Going inside the glass box, he extracted coins from his pocket, then at the right moment pressed numbers to call Park Crescent.

'Monica, Tweed here. I'm calling from a public phone. More secure . . .'

'I'm so glad to hear from you. Happenings. The Bomb Squad checked a key telephone exchange, found two huge bombs, made them harmless. Same thing at Mount Pleasant sorting office. But another bomb had been placed inside a major Knightsbridge store. Blew the first and second floors to smithereens. At least fifty dead and many injured. The number of casualties is rising. That's it.'

'Thank you. I'll keep in touch.'

Outside the box he told the others what Monica had reported. Paula, particularly, was shocked. She stared at Tweed and had trouble getting the words out.

'When is this horror going to end?'

'When we've finished them off. Let's get back to the hotel. I am so cold I feel like a snowman.'

They had reached the end of the side street, had walked a few paces back the way they had come, when Marler held up a hand. He spoke very quickly.

'The Umbrella Men are back. *Drop flat!*'

Too close for comfort a cluster of four black umbrellas, held low so they concealed their owners, were advancing towards them. For a second Paula was hypnotized by the weird spectacle – the way the dark cones moved towards her, the rims just not touching each other, the umbrellas held quite still, not wavering an inch.

She dropped beside her three companions, who were already flat on the pavement. Fascinated, terrified, as though watching a macabre stage performance, she saw the four umbrellas elevate as one, with martial precision, exposing the four men beneath them. Each wore a dark overcoat, held their umbrellas with their left hands. Their right hands dipped inside canvas bags similar to Marler's, but larger. The hands emerged with astonishing speed, holding machine-pistols. The barrels of the deadly weapons elevated, again as one, again with military precision, aiming at their targets lying on the pavement. Paula was struggling to extract her Browning, knowing it would be too late. She saw all this as though her vision had quickened.

As he fell, Marler had dived a hand inside his holdall, the flap open. His hand came out holding a grenade. Newman hissed out the words.

'That trick grenade won't work this time. It's probably the same lot we met before . . .'

Paula stiffened. She was waiting for the thud of bullets into her body when a fusillade hammered them. Marler lobbed his grenade over-arm. It sailed through the night air in an arc, landed amid the group of men under the umbrellas. There was a brief flash of light, a loud *crack!* as the grenade detonated.

Two of their attackers staggered backwards, hit the pavement with heavy thuds. Another one tried to stagger into the empty street, fell forward. The fourth man slumped against a wall, slid down it. Paula had felt vibrations from the detonation passing under her. She stared again. Three of the umbrellas had shattered into shards, chips of stone from the nearby building had been hurled across the street. The man who had slumped against the wall had fired a short burst as he collapsed sideways, but his weapon had been pointed upwards. The burst had shattered a street lamp, showering the body with fragments of glass. What remained of the Umbrella Men were four still bodies.

'We'd better get out of this,' Tweed snapped, jumping agilely to his feet, slipping on ice, recovering his balance. 'Police headquarters are in the next street. The buildings may have muffled the sound but we'll take no chances. We'll go back down the opposite side of the street.'

He was walking down the opposite pavement, Paula by his side, when Newman and Marler came up behind them. Marler glanced at his companion.

'That, as you'll now have gathered, was the real McCoy. Have faith in me.'

'You certainly saved our bacon,' Newman said with feeling.

Ahead of them, Paula grasped Tweed's arm. She nodded her head in the direction of the other side of the street. The thug who had collapsed over the pavement edge was almost invisible. His umbrella, the only one to remain intact, had fallen over his prone corpse. It looked as though he was taking a nap and had used the umbrella to shelter under.

'It's surreal,' Paula whispered.

Then she saw on a shop window they were passing a huge smear of blood. The temperature was so low it had congealed in the shape of a hand. She shuddered. Tweed hurried her back to the Three Kings. They paused outside to brush snow and dirt off their coats, then walked into the warmth of their hotel.

'Heavenly,' Paula said to herself.

The concierge came from behind his counter to press 'one' by the side of the lift. All four of them were just able to squeeze their way inside.

'We'll all go to my room. Have a drink,' said Tweed.

He poured wine from an ice bucket into four glasses. Before the others sat down they took off their coats. Tweed sat on a couch next to Marler, so they faced Paula and Newman on another couch. Tweed raised his glass.

'Here's to survival.'

'I'll drink to that,' said Paula with enthusiasm.

'I must apologize to one and all,' Tweed began. 'For being an idiot. I said something like, "It's lucky they don't know we're here." They do. Very significant.'

'You're not going to tell us why, of course,' Paula teased.

'I have other things on my mind.' He smiled to take the edge off ignoring her question. 'When Bob went to fetch his coat Keith Kent phoned me. He's coming to see us in the morning.'

'My tummy's rumbling,' Paula remarked.

'Bob,' Tweed requested, 'could you phone down and make sure they'll serve dinner for us? It's a bit late.' He drank some more of his wine. 'Well, that's four of them disposed of, thanks to Marler. A long way to go yet.'

'They'll serve dinner when they see us,' Newman reported, returning from the phone.

'Tweed,' Paula pointed out, 'you're still wearing your overcoat.'

'So I am. Mental concentration,' he explained, taking off the coat. 'I want us to get cracking tomorrow. I sense we have very little time left. Oh, Paula, could you tell us the three different names for this city?'

'I suppose I could,' she said, puzzled. 'first, Basle, which is the English version. Then Bâle . . .' She spelt it out. 'I just gave you the French version. Third, B-a-a-sel.

198

I have just pronounced the German version.' She spelt it out.

'B-a-a-sel,' repeated Tweed. 'Exactly. The German pronunciation. Sounds rather like Basil – especially the way Windermere pronounces his name in his high-falutin' voice.'

'What's the point?' asked Marler.

'*Basil . . . Schwarz.* Isn't that what you heard the Ear say as his last words?'

'Yes, it was.'

'You overlooked the fact that when a man knows he is dying, is desperate to get a message across to you, he's likely to revert to his natural language. Which was German. Poor Kurt was pointing his finger at this city. Which is the main reason we're here when I'd realized what he'd really tried to say.'

'But why use his real name? Schwarz?'

'For the same reason. He'd reverted to German. In that language *schwarz* means black. Hence the Schwarz-wald – the Black Forest. There was mention that the Americans had a secret base outside Basle. I think it's somewhere in the Black Forest. So our next job is to locate it – bearing in mind it's likely to be heavily protected.'

20

In the morning Marler was early down to breakfast. He had called on Tweed first, but his chief was studying a large map of the Black Forest. He told Marler to go down and he'd join him later. The dining room was almost empty at that early hour. Seated by herself at a table, Marler saw Denise Chatel.

'May I join you?' he suggested. 'Or if you're one of those people who prefer to breakfast alone I'll understand.'

'Please sit down, Alec. Sharon went out somewhere, said she'd be back later. And I do prefer company at this hour.'

'Then I'll join you.'

He ordered a full English breakfast. The pleasant waitress was pouring him coffee as he broke a roll and began eating. He was famished. Denise, he noted, had contented herself with coffee and croissants.

'Are you alert?' he asked quietly.

'You have news for me?' she reacted eagerly. 'If so, I want to hear it. I'm a lark, on top of everything as soon as I get out of bed.'

'It's rather grim.'

'Just tell me, please. All the details you have.'

She was dressed in a thick beige two-piece trouser suit with a poloneck. He thought she looked very smart. Her blue eyes were fixed on him and she stopped eating as he recounted what he had learned from Cord Dillon. There was still no one else in the dining room as he concluded and his bacon and eggs had just been put before him.

'I'm sorry,' he said, 'but there seems little doubt that it was cold-blooded murder. And it was covered up by Washington. Possibly on the orders of the mysterious Charlie. I must have given you a shock.'

'You haven't. It just confirms finally what I suspected. I wish I knew who Charlie was,' she said vehemently. 'I have heard his name mentioned just once at the Embassy.'

'Who mentioned it?'

'A very unpleasant-looking man. Someone told me he was called Jake Ronstadt. I was walking along a corridor in rubber-soled shoes when he came out of a

200

room with another man. I heard him say, "I told you. First I have to check it out with Charlie." Out of the corner of my eye I saw him stare at me but I kept on walking.'

'Any idea at all who he was referring to?'

'None at all. It's the only time I've heard the name. What made me remember it was the venomous look Ronstadt gave me as I passed him.'

'Well, have you any idea what Ronstadt's job is?'

'None at all. He was pointed out to me by a friend when we were in the Embassy canteen. My friend told me to keep well away from him. She'd heard he was dangerous. That's all I know about him.'

'I think I've upset you. You haven't eaten a thing since I started talking.'

'Don't worry, Alec.' She gave him a radiant smile. 'It's a kind of relief to know my suspicions were justified.' She began eating again. 'And thank you very much for finding out what really happened to them. I was very fond of my parents, especially of my father.'

'Does Sharon know I'm here?'

'No. I didn't even know until you walked in to the dining room. She doesn't know you exist. I'll keep it that way.'

'Please do. Has she any idea that Tweed is staying here?'

'Oh, yes. She mentioned to me she'd seen him arrive with Robert Newman.'

'Oh, of course. Tweed told me she'd been in the lobby when he arrived. Have you any idea how long Sharon plans to stay here?' Marler asked casually.

'None at all. I get on very well with her, but she's rather reserved. Very English, is how she strikes me. I hope you'll excuse me, I have to go now, get some work done. Maybe, if you're free one evening, we could have dinner together outside the hotel?'

'That is something I'd look forward to. Trouble is I'm pretty busy myself. Working on an investigation job with Tweed. If I get the chance I'll certainly contact you.'

'It's been lovely talking to you.' She took out a small notepad and scribbled on it, then tore out the sheet and handed it to him. 'That's my room number. I really do have to dash now . . .'

Marler was facing the exit. As Denise reached the door Tweed appeared on the other side, opened it for her. He smiled and Marler heard what he said.

'Good morning.'

He had spoken rather formally, as though his only contact with her had been when she had come to his office. Marler smiled to himself, recalling how he had seen Tweed leaving her flat in Belgrave Square.

'Newman will be joining us in a minute,' Tweed said as he sat down opposite Marler. 'Paula's coming too.' He lowered his voice. 'Sorry I've been awhile. Beck paid me a quick visit. Armed with the photos, he'd sent a couple of his men in a car to watch the Euler. Early this morning two of the thugs came out, got into a car and drove off. Beck's men followed them to the border. They drove on through the checkpoint along the autobahn into Germany.'

'Which leads to where?'

'A small town called Breisach, if you turn left off Autobahn 5. On the other hand, if you turn right you arrive in Freiburg.' He paused. 'That's the route into the Black Forest.'

'Pity we couldn't have followed them. But the tracking signal is under Ronstadt's car. You could be right about the Black Forest. Maybe we ought to take turns in driving up close to the Euler, standing watch on Ronstadt's car. Newman and I would be the best bet, taking pre-arranged watches.'

'I don't think so.' Tweed shook his head. He looked

up. Paula and Newman had entered the restaurant, came to join them. 'I've something to tell you while this place is quiet . . .'

Tweed then repeated what he'd told Marler about Beck's visit to him. He also told them about Marler's suggestion, that he had turned it down.

'Why?' asked Paula. 'If we're not careful we'll lose Ronstadt. Then we have no way of locating their base.'

'Yes, we have. Beck is very clever. He gave me this.' He took from his pocket a small mobile phone of a type Paula had never seen before. 'I vetoed Marler's suggestion because I'm sure we need a large force when we do locate that base. All of us, in fact.'

'So how on earth do we manage that?' Paula persisted.

'I said Beck was clever. He'd heard about the bomb outrages in London and he takes as savage a view of them as I do. He has arranged for a succession of his own men – in unmarked cars – to watch the Euler. The ones on duty will carry a mobile like this one. It's specially coded and can't be intercepted. The moment Ronstadt leaves in his car they'll inform Beck, who will immediately inform me.'

'We might still miss Ronstadt,' Paula objected.

'Wait, please, until I finish. If Ronstadt takes the same route as his two thugs did earlier, he'll have to pass through the checkpoint on the Swiss side before you drive through on to Autobahn 5. Beck will instantly phone the officer in charge of the checkpoint, giving him the number of the Citroën. He will stop Ronstadt.'

'Stop him? What's the good of that?' Paula wondered.

'You really are in an argumentative mood this morning,' Tweed chided her.

'Very sorry. Please continue.'

'As I said, the officer will stop Ronstadt at the checkpoint. He will take his time searching the car, explaining that they conduct random searches for drugs. Briefly, he will delay him until we arrive. You and I, Paula, have to be in the lead car. I will be driving. As we approach the checkpoint you take out a cigarette and make a big fuss of lighting it. The checkpoint officer has a clear description of both of us – given to him by Beck.'

'This is clever of Beck,' Paula agreed. 'We'll have to stay out of sight of Ronstadt – that villain met both of us briefly at Goodfellows.'

'I think I can manage that. Marler, you'll follow in your car. Bob, you bring up the rear in your car. I wish Butler and Nield were with us. Butler could have travelled with Marler while Nield came with Bob . . .' He paused briefly. 'This investigation is going to take longer than I'd expected,' he said in a louder voice, sitting erect in his chair.

Paula glanced over her shoulder. Sharon Mandeville had entered the dining room. She headed straight for their table.

'I thought I could rely on you, Tweed, she said in a quiet voice. 'Yesterday we were going to have drinks.'

'I'm so very sorry, Sharon,' Tweed responded, standing up. 'I was caught up in a business meeting I couldn't get away from.'

'You're forgiven. Thank you, Bob. Or am I interrupting?'

Newman had jumped up, brought her a chair which he placed next to Tweed's. When Sharon sat down she was facing Paula.

'I feel out-gunned,' Sharon said with a smile. 'So many men.'

'I'm here,' Paula reminded her. 'I'll give you moral support.'

'That's very sweet of you.'

'You look dressed magnificently,' said Newman. 'Ready to set the world on fire.'

He was referring to the smart red trouser suit she wore. She gave him a warm smile of appreciation, then frowned before she spoke.

'Talking about setting the world on fire, somebody tried to do just that last night to the American Embassy in London. Smoke and flames were pouring out of a window, the fire brigade was called, Grosvenor Square was in chaos.'

'How do you know this?' asked Tweed.

'I called the Embassy this morning. What is happening? I don't know.'

'Which part of the Embassy was set on fire?' Tweed enquired.

'The office next to the Security room on the first floor. My office is OK, thank Heaven. I'm glad I wasn't there.'

'So am I,' said Newman.

'Hi, everybody. Mind if I join the party?' a voice boomed behind Newman.

Tweed was looking up. He smiled ironically. The large figure of Ed Osborne had come into the dining room. Dragging a chair from another table, he placed it at the end, eased his bulk into it, clapped his large hands together, a grin on the outsize face above a bull neck.

'Great to see you guys again,' he said, looking at Paula and then Tweed. 'What brings you to this hick town?'

'First of all,' Newman rapped back, 'it's not a hick town. It is a more ancient and interesting city than you'll find in the whole of America.'

'Naughty.' Osborne slapped a hand against the wrist of the other hand. 'Keep your big mouth shut. Trouble is,' he went on, leaning forward, 'the mouth opens and it all hangs out. Coffee, *garçon*,' he demanded, addressing the waitress. 'PDQ. And since I guess you don't understand the lingo, that means pretty damned quick.'

'And for breakfast, sir?' she asked quietly.

'Just the coffee, honey. Didn't get that it was a girl at first,' he remarked as the waitress moved away. 'Her hair is trimmed so short.'

'Men don't wear skirts,' Paula snapped.

'They sure do – when they're transvest—' He broke off. 'Guess that's not a subject for breakfast.' He gazed at Paula. 'You enjoying a holiday out here?'

'We were. Until you arrived.'

'Great!' Osborne grinned broadly. 'I like a lady who answers back. You and I must get into a huddle soon as we can.'

'Don't go in for huddles,' Paula told him. 'And what are you doing in Basle anyway?'

'I get around. Why I am here?' He gave a belly laugh. 'Business, honey. Monkey business.'

Tweed pushed back his chair. Before he could stand, prior to leaving, Sharon leaned over, whispered in his ear.

'Now you won't forget we're having a drink together. Would noon in the bar behind us suit you?'

'Perfect,' Tweed whispered back.

'Hey!' Osborne boomed out. 'You two got a thing going together?'

'You'll excuse us,' Tweed said, standing up. 'We have an appointment to keep. We enjoyed your company, Mr Osborne.'

'Ed! I keep tellin' you, it's Ed . . .'

They were on their way out of the restaurant. Tweed had Paula by his side while Newman and Marler followed behind them. As the door to the restaurant closed behind them Paula exploded.

'What a coarse man!'

'Don't underestimate Osborne,' Tweed warned. 'Under that brash manner I suspect is a shrewd operator. Ruthless, too. I bet he could recite how all of us were dressed. His eyes were all over the place.'

206

'Well, he could do with a few lessons in how to dress. That loud jacket, striped shirt, flashy tie, dingy corduroy slacks. It was all wrong. Like his conversation. If you can call it that.'

'Can we all have a quiet word?' Marler had caught up with them. 'Maybe over there in that far corner?' he suggested.

'Since you want to,' Tweed agreed.

They sat in a circle round a small corner table in the lobby, well away from the reception counter. Marler was about to explain when he stared. Pete Nield had appeared from the direction of the lift. He fingered his moustache as he greeted them.

'Harry and I just got here from the airport.'

'Enter the Knife Man,' Marler commented.

'And what does that mean?' demanded Tweed.

'Pete has added to his talents. During the past month or two he's been practising knife-throwing,' Marler explained, keeping his voice down. 'He's become fantastic. He invited me to go with him to a low-down pub in London. They were playing darts and Pete bought drinks all round, then asked if he could use a knife instead of darts. Everyone thought he was a lunatic but let him have a go. He stood well back from the target, threw his knife six times. Result? Six bull's-eyes. I lost a packet. I'd bet him he couldn't do it from that distance.'

'Could come in useful,' Tweed commented. 'Now what were you going to tell us, Marler?'

'It's about the Ear. Poor Kurt. He gave me an address where I could meet him in Basle in an emergency. Drew a map.' He produced a folded sheet of paper from his pocket. 'As you'll see it's a five-minute walk from here – as long as you're good at climbing steps.'

'So what is your idea?'

'That we go there and check out this place. It's not

where he lived, wherever that might be. There might be a note left for me there.'

'Who is going?' asked Newman, studying the map.

'All of us,' said Tweed.

'Any thugs in Basle?' Nield enquired.

'The place is crawling with them. They appear to be based at the Euler with more at the Victoria. Two hotels close to the Hauptbahnhof.'

'I know where those hotels are. I came to Basle for you once before,' Nield said. 'I know the place pretty well. And after what you've told me I don't think it's a good idea you trooping up to this place *en masse*.' He took the map back from Newman.

'Then what do you suggest?' Tweed asked.

'I'm going up to have a quick look at this address by myself. I can be back in a few minutes. I'm off now. Harry will be down soon.'

Before Tweed could protest Nield, taking the map with him, had walked away. Prior to going through the revolving door he slipped on the coat he'd held over one arm. Then he was gone.

'Do you think that's a good idea?' Marler queried. 'I don't. I just hope he'll be all right. He's got the map, so we'll have to sit here and hope for the best.'

Even though it was morning it seemed like night to Nield as he headed along the pavement. The heavy overcast appeared to be almost touching the tops of the old buildings, making the atmosphere even bleaker. There was no one about. All the workers would be thankfully inside their centrally heated offices. Anyone who could would stay in their apartment. It was very quiet. The only sound was the crunch of a tram's wheels as they passed over ice.

Nield had turned left after leaving the hotel. The map

was in the breast pocket of his jacket now – having once seen it he knew where he was going. He passed the steps leading down to where, in summer, ships took tourists on short cruises up the Rhine, crossed the street, came to the entrance to the Rheinsprung, a steep street leading upwards for pedestrians and cyclists only. He knew that if he followed that eventually it would lead him to the Münster, a great feature of Basle overlooking the river from a considerable height. Instead, he was treading carefully on the icy slope, looking to his right. He saw what he was looking for very quickly.

A plate on a wall identified it as a *gässlein*, a narrow alley of endless steps leading up between two high vertical walls. The plate gave the full name, a trainload of German letters. Nield, skilled in speaking and reading German, translated it.

'Alley of the Eleven Thousand Virgins. Sounds hopeful,' he said to himself.

It was a stone staircase mounting upwards into the distance. Very dark, very lonely. Remembering to bring his coat from his room, he had forgotten his gloves. His fingers were beginning to tingle with the cold when he thrust them into his coat pockets. He started climbing his staircase to heaven.

Despite the icy surface of the worn steps he climbed steadily. One advantage of the eerie quiet was he would hear anyone who might be about. He counted as he climbed. It was sixty-eight steps to the top. He paused on the last step, listening, looking. A brand-new Yamaha motorcycle was perched against a wall. A BS registration number – Basle.

Nield knew he was gazing into Martins-platz, a small cobbled square enclosed by old buildings, hidden away from the city. He walked into the deserted but claustrophobic square. No sign of anyone. He knew the address he was looking for was just beyond where the motorcycle with the large saddle had been left. The heavy wooden door was closed, but when he turned the handle slowly it opened. Warmth flooded out to meet him. He pushed the door open slowly, soundlessly. The hinges were well oiled. A dim lamp illuminated the interior. He walked in a few paces and then stopped.

An old woman wearing a dark ankle-length dress sat in a chair, her grey hair tied back in a bun. An ape of a man had been holding a lighted cigarette close to her right eye. The ape was very big, very fat, clad in a black anorak, black slacks, a black beret on his melon-like head. He spun round, holding in his other hand a Magnum pistol, pointing it at Nield. The end of the muzzle seemed like the mouth of a cannon. Like so many fat men, the ape moved swiftly. Dropping the cigarette on the stone floor he leapt forward. The barrel of his weapon struck at Nield's head. He moved slightly so the barrel slid off the side of his face, but the force of the blow made him dizzy. The ape grasped him by the collar, threw him back with a vicious shove. He went backwards, dipped his head at the last moment so his shoulders took the impact of colliding with the stone wall. His legs gave way and he sank down, back resting against the wall.

He felt groggy, but was aware of the ape's hand feeling under his armpits, sliding down his sides, then down his legs, searching for a concealed weapon. Nield was not carrying a gun. Dimly, he saw the ape straighten up, his body enormous. He spat at Nield.

'Whoever you are, you can have the pleasure of watching me torture this stupid woman.' The accent was heavily American. 'I will then deal with you after she's talked – which she will.'

Nield tried to straighten up, sagged again. His vision was beginning to clear. He was in a square stone-walled room. The warmth came from an old ceramic wood-burning stove in a corner. The ape grinned, sharp teeth showing behind his thick lips. He lit a fresh cigarette, held it between his fingers, went over to the old woman, the burning end pointed towards her. On his way, he shoved the door closed.

21

Rage was growing like a fire inside Nield. It started the adrenalin flowing. The burning end of the cigarette was close to the old woman's eyeball. He eased himself a little higher up the wall. He dared not move much – it would attract the attention of the ape. His right hand crept up over his side. He leaned forward a few inches. His hand was behind his back. The ape became aware of movement. He turned round. In one hand he was still holding the huge gun.

Nield withdrew the stiletto-like knife from the sheath strapped round the top of his back. The stiletto flew across the room with great force and speed. It embedded itself in the throat of the ape. For a moment nothing happened. Then the ape dropped the cigarette, followed by the gun. One hand reached up to the knife, then fell to his side. He gurgled. Blood began to stream down his neck. His massive weight fell forward, his head and neck striking the stone floor. The hilt of the knife was rammed upwards, the point of the stiletto projected out of the back of his neck. He lay still.

Nield let out a deep breath of relief. The door opened. Marler came into the room, Walther automatic in his hand. He was followed by Tweed, Newman and Butler. Newman took in the situation in a glance, ran to help Nield who climbed shakily to his feet. He stiffened both his legs as Newman held on to him. He managed a weak smile.

'In the films they'd say, "What kept you?"'

'Who is this lady?' Tweed asked quietly, going to her.

'No idea.'

Tweed looked at her carefully. In her seventies, he estimated. Her face was lined, her hair was thinning. But her hazel eyes were clear as she looked back at him. He laid a gentle hand on her shoulder. He smiled sympathetically.

'It's all right now. Do you understand me?'

'I understand.'

'What's happened?' Tweed asked Nield.

Clearing his throat, Nield told them, in as few words as possible, his experience since reaching the top of the stone staircase. As he listened, Tweed bent down, checked the neck pulse of the body on the floor. He turned round, mouthed the word 'Dead' without saying it aloud.

'Good,' said Nield with grim satisfaction.

He then continued telling them what had happened up to the moment his knife had flown through the air like a dart. Marler whispered to him, 'Bull's-eye.'

'So,' Nield concluded, 'after the ape hits the floor you lot come charging in when you're not needed.' He grinned. 'I'm joking.'

'Could you tell me, please, who you are?' Tweed asked, turning back to the old woman, still sitting in the chair.

'You haven't said anything to me,' she told him in a clear voice.

'General Guisan,' Marler said suddenly.

'So, you are the right man,' the old lady replied. 'Kurt said you would come. You have come.'

'I come with bad news,' Marler said quietly.

'I know.' The old woman put a hand on her heart. 'I felt it here. Kurt, my husband, is dead.'

'I am sorry. He died very quickly.'

212

'I am Helga Irina,' she went on. 'Many years ago I was Russian. I met Kurt in the cheap bar. We fell in love then. He was clever man. He helps me to escape from Moscow. Terrible life. He takes me out to Finland. Secret route. To Helsinki. Then to West Germany. We come here, his home. We marry. He was the great man. He tell me if he loses his life his friend, the Englishman, comes. I know him if he says General Guisan. This KGB kind of man on floor follows Kurt. One day in a bar Kurt talks to his Swiss friend. This KGB man sees them. When Kurt goes his friend is made drunk by this man. Barman tells Kurt later. In his drink friend tells Kurt has wife, Irina. Me. Must be how torture man found me. The week later, after friend of Kurt is dragged from river, his head smashed.'

'Can I make sure you get home safely?' Tweed suggested. 'You have had a terrible time. I am sorry.'

'No!' Irina jumped up from the chair quickly, looked at Marler. 'Kurt tells me give the little black book to the Englishman who says General Guisan.'

She staggered as she began to walk. Tweed grasped her arm, helped her to walk. After a few paces her legs moved normally. She went to the wall to one side of the stove, her gnarled right hand reaching up to a section of the wall. Her fingers worked with surprising agility, Tweed noticed, as she slowly eased out a stone which appeared to be firmly embedded in the wall. She seemed to read Tweed's thoughts.

'I was seamstress in Russia. I am seamstress in Basle when Kurt has married me. It gives me good money to live with.'

She had released the oblong stone which Tweed took from her. Behind where the stone had rested was a cavity. Reaching inside, she brought out a small black book with a faded cover. She walked across the room, handed it to Marler. Behind her back Tweed took out his wallet, extracted ten one-thousand-franc Swiss bank-notes, put them in his coat pocket.

'Thank you,' said Marler, taking the notebook from her.

'That is what I would never give to the torture man – no matter what he does to me. Kurt says it has important information.'

'I must pay you the fee Kurt earned.'

'No! It is his gift for you.'

Staring at Marler, Tweed jerked his head towards the door. It was a gesture Marler grasped immediately.

'Now I will take you safely home,' Tweed said.

'It is not needed,' Irina protested. 'I know the way.'

'There may be more bad men outside. I will take you home,' insisted Tweed.

'The stove!' Irina turned, walked to it, bent down and turned something. 'Now it goes cool, then out.'

'We'll deal with that,' said Marler.

'Get out of here as soon as you can,' Tweed whispered to Newman. 'If the police arrive that dead body would take some explaining.'

'Will do . . .'

Irina had picked up her coat which lay in a heap behind the chair she had sat in. Marler presumed the thug had torn that off her, thrown it down before he began his foul work. He waited until Tweed had escorted Irina halfway across the square and then slipped outside. It was his job to shadow them, then keep out of view while he followed Irina to her home – to make sure she arrived there safely.

'You said at one moment your name was Helga Irina,' Tweed began. He was steering her mind into another direction, hoping it would help her to forget the dreadful ordeal she had suffered. 'Irina is Russian,' Tweed went on as they continued walking. 'Helga is German. I do not understand.'

214

'You are the boss? The Englishman's boss?'

'Yes, I am.'

'Thank you for what you save me from. I did not thank that nice young man who save me. Please give him my love.'

'I will do that.'

'You were asking me about Helga.' She had slipped her arm inside Tweed's, so he knew he had at last established her confidence in him. 'My mother was Russian,' she explained. 'She met a German prisoner-of-war who escaped from Stalin's gulag. They fell in love and were married secretly by a priest who had an underground church. So I am Irina for my mother, Helga for my father. They worked for the anti-Communist opposition. I was told by a friend they were trapped trying to escape from the meeting in a cellar. Both were shot dead. I was ten years old.'

What hellish lives some people have led, Tweed was thinking. They had crossed another deserted silent square and eventually walked into the Rheinsprung, high up and close to the Münster. Irina slipped her arm free of Tweed's and stopped. As she did so he pushed the folded banknotes into the pocket of her coat. She frowned, slid her hand inside the pocket, feeling what he had put there.

'This is a lot of money. Too much. The black book was a gift from Kurt. I leave you here, but I give back the money.'

Tweed moved away from her so she couldn't hand him anything. He spoke briefly before he began to make his way back down the Rheinsprung, knowing it would lead him to the hotel.

'Kurt earned a big fee. He gave us very valuable information. You cannot give back what Kurt earned. Take care . . .'

Then he was walking carefully down the steep

cobbled slope, wary of its icy surface. He knew that Marler would be somewhere close by, the Invisible Man making sure Irina reached her home safely. Arriving at the bottom, passing the Alley of the Eleven Thousand Virgins, he stopped as Newman appeared out of nowhere.

'She's on her way home,' Tweed told him. 'Marler is secretly following her to make certain she gets there.'

They were crossing the empty street, stepping over the tramlines, when Nield and Butler appeared, also out of nowhere. Tweed spoke rapidly before they entered the hotel.

'Pete, you did a great job, saving that poor lady from hell. Now, all of you, we must keep away from that area.' He took a notebook from his pocket, opened it at a certain page, handed it to Nield. 'Pete, that's the phone number of Beck's temporary headquarters. Could you call him, disguise your voice, give him the address? Tell him he'll find a corpse there. Be brief – so he can't trace where you're calling from.'

Entering the hotel, he met Paula who had just emerged from the lift. She lowered her voice.

'Keith Kent has arrived. He's in your room. He told me the Americans are going berserk.'

22

Paula unlocked the room door with the key Tweed had left with her. He had asked her to stay behind in case Kent arrived during his absence. They all followed her inside, with the exception of Nield, who said he was going to his room to make a phone call.

Keith Kent was sitting in an armchair. In his hand he nursed a glass of brandy. Introductions were not necessary. They all knew the visitor. Kent lifted his glass.

'With the compliments of Paula. Central heating to warm me up. At least, that's my excuse.'

'I hear you have news,' Tweed said, taking off his coat while the others did the same. Paula took them to hang them up. 'I'd like to hear it,' he said, occupying an armchair close to Kent.

'And I expect you'd all like some hot coffee,' said Paula as she picked up the phone without waiting for a reaction.

Keith Kent was the soul of relaxation. No matter how tense a situation might be, he never showed any sign of nerves. As usual, he was smartly dressed, clad in a dark blue suit, pale blue shirt and a Chanel tie with a motif of peacocks.

'I expect Paula has told you,' he began, 'that the Americans are in an uproar. Behaving as though they don't know what to do next. And don't like it.'

'How do you know all this, Keith?'

'This morning I called in at the Zürcher Kredit Bank again – to check that my transaction with the fortune in dollars had been completed. Turned out I didn't even have to speak to the teller. She was occupied – in a big way. A couple of Americans, one of them banging his ugly fist on the counter and shouting at her.'

'Could you describe him?'

'Not very tall. He has a very big head, clean-shaven, with a boxer's face – slit mouth, tough jaw. Very wide across the chest, tapers down to small feet. Hair brown. He glanced at me once – eyes hard as diamonds.'

'Jake Ronstadt,' Paula said to herself.

'Would he recognize you?' Tweed asked.

'Doubtful. I wore a scarf pulled up over my chin, a hat with the brim pulled down. Normal wear, considering the weather.'

'Go on.'

'As I said, he was shouting at the girl. "There was a

217

fortune in this account and now you show me a balance sheet with zero funds." Then he lowered his voice but I have acute hearing, as you know. He went on raving. "I want to see a friggin' director. I want to see him now. Got it?" That was when he started crashing his fist down on the counter. What the girl said next didn't help.'

'What did she say?'

'That there wasn't a director on the premises. They were away, holding an executive meeting. He really blew his top at that. "Get on that friggin' phone and tell a director to get back here before I bust this place to pieces. Millions and millions of dollars can't vanish, you stupid twist." That was when I quietly left the bank.'

'You said there were a couple of Americans. Can you describe the other one?'

'A tall thin man with a hard thin bony face. I heard the short one call him Vernon.'

'Sounds like that could be Vernon Kolkowski,' Newman interjected. 'I was shown photos of various thugs when I was in New York. The police captain said he was called the Thin Man, a notorious killer. They could never get him. If there were witnesses willing to testify they ended up floating down the Hudson River.'

'Sounds like a suitable candidate for the people we are up against,' Tweed commented.

'After I left the bank,' Kent went on, 'I sat in my parked car to see if anything else happened. It did. About five minutes later the short man with the big chest stormed out of the bank. He walked straight across the street. A car had to come to an emergency stop to avoid running him down. The American crashed his fist down on the car's bonnet, swore foully at the driver and went on to his car. Vernon followed more slowly, as though he didn't want to be too close to the other one. He had to dive into the car as it started moving off.'

'Paula told me the Americans had gone berserk. Probably your word.'

'It does mean,' Kent pointed out, 'that my conjuring trick has worked. Their millions have disappeared into thin air. Could take them weeks, even months, to trace them.'

'Thanks, Keith. You've really achieved something. Don't forget to send me a bill.'

'Oh, I'll bill you.' Keith finished off his brandy and grinned. 'Should I hang around a bit longer?'

'Yes. Where are you staying?'

'At the Hilton.'

'That's fortunate. The thugs are at the Euler, more at another hotel, the Victoria.'

'I'll show you out,' said Paula as Kent stood up. She fetched his coat. 'Yes, I'm coming down in the lift with you.'

'Let's keep in touch,' said Tweed. 'And thanks again . . .'

Less than a minute after they had left Nield arrived. He accepted Tweed's offer of coffee, settled himself on a couch next to Newman.

'I waited until Kent had left. I made the call a while ago. I had to slam down the phone when Beck tried to ask me questions. He was trying to keep me on the line while he had a trace put out.'

'You kept it brief, then,' Tweed said.

'Simply asked him to take down an address as soon as he came on the line. Then told him he'd find a body there. I had a silk handkerchief over the mouthpiece. Then Beck started to ask me something. I slammed the phone down. Couldn't have been on the line more than thirty seconds.'

'Good.' Tweed looked up as Paula let Marler into the room. 'I trust Irina got home safely – and without your being seen?'

'Of course she did.' Marler went across to a wall, leant against it. 'And of course she didn't see me.'

'What was that General Guisan business? I gathered it was a password.'

'Exactly that. Kurt once told me that if he went down and later I could get here, I should meet someone in that room. He said if I used "General Guisan" I'd get some valuable information.'

'General Guisan,' Tweed mused. 'The C-in-C of the Swiss armed forces during World War Two. He stopped the Nazis from invading Switzerland by clever threats.' He stopped speaking as the phone rang. Paula answered it. She put it down quickly.

'Beck is here. On his way up.'

Tweed braced himself for an aggressive Beck. Instead, the Swiss police chief came into the room with a quizzical expression. He accepted Tweed's offer to sit down, refused his offer of coffee. He gazed round at them all, one by one.

'All present and correct. I think that's the English phrase.'

'It is,' Tweed agreed.

'In case it's news,' Beck continued, his tone ironic, 'four corpses were found in a street near Market-platz early this morning. All Americans. All with diplomatic passports. All blown to kingdom come by a grenade.'

'Disturbing,' said Tweed.

'So, well before dawn, I phoned the Euler. The night receptionist knows me, recognized my voice. I asked him to read out a list of Americans staying there. Recent arrivals. Only one had a suite. I guessed he was the top man. A Jake Ronstadt.'

'We met the gentleman briefly in London.'

'So,' Beck went on, 'I asked to be put through to him.

He was not happy at being woken at that hour. He was even less happy when I gave him the news, read out the names of the deceased. He admitted they were members of his staff, as he put it. Had to. They were registered as staying there.'

'What was his exact reaction, Arthur?'

'Thunderous! Had I caught the villains who committed this foul crime? I hadn't? Why not? He was reporting this to the American Embassy in Berne. I told him it would take time, that I had only just begun the investigation. He swore at me. I asked him what their profession was.'

'That must have foxed him,' Tweed commented.

'It didn't. He repeated he was getting in touch with Berne. I said I thought that was his best move. He slammed the phone down on me.'

'He sounds to have been disconcerted.'

'He was in a towering rage. I had to phone him again a short time ago. Another body was discovered after I received an anonymous phone call. Wonder who that could have been? This corpse was in a ground-floor room near the top of the Alley of the Eleven Thousand Virgins. Had a knife through his throat. It had penetrated through the back of his thick neck.'

'Who was this one?' Tweed enquired.

'Another American. Another with a diplomatic passport. A Rick Sherman. Also registered as staying at the Euler.'

'How did Mr Ronstadt react to this further news?'

'He was apopoplectic. Raved on about how I was the Chief of Police and Basle was becoming the murder capital of Europe. He slammed the phone down on me before I could advise him to get in touch with his Embassy in Berne.'

'Things do seem to be warming up,' Tweed remarked.

'I know these men are gangsters,' Beck said, his tone grim. 'I still have to investigate.' He paused, looked at Newman and then at Butler, both of whom sat with their legs crossed. 'I wondered whether you had been outside this morning. I notice that Newman's shoes are drying out in this warmth, but the soles are still damp. As are Mr Butler's.'

'We went for a breath of fresh air along Blumenrain,' explained Tweed. 'Very fresh it was. I noticed your river police still have that boathouse under the lee of the promenade.'

'We have to watch the river. Along Blumenrain? Well, that is in the opposite direction from the Alley of the Eleven Thousand Virgins.' Beck stood up. 'Thank you for allowing me to question you.'

'Any time, Arthur,' Tweed replied, standing up. 'Any time.'

Paula was about to open the door when Beck turned back. He smiled at Tweed.

'Incidentally, whatever the plans of the Amerians were they seem to have put them on hold.'

'How do you mean?'

'Well, the car with two Americans which drove them through the checkpoint towards Freiburg – and possibly on to the Black Forest – has returned here. The officer at the checkpoint has told me he had the impression they have been recalled in quite a hurry. Take care of your-selves, everyone . . .'

When they were alone Tweed rubbed his hands. Paula poured him more coffee, then looked at him as she spoke.

'You look pleased with yourself.'

'Pleased, but not with myself – and not complacent. I

222

just knew Ronstadt would be checkmated, at least temporarily . . .'

'Knew?' queried Paula.

'Wrong word, my sixth sense told me.'

'And how did you know the boathouse for police launches is still there?' she asked. 'We never walked along Blumenrain.'

'If you lean out of my window, as I did when we arrived, you can see it. You're interrogating me,' he joked. He looked at Nield. 'Pete, I meant to ask you earlier. Did you think to do something about your fingerprints on the handle of that knife you threw at Sherman?'

'Naturally. It was a bit of a job with Sherman in that position, but I managed it.'

'While I gently lifted the corpse,' Butler added.

'Thank heavens for that,' Tweed told them. 'Then there was that brick Irina removed from the wall.'

'Which we carefully put back in place,' Newman confirmed.

'You seem to have thought of everything.'

'That is our job,' Newman remarked.

'I'm sure that sooner or later Ronstadt and his thugs will drive to the Black Forest – Kurt did tell us with his last word that the base is there. But recent events have thrown Mr Jake Ronstadt off balance – the loss of the money at the Zürcher Kredit, plus the loss of five of his men within hours. It does give us a breathing space.'

'I have something for you,' said Marler.

He handed to Tweed the small black book with a faded cover extracted from the cavity behind the brick. Tweed was about to examine its contents when Nield spoke.

'And I've got something for you. I'll fetch it from my room. Back in a minute.'

Tweed had started to read the brief notes in English

223

in the notebook when Nield returned. He handed Tweed a file. Tweed's mind flashed back to the American Embassy in London, when he had seen Jefferson Morgenstern placing a file into a safe which had looked like a bank vault. He looked up.

'Pete, is this what I think it is?'

'It's the file you asked us to grab from the safe inside the Security room at Grosvenor Square.'

'How on earth did you manage it. I thought afterwards I'd given you an impossible task.'

'Simple, really,' Nield explained. 'Most of it was down to Harry, expert locksmith and safe-cracker. We went in late evening by a door in a side street. Harry spotted it was equipped with a concealed alarm. Took him no time to deal with that, to open the door. There were still people in the building. We crept up a side staircase, got into the room next to Security, left a special firebomb with timer under the window, then Harry unlocked the door into Security . . .'

'Pete did act as lookout,' Butler added, 'so I could concentrate on my bit.'

'His bit involved opening the safe. Biggest job I've ever seen.'

'The more complex they try to make them,' Butler remarked, 'the easier they are to get into. I closed it after we'd got our hands on the file.'

'About that time the firebomb went off,' Nield continued. 'It gave off a lot of heat, which cracked the glass of the window. Important, that. The bomb contained a huge amount of smoke which flooded out of the window. We heard alarms going off, people rushing up and down the corridor outside.'

'How on earth did you get out?' asked Tweed.

'Simple. Opened the window when the fire brigade arrived – in no time at all. Saw them using a telescopic ladder to rescue a few people from another window. We waved like mad, they moved the ladder along, sent it up to us. Helped by a chap in a helmet, we climbed down the ladder, walked away. We wore charcoal black business suits – the type Americans pretending to be English are wearing at the moment. Walked to where we'd left our car, drove back to Park Crescent. Simple.'

'Nothing like as simple as you make it sound, I'm sure.'

Tweed opened the file. He sat back to read the first typed sheet. He read it again. Then he sat up straight.

'Oh, my God.'

'What is it?'

Paula had asked the question. She had rarely heard Tweed use the words he had just uttered. He sat rigid. He handed the file to her.

'Read that first sheet. The Americans are moving much faster with their operation than I'd anticipated. Which means we may have very little time left to stop them . . .'

The vast task force sailed on into the night, leaving behind Newport News, the naval base on the east coast of America. The centrepiece of the force, a main asset of the United States, was the gigantic 110,000-ton aircraft carrier *President*. The colossal ship had a crew of 6,500 men aboard, was armed with a devastating collection of nuclear missiles. Such ships do not put to sea without a fleet of powerful escorting vessels – distributed at a distance to port and starboard, way behind the stern, way ahead of the immense bow. No nation in the world could have mustered a fleet as advanced and numerous as the escorts.

Aboard one escort vessel was a unit of SEALs. These were naval men trained to be the toughest fighters on the planet. On the same vessel were new fast-moving amphibious craft which could carry the SEALs to land them on any beach, put them ashore so they could drive inland to destroy their target.

Perched on top of the endless deck of the aircraft carrier, reared the Island – the control tower, over forty feet high and composed of several different levels. The *President* was one of the jewels in the crown of American world power. The movements of this terrible weapon of war were controlled by Rear Admiral Joseph Honeywood. Six feet two tall, he was built like a quarterback and had a craggy face, which was why he was known throughout the US Navy as Crag. He sat relaxed in his chair at a lower level inside the Island. His eyes were blue, his hair dark, his movements slow and deliberate.

Outwardly he was a calm man. He had never been known to allow a crisis to disturb him. He issued orders tersely, in a quiet voice. He abhorred anyone showing excitement on the bridge and an offender would be demoted on the spot. Which is why it was surprising that he had been startled when he had opened his sealed orders. Not that anyone observing him would have known his reaction. He read them twice, then handed them to his Operations Officer.

'Say, Bill, you might like to take a look.'

It was the opening, brief paragraph which caused the officer to muster all his self-control not to show surprise. That paragraph was followed by route instructions, ordering them to steer clear of all shipping lanes and flight paths of commercial airliners. As the Rear Admiral had done, the officer read the opening paragraph twice.

Objective: Great Britain. The English Channel off Portsmouth.

'I reckon, Bill,' Crag said in an offhand way, 'it should take us no more than seven days to reach our objective.'

23

'It's time we killed some of Tweed's people.' Vernon grunted, then continued. 'Better still, wipe out all the m *********** with one bomb. Put them underground for good.'

'Or underwater,' Ronstadt said viciously. 'You've given me an idea.'

He had called a meeting in his suite. Only three people were present, Ronstadt, Vernon and Brad. Recently Ronstadt had promoted the two men to be his deputies. He played with his pack of cards. That had been a smart move, he was thinking. If he gave them a task which was dangerous they'd go for it, puffed up with pride by their new status. Which left him in the clear if anything went wrong.

'Underwater?' queried the squat Brad. 'Don't get it.'

'Wouldn't expect you to – otherwise, feller, you'd be sitting in my chair. Like this suite?' he asked suddenly.

'It's great, Jake,' Vernon said quickly.

'It's really great,' Brad agreed.

'Play your cards right and maybe – just maybe – you'll have a suite like this one. Play your cards,' he repeated, then held up his pack. 'See what I mean, dopes?'

'Sure, Jake,' they both said at the same time.

'It was a joke, morons,' Ronstadt snarled. 'Trouble with you guys is you ain't got no sense of humour. Remember what we pulled off outside Paris last year? You do? Amazing. Guess we could do the same thing here. We need a whisperer. Has to convince that bastard Tweed. Guess I know who could do it for us.'

Standing up, Ronstadt left the table, walked over to a window, gazed at the traffic outside the Euler. He was turning the idea over in his mind. He suddenly returned to the table, where his two deputies were waiting for him.

'I've got it, you guys. We use the bar here at the Euler. I hope you brought back the explosive when I recalled you from Höllental on my mobile. Höllental!' He grinned nastily. 'I've heard that's German for Hell's Valley. That's what we're going to give them. Hell.' His tone became savage. 'Tweed's mob has eliminated five of my men. I always pay back. And do I have to ask you again? Did you bring back the explosive?'

'We did,' Vernon said hastily. 'Enough to blow the Three Kings Hotel sky-high.'

'We'll need that kind of amount for this job. Give you details later. Stay in your rooms. Don't drink. Why are you still here? I have phone calls to make.'

'We're going now,' Vernon said, jumping up, followed by Brad.

Alone in the room, Ronstadt shuffled his cards, almost without realizing he was doing so. He'd had to tell his deputies about the five dead men – they'd soon notice they were missing. What he had kept to himself was the disaster at the Zürcher Kredit. He'd threatened Vernon with mayhem if he mentioned the scene he'd witnessed. In any case, what did Vernon know about money?

The one thing Ronstadt had hated doing was having to explain to Charlie what had happened. On top of that he'd had to ask Charlie to have more funds transmitted electronically from the US to the Zürcher Kredit. Charlie had given him a roasting.

Standing up again, he went back to the window. He'd better make that phone call, get the show on the road.

He grinned as he visualized what was going to happen this evening. He waved a hand behind the net curtain.

'Bye-bye, Mr Tweed . . .'

Paula stared with shock at the document, the typed sheet Tweed had passed to her. She could hardly believe what she had just read.

THE COMMONWEALTH OF BRITAIN.

Governor – Tweed.

Following Tweed's name was a list of other positions. One was Chief Medical Examiner. Each position had the name of a well-known Englishman or Englishwoman shown. She stared at Tweed as he spoke.

'Hand it round to everyone.'

'What does it mean?' she asked, passing the sheet to Newman. 'Why is the word Commonwealth used?'

'Because in America a number of states are called by that name. The Commonwealth of Virginia is one example. You're looking at a blueprint of Britain to be absorbed into the United States. If they pulled it off we'd be the fifty-first state.'

'You really think they're going to try and do this?'

'I know they are. Morgenstern practically said so when I had dinner with him. Gave me a lot of plausible reasons why they had to do it – from America's point of view. I just listened most of the time, to find out what they were up to. For some reason Jefferson has great faith in me. Hence my appointment to the top job – Governor.'

'You'd make a good one,' Newman commented.

'Except I'd slip abroad rather than have anything to do with their plan. When you've all seen that sheet you'll realize what a supreme effort we have to make to defeat them. And I have a horrible feeling we're up against a tight deadline.'

229

'So how do we hit them?' asked Marler, who had just read the sheet.

'In Kurt's black book he mentions a place called St Ursanne. I happen to know it. It's an attractive village, or small town, south of here, in Switzerland, the French-speaking part, and close to the border with France. That's where we're going this morning.'

'Why?' asked Paula.

'Because in his little book Kurt has written after St Ursanne the Hôtel d'Or, in La Ruelle. And a name, Juliette Leroy. He has scribbled after that General Guisan. I assume I have to use the same password when I meet Leroy as Marler used when he met Irina. I think Kurt Schwarz had great faith in women keeping secrets – providing he chose the right women.'

'He could make friends with women easily,' Paula said. 'I was very taken by his gentle personality when he had dinner at my flat.'

'Hold on,' said Marler. 'We all come with you? I think we should after what's happened. But what about the Black Forest? If Ronstadt and Co. take off for that area we won't be here to follow them.'

'Ronstadt isn't going anywhere at the moment. He's waiting for more funds to arrive after Keith's conjuring trick at the bank.'

'You sound as though you know,' Paula said.

'I'm betting on being right. I'll cover the Black Forest before we go, by phoning Beck. No, I'll pop across the road, hope he's in, and see him. I think I can persuade him to get two off-duty officers to stand by the check-point in an unmarked car. If Ronstadt leaves they can follow him. We have to find out what there is in St Ursanne. I have great faith in Kurt Schwarz.'

'When are you going to see Beck?' Newman asked.

'Now.'

'Then I'm coming with you.'

'I welcome your company. The rest of you get ready for this trip. Incidentally, we're going by train. Paula, find out train times to St Ursanne. We have to change at a place called Delémont.'

The phone rang, Paula answered it, asked the caller to hang on just a minute. She extended the phone to Marler.

'It's for you. Denise Chatel. She says she has urgent news. She wants to meet you immediately. She's in the hotel.'

'Ask her to go to my room. Give her the number. Tell her I'll be waiting for her . . .'

'I wonder why he gave her his name as Alec,' Paula remarked when Marler had gone. 'Good job he told us all.'

'Probably the first name that came into his head,' Tweed surmised. 'Bob, we'll wait until Marler gets back. I'm intrigued by what Denise calls urgent.'

'Come in, Denise,' Marler said at the open door of his room. 'I must say you look great in that outfit.'

She wore a navy blue trouser suit, a colourful scarf at her throat. She looked pleased at the compliment even though she dismissed it.

'It's just workaday clothes, but they're warm. I'm in a rush.'

'Well, at least you can sit down. Care for some coffee? I think it's probably still fairly hot.'

'No, thank you.' She was breathless, sat down in an armchair. Her small hands twisted in her lap. She was nervous. 'I can't really understand what I'm going to tell you, but it sounded threatening.'

'I'm a good listener.'

'I had a phone call in my room here a little while ago. It was from a man. I didn't recognize his voice. An

231

American. I'm not telling this very well. He said he had a message from Sharon who had had to leave in a hurry. She wanted to meet me immediately at the bar in the Hotel Euler. So I grabbed a cab and went there.'

'What sort of voice did the caller have?'

'Oh, very polite and smooth. He talked quickly. An educated voice. I should have asked his name but it all happened so quickly.'

'I understand. Do go on.'

'Outside here I was lucky. I grabbed a passing cab and it dropped me outside the Euler. I found the bar quickly. It was almost empty and there was no sign of Sharon. I ordered coffee and sat in a booth. I thought she'd been held up. Soon afterwards two men came in and sat in the booth behind me. Americans.'

'Ever seen them before?'

'No, never.'

'Can you describe them briefly?'

'Up to a point. They walked past where I was sitting to get to their booth. Funny pair. One was quite short, squat might be the right word. The other was very tall and thin. I didn't like the look of either of them.'

'What happened next?'

She was still tense, nervous. She unconsciously ran her fingers through her long dark hair.

'They ordered drinks. As soon as they'd been served they started talking quietly, but I could hear every word. The thin man said a meeting of everyone, including Charlie, had been arranged for later today. It would take place aboard a barge on the Rhine called the *Minotaur* . . .'

'Are you sure you got that name right?'

'Certain, Alec. *Minotaur*. Like the legend about the monster on Crete thousands of years ago. He said they'd cruise down to the harbour before dark, about four in the afternoon. They were meeting to work out a plan to destroy Tweed and his whole organization. That's why I

232

used the word threatening. I just wouldn't like anything to happen to you, Alec.'

'I really appreciate your concern. Hear anything else?'

'Yes. Incidentally, the thin man is called Vernon. The squat man used his name once. He went on to say that at long last they'd meet the mysterious Charlie. Then they got up and left. I was lucky again outside the Euler. I grabbed a cab and came back here to tell you. Heaven knows what happened to Sharon.'

'Will you tell her about this experience of yours?'

'No, I won't. She has her own problems. The Swiss couple she goes to see are thinking of separating. She's known them for years. She's trying to persuade them to stay together while they give it some more thought.'

'I'm very grateful to you, Denise, for passing on this news.'

'I must go now. Sharon has given me a ton of backlog work she brought from London.' She had stood up, was near the door when Marler gave her a hug. She smiled. 'You take good care of yourself.'

'I've had a bit of experience at doing that.'

'Oh, I forgot something.' She paused before he had opened the door. 'The thin man said Jake was organizing the meeting on the *Minotaur* . . .'

'Quite a bit to tell you after listening to Denise,' Marler said after returning to Tweed's room.

'We have time,' said Paula. 'I phoned the station. We've just missed a train to Delémont. The next one is not departing for an hour.'

'We've still a lot to do,' warned Tweed. 'We have to see Beck before we leave. Paula phoned the Spiegelhof – Basle police HQ, just across the road. Beck is waiting until we arrive. Now, Marler, I'm listening.'

There was complete quiet in the room as Marler

recalled every word Denise had said to him. Tweed sat back in his chair, his eyes half-closed as he absorbed the information. Marler waved a hand when he had finished.

'Interesting that Charlie will be aboard that barge. And now we have even more to tell Beck,' Tweed remarked. 'You get on rather well with Denise, don't you, Marler?'

'She's a nice lady.'

Something in the way he'd said the words made Paula glance across at Marler. Was he falling for Denise? Then she also wondered about Newman – who seemed so enthusiastic about Sharon. Newman spoke just after the thoughts had passed through her mind. He addressed Marler.

'Could you repeat Denise's description of the man she heard called Vernon?'

'First, she called him very tall and thin. Later she referred to him simply as the thin man.'

'And she said his name was Vernon. I think we're encountering at a distance – which is safest – Vernon Kolkowski. He was the man in the Zürcher Kredit Kent described as accompanying Jake Ronstadt. We'd better watch out for him – I told you I saw his mug shot when I was in New York. He's already killed several times and got away with his murders.'

'Time to go and see Beck,' Tweed said briskly, standing up. 'I will take Bob with me. Paula, I've made a note of the train time you gave me, the one to St Ursanne, while Marler was out talking to Denise. Scribble those details down on a bit of paper and give it to Marler.' He looked round the room at Butler and Nield. 'You go with Paula and Marler so you're at the Hauptbahnhof in good time. It's a weird set-up – you go to the section known as the French station. Make sure you have your passports. Bob and I will get there as soon as we can – we have a lot to discuss with Beck, including that meeting on board that barge. The tram stop is near where we had the episode with the Umbrella Men. A No. 1 or a No. 8 will get you there.'

With his coat on Tweed paused at the door. He looked back at Marler.

'You called Denise Chatel a nice lady. You'd all better get it through your heads we can trust no one. No one at all.'

Jake Ronstadt, in his suite at the Euler, made a phone call to another room standing up. Ronstadt had always disliked sitting down – it made him restless. Ever since he was a kid in Hoboken, not the best district in New York, he liked to keep moving. When his number was answered he was cautious. Wouldn't do to have someone listening in to what he was going to say.

'That you, Leo?'

'Operator!' he snarled suddenly. 'Something wrong with this goddamn line.'

He waited for a reply. Nothing. The line was clear, safe.

'Leo, you have started sending down men in relays to watch the Three Kings Hotel?'

'Sure, boss. Got a man on duty now. Just about to drive down myself and take his place.'

'This is a smart mob we're watching. Would they spot the guy there now – or you?'

'No way. We're dressed as Swiss. We pretend to be waiting for a tram. There's a stop close to the hotel. Don't matter that we don't get aboard one. Looks like we're waiting for another one going to a different destination.'

'Sounds like you've got it tied up,' Ronstadt agreed reluctantly. 'Get on down there. You've all got mobiles. You see any of them, report back to me instanter. I gave you a description of Paula Grey and Tweed. You have pics of Newman from the reference library back in London. Get off the line. *Move!'*

24

Paula boarded the tram for the station first, followed by Nield and Butler. Butler chose a seat by himself, as though they didn't know each other, and Nield followed suit. The tram was made up of three green cars, joined to each other. It was only about a quarter full.

Marler was the last to mount the steps. He was checking the other passengers who had been waiting at the stop. They all seemed to be local Swiss, wearing heavy winter clothes. Ahead of him a moon-faced man made his way to the very back of the car. Marler decided to join Paula.

'What I can't understand,' she said as he settled beside her, 'is why Tweed thought it necessary to give the train details to you. I've got them.'

'He was being clever. When we get to the station you can buy tickets for yourself and Nield. I'll buy them for Butler and myself – in case any of the opposition are watching the Hauptbahnhof. Don't forget it's very close to the Euler.'

'Of course. I must be half asleep. I must get my wits about me.'

'You'll be all right if we run into a spot of trouble.'

'What's in that holdall on your shoulder?'

'A flask of coffee sticking out, oranges and other food. In case we have to picnic.'

'Heaven forbid. In this weather.'

Earlier Paula had stared straight ahead. Marler knew why – they had been passing the scene of the massacre of the Umbrella Men. The tram swayed round corners, climbing all the time. Basle, Paula remembered, sloped down from the station until it reached the Rhine.

They stopped briefly at Bankverein. Looking out of the window she saw the Zürcher Kredit Bank. Then they were moving on.

She glanced back once at the other passengers. They all had a glazed look as they stared out. It must be even colder than they were used to, she thought. She looked again at Marler's canvas holdall.

'Is that all you've got inside there? Food and drink?'

'Well,' he drawled, lowering his voice as she had done, 'there is the odd weapon at the bottom, including a .32 Browning so you won't feel naked.'

'We may have to pass through French Customs. Let's hope you make it.'

'Another reason for separate tickets. If I don't you'll get through – and so will Tweed and Newman.'

'We're nearly there. You do think of everything.'

'I try.'

At the rear of the car the moon-faced man had slipped his phone out of his coat pocket. Well away from any other passengers, he whispered into it. He kept his message brief, then put his instrument away. It was Paula he had recognized – from the careful description Jake had given him.

'Who is it?' Ronstadt rapped out on his mobile.

'Leo Madison here . . .'

'How goes it, Moonhead?'

'I just said it was Leo here.'

'Heard you, Moonhead. Get to it. Any news from the Three Kings?'

'Paula Grey, Newman, Tweed and some other people

237

are leaving the French station for some burg called St Ursanne. They change on to a local train at a place called Delémont. I bought myself a ticket—'

'Hold it. Where's this friggin' place, St Whatever?'

'Down in the Jura. To the south. French-speaking Switzerland.'

'Got it.' Ronstadt had looked at the map of Switzerland spread out on a table. 'Tear up your ticket.'

'Do what?'

'You heard. On a train – two trains – they'll spot you. Get a cab to the airport. We have a chopper there, as you know. I'm calling the pilot. He'll fly you – he can follow that train, see them change at Delémont. You've got that fancy disguise?'

'With me. The telescopic stick is down my belt, with the dark glasses.'

'Use them when you track them to where they're going. My guess is they're meeting someone. Whoever it is, wipe them out. Got it?'

'The train leaves in five minutes—'

'Moonhead, tear up your friggin' ticket. Get to the airport. Last time you called you said you're on the tram with them. They're smart. They'll spot you. Grab a cab. For the airport. *Now!*'

'The name is Leo. Next time you call me Moonhead I'll headbutt you in your face. On my way. Airport—'

'You talk to me like that again you won't have any head!'

Ronstadt slammed the phone down. Moonhead had disconnected. 'I am going to kill that guy,' he said to himself. Moonhead was the one member of his team he couldn't tame. Then he remembered it was Moonhead who had once shot a baby in the back of the head. Ronstadt shuddered, called the pilot at the airport.

*

238

There was Passport Control before they passed through on to the platform of the French station, but no one behind the Customs counter, which was a relief to Marler. Tweed and Newman arrived to join the others minutes before the train was due to depart. Paula had given them their tickets, then the three of them ran. Nield and Butler had boarded the last coach, which was empty when they entered it. Marler had followed them and was leaning out of the window when Paula and her two companions jumped on to the train.

'That was a near-run thing,' Paula commented as the train moved off.

'As Wellington said about Waterloo,' Tweed replied.

Marler had continued leaning out of the window until the train was clear of the platform. As he sat down Tweed asked him what he had been looking for.

'I memorized the faces of all the passengers on the tram which brought us here. None of them has boarded this train.'

'So we've given them the slip,' said Paula.

'We *hope* we've given them the slip,' Tweed corrected her.

'You're never sure of anything,' she chided.

'Which is why I'm still alive.'

'Let's be positive,' she responded. 'How did you get on with Beck?'

'We made a lot of arrangements. We have to be back at police headquarters before four this afternoon. Beck was very helpful.'

'We should just make it, with a bit of luck,' she said after consulting a timetable.

'From the station at St Ursanne it's a good ten-minute walk down to the village.'

'Then we'll make it, with a lot of luck. I sense you're very anxious to meet this Juliette Leroy at the Hôtel d'Or.'

239

'I have great faith in Kurt Schwarz.'

'What was the outcome of your talk to Beck?'

'A very important decision concerning that barge, the *Minotaur*. I learned from Beck the vessel isn't used for transporting cargo any more. Some Swiss entrepreneur has converted it to a floating hotel for business conventions. It has conference rooms, a bar, a restaurant and all modern communication facilities. Today an American called Davidson phoned the owner, hired the *Minotaur* for a week.'

'Davidson?'

'I think Mr Davidson is really Jake Ronstadt. Beck has laid plans to follow the vessel, to board it from police launches, then to arrest everyone on board for interrogation. He's going to use the dead Umbrella Men as a lever.'

'How?' she wondered.

'They were all carrying guns. They were all staying at the Euler. That's enough for starters. He thinks he'll find the people at that meeting are also carrying weapons.'

'Pity we aren't going to see it happening.'

'We are. He's loaning us an unmarked launch. I asked him to let me have a loudhailer, which he did. I dashed back to the hotel with it, left it in my room before Bob and I raced up to the station in a taxi.'

'What do you want with a loudhailer?'

'Might come in useful . . .'

Tweed lapsed into a brooding silence and Paula looked out of the window. They had left Basle behind and it was a bright sunny day with a crystal-clear sky. She felt relieved to be away from the city. She liked Basle, had loved it the last time she had been there with Tweed, but this time she was depressed by the grim ancient buildings looming over her everywhere, like being inside a sinister fortress.

She decided her reaction was partly due to the weather – and to the events which had occurred there. The Umbrella Men, then Nield's description of the last-minute rescue of Irina, of the ghastly ape man who had come so close to torturing Irina. The train entered a deep gorge. On either side rose sheer walls of jagged lime-stone. Peering out, her face close to the window, she could just see the crests, tipped with snow. It was so warm inside the train they had all taken off outer clothes.

'We're in the Jura Mountains,' Tweed remarked. 'Nothing like the enormous heights of the Bernese Ober-land but I'm fond of the Jura. You don't feel a million tons of rock is going to fall on you.'

The train emerged from the gorge and open fields stretched away into the distance. Here and there was an isolated wooden farmhouse, sometimes with a ramp at its side leading up to a storage barn attached to the house. They were seeing the Switzerland so liked by more sophisticated tourists.

'Looks like we got clean away from Ronstadt and his thugs,' remarked Newman.

'There aren't any on the train,' Marler agreed.

'I feel safe,' said Paula. 'At peace with the world. The sun is wonderful.'

She had just spoken when she saw the helicopter, flying on a course parallel to the train, about a quarter of a mile away. She stared at it, all her misgivings returning. Tweed caught her change of expression.

'It's probably just a traffic helicopter. The Swiss use them a lot.'

'That reminds me,' Paula told him. 'I forgot to tell you that when I was driving to the Bunker on Romney Marsh I heard a chopper. It was flying straight towards me. I was still some distance from the Bunker when I saw an open barn by the roadside. The chopper was temporarily hidden in a cloud so I drove inside the barn out of sight. I had to wait a while. The chopper came closer, sounded to be circling above the barn. Then it went away and I didn't see it again. I drove on to the Bunker.'

'You are wise to take precautions,' Tweed assured her. 'The Bunker has become our main operational centre. Before we left I sent down more personnel. There's only a skeleton staff left at Park Crescent. Howard agreed it was a good idea. He'll keep in touch with the Bunker.'

'Pretty drastic,' Paula commented. 'Why did you do it?'

'I think you all realize now we're up against the most powerful state on earth. America has limitless resources, vast sums of money. It took me a while to grasp that it was really planning on taking over Britain. The idea seemed so momentous. I'm convinced now – after my dinner with Morgenstern – and after reading that file Pete and Harry grabbed from the Embassy in Grosvenor Square. We can only stop them by superior cunning and a certain amount of luck. Don't look so serious, Paula. We're coming into Delémont, where we change trains. You're really going to like St Ursanne.'

Aboard the helicopter Leo Madison – or Moonhead, as Ronstadt sneeringly called him – grasped hold of the powerful binoculars hanging from a strap round his neck. He glanced at the pilot in the seat next to him.

'From now on we must change our flying tactics. Don't want to make the targets suspicious. Train's comin' in to Delémont. Can you hold us still while I check the platforms?'

The pilot slowed the machine, hovered. Through his binoculars Leo clearly saw Paula Grey, Tweed and Newman alight. Two more men appeared to be with them but they were strangers to him. In the lenses he could see the faces of the trio he recognized. He saw them hurry across the platform, climb aboard a smaller train. He lowered his binoculars, waited until the little train started moving.

'Now you follow that little job. But do change your angle of flight.'

Again they had a coach to themselves. As the small train moved on into open country Paula had her eyes glued to the window. The scenery was superb, with large fields showing a froth of green sweeping up the slopes of high, hump-backed hills. She was looking out at a panorama as far as the eye could see – with here and there a lonely village of wooden houses clustered together and the tiny spire of a church. The helicopter had disappeared.

'You see,' Newman reassured her, 'that machine in the sky has gone.'

The next moment they entered a long tunnel. The wheels of the train made a quiet drumming sound. The lights had come on, Paula relaxed, looking forward to seeing the village Tweed had recalled with such enthusiasm. Her eyes closed and she almost fell asleep. Suddenly they emerged from the tunnel. She was alert instantly.

In the near distance the hills were higher, the slopes steeper. There were no villages anywhere. She saw a car driving along a road which seemed to follow the railway. They were climbing.

'It's back,' she said.

'What is?' Marler asked.

'The chopper. Can't you hear the beat-beat of its engine? I think it's flying directly above the train.'

'And I think you're right,' Marler agreed.

'I don't honestly see how they could have known where we are going,' Nield interjected.

'Pete has a point,' Tweed agreed.

He was anxious to reassure Paula. But he didn't believe what he said. He was beginning to think that it had been a good idea of Marler's to distribute weapons from his canvas satchel earlier. A chopper near Romney Marsh. Now another one out in the wilds of the Jura. The Americans, as he'd pointed out earlier, certainly had unlimited resources. He checked his watch. They were almost arriving at St Ursanne.

'We'll soon be there,' Tweed said. 'A good job it's such a perfect day. As I mentioned earlier, we have a good ten-minute trot along a road before we reach the village. Maybe fifteen minutes . . .'

The helicopter swung away from the train after climbing directly above it. By this tactic the pilot hoped the targets aboard the train would not think he had been following them. A minute before giving the pilot his instructions Leo had focused his binoculars on the small station – just one platform – the train was nearing. The signboard read St Ursanne.

'Let's get clear away from the train,' he began. 'See that small village in the distance?'

'Got it.'

'I want you to land me as close to it as you can – within close walking distance of the place. You should be able to drop me somewhere. Then wait until I return to take me back to Basle.'

'Will do.'

The chopper was already climbing vertically. The pilot became aware that his passenger was wriggling around a lot, that he had removed his safety belt. He had no time to look at him as he concentrated on his manoeuvre, then high in the sky swung away from the railway. Now he was searching for a landing point. He saw one at the edge of the village.

'Here we go.'

'Try and land before the train stops at the station. I'll tell you when.'

'Will do.'

It was then that he glanced at his passenger and had a shock. He would never have recognized the man seated next to him as Leo.

25

'Back of beyond out here,' Tweed remarked as they alighted on the deserted platform.

'Nobody else has got off except us,' Paula observed.

'Who would? At this time of year? At this time of day?' Marler replied.

Tweed was hurrying. They followed him as he went down a ramp and started walking along a narrow road alongside the station. The road led steeply downhill with a high rock wall on one side. No traffic. They turned a bend and for a moment Tweed stopped and pointed.

'St Ursanne.'

Paula almost gasped with pleasure at the beauty of the scene in the sunlight. In the distance, where Tweed had pointed, way below them, an ancient village was huddled inside a valley, the old houses close together, with the spire of a church spearing up amid the dwellings which must have existed like this for centuries. It was idyllic. To their left, beyond the empty road, the ground fell steeply for quite a depth. At the bottom a small river meandered through meadows until it passed the edge of the village. Paula gestured down.

'Any idea which river that is?'

'The River Doubs,' Tweed told her. 'It figures in the famous and controversial novel, *Le Rouge et Le Noir – The Red and the Black,* by Stendhal. Now we must keep moving. I have a growing sense we have very little time left.'

Almost before he had finished speaking Tweed was hustling ahead down the road which had become even steeper, his legs moving like pistons. The others had to increase pace to keep up with him.

'Where's the fire?' called out Nield.

Tweed didn't reply. He seemed intent on reaching their destination in the shortest possible time. Lower down there was a pavement on the left side but he ignored it, keeping to the road. Paula caught up with him. If she had to move any faster she would be running. It was only when they were very close to the village, and old houses appeared to their right, each with plenty of land and perched on a slope, their entrances small gates in their garden walls positioned well below them, that Tweed stopped.

'We'll be cautious now,' he said as the others arrived.

'Well, at least the chopper has vanished,' Paula remarked. 'And I am wondering whether we ought to have phoned Juliette Leroy before coming all this distance.'

'That would have been a mistake. Like Irina, I think Leroy has to see us before she will talk.'

'Hear it?' Marler asked. 'Behind us?'

Tap . . . tap . . . tap . . .

It was a weird sound in the serene silence of the sunny afternoon. As one, they all turned to look back. A man was emerging from one of the gardens they had passed, his stick tapping on the stone steps leading down from the house. Arriving at the gate, he fumbled with the catch, opened it, came out slowly, closed the gate and came trudging slowly towards them.

Tap . . . tap . . . tap . . .

He wore an old coat, which Paula thought must be too heavy for a sunny day. But he was old. He wore a floppy brimmed Swiss hat and beneath it very dark glasses were perched on the bridge of his nose, his head bent. In his right hand he carried a white stick, ringed at intervals like a bamboo cane. It was tipped with a rubber at the end. He was tapping the stick against the edge of the pavement.

'Poor devil. He's blind,' Paula whispered.

'Better let him pass us,' Tweed suggested. 'We'll move out of his way.'

They crossed to the far side of the road and waited. The man with the dark glasses trudged on. They kept quiet as he passed them, seemingly unaware of their presence.

The handle of his white stick was curved like a shepherd's crook. Paula noticed it was flexible, moving in the hand which gripped it as the cane tapped. Immediately ahead of him was an ancient stone tower with an archway below it, high and wide enough to let a farm cart pass through. They watched the man raise his stick to tap at a side wall of the archway, then make his way through it.

'Must be a local,' Paula mused. 'Probably knows his way about the place better than we ever shall.'

They waited while the man tapped his way carefully along the street beyond. He was some distance away when he paused with his back to them. Taking an old pipe out of his pocket he half-turned, used the side of a lighter to tamp the bowl, then lit it. He resumed his slow progress away from them.

'Let's get on with it,' said Tweed.

Walking through the archway, Paula noticed the street ahead had a plate on the side of a wall. *Rue du 23 juin.* Tweed had stopped by her side, looking to his left.

Steps led up to the Hôtel La Couronne. The door at the top was closed.

'We might enquire here,' he suggested.

'I don't think so.'

Paula pointed to a small notice in the window near the door. It had a simple message. *Fermé*. Closed. Tweed shrugged. Paula was gazing down the main street, fascinated. On either side ancient houses, joined together, had tiled roofs at different heights. Like something out of a child's fairytale. The walls were covered with plaster, each house painted a contrasting muted colour – yellow, ochre, cream and other attractive tones.

'It's like Paradise,' she said. 'And so quiet. Apart from that blind man there's no one about anywhere. I wonder how we're going to find that street?'

'La Ruelle. Look at that plate on the wall over there. It's in this side street.' He peered down it. 'There's the Hôtel d'Or. Not twenty yards away.'

They walked down the street and Paula followed Tweed up stone steps to a landing on the first floor. It had a door with a window masked by net curtains. Tweed pressed a bell by the door's side. The door opened and a tall attractive slim woman in her fifties stood looking at them, as she quickly removed an apron.

'Do you speak English?' Tweed enquired.

'I do, Monsieur. How can I help you?'

'I have come from the late General Guisan, so to speak.'

'Please to come in.' She peered down the steps. Newman was waiting with the others, not wishing to crowd the flight of steps. 'Those are your friends?' she asked.

'You are Juliette Leroy?'

'I am.'

'Yes, they are my friends, but there are rather a lot of us.'

'Please to ask your friends to join you.'

They walked into a large room which was obviously a dining room with a bar at the back and the kitchen in the rear. The walls and ceiling were covered with pinewood, which gave the place a cosy atmosphere. Extending close to the kitchen area paintings of scenes in the Jura hung from hooks and with very heavy-looking gilt frames. One long table was laid for a meal with ten places but the other tables were bare of cloths.

'I have waited for you,' said Leroy. 'I have something for you from Albert.'

'Albert?' The surprise showed in Tweed's voice. 'My friend is called Kurt.'

'Please to excuse me. That was a little test. I will get it for you now.'

She hurried to the kitchen, hauled out a drawer full of cutlery. Balancing it on a work surface, she detached an envelope taped to the underneath. She handed it to Tweed.

'There you are. You will see Kurt signed it on the back with his Christian name. You are hungry?'

'We can't impose on your hospitality . . .'

'I ask if you are hungry.' Her blue-grey eyes held his and he had the impression of a forceful personality. At the same time she gave him a radiant smile. 'You like *Filets des Perches* with the *pomme frites*? Most Englishmen do. The table is already laid, as you see.'

'For someone else, I suspect, Mademoiselle.'

'I am a widow. The table is laid for a group of farmers – they will not be here until this evening. I have plenty of food for them and for you and your friends.'

Tweed glanced at his watch. He suddenly felt terribly hungry. And what she had offered was one of his favourite dishes.

'We have to leave in an hour at the latest – to catch a train back to Basle.'

249

'Then please sit down, everyone. You have plenty of time.'

She was already returning to the kitchen. She produced several pans, opened the large fridge-freezer. Everyone was sitting down when Paula noticed the entrance door had not been closed properly. She went to shut it and thought she caught sight of someone moving in the street.

Opening the door wider, she went out on to the landing. There was no sign of anyone. Nearby several narrow alleys led off the street. Must have been my imagination, she thought. She closed the door and sat next to Tweed at the table.

The plates of food, which smelt wonderful, were placed before them more quickly than Tweed had expected. Juliette sat down opposite him, noticing he had already broken some crusty bread. She smiled.

'You were hungry. You have started eating the bread.'

'It's some of the best bread I've ever tasted,' he answered honestly. 'This is very good of you, Madame Leroy.'

'I enjoy this.' She looked round the table at Newman, Nield, Butler and Marler, then at Paula. 'It gives me much pleasure to watch you eating. You are all most hungry.'

What a nice woman, Paula thought. She radiates good humour. She loves to see people having a good time. What a pity there aren't more like her in the world.

'I fear we must go now,' Tweed said a short while later. 'I don't want to but, as I said, we have to catch that train. Something important waits for us in Basle.'

They stood up from the table, their plates cleared of food. Then Tweed had a friendly argument when he insisted on paying. He became emphatic.

'You are running a business here. I must pay.'

'You come here for holiday with me. All who can. All, I hope.' She laughed. 'Then you pay through the nose. Is that correct?'

'Perfect English.' Tweed reluctantly put away his wallet. He could argue all night and she wouldn't give way. He made a gesture of resignation.

'Madame Leroy—'

'Juliette. Please.'

'Juliette, we will come here on holiday – to your beautiful village. To sample your superb cooking. You gave us a meal to remember.'

'Go and catch your train. And may God go with you.'

When they reached the archway under the ancient tower Paula paused and they waited for her. She was looking back at the beauty of St Ursanne. She wanted to be able to visualize the village later when they were gone. Then she forced herself to turn round and they started to hurry up the road which seemed steeper climbing it. They were halfway to the station when Newman stopped, swore under his breath.

'Something wrong?' asked Paula.

'I've left my gloves, my motoring gloves in the restaurant. I'm going back to get them. They're the ones you gave me for Christmas, Paula.'

'You'll miss the train,' Tweed warned.

'No, I won't. Remember, I came in the first ten in the London marathon.'

He began to hare off down the hill. Paula paused briefly to take one last look at St Ursanne. Soon the sun would drop behind a nearby mountain and the village would be swallowed up in shadows. At the moment she could see every detail in the crystal-clear light.

'It's a dream village,' she said as she resumed climbing upwards alongside Tweed. 'I'm looking forward to a wonderful holiday.'

'So am I,' Tweed agreed.

251

Behind them Newman, running, was about halfway to the old stone tower. His right foot slipped on a large stone and he sprawled full length. He took the worst of the impact on his forearms. When he began to get up he realized his right ankle was hurting. He sat up in the road, pushed down his socks, examined it. Wiggling his foot, he was relieved to realize he had neither broken nor sprained it. The only sign of his minor accident was a faint bruise.

He stood up, tested the foot. When he glanced back up the hill the others were tiny figures approaching the bend below the station. He was glad they hadn't seen him fall and he found he could move at a brisk pace back to St Ursanne.

Tap ... tap ... tap ...

Juliette Leroy frowned as she heard the strange sound coming closer and closer, mounting the steps outside. She went to the door and opened it. A man with very dark glasses, holding a white stick, stood motionless.

'I am sorry to disturb you,' he said, his accent American. 'I am very thirsty. I have walked a long way. Could you give me a glass of water?'

'Of course. Please come in.'

Juliette was disappointed. She had just found a pair of gloves on a chair. She had hoped it was one of her new friends returning to collect them. At the same time she felt sorry for the blind man. He had looked so lonely. It must be awful to go through life like that.

Tap ... tap ... tap ...

She turned and saw her visitor coming across the room, his stick guiding him between the tables. She remembered reading somewhere that the blind developed a keen sense of hearing. He must have picked up

252

the sound of her footsteps walking across the floor to the kitchen.

With her back to him, she took a clean glass from a cupboard. She wiped it carefully on a clean cloth although it had been washed recently. Juliette was a stickler for all forms of hygiene. She turned off the tap when the glass was three-quarters full.

Behind her, Leo moved swiftly. Reversing his stick, he held it close to the tip. Elevating it, he hooked the flexible handle round her neck and throat, pressing a button which tightened the grip remorselessly. Juliette dropped the glass, tried to scream. Her air supply was cut off and she managed no more than a gurgle. The rubberized handle tightened. She reached up with both hands, trying to insert her fingers inside it. This was the moment when Leo jerked her backwards.

She toppled, hit the side of her head on the edge of a wooden working surface, sagged to the floor. Leo pressed the button again, releasing the grip of the handle. Bending over her unconscious form he checked her pulse. It beat steadily. He swore foully.

He glanced round, saw the heavy framed pictures hanging from the wall. Moving with great speed, he lifted one of the pictures, surprised at its weight. But that meant the hook left on the wall as he propped the picture against a cupboard was more than strong enough for his purpose.

From his pocket he pulled out a coil of thin strong rope – as strong as wire. Holding on to one end, which had a small wooden handle, pencil-thin, he whipped out the rope. The other end had a curved hook firmly attached. Bending down, he fashioned the first end into a loop with a hangman's knot. Slipping the loop over the unconscious woman's neck with the knot at the back, he used one strong arm to lift her. When he had her pushed close to the wall he slid the curved hook over the hook high up on the wall which had held the picture. Then he let go.

He had calculated the length of the rope perfectly. She was hanging with her feet well clear of the floor. That was when consciousness briefly returned to her. Leo stood back as her eyes opened, her heels thudded against the wall, then the rope tightened round her neck. The thudding of her heels ceased. Her eyes stared out of her head. She hung motionless.

Leo grabbed his stick, twisted a band round it, closed it with a telescopic motion, thrust it down inside a pocket. He opened the door slowly, peered out. No one anywhere.

He ran down the steps, along the street. Reaching the archway exit he paused, looked round it. He saw Newman running towards him, then collapse, stretched out in the road. He waited. He chose the moment when Newman glanced back up the road to dart across the arch, then down a side street opposte La Ruelle.

Above this part of St Ursanne a steep slope climbed behind the buildings. Its crest was topped with a dense palisade of leafless trees. The helicopter which had brought Leo had landed on a wide secluded plateau. From there he had found a way into a large garden of a house which appeared unoccupied. He knew he must not go back the same way. At the end of the street he found a footpath climbing up. It should not be difficult to find the plateau where the chopper was waiting to take him back to Basle airport.

26

Paula had the train door open. Newman hurtled up the ramp into the station, dived inside the coach, Paula shut the door as the train started moving. Newman, streams of sweat pouring down his face, sank into a corner seat, stared round. They were now all aboard.

Tweed sat opposite him, next to Marler. Butler and Nield were in seats on the other side of the central corridor. Once again they had the coach to themselves. Gradually Newman's breathing became normal. He took out a handkerchief, wiped his face and the handkerchief was sodden.

He had never run so fast in his life. Not even for the marathon. And all the way it had been uphill. Everyone was staring at him. He didn't like it. He'd sooner have been alone. Paula was the first to speak to him. Quietly.

'I see you got your gloves back.'

He looked down. His right hand was still clutching the motoring gloves he had picked up. He had forgotten about them. He wasn't really in the train carriage at all. In his mind he was back at the Hôtel d'Or in St Ursanne. He had been suspicious when he saw the door was half open. He had crept silently up the steps, his Smith & Wesson in his hand. When he had walked in, seen what was there, he had automatically closed the door behind him.

He could see it now vividly. Juliette's body hanging from the picture hook like a side of beef. Her body limp, her eyes wide open, lifeless. His training had asserted itself. He had forced himself to search the place first, checking to see if the killer was still there. Then, futilely, he had reached up and checked her neck pulse. She was dead. Dead as anybody could be. He remembered thinking he should have checked her pulse first.

Holstering his gun, he had reached up again, one hand round her body, the other lifting off the hook. He was surprised at how light she had felt. Tenderly, he had placed her on a couch. Finding a knife in a kitchen drawer, he had carefully cut through the hangman's knot, removed the rope from round her neck, which was already swelling up.

He had thought of calling the local police. He had rejected the idea quickly. He could be held there for days. As a witness – more probably as a suspect. And there was work to do in Basle. Tweed needed him. That was when he had seen something lying on the floor under a table. He had picked it up, examined it for only a moment. Then he had known who the brutal killer was.

He had gone back briefly to the couch where she lay. He put a hand on her face. It had felt so cold. Then he had moved like a robot, using his handkerchief to wipe his prints off the handle of the knife, to open the door to the outside world, his gun by his side in his left hand. He hadn't thought he would see the murderer in the street but he had looked anyway. Nothing. Nobody.

He had checked his watch. He would never make the train. He had walked to the arch, had taken a deep breath, had begun running up the road beyond nonstop. His brain had dulled, all his concentration on running. Now the shock was receding, he was thinking clearly.

'Let's change seats, Paula,' he said in a normal voice. 'You like to look out of the window.'

They had changed seats but she hadn't looked out of the window. She was looking at him. Newman didn't realize that his complexion was ashen. Except for Tweed, the others were now being careful not to look at him. They were giving him time.

'You look washed out, Bob,' Tweed said casually. 'Has something happened?'

'You could say that.'

'I'd like to hear about it. When you're ready.'

Aware of Paula beside him, Newman phrased it carefully. He kept it simple. She had gone through enough already with her experience in Eagle Street – and then, more recently, the Umbrella Men.

'It's not good news, I'm afraid.'

'I didn't think it would be,' Tweed said in the same casual tone.

'It's about Juliette Leroy?' Paula whispered.

'When I got back I found her – strangled.'

'Oh, no . . .'

Paula tightened her lips. Newman had decided to give no details. They could come later. Any description now would be too horrific. He felt in the pocket of his coat. He had the attention of everyone now. He took the coat button he had picked up off the floor, handed it to Marler.

'Recognize that?'

'Can't say I do.'

'For once you slipped up.'

'I'm not with you,' said Marler.

'The killer walked past you before we went into St Ursanne. A fake blind man. Put on a clever show. As I think Tweed once said, we're up against professionals.'

'I'm still not with you,' Marler repeated.

'He wore an old coat with unusual buttons. They almost merged with his coat. But I noticed them because the symbol on them is unusual. Couldn't identify it at the time. Look at it again. Looks like the torch held up by the Statue of Liberty outside New York.'

'So it does.' Marler handed back the button. 'Where did you find it?'

'Under a chair in the room where we had a meal at

the Hôtel d'Or. There must have been a struggle. Or maybe the thread holding it was hanging loose.'

'And we saw him walk past us,' whispered Paula. 'And I thought, poor old thing.'

'Which was what you were intended to think,' Tweed remarked.

'Poor Juliette,' Paula went on. 'She was such a nice kind person. And I was looking forward to seeing her again. Dream village? It's turned into a nightmare.'

She stared out of the window. Sunlight still shone brilliantly on the greening landscape. She wasn't taking it in. Her mind had gone back to their lunch at the Hôtel d'Or. Tweed and Juliette had got on well together, their conversation easy. Maybe if they had returned for a holiday the two of them would have struck up a warm companionship. Years before, Tweed's wife had run off with a Greek shipping millionaire. He had never bothered to divorce her.

Tweed was also gazing out of the window, his expression pensive. The sunlight vanished. They had entered the tunnel. When they emerged from the other end Marler spoke.

'A second before the train left I thought I heard a chopper taking off.'

'You did,' agreed Newman.

'Probably the machine which brought the assassin, then flew him out afterwards.'

'That's what I thought,' Newman agreed again.

Arriving back at the Three Kings, Tweed followed Paula inside and stood stock-still. Standing by the reception desk was the last person in the world he expected to encounter. Sir Guy Strangeways.

'Hello, my good friend,' Strangeways greeted him. 'Small world.'

258

'As you say.'

'I'd appreciate a word with you. The writing room opposite the lift do you?'

'Just for a short time.'

As Strangeways disappeared into the room Tweed joined the others waiting for the lift. He kept his voice down.

'In half an hour's time we have to be in Beck's office across the street. You go on ahead when you're ready. I'll follow you. Guy has something on his mind.'

The door to the small room was closed. When Tweed opened it, shut it behind him, Strangeways was seated at a desk, writing furiously. There was no one else in the room as Sir Guy, hearing the door close, dropped his fountain pen, twisted round in his chair with a worried expression.

'Good of you to come so quickly. Please do sit down.'

'How did you know I was here?' Tweed demanded, still standing.

'That's hush-hush. Sorry, I gave my word.'

'What was it you wanted to see me about? I haven't much time.'

'I have problems.'

'We all have. What are yours, Guy?'

'Rupert, for one thing.' Strangeways grimaced. 'I told you – he owes that casino at Campione a packet. They're turning nasty. They even had the nerve to call me at Irongates.'

'So where is Rupert?'

'I do wish you'd sit down, Tweed.'

'I can only give you a few minutes just now.'

'Rupert's here. With me.'

'In this hotel?'

'Yes. Situation being what it is, thought I'd better keep him under my wing, so to speak.'

259

'He may sneak off,' Tweed warned. 'To borrow more money.'

'He's tried that back home. No one will give him a *sou*. Didn't know I was going to have to buy three tickets when we came out here.'

'So who is the third party?'

'Basil Windermere.'

'And has he a room in this hotel?' Tweed asked, suppressing his annoyance.

'He has. Not the sort of chap I want within a thousand miles of me, but I hadn't much choice. They're close friends. I know at one moment they'll be snarling at each other, then the next they're bosom pals. I thought Rupert needed someone of his own age to keep him company.'

'Where did you think I come in on this domestic problem?'

'Well ...' Strangeways capped his pen, began twirling it between his fingers. 'I thought maybe Bob Newman could phone the boss at Campione, threaten to write an article exposing him.'

'Threaten? He doesn't know anything about the place.' Leaning on the edge of the desk, Tweed folded his arms. He stared down at the worried man.

'I don't think that's the real reason that you – somehow – found out where I was and hopped on a flight to see me.'

'There was something else.'

'I've got a couple of minutes left before I have to go.'

'Morgenstern called me, urged me to come and see him right away at the Embassy. You know what he's like – wants everything yesterday, if not sooner. I drove up for the meeting. His one theme, hammered away non-stop, was that the special relationship between Britain and America must be enormously strengthened. And quickly. He thinks you're a key element in the plan. He

260

said he'd seen you once. Now he wants to see you again. I'm worried.'

'Why?'

'As you must know, recently American companies have taken over electricity companies in Britain. Also water supply companies. Soon they'll control our country. Do we resist – or do we go along with them?'

'Guy, you were in the Gulf War. Did you ever wonder whether to fight the enemy or to go along with him?'

'Put that way, we have no alternative. I'd still like to talk to you about what Jefferson Morgenstern said later.'

'Later, we will. I must go now . . .'

Tweed had just entered his room, the coat he had taken off earlier over his arm, when someone tapped on his door. It was Paula. He had called her from the reception desk before coming up in the lift. She carried her own fur-lined coat over her arm, had her gloves in one hand, and was wearing knee-high boots. She went straight to a table, poured a glass of water from a bottle on the table, took it to him. She had dropped her coat on a chair and held out the other hand.

'Take this now. We have fifteen minutes. You should have had it earlier. A Dramamine tablet. Don't look out of the window but the river is rough. You know you hate being on water.'

'Thank you.'

He swallowed the tablet, drank the whole glass of water. Then he sat down. Paula noticed he looked grim, sat beside him on the couch.

'Want to tell me about it?'

'First, we can expect Keith Kent very shortly. I phoned him to come over from downstairs. I want to show him what was inside the envelope Juliette gave me which I opened in the taxi on our way from the station.'

261

'I didn't see what it was. I knew you'd tell me if you wanted to.'

'These were inside. No note. Just these.'

Taking the envelope from his pocket, he extracted two banknotes. He handed them to Paula. She stared at them, examined them, then looked at him with a puzzled expression.

'One English twenty-pound note, one English ten-pound note. I am mystified. Why would Kurt travel all the way to St Ursanne to see his friend, Juliette, just to leave these with her? And then put her details in that little black book Irina extracted from behind the brick in the wall?'

'He was leaving us a secret paper trail for us to follow. I imagine he knew he had a tail. That's a guess. So he evades the tail and goes to St Ursanne.'

'Just to hide two ordinary banknotes? Why?'

'I haven't a clue.'

'Was there anywhere else written down in the little black book?'

'Yes, but we haven't time to follow it up at the moment. Now, I had a chat with Strangeways . . .'

He told her all about their conversation. She listened, memorizing every word. When he had finished she sat lost in thought before she reacted.

'Something very weird's going on. And I could have told you Rupert is here. He's on the same floor as me.'

'He saw you?'

'No. I dodged back in my room until he'd gone off down the corridor. He definitely did not see me. And how, in Heaven's name, did Strangeways find out you were here? Monica would never tell him.'

'I told you what he said. I don't like his finding me any more than you do. There's a leak somewhere.'

He stopped talking as the phone rang. Paula jumped up, answered it. She called out to Tweed.

'Keith Kent's in the lobby.'

'Ask him to come up immediately.' He checked his watch. 'We have about five minutes before we rush across to Beck. I see Marler remembered what I asked him to do. He must have given it to a maid and asked her to use her pass key.'

He walked quickly to where a canvas holdall was perched by a settee. Picking it up he opened the flap, turned it upside down to show Paula it was empty. Wondering what the deuce he was up to, she watched as he unlocked a cupboard, took out a powerful cone-shaped loudhailer, slipped it inside the holdall, closed the flap.

'What do you want that for?' she asked.

'I hope you'll never know. If you do, it will save lives.'

Before she could ask him what he was talking about someone knocked quietly on the door. Paula, shoulder bag over her arm, took out her Browning. She opened the door a few inches, then threw it wide. Keith Kent strolled in.

'Warm in here,' he remarked, taking off his overcoat. 'Don't go out. You'll freeze to death.' He smiled at Paula. 'Normally the service here is first rate. I get a cup of steaming coffee.'

Paula went to the largest table, felt the silver pot, took her hand away quickly. One of the staff must have brought up a fresh pot with new cups when they had seen Tweed return. The service at the Three Kings *was* first rate. They had noticed the amount of coffee Tweed consumed. She poured a cup for their guest.

'Thanks.' Kent had sat down. He drank half the cup. 'Makes really good central heating. Now, what can I do for you?'

'These mean anything to you, Keith?' Tweed asked.

He handed him the two British banknotes. Kent felt them with his sensitive fingers. Standing up, he took them over to the window, held them up to the light. Returning to the couch, he sat down, took an eyeglass from his pocket, screwed it into his right eye, examined the banknotes again. Then he removed the eyeglass, put it back in his pocket.

'I'm sorry, Keith,' Tweed said, 'but we do have to leave here in about three minutes.'

'That's all right. Where did you get these?'

'Can't tell you that. Does it matter?'

'Not really.' He drank more coffee. 'I just wondered.'

'Have you any comment?' Tweed persisted.

'Yes. They're fakes. Paper they're printed on seems OK. Can't imagine how whoever printed them got hold of it. But they are quite definitely forgeries. Some of the best I've seen. But they do have an error.'

'Would it be spotted by a bank teller?'

'Yes. Especially if someone walked into a British bank with a wad of them. As the teller riffled through them the error would jump out at him. If a lot of these were in circulation they'd be detected very quickly. Good as they are.'

'Thank you. It's a breakthrough. Keith, would you mind moving from the Hilton to this hotel? They're more than half empty. Time of the year.'

'I'll go and collect my things now.'

'Thank you again.' Tweed was putting on his coat, picking up the canvas holdall. 'We have to rush now. Book yourself a room here on your way out. Get one overlooking the Rhine, if you can.'

'All mod. cons. I do like the life of luxury,' Kent said.

27

They were transported in unmarked police cars from headquarters to the far side of the river. The route took them over the bridge Tweed could see when he looked right – upstream – from his bedroom window. Beck drove the first car with Tweed sitting next to him, nursing the canvas holdall in his lap. In the rear sat Paula and Newman. The others were in a similar car following behind them.

'The *Minotaur* will come downriver on this side,' Beck explained. 'I've had a report from my officer watching the vessel that a number of people in cars drove into the yard, then when they came out they only had the driver in each vehicle. So the party is aboard.'

'Did your officer wait – to see if those cars returned?' Tweed asked.

'No, he didn't. Why would the cars return so quickly?'

'I just wondered.'

A strong wind had blown up suddenly. Crossing the bridge, Paula noticed wavelets ruffling the surface of the Rhine. She hoped the tablet she had given Tweed would work. It was likely to be choppy aboard a launch. Added to the wind, an army of low dark clouds swept over the city, creating a heavy pall. Beck had driven into the city on the other bank and then turned right along a course parallel to the river.

'You have your own launch, as requested,' he told Tweed. 'I am in the big one brought out of the boat shed. There will be three other launches, packed with my men. One of them has boarding equipment – just in case we meet resistance when I order the *Minotaur* to heave to. I shall do that further downriver, near the harbour.'

'I have a loudhailer here. If I order all launches to speed away from the barge they must do so very quickly.'

'What would cause you to do that?' Beck asked in surprise.

'An emergency. A dangerous one.'

'If you say so. You usually know what you're doing. All launches have wireless communication, but the skipper of each one also has a mobile phone, as I have.'

'If it comes to it, use the mobile. It will be quicker.'

'I should have checked earlier. You do have someone experienced in handling a high-powered launch?'

'Two,' Tweed replied. 'Newman and Marler.'

'We have cordoned off a section of the riverfront with police tape,' Beck went on. 'To keep the public away from where our launches are assembled.'

'You seem to have thought of everything.'

'I believed so – until you made your remark about your loudhailer. I expect this to be a straightforward operation. We shall arrest everyone on board, saying we have been tipped off that the barge is carrying drugs. They'll wave their diplomatic passports, particularly if Ronstadt is aboard. I'll say I think they are producing phoney documentation and have to check with their authorities. Ronstadt will think I mean their Berne Embassy, but in due course I'll contact Washington. Meantime we interrogate the passengers.'

'You've thought it out well. Have you had a complaint from the Berne Embassy?'

'Not a cheep, as I think you sometimes say. Obviously he was bluffing. Rather a giveaway.'

'It's after 4 p.m.,' Tweed said. 'If they stick to their timetable the *Minotaur* is coming.'

'And here we are at the landing stage.'

*

266

To Paula's surprise Tweed hurried aboard the large launch allocated to them. He then made his way to the bow, one hand holding on to the gunwale, the other gripping the loudhailer.

Even while berthed at the landing stage the launch was swaying. The motion seemed to have no effect on him. He gazed back upriver for his first sight of the barge. The other four launches, crammed with police, were waiting to take off.

Beck's very large launch had a bridge at a higher level. The word *Polizei* appeared on its sides and stern. Above the bridge was mounted a large searchlight and a prominent horn. Beck came back from his vessel to Tweed's launch.

'The plan is to let the *Minotaur* pass us, then we go after it when it has gone under the bridge. The current is flowing stongly, so you may be surprised how quickly it will reach the bridge. Good luck . . .'

The wind cut through Paula's coat like a knife. She was hoping the barge would appear soon. Then one of the policemen from Beck's launch appeared, carrying an armful of oilskins. Handing them to Newman, who had been experimenting with the engine, he called out above the wind.

'All of you put these on. Extra warmth. Stop you getting soaked.'

'Thanks a lot,' said Newman.

'This is better,' said Paula, putting the oilskin over her coat.

Tweed sat down to put on his oilskin, then immediately stood up again. There were no other craft on the Rhine and no public to gawk at them from behind the distant tape. The weather had kept them indoors.

'Here she comes,' Tweed called out.

Round a bend in the river a massive barge loomed

into view. The conversion to a passenger craft had been extensive. Huge portholes like giant eyes had been cut out of the hull. Tweed noticed that curtains were closed across all of them. Behind each one a light glowed.

'They've got music,' he called out.

'Didn't expect this,' Paula responded.

'Well, it's supposed to be a pleasure craft,' Newman remarked as he turned off the engine.

He had been surprised at the power it generated. These launches could really move, he decided. The strains of the 'Blue Danube' waltz grew louder. Hardly appropriate for the Rhine, Paula was thinking. There was no sign of anyone on board, but she wouldn't expect passengers to be flaunting themselves on deck in weather like this.

'I can see the helmsman,' Tweed called out. 'In the cabin at the stern.'

'Appears to be by himself,' Marler commented.

'Only takes one man to hold the wheel,' Newman told him.

None of the launches had started their engines. Tweed guessed that Beck had ordered them to maintain silence until the huge barge had passed them. He wouldn't want to alert the people on board to his flotilla waiting to pounce.

Even though she was wearing her gloves Paula's hands were beginning to chill. Butler and Nield, standing up, were slapping their arms vigorously round their bodies. Despite the cold, Paula sensed an air of tension, of suppressed excitement aboard their launch. They were within a few minutes of rounding up the whole American gang which had descended on Basle.

Coming closer and closer, the barge seemed even more enormous than she had expected. Its bow wave swept out like a minor tidal wave, causing their launches to rock madly when it reached them. Tweed remained standing up, still gripping the gunwale, staring fixedly at the monster.

As far as Paula could tell, he seemed focused on the shadowy silhouette of the burly helmsman inside his cabin. He was standing stock-still, his hands moving the wheel slightly for a moment. He never glanced to port or starboard. His whole concentration was ahead, on the bridge where he would soon pass through one of the large arches.

Beck, inside his own bridge, was equally motionless. He did not give the barge a glance as its immense hull started to sweep past. The *Minotaur* was so long it seemed to take ages to pass them, even though travelling at speed with the current. There were a number of dinghies, powered by outboard motors, on the main deck. A poor substitute for lifeboats, Paula was thinking.

Eventually the stern of the *Minotaur* loomed above them and the vessel approached the arch under the bridge. Paula saw Tweed had put his loudhailer down at his feet, and was now using a pair of binoculars to scan the barge. As far as she could tell, he was focused on the cabin and the helmsman inside.

The barge passed under the bridge, was now opposite the Three Kings. It struck her that anyone sitting by the windows at the rear of the lobby would have a ringside view. Beck was still erect and still as a statue, his eyes glued to the receding barge. Once he glanced at his watch. Paula guessed he had estimated the barge's speed, was waiting for it to reach a certain point on the river.

Looking back onshore, she noticed the cars which had brought them had disappeared. She wondered where they would eventually land. Then she remembered Beck had said something about ordering the barge to heave to

269

further downriver, near the harbour. Maybe the cars had been driven there, waiting to pick them up as passengers again.

The stern of the barge had vanished from sight. Surely Beck was cutting the timing a bit fine? As though he had read her mind, he raised his right hand, held it aloft, staring at his wristwatch. The engines of the launches burst into action, but remained at the landing stage. Then Beck dropped his hand.

The launch he was aboard moved off when one of his men freed the rope holding it to a bollard. Marler unleashed them in the same way and they sped out on to the Rhine. Paula noticed that the strong current was giving them extra speed. Tweed, the binoculars dropped from a loop round his neck, the loudhailer gripped in his hand, turned to shout at Newman, who was gripping the wheel.

'Bob! Get ahead of Beck. Get this damned launch moving!'

'Doesn't expect much, does he?' Newman said to Marler.

He opened full throttle and the launch soared forward while Tweed gripped the gunwale with both hands. They were skimming over the waves as Beck passed under the bridge. Newman was still behind him as their launch sped through the arch under the bridge. In the distance Paula could see the *Minotaur* again. The barge was about to pass under another bridge. Tweed again turned round to shout a fresh order at Newman.

'Keep us as close to the shore as you safely can. Do get a move on!'

'What does he think I'm doing!' Newman snapped to Marler. 'Paddling across the Serpentine?'

He changed course to obey Tweed's command. Paula couldn't understand what Tweed was up to. Beck's craft was in the middle of the Rhine – or as close as he could be without leaving the official channel for vessels moving downstream. Paula was so intent on watching what was happening ahead she forgot to glance at the Three Kings as they passed it.

Newman was coaxing an extra burst of speed out of his engine after changing course, which had lost him a few seconds. Seated, as everyone else was, except Tweed and Newman, Paula looked back quickly. The other police launches were racing close behind them. It was then that she remembered Newman had once taken part in a powerboat race off Cannes. Up against some well-known names, he had won the race.

Beck's launch passed under the second bridge. Newman, with a determined look on his face, roared through the arch, was now almost alongside Beck with a safe distance between the two craft. Beck was waving him back but Newman thundered on, inched his way ahead. Paula, who had been gazing back at Newman, turned to face the way they were going and was taken aback when she saw how close they were to the *Minotaur*, passing a well-known pharmaceutical firm's headquarters on the opposite bank.

Now they were a short distance ahead of Beck. In the bow Tweed was hanging on to the gunwale with one hand. With the other he had the binoculars pressed against his eyes. He saw the helmsman leave his cabin, throw overboard a dinghy attached to the barge with a tow rope. He followed this by throwing over the side a rope ladder, was starting to descend it when Tweed dropped his binoculars, snatched up the loud-hailer.

'Everyone get away from that barge. Move away at top speed as far as you can. MOVE!'

'*Flee for your lives . . .!*'

To Paula, his thunderous commands reminded her of

271

recordings she had heard of Churchill speaking. The moment he began his warning she saw Beck using his mobile. The helmsman from the barge had landed in his dinghy, cut the rope linking him to the barge, started his outboard, moving towards the shore.

'Hang on like grim death!' shouted Newman.

Paula, one hand already holding the gunwale, used the other to grip the underside of the plank she was sitting on. She leaned back. Newman swung his wheel hard over. The launch swung in a violent U-turn, so fast, so suddenly, Paula knew they were going to capsize. For the first time Tweed had sat down, had both hands gripping the gunwale.

The launch swung over at an angle of almost forty-five degrees. Vaguely, as in a film speeded up, Paula saw Beck's craft heading back upstream. The other police launches were also swinging round, speeding away. She shook her head to clear her vision, looked back, froze, still looking back.

The *Minotaur* exploded like a giant bomb. The *boom!* echoed down the Rhine. A huge piece of the hull rock-eted across the water, struck a large craft anchored to a buoy near the opposite shore. The craft, fortunately empty, disappeared altogether. Another section of the hull broke off, elevated high above the river, then plunged downwards, landing in the river at the very point where Newman's launch had been. It plunged below the surface. Half the stern broke away, skidded across the water, dived out of sight where Beck's launch had been a few seconds earlier.

Newman had just successfully completed his manoeuvre, was racing upriver in the wrong channel, when the shock wave from the explosion hit them. Like a blast of hot air from a furnace it hit their launch when it had just stabilized. They were rocked from side to side but Newman continued speeding them away from the

272

inferno. The other police launches had escaped certain destruction.

Paula's teeth were chattering – whether from fright or the cold she wasn't sure. Then Beck's calm voice was carried over the water through his loudhailer.

'Everyone follow me. I'm taking you in to a landing stage.'

'I could do with a bit of *terra firma* under my feet,' called out Tweed, his voice as calm as Beck's.

When they climbed, stiff-legged, out of the launch, Beck's craft was already moored to the other side. As he walked across to speak to Tweed Paula looked back down the Rhine. From what remained of the wrecked barge flames were blazing upwards, a glare in the near-dark. Fire-boats, which had appeared from nowhere, were directing great jets of water from hoses onto the fire.

'What about the passengers?' she asked.

'There weren't any,' Tweed told her. 'Otherwise we'd have seen at least a few of them on deck. Only the helmsman was aboard. I think he fixed the wheel to keep the barge on course before he escaped in his outboard. I caught a glimpse of him diving into a waiting car after he'd reached the shore. The bomb, I feel sure, was detonated from a distance by radio – once the helmsman got clear.'

'You expected something like this?' demanded Beck grimly.

'I didn't know what to expect – whether, in fact, to expect anything. I was just suspicious of the way the information reached us.'

'You can see your cars have arrived. I called them on my mobile. We'll drive you back to your hotel. Paula, are you in shock?'

'No. But thank you for asking. What I do need is a cup of something hot to drink.'

'You'll get that at the hotel. Tweed, I'll want to talk to you later,' Beck snapped.

28

Arriving back at the Three Kings, they climbed out of the two unmarked police cars. Tweed bent down to speak to Beck, behind the wheel, through his open window. The second car deposited Marler, Butler and Nield, who waited.

'Thank you for the lift,' Tweed said. 'I'm sorry it turned out to be such a grim fiasco.'

'We'll talk later,' Beck replied abruptly.

Newman was the last to enter the hotel. He had hung around outside, on the lookout for hostile watchers. There didn't seem to be any. He went inside and bumped into Basil Windermere, as always smartly turned out. He wore a new camelhair coat.

'How are you, Bob?' he began. 'Just the chap I was hoping to meet. Tell you what, we'll go into the bar, have a drink and a chinwag.'

It was on the tip of Newman's tongue to refuse. But he was startled to see Windermere in Basle. Tweed had not had time to tell him of the presence of Rupert and Windermere. He decided he'd better find out what was going on. Reluctantly, he agreed. They took off their coats on the way to the bar, which was beyond two restaurants adjoining each other.

'What are you having to celebrate?' Windermere enquired.

They were sitting in two comfortable seats uphol-stered in red leather. No one else was in the bar except for an attractive blonde waitress, who immediately came to them. Windermere looked her up and down appreciatively. Newman sensed the girl did not like the way he looked at her.

'I'll have a double Scotch,' he said.

After what's just happened I think I need it, he was thinking. And I'm not staying here a moment longer than I have to. Not with this piece of rubbish.

'Cheers! To eternal friendship, my dear chap,' said Windermere, raising his glass.

'What are we celebrating?' Newman asked without enthusiasm.

'The fact that we're together again, of course. I must say you're looking chipper.'

'Why are you here?'

'Just like the old Newman, foreign correspondent *extraordinaire*.' Windermere gave a saturnine smile. Newman realized he'd never before noticed how like a handsome fox the playboy was. A smile which probably had rich dowagers swooning. 'Always digging for info,' Windermere went on.

'You haven't answered my question. Why?'

'To keep dear Rupert company, of course.'

'Rupert is in Basle?'

'Ectually, like me, he has a room in this hotel. Sir Guy also is here.'

'I get it. He's paying for you both.'

'You could be a little more diplomatic at times, Bob.'

'When it's staring me in the face, I tell the truth.'

'See you've finished your drink.' Windermere summoned the waitress. 'Same again?'

'I'll have a single this time, thank you.'

'You know, Bob,' Windermere remarked when they were alone, 'at times life can be hard. A chap doesn't know where the next penny is coming from.'

Windermere was wearing a new blue Armani suit, an

expensive starched white shirt, a Valentino tie. He sat with his long legs sprawled out, crossed at the ankles. His feet were clad in handmade shoes.

'From the way you're dressed I'd say you were doing all right.'

'Ah! Appearances can be deceptive.' He placed a finger along the side of his Roman nose. 'Not a word to Betty. At the moment I haven't a bean. Thought you might help me out. Twenty thousand pounds would help me to get by. Just as a loan,' he added hastily. 'Pay you back as soon as I get on my feet.'

'I know. This year. Next year. Sometime. Never.'

'You know you could afford it – never even notice a difference in your bank balance. You did write that book – world bestseller. *Kruger: The Computer That Failed.* Must have made you independent financially for life.'

The book had done just that for Newman. He had no intention of confirming the fact to Windermere. He finished his drink, turned in his chair to face Windermere.

'Basil, I never borrow, I never lend. A maxim you might like to think about.'

The waitress had placed the bill on the table. It was left there for Windermere to sign. His expression turned ugly. He lifted his glass, drank the contents quickly, hammered down the glass.

'I thought you'd get me out of a hole. I've got back rent due on my flat . . .'

'You will live just off Regent Street. Move to Clapham.'

'You know I couldn't possibly receive my friends in Clapham . . .'

'Your rich widows. Ever thought of getting a proper job?'

'If you don't mind my saying so,' Windermere said with an edge to his voice, 'I don't too much care for what you're saying.'

'It's not an ideal world, Basil.'

Newman stood up to leave. Windermere caught him by the sleeve. The smile was a memory. Newman was surprised at how vicious Windermere looked.

'You've forgotten the tab,' he said, pointing to the bill.

'And you've forgotten you invited me to have a drink.'

Without waiting for a response he left the bar. On his way up in the lift to his room Newman had a thoughtful expression. He was recalling his conversation with Basil Windermere. He was also remembering the vicious expression which had crossed Windermere's face at one moment. It didn't fit in with his previous impression of a playboy who preyed on rich woman. He'd have to see Tweed a little later.

Tweed was alone in his room. He had taken his time having a hot bath, changing into fresh clothes. His mind was racing round in three or four different directions. He was just about to call Newman, Marler and Paula when the phone rang. To his surprise the hotel operator told him Beck was waiting downstairs to see him.

'Please ask him to come straight up . . .'

It was a solemn-faced Beck who entered. He accepted Tweed's invitation to sit down, refused his offer of coffee. Crossing his legs, he sat quite still, as though gathering his thoughts, or wasn't sure how to start. Tweed sat opposite him and waited.

'That was a grim business,' Beck began. 'Fortunately there were no casualties, which was a miracle.'

'You know what it was all about? A determined attempt to wipe out me and my team at one blow. I doubt if you would have survived.'

'I'd worked that out for myself. I've just had a stormy

277

phone conversation with Jake Ronstadt. I called him. I told him what had happened, that I was just about to report the incident to Washington – together with the fact that five of the men staying with him had been killed in Basle, that all were found to carry weapons. He didn't like it at all.'

'What was his reaction?'

'Oh, what I expected. Raved on, saying it was nothing to do with him, that he had diplomatic status. I interrupted him, said that after I had spoken to Washington I would want to see him here at police headquarters. He erupted.'

'In what way?'

'He said he'd not stand any longer being harassed by Swiss police. In any case, he was leaving Switzerland for good during the next two or three days. And he'd be taking his staff with him. Then he slammed the phone down.'

'So you got what you wanted.' Tweed smiled ruefully. 'What you are after.'

'I'm not sure I understand you.'

'Arthur, you understand me only too well. Your phone call was intended to drive Ronstadt and his men out of the country. And you succeeded.'

'I must admit I'm sick and tired of the violence the Americans are causing.'

'And,' Tweed said quietly, 'you'll be glad to see the back of us.'

'I don't remember saying that.'

'Because you're tactful. But you know when Ronstadt and Co. do leave – probably to Germany – we'll go after them.'

'My job is to protect Swiss civilians,' Beck admitted. 'Luckily, so far there haven't been any casualties among our people. But if what has happened continues, then it's only a matter of time.'

278

'I think you're absolutely right. You said Ronstadt told you he would be leaving in two or three days. I think he may slip away tomorrow.'

'I'm still keeping officers on watch at the exit to autobahn 5. When Ronstadt and his thugs do move they'll be detained at the border; as I said before, on the pretext that we suspect they're smuggling drugs. Then I'll inform you, give you time to get there and track them.'

'For that, I'm very grateful. Over the years you have always been a reliable ally.'

'That has worked both ways. I'd better go now. You take care of yourself.' Standing up he took a compact mobile phone out of his pocket, placed it on a table close to Tweed. 'I know you mistrust these things, but it will let me contact you urgently – wherever you may be at the time. Incidentally, I think Ronstadt is tricky. Don't overlook the possibility he might leave in the middle of the night . . .'

When Beck had gone Tweed used the phone to summon everyone to his room. Paula arrived first, followed almost immediately by Newman, Marler, Butler and Nield. Tweed had also ordered three pots of coffee and cups for seven people. Afterwards he had called Keith Kent and asked him to come and see him.

Tweed was standing by the window, hands behind his back as he gazed into the night. It was a stance Paula recognized – he had at times done the same thing at Park Crescent when he was working out a problem.

'Coffee!' she called out with enthusiasm. 'How about the rest of you?' she asked when they had all arrived. 'Put a hand up if you want a cuppa.'

Six hands rose in the air. She started pouring as they found somewhere to sit or perch. Keith Kent looked round, saw he had met everyone present in London, clasped both hands and made a shaking motion. Unusually, it was Marler who spoke first.

'Tweed, when we reached safety on the landing stage, I heard you say to Beck that you were suspicious of the way the information reached us. You were referring to the earlier news that Ronstadt and his gang would be holding a meeting aboard the *Minotaur*. So you had to be talking about what Denise Chatel told me.'

'I was,' Tweed agreed.

'You think she made up the story?'

'I'm not sure. But it all seemed rather neat. Denise being called by an unknown American. Then told that Sharon wanted to meet her at the bar in the Euler.'

'So we can't trust her?' Marler remarked, now leaning against a wall.

'We can't trust anyone,' Tweed said emphatically.

'I have good news for you,' Newman said ironically. 'Dear Rupert is here. Staying at this hotel.'

'I know,' Tweed replied. 'Sir Guy told me.'

'And he has his pal Basil with him,' Newman went on. 'Also staying in this hotel. I had a drink with Basil, the ladies' dream. You'll never guess what he wanted to cadge off me . . .'

He relayed what had happened in the bar. He abbreviated their conversation but gave them the flavour of it. Paula gasped.

'Twenty thousand pounds! The nerve of the pimp.'

'He wasn't best pleased,' Newman told her, 'when I told him to go jump in the Rhine, or words to that effect. I was surprised at how ugly he turned.'

'Must be desperate,' Paula commented.

'Desperate men are dangerous,' Tweed mused. 'What I can't understand is how Guy found out we were here. And he wasn't prepared to tell me.'

'Could Ronstadt have told him?' Nield wondered. 'It

stands out like a sore thumb that Ronstadt has known we are here for a while.'

'Why would he do that?' asked the normally taciturn Butler.

'Possibly to confuse me,' Tweed suggested. 'Have me looking in all directions so I'd miss something obvious.'

'That would mean Strangeways is one of them,' objected Butler.

'I did say a few minutes ago we can't trust anyone,' Tweed reminded him.

'Not even Denise Chatel,' said Marler.

'Beck has been over here to see me,' Tweed began. He told them everything the Swiss police chief had said. 'So if he's right,' he concluded, 'we had better be ready to leave at any time. Better get some packing done when you leave here.'

'You still think it's the Black Forest?' Newman queried.

'You should know. Kurt's last word was Schwarz, which, as I remarked earlier, is German for black. If I had to gamble I'd say it will be the Black Forest.'

The phone rang, Paula answered, told Tweed Beck was on the line for him.

'Yes, Arthur . . .'

'Just heard a weather report. Thought you ought to know there's been a heavy fall of snow in the Black Forest. More on the way. Unusual for this time of year, but occasionally it does happen. Excuse me now, I'm up to my neck in work.'

Tweed put down the phone. He told them what Beck had said. Paula sighed.

'Just what we needed. If I have time I'm going to shop for warmer boots.'

'Incidentally, Keith,' Tweed said, 'I'd appreciate it if you would come with us when we leave here.'

'Go to Singapore as long as you pay me. If you don't need me I'd better go and start packing.'

'Good idea.'

'What sort of game do you think Strangeways is playing?' Newman asked when Kent had gone.

'I wish I knew,' replied Tweed. 'But I'll tell you one thing. As soon as I can I'm going to make him tell me how he knew we were here. I think I can get it out of him. He's in a highly nervous state. When I went into the writing room the hand holding his pen was trembling. Then later he started fiddling with it.'

'I think,' said Newman, standing up, 'we'd all better get back to our rooms and start packing. Beck could be right. Ronstadt might try and do a moonlight flit.'

Paula waited when everyone except Tweed had gone. She was curled up like a cat in an armchair. Tweed refilled her cup before he spoke.

'You have something on your mind.'

'Yes. Don't worry about my being ready if we have to leave at a moment's notice. I'm half-packed already.'

'Knowing how methodical you are, I thought you might be. Now, what's bothering you?'

'Not bothering. I admit it's sheer curiosity. But why is Keith Kent coming with us when we leave?'

'I told you in the car on our way to the launch what he had said.' Tweed produced an envelope, took out the two banknotes, a British twenty-pound note, a ten-pound note. 'Fakes. Good ones. They really worry me.'

'Why?'

'Remember that letter from the dead, as Marler called it – from Kurt Schwarz? The wording was brief. *Be very careful of the barges.* At Park Crescent I thought he was referring to Thames barges. When we arrived here and I saw barges on the Rhine I began to think they were what Kurt had referred to. We now know it was. We'll never know how he suspected what might happen.'

'But he was right. So what about the banknotes?'

'The second sentence in Kurt's letter said: *You must locate the printing presses.* So what prints banknotes? Printing presses. I think Washington has devised a diabolical plan to destabilize Britain. There may not be much time to stop them. And I think the secret lies at their base in the Black Forest.'

29

Tweed received the invitation soon after Paula had left him. When he picked up the phone it was Sharon Mandeville. He remarked he hadn't seen much of her since arriving in Basle.

'Well, some people would say that's your fault,' she chided him gently in her soft voice. 'You stood me up for drinks.'

'I was about to apologize for that. Something I couldn't ignore turned up. And I had to rush out.'

'You're forgiven. I'm calling you because I thought it might be nice if you and Bob Newman had dinner with me this evening. Here at the hotel, if that suits you.'

'Suits me down to the ground. What time?'

'Would eight o'clock be all right? Maybe afterwards we could all adjourn to the bar.'

'Sounds like a great programme. I could phone Bob Newman to save you the time.'

'Would you? I'm about to dash out to see my Swiss couple again. They're getting wearing, but I agreed to go. See you tonight . . .'

Instead of phoning Newman, Tweed called him to ask him to come to his room. He was staring out of the window when Newman arrived. Then he told him about the invitation.

'I hope you don't mind,' he said, 'but I accepted on your behalf.'

'I'm glad you did. I'm just wondering what she's up to.'

'She sounded a bit fed up. I got the impression she's in need of some company. I'm hoping to lever information out of her.'

'What could she possibly tell us?'

'Maybe something she's observed while at the Embassy in London. Now, I'm popping down to the reception desk. There's something I want to ask whichever girl is on duty.'

'I'll continue with my packing, then.'

'Hurry. As I told you, Beck phoned to say there's been a heavy fall of snow in the Black Forest, with more to come.'

'In that case we're going to need cars with snow tyres. I'll call in on Marler to give him the good news. He won't find a car hire place open now, but he can organize things in the morning. We'll just have to hope Ronstadt and Co. don't leave tonight. Oh, what time is the dinner?'

'I should have told you. Eight o'clock in the main restaurant downstairs. Don't forget to put on your best suit for Sharon . . .'

Tweed walked down the wide flight of stairs instead of taking the lift. The lobby was empty. No one was sitting at any of the tables overlooking the Rhine. He smiled at the receptionist, kept his voice quiet.

'I expect you've heard about the barge disaster near the harbour?'

'Yes, sir. Everyone is talking about it. Apparently it exploded but I heard no one was hurt.'

'That's right. No one was. And the trouble was one of the boilers blew up.'

'Oh, that is what caused it.' Tweed guessed that at the earliest opportunity she would pass his fictitious explanation down the grapevine. Which would soften rumours. 'Anyone sitting by the windows over there must have seen it pass,' he suggested.

'Two guests did. One was Ms Mandeville. She was sitting by herself at the corner table when the barge passed us. Then there was Mr Osborne, sitting in a chair near the restaurant. Both of them had binoculars. We all heard the sound of the explosion – of the boiler blowing up. It's never happened before. Someone's coming,' she ended in a whisper.

'Hi, there, Tweed!' Osborne's very American voice boomed behind him. 'Been lookin' for you, feller.' A strong hand grasped his arm. 'Time we had a drink together. Mebbe more than one. Nobody over by those windows.'

'I haven't a lot of time,' Tweed warned.

'Always time for a drink – or two.'

Osborne guided Tweed to the corner table he had sat at before. He boomed across to the receptionist.

'Send a waiter, would you? Toot sweet, as the French say.'

'They do speak excellent English,' Tweed remarked as they sat at a table next to a window.

'Guess I like to try out my foreign languages. When in Rome . . .'

'I'll have a glass of French white wine, medium dry,' Tweed ordered as a waiter appeared swiftly.

'You ain't got Bourbon. Don't know why,' Osborne complained. 'I guess I'll settle for a double Scotch on the rocks.'

'You know about the barge which blew up?' Tweed enquired.

'Sure. No bodybags needed, so I heard.'

'Ed, why are you here in Basle?'

'*Ed.* That's better, much better. Why am I in this weird town? Embassy sent me to check on a Swiss PR firm. See if they know their stuff. I guess they're OK. We might pick up their key people. Take them to New York. Boy, here are the drinks. Your good health, Tweed.'

'Yours too.'

'Now the job's done, guess I may soon move on. To Freiburg – near the Black Forest. They tell me there's a nice place there. Hotel Schwarzwälder Hof. Some street called Konvikstrasse. I like that. Convict Street.' Osborne gave a belly laugh. 'Just the place for me.'

'When are you thinking of going there?'

'Haven't decided.' He paused. 'Could be in the next few days.'

Osborne shifted his large bulk. His chair creaked under the weight imposed on it. He was wearing a cream jacket with orange stripes, pale yellow slacks and a white shirt with a flashy tie. His outfit struck Tweed as loud, the kind he'd seen in California.

'What made you choose this hotel?' Tweed asked.

'There's an interesting story behind that.' Osborne had lowered his voice. 'Back at the Embassy in London I hear Sharon is also comin' to Basle. So I ask her where she's stayin' and – without much enthusiasm – she tells me about this place. Thought I'd have a bit of company. I can be a naive guy. Hardly seen sight or heard sound of her since I got here. That's the way it goes.'

'Do you mind if I ask what exactly is your job?'

They were both talking quietly now. Osborne took out a cigar case, offered it to Tweed, who refused. The American took his time clipping off the end, lighting it with a match, moving it round the exposed tip.

'I'm forming a propaganda outfit,' he said. 'A team

of spin doctors and all that crap you have in Britain at the moment. I guess the purpose is to fool the voters, brainwash 'em, repeat the same line over and over again. Sounds like Dr Goebbels, doesn't it? Smells like him.'

'This outfit is for Washington?'

'Sure.' Osborne turned to Tweed, smiled drily. 'Where else?'

'Wasn't it Abraham Lincoln who said you can't fool all the people all the time? Something like that.'

'It was.'

'You like doing this?'

'Sure.' Again he smiled drily. 'It's a job. Until something else comes along.'

'Thank you for the drink,' Tweed said, getting up. 'Excuse me, I have work to do.'

'Let's have another drink tonight,' Osborne called after him.

Angled in his chair so he could see the whole lobby, Tweed had seen Denise Chatel emerge from the lift. She had walked into the writing room. At the same moment Paula was descending the flight of stairs behind him. Tweed walked to the writing room door, opened it and Denise swung round in her chair in front of a desk as he shut it. Her expression was startled, uncertain. Tweed wondered whether the psychiatrist who had said she was highly strung was right.

'If I'm disturbing you I'll leave,' he said.

'Of course you're not. Please sit down,' she said stiffly.

She was tense, almost had a hunted look on her attractive face. He sat in a chair close to hers, smiled.

'How are you getting on? That file in front of you isn't more work, I hope.'

'Yes, it is – a whole load of work I have to finish

287

before I have dinner.' She was rattling out the words. 'Sometimes I've got the impression Sharon invents work to keep me busy. Don't tell her I said that, will you?'

'Of course not. Tell her you're tired, that you need a break.'

'She doesn't believe in breaks. She never stops working herself. Even going out to see someone she takes a file with her so she can work on it while she's in the car. She always has a driver to take her round. She's a fanatic for work. The ultimate career woman.' She was rattling on again. 'At times I admire her incredible drive. She gets by on hardly any sleep.'

'Have you talked to anyone this afternoon? To give yourself a bit of variety?'

'I've chatted to quite a few of the staff, including the duty manager. They're very sociable here. I think they've noticed I'm on my own a lot.'

'Have you seen Marler this afternoon?'

'Only briefly. I passed him in the hall on my way to my room.'

'Well, I've given you a little break.' He smiled again. 'But I think I'm interrupting your work.'

'I should get on if I'm to get through it.'

'Don't push yourself too hard. I'll leave you to it.'

He was walking back upstairs to his room when he met Marler on his way down. They were alone on the staircase and no one was within hearing distance.

'Marler, I gather you saw Denise briefly after we'd got back from the barge disaster.'

'Briefly is the word. She just said, "Hello, there," and kept on walking to the lift. Struck me she was pretty busy.'

'I'm sure you're right. No luck with cars equipped with snow tyres at this time of day, I imagine.'

'I did get lucky. I phoned the hire people who had cars waiting for us at the airport. They were just closing.

I managed to persuade them to deliver cars with snow tyres – a couple of white Audis. They're in the garage here. They took the other cars back.'

'So we can leave at any time. That might be soon. Good work, Marler.'

Tweed continued on up to his room, thinking. His thoughts disturbed him. Denise had warned Marler about the supposed meeting aboard the *Minotaur*. Denise had talked to staff inside the hotel since they'd got back from the Rhine. It was obvious their main topic of conversation was the explosion aboard the huge barge. Denise had since met Marler briefly. *Yet Denise had made no mention of the barge to Marler – or to himself.*

30

At about seven in the evening Paula was wandering around the hotel on her own. She wanted to see what, if anything, was going on.

'There are two hostile elements in this place,' she said to herself. 'Ed Osborne and Denise Chatel. On someone's instructions – maybe Ronstadt's – Denise made up that story about a so-called meeting on the *Minotaur* to lure us into the trap. When the barge exploded we'd all be killed.'

She had descended from the second floor and started walking down the corridor on the first floor. Suddenly a door further along opened, Denise came out of Tweed's room, turned to say something and closed the door. She walked towards Paula with a blank look. Then she walked straight past her as though she didn't exist.

'What the hell's going on now?' Paula said to herself.

The hotel was strangely quiet and there was no one

else about. She continued prowling. Downstairs there was no one in the lobby and the restaurant wasn't open yet. She opened the door to the writing room, peered inside. No one there. She went back upstairs to see Tweed.

For a moment she thought the same scene was being replayed – like a film turned back and then run forward again. The door to Tweed's room opened, Sharon came out, turned to say something, then closed it. She began to walk in her elegant way towards Paula.

'Just the person I was hoping to see,' Sharon greeted her with a warm smile as she stopped. 'I'm organizing a small dinner in the restaurant here this evening. Bob Newman and Tweed have agreed to be my guests. I'd like you to be there.'

'Well . . .'

'Don't think about it, just say yes.' Sharon smiled more radiantly, her green eyes holding Paula's. 'Take pity on me. One woman and two men doesn't work. I'll be outgunned. You can give me moral support. Please!'

'I'd love to come. Thank you so much.'

'Eight o'clock. In the main restaurant – not the Brasserie next door to it.'

'I'll be there.'

Paula watched her walk away. Sharon almost glided, her figure erect, the waves of blonde hair just touching the top of her shoulders. Then she was gone. Paula frowned, then remembered a friend who had told her she'd develop creases in her forehead. Turning round, she went to Tweed's door, tapped on it, he called out, 'Come in.'

'It's just me. I was passing so thought I'd see how you were.'

'I'm fine. You know I like to get ready for a meal in good time. A little while ago Sharon phoned me, invited

Bob and me to have dinner with her tonight. Here in the hotel, bless her – considering what it's like outside.'

He'd put on his best suit, a blue bird's-eye. Now, seated on a couch, he was bent over, buffing his shoes. He seemed very relaxed.

'I've just bumped into Sharon in the corridor,' she said, perching on the arm of the couch. 'She's invited me to join the dinner party. I accepted.'

'I'm glad. That makes us a foursome. You know something? Apart from Sharon's call a while ago that phone hasn't rung once. Peace and quiet. It seems a novelty.'

'I think I'd better go to my room and get changed. Competing with Sharon takes some doing.'

'Oh, I don't know. You always look so perfectly turned out.'

'Thank you, sir.'

She bent down, kissed him lightly on the cheek, then left as she checked her watch.

She'd had a bath earlier but decided she'd have a quick shower.

They kept it very warm in the hotel. She was on her way to the bathroom when she paused before a large wall mirror. She looked at her dark, glossy hair, her large blue-grey eyes, her thick brows, her well-shaped features, her good complexion.

'I'm a brunette, Sharon is a blonde,' she said aloud. 'What is it about that lady which makes her so striking? I'll study her over dinner. No! Admit it – you're an envious witch.'

There was a knock on the door. When she unlocked it Newman was standing outside. She invited him in with a smile. He had on his best suit and a brand-new tie she hadn't seen before, a Valentino. How *was* Sharon able to mesmerize such different men?

291

'I just called in to let you know Sharon has asked Tweed and me to dinner at the restaurant downstairs.'

'She's just asked me to join the party. I said I would.'

'That's great, really great. I was getting bothered you'd feel left out when you saw us.'

'That was nice of you, Bob. Now you can stop getting bothered.'

'I rather think you'll be changing, so I'm holding you up.'

'That's all right. But I was about to dive into the shower.'

'Then I'll leave you to it.'

'Bob, just before you go. Have you noticed Tweed often seems to know what's going on in the enemy's mind? Calls it his sixth sense.'

'Yes, I have.'

'Well, I think he has an agent inside the American camp.'

Newman headed for the ground floor after he'd left Paula. Unusually for him, he stopped for a moment to check his appearance in a mirror on the corridor wall. It was seeing Windermere's Valentino tie, when they had a drink in the bar, which had caused Newman to dig out his own new tie. He walked downstairs, looked in the lobby, wished he'd stayed in his room. Seated by himself at a table overlooking the river was Rupert Strangeways.

'I say, Newman, do trot over and join me for a drink. A chap gets lonely, don't you know.'

'And what brings you to Basle?' Newman asked as he sat down.

He had been told by Tweed what Sir Guy had said, but he wanted to see whether the stories of father and son tallied. Rupert waved a commanding hand.

'First things first. A waiter chappie is coming. What's your tipple?'

'I'll have a double Scotch, no ice.'

I'm going to need it to get through this, he thought. Rupert, heavily in debt, wore an expensive dark smoking jacket, a pair of dark trousers with a razor-edged crease, a crisp white shirt and a polka-dot bow tie. Newman had always mistrusted men who sported bow ties.

'Mine is a very dry martini, shaken, not stirred,' Rupert ordered with a dry smile. 'I was always a follower of James Bond,' he told Newman when the waiter had gone. 'Poor joke, I know. Maybe I'll sparkle after a few drinks.'

'I think I asked you what brings you to Basle.'

'You most certainly did. Amazing memory you have.' Rupert grinned. 'I'm not being sarcastic. Meant to be a joke. Not doing very well, am I?'

'You'll liven up. I'm listening.'

'Pater put on his military uniform, in a manner of speaking. Told me to come with him. The idea, I'm sure, was to keep me out of mischief. And here I was, waiting for a pair of gorgeous female legs to appear, and what happens? You turn up. Again, no offence meant.'

'None taken. I had a drink with Basil earlier. I suppose that he came along for the free ride.'

'You've got it.' Rupert snapped his fingers, grinned wolfishly. 'Literally.'

'I think I missed something there.'

'Pater's paying for all Basil's expenses, including the air ticket. The idea is I need someone to keep an eye on me. Basil was elected.'

'As a nursemaid,' Newman joked.

'Can't say I find that tremendously funny. Comes from being one of those reporter chappies, I suppose. They all develop a rather weird sense of humour. Of course you made a mint out of that huge bestselling book you wrote, *Kruger: The Computer That Failed*. I've met reporters who failed – ended up behind some crummy desk subediting other people's stories. On a clerk's pay.'

'So what are you going to do when you get back home?'

'I rather fancy the idea of becoming manager of a mutual fund.'

Newman could hardly believe his ears. He had never heard Rupert talk like this before. He'd always thought the prospect of doing a proper job had never occurred to him. That was for the peasants.

'I'm surprised,' he said.

'Thought you might be, old boy. Oh, is the divine Paula about?'

'Yes, she is.' Newman became wary. 'She's very booked up now. Tonight she's having dinner with a party of us. Think I'd better make a move.' Newman reached for the bill the waiter had left so he could sign it. 'I'll handle this.'

'No, you won't.' Rupert's hand grabbed the bill. 'I invited you for a drink.'

Newman got up to go. He had left the table when Rupert called out to him. He swung round and Rupert was smiling sardonically.

'Bob. Give my love to Paula when you see her . . .'

Jack Ronstadt sat at the head of the long table in his suite at the Euler. He was in a towering rage. He spoke very quietly, which alarmed everyone sitting with him. They knew when he was quiet it was a very bad sign.

'You bombed,' he began, using the American expression for falling flat on your face. 'First, four of our guys are blown to hell by a grenade. Second, Rick Sherman, sent to torture information out of the Irina

294

crone before he breaks her stupid neck, ends up with a knife in his throat.' He looked round at the tense faces. 'Any more contributions? What about you, Vernon?' he asked the thin man.

'Well, Chief . . .' Vernon cleared his throat. 'Guess you're talkin' about the barge.'

'You're goddamn right I am.' His fist crashed down on the table. 'I put you in charge of organizing what should have been the end of Tweed and his mob. What friggin' happens?'

'It kinda didn't work out . . .'

'*Kinda?*' Ronstadt was going full throttle now. 'Don't mess with me. It was a friggin' catastrophe.'

He bunched his fist. It moved so quickly no one saw what was coming. The large fist connected with Vernon's jaw. He fell over backwards, taking his chair with him, lay sprawled on the floor. Vernon kept his eyes lowered, concealing hatred welling up inside him. He clambered to his feet, lifted up the chair, resumed his place at the table.

Ronstadt's expression was passive, as if nothing had happened. He had hit his subordinate with only half his strength. If he had really hit him Vernon's jaw would have been broken – and he needed Vernon.

'So we move on,' he continued quietly. 'First thing tomorrow Vernon and Brad are turning in all our cars. They're gettin' vehicles with snow tyres for us. There's been a big snowfall in the Black Forest. My idea is we leave tomorrow night. I do mean in the middle of the night. We collect a big cargo waitin' at the base. It has to reach Britain very fast.' He smiled for the first time. 'Any questions?'

There was silence. No one felt like opening their mouths after witnessing the punishment meted out to Vernon. Ronstadt sighed. He started shuffling the pack of cards he'd picked up.

'Some smart guy might have asked, "What about weapons?"'

'What about weapons?' Vernon asked obediently.

'Vernon, you'se comin' on.' Ronstadt reached out a hand, grasped Vernon's shoulder, squeezed it in a friendly way. 'You'll make it yet. Tomorrow mornin' all weapons and explosives left are to be dumped in the Rhine. That officer at the checkpoint close to the autobahn is a nosy bastard. When we're on the way, across the border, a car from base will meet us with more weapons. Don't no one go to bed tonight. I may call another meeting middle of the night. After I've contacted Charlie, got the OK . . .'

Paula was ready early for the dinner. In her room she began thinking about Denise Chatel. It struck her Denise was lonely. She might be upset if she saw the dinner party to which she had not been invited. She picked up the phone, spoke to the operator.

'Could you put me through to Denise Chatel's room, please.'

'Sorry. I can't do that. Ms Chatel has checked out.'

'Checked out? What do you mean?'

'She asked me to have her car brought to the entrance about three-quarters of an hour ago. Then she checked out. Left the hotel.'

'Did she leave any forwarding address?'

'No, she didn't.'

'Thank you.'

Paula hurried along to Tweed's room. He opened the door and she waited until she had sat down. She was feeling stunned. Normally she was quick when it came to working out relationships between people. Now her mind was circling round at speed like a whirlpool.

'I've just heard that Denise Chatel has checked out of here,' she announced.

'When?' Tweed rapped out.

'Over three-quarters of an hour ago. Had her car brought to the entrance, then she was off.'

'Any idea where to?'

'None at all. She didn't leave a forwarding address. Tweed, I just don't know what's going on any more.'

'Have some more coffee . . .'

'No! I don't want any more coffee. I'm up to here with it. And I think you're drinking too much of the stuff. Caffeine sets your nerves on edge.'

Tweed sat down in a chair opposite her. As he poured himself another cup he glanced across at her, then concentrated on what he was doing. Sitting back, he sipped at his cup.

'I'm sorry,' said Paula. 'That outburst was very rude. Don't know what's got into me.'

'Too much coffee,' Tweed said with a smile. He put down his cup. 'Newman and Marler will be arriving in a minute. I want a word with them before our dinner. And I want to tell them while you're here. It's important you're fully in the picture. I'm not surprised you felt confused. So did I – until I realized certain people are feeding me with smokescreens. Verbal camouflage is a better description. They're trying to conceal from me who is who – and what is really about to happen.'

'I feel better. I thought it was me.'

She had just finished speaking when Newman and Marler came in. Paula decided to speak up first when she saw Marler. He stood against a wall, lit a king-size.

'Marler,' she said, 'Denise checked out of the hotel less than an hour ago. Drove off by herself . . .'

'What?'

It was rare to be able to gauge his reactions from his expression. Now he looked staggered, mystified.

297

'She didn't leave a forwarding address. So we have no idea where she's gone, why she left so suddenly, anything.'

'And she didn't say a word to me. Don't understand it.'

'There may be quite a simple explanation,' Tweed interjected. He looked at Marler. 'Paula, Bob and I are having dinner with Sharon downstairs this evening. I'd like everyone to leave this to me,' he warned. 'At a suitable moment I'll bring up the news about Denise. Incidentally, I shall be playing a power game, so don't be surprised when I say something odd to our hostess. My objective now is to disturb the enemy. I think I can use Sharon without her realizing it.'

'Shouldn't we pass on this strange business about Denise to Pete Nield and Harry Butler?' Marler suggested.

'I was going to ask you to do just that. At the moment they're testing out the new Audis with their snow tyres. I had an interesting chat, by the way, with Ed Osborne down in the lobby.'

'You must have enjoyed that,' Paula commented.

'He apparently let slip that soon he's moving on to Freiburg at the edge of the Black Forest. He even gave me the name and the address of the hotel he'll be staying at. The Schwarzwälder Hof.' He looked at Paula. 'Before dinner could you phone up the place, book rooms for all of us? I've scribbled details of the hotel and its address on that pad over there.'

'Book rooms? In our own names?'

'Yes. Exactly. Tell them we may arrive tomorrow, but they're to hold the rooms until we do arrive. We'll pay for them even if they're unoccupied for a day or two.'

'Is this a good idea,' Paula questioned, 'all of us in the same hotel in the Black Forest area?'

'Yes. I think we'll need as heavy a force close together as we can muster.'

'Before I forget,' Newman began, 'I had a drink with what sounded like a reformed Rupert . . .'

He went on to describe his conversation with Rupert Strangeways. They all listened with a mixture of surprise and disbelief. As he finished Paula burst out.

'Do you believe a word of this? Rupert getting himself a proper job? The mind boggles.'

'It could be,' Newman speculated, 'that Rupert wants to get into his father's good books. After all, Sir Guy is a millionaire.'

'What do you think?' Paula asked Tweed.

'I don't think anything.'

'Going back to Osborne,' Newman said, 'you used the words "he apparently let slip" when you told us about Freiburg, the hotel he's staying at, the address. Did it occur to you he might have deliberately told you this?'

'Indeed, it did.'

'Then I vote that Paula does nothing about booking rooms in the hotel he mentioned.'

'Sorry, Bob, you're outvoted. By me. I want Paula to do what I requested.'

'I don't understand it.'

'I thought I'd made myself quite clear.'

'It's a trap,' Newman told him vehemently.

'So we walk into their trap.'

When Tweed, Paula and Newman arrived in the dining room Sharon was already waiting for them at a table by a window. There were place cards and Tweed sat next to Sharon by the aisle. Paula's card put her by the other window, facing Sharon with Newman alongside her.

'I think we're dead on time,' Tweed had greeted his hostess.

'Dead on time,' Sharon agreed with a smile.

'Don't use that phrase,' Paula whispered under her breath.

Only Newman heard her. He realized Paula was tense, on edge. Outwardly she was the model of composure. She smiled at Sharon.

'I think your ensemble is one of the smartest I've seen this season.'

'Thank you, Paula. That is generous of you.' She looked at two waiters who had arrived. 'Let's get the party going. What are you all going to have for aperitifs?'

As they ordered Paula found herself studying Sharon, despite her previous determination not to. She wore an emerald-green dress with a high collar. Round her slim waist was a gold belt. It was all perfect. She sat very erect, very much in control of herself but without a trace of arrogance.

She exudes an air of complete calm, Paula thought. She moved her head constantly, but slowly. Her green eyes also swept the table slowly and Paula had the impression she was taking in every little detail about her guests. She didn't fiddle with her magnificent mane, as so many women do. Her white, beautifully moulded face would attract the attention of almost any man the first moment he saw her. But there was not a hint of flirting with the men as she chatted in her very English accent.

'I propose a toast,' Tweed said, raising his glass and turning towards Sharon. 'To our hostess, Sharon, one of the most remarkable women in the world.'

'I'll second that,' Newman said instantly.

'I'm going to blush,' Sharon replied, then sipped her drink. 'I've dined with Heaven knows how many people in America,' she went on, 'but I haven't, until tonight, been honoured with a group of such talent and dynamism.' She looked straight at Paula. 'And what I have just said very much includes you.'

300

'Thank you. I fear you exaggerate.'

'No. It is the Americans who exaggerate.'

Paula had listened carefully to Sharon when she was speaking in her soft voice. She had also been watching her. As far as she could tell Sharon spoke with absolute sincerity. It was at this moment that Newman said something Paula thought would ruin the pleasant, relaxed atmosphere.

'I imagine you should know, Sharon. About exaggeration. After all, you have been married to four Americans.'

'Oh yes, I have.' Sharon broke into peals of laughter. Then she concentrated on Newman, her wide mouth smiling. 'It would be you, Bob, who brings up the subject of my adventures – experiments is a better word – with four American husbands. I was very young when I was first taken to the States. I was dazzled. Then after a year I realized I couldn't stand my husband. Always boasting about his big deals, running after other women. I left it to my lawyer to arrange the divorce settlement. I was staggered when he told me what he was going to get me. It was then it dawned on me.'

'What did?'

'Bob, do go ahead and have a cigarette.'

Paula realized that Sharon had noticed Newman reach for a packet in his pocket, then think better of it. He nodded, took out the pack and lit a cigarette.

'What did?' Sharon repeated. 'It dawned on me that in America the only people looked up to are the rich. So I thought, if this is the game over here, I'll play it. I was still very young. I had been elevated by my first husband into the world of country clubs, top hotels, Cadillacs, you name it. Which is how I fell for my second husband.' She burst out laughing again. 'I'll go on in a minute. We must study the menus.'

Paula was fascinated. Sharon's personality had

suddenly – at the mention of husbands – become amazingly animated. She glowed with life and Paula realized even more why men would, at their first meeting, be hypnotized by her.

Once everyone had decided on their main courses, refusing starters, Sharon consulted Tweed about the wine list. After telling the wine waiter what they wanted, she looked at Tweed.

'I've been chattering on too much. Your turn now.'

'Did you know that Denise Chatel has booked out of this hotel – and driven off in her car? Someone told me before dinner.'

'Yes, I found that out too.' The animation was replaced by her deep calm. 'She didn't say a word to me. I can't understand why she did it. Or where she's gone.'

'So she's disappeared?'

'Vanished into thin air. And after working for me for two years. I'm puzzled – and worried.'

'Would it be worth informing the police?' Tweed suggested.

'I thought of that, then rejected the idea. After all, she's a free soul. She was a good worker, but often I was never sure what was going on in her mind.'

'Sorry to bring that up,' Tweed replied. 'Let's settle down and enjoy ourselves, as we were doing.'

'Husband Number Two,' said Newman.

'He doesn't let go, does he?' Sharon put her hand across her mouth to suppress a giggle. 'I really did fall for him. After we became engaged he took me to Hawaii. Before I knew what was happening we were married – on the beach. It all seemed very romantic. Then after six months he was running after other women. By then my lawyer, Joshua Warren, had become a friend. After a year I'd had enough of it. Joshua again took over – and again I was astounded at the size of the settlement. I won't bore you with Number Three, which followed the same pattern.'

'Where were you by then?' Newman asked.

'Washington. The trouble there is a single woman is suspect – the wives of high society men think you're after their husbands. So you don't get invited anywhere. I'm all right on my own – I love reading, but there's a limit to the number of books you can occupy yourself with. Then Joshua introduced me to Number Four. I admit I married him so I could lead a more social life. When my fourth husband went off the rails Joshua was in attendance to handle the divorce.' She paused. 'I was rather naive. It was only then I understood the enormous fees Joshua was making out of my divorces. Enough to set him up for life.' She went very quiet, staring at the table. 'I began to feel like a high-class call-girl – with Joshua manipulating me like a pimp. That's the way it goes in America – they're all corrupt. Which is why I hanker for England.'

She looked up as the wine waiter showed her a bottle. He waited while she looked at it, then at him.

'I ordered 1992 – that's 1994,' she said sharply.

'I'm sorry, madame. I must have misunderstood you.'

'I spoke clearly enough.'

Tweed glanced down towards the main entrance. Rupert and Basil had just come in together. They strolled along the aisle and then Rupert paused by their table. He was staring at Sharon.

'I can recognize Venus-like beauty soon as I see it.'

Sharon glanced up with a blank expression. She stared at him, then lowered her eyes, her mouth tight with annoyance.

'Bob, aren't you going to introduce me?' Rupert persisted.

Basil stood by his side, smiling blandly. He adjusted a silk handkerchief in his top pocket.

'No, I'm not,' Newman told Rupert brusquely. 'And for your information this is a private dinner party.'

'I say, I say. A *cordon sanitaire*, as the French would say. Excuse me for being alive. Basil and I are on the way to the bar.'

'Your usual watering hole. I suggest you shove off there now.'

Newman had pushed back his chair. If necessary, he was ready to grab Rupert by the scruff of the neck and escort him through the Brasserie next door into the bar beyond. At that moment the head waiter, sensing trouble, appeared.

'Is everything all right – to your satisfaction, I hope?'

'It's tewwific,' Rupert told him. 'They want the same all over again.'

Before Newman could intervene Basil pulled at Rupert's sleeve. He said something in an undertone and guided Rupert away from them into the Brasserie.

'Everything is perfect,' Tweed told the head waiter. 'You have served us a meal to remember.'

'Thank you, sir . . .'

By then they were well into their main course. Tweed and Newman had chosen fillet of turbot. Sharon and Paula were both eating skewers of scallops and lobster on a bed of mashed potato with diced vegetables. During brief pauses in her conversation Sharon had delicately devoured large portions of her meal. Now she put down her knife and fork and looked at Paula.

'Who was that silly schoolboy?'

'Oh, that was Rupert Strangeways. His father is Sir Guy Strangeways.'

'I met him several times in Washington – Sir Guy, I mean,' Sharon explained. 'A nice man. I shouldn't say it, but he deserves a better offspring.'

'If you hadn't said it,' Newman told her, 'I would have done. Anyway, he's gone now . . .'

There was silence for a while as they concentrated on the meal. After dessert had been served and consumed Tweed posed his question to Sharon.

'Have you encountered a man called Jake Ronstadt?'

A heavier silence descended on the table. Sharon was dabbing at her lips with her serviette. She turned to look at Newman.

'Tweed is an interesting man. He fires intriguing questions at the most unexpected moment.' She smiled warmly at Tweed. 'Like a detective. Yes, I have encountered Ronstadt twice at the Embassy in London. Briefly on both occasions. I think he's a horrible man. Like a gangster. I can't imagine what he's doing at the Embassy.'

'He's not there now, Sharon,' said Tweed.

'Oh, have they sent him back to Washington?'

'No, he's at the Euler.'

'The Euler?'

'It's a top hotel here in Basle, no more than a mile from where we are sitting.'

'I find that very peculiar. Why here in Basle?' Sharon asked.

'I've no idea. Someone who knows him by sight spotted him, told me. I was just curious.'

'So am I,' she said. 'Well, I'll be moving on soon. Not sure exactly when.'

'Moving on?' Tweed queried.

'Yes.' She turned, gave him her full attention. 'I was going to suggest we have coffee in the bar with a liqueur. That's when I was going to tell you.' She looked up as the waiter appeared. 'Can we have coffee in the bar? A quiet table if you can manage that.'

'Certainly, madame.'

Newman had turned round in his chair to survey the restaurant behind him. There were just a few couples here and there. He then saw Ed Osborne sitting at a table

305

by himself. Osborne had a grim look on his face. Newman gave him a small salute. Osborne pretended not to see it, bent his head over a newspaper. What has disturbed him? Newman wondered.

Earlier, when Basil guided a wobbling Rupert through the Brasserie, the second restaurant in the hotel, and on into the bar, he had to hold him up. He had found Rupert at a table in the lobby. There were several empty glasses on the table Rupert was sitting at.

'Need another drink,' Rupert mumbled.

'Are you sure?'

'When I say need 'nother drink, I need 'nother drink. Wha's the matter, Basil? Don't understand the King's English?'

'It's the Queen's English these days. Has been for long as I can remember.'

'Basil!' Rupert said aggressively. 'You tellin' me how you want me to speak my own language? 'Nother Scotch. Wanna sit down.'

The bar was empty. For the moment there was no one behind the serving counter. Basil guessed the girl had taken an order into the restaurant. He kept Rupert moving. There was another exit which led out straight on to the street.

'You need some fresh air first,' Basil said firmly. 'Then we can come back and get something to drink.'

'Fresh air? Can't drink fresh air. Didn't you know that?'

'I'll bring you a drink outside,' Basil lied.

'Against Swish law. Drinkin' in the street. End up in pokey, we will.'

'Almost there.'

Basil was anxious to get Rupert out of sight before someone returned to the bar. He got a strong hold on

Rupert, propelled him to the door at the rear. He opened it with his back, hauled Rupert out with him. The outside air hit them like a blast from the Arctic. Rupert's legs gave way. Basil let him slide down until he was slumped with his back inside the alcove. Then he left him there, confident he would recover swiftly. He had no doubt Rupert would go straight back inside the bar to order another drink.

Basil hurried the short distance along the road, entered the hotel by the main door, took the lift to his room. He reappeared very quickly. He was wearing a long black overcoat which almost came to his ankles. He walked off into the night.

When Sharon's party walked through the Brasserie Tweed saw Nield and Butler having dinner at a table on their own. Neither of them looked up or said a word as they walked past. At another table, by himself, sat Marler. When he saw them coming he picked up his newspaper and began studying it.

'I'll go in first,' Newman said to Sharon. 'See if it's all clear.'

'I'm coming with you. People like that schoolboy don't worry me.'

A little distance behind them Tweed followed with Paula by his side. She kept her voice down.

'Rupert seems to have reverted to his normal obnoxious self.'

'I was sceptical about what he said to Newman. No more than a pipe dream, I'd say. He probably believed what he was saying at the time.'

'You really think so?'

'You sound dubious.'

'I think he was putting on an act. Here we are. And no sign of either of them, thank heavens.'

They ordered liqueurs from the girl who, at that moment, took up her position behind the bar counter. As soon as she saw them she came over and took their orders.

'Sharon,' Tweed began, 'I got the impression from what you said in the dining room that you are really fed up with the Americans.'

'I am. Which is why I'm out here. I was appalled to hear Ronstadt is in town. I can't stop myself working, but officially I'm here on holiday. I'm floating around while I take a big decision. I'm getting away from it all so I *can* think. I'm playing with the idea of moving to living in Britain permanently. Down at my manor in Dorset.'

'So you're staying on in Basle?'

'No. I need different surroundings. I'm soon going to Freiburg, staying at the Hotel Colombi, which has five stars. You know, you look very smart in that blue bird's-eye suit. Pity that pocket bulges.'

Tweed put his hand in his pocket, brought out Beck's mobile. He smiled with resignation.

'Should have left it in my room. Picked it up automatically.'

He had hardly spoken when the mobile started buzz-ing. He stood up, shrugged, looked at Sharon apologetically.

'Excuse me. I refuse to use these things when I'm with guests in a restaurant or bar. I'll be back in a minute . . .'

He walked over to an empty table well away from anyone else. Only then did he answer the mobile phone. It was Beck on the line.

'Tweed, where are you now?'

'Just finished dinner in the hotel.'

'Please get over here quickly. It's an emergency.'

Tweed returned to the guest table, apologized,

thanked Sharon for a marvellous evening, explained he had to rush off to a meeting. He then walked swiftly into the Brasserie. Marler, drinking coffee, looked up as Tweed swept past him. Tweed was about to step in the lift when he found Marler behind him. As they ascended he told Marler what had happened.

'I'm coming with you. No argument . . .'

31

'All hell has broken out in London,' Beck said grimly.

Tweed was taking off his coat. A uniformed policeman took it and also Marler's. Beck's office at police headquarters was bleak. The police chief was sitting down at a large wooden desk, its surface empty except for two phones and a pad with scribbles on it. Tweed sat down facing him, with Marler by his side.

'Tell me,' Tweed said.

'Late this morning a huge bomb exploded inside a store in Regent Street. There was a sale on. Crowded with shoppers. Reports say there are at least a hundred dead, many more injured. I had all this from Chief Inspector – now Superintendent – Roy Buchanan. Monica had phoned Berne. Luckily spoke to my assistant, who knows her. He gave her my number here. She passed it to Buchanan, who has phoned me, wants you to call him.'

'Then I'll do that from here, if I may.'

'There's more. Buchanan said an American syndicate has bought the *Daily Despatch*. One condition was they took over as soon as the deal was signed. An American editor has arrived. His first edition has a huge splash headline – FBI MUST TAKE OVER.'

'The net tightens,' Tweed said quietly.

'I can get Buchanan for you now.'

'Do it, please . . .'

Marler was looking round the office. The walls were painted an uninviting green. Two metal filing cabinets stood in one corner. The room was illuminated by fluorescent tubes suspended from the ceiling. The blinds over the windows were closed.

'Tweed here, Roy.'

'Beck has told you?'

'Yes. About Regent Street. The American takeover of the *Despatch*. Its damnable headline.'

'So you're partly in the picture. At lunchtime the Commissioner asked me to take over as head of the Anti-Terrorist Squad. I told him I must have full powers. He said the PM had already agreed that.'

'Sounds as though the PM's backbone has stiffened.'

'Regent Street was the last straw. They also tried to blow up a major power station. We had it covertly guarded. Two cars drove up close to it. They were stopped. The driver in the first car dived out, ran back to the second vehicle, dived into it. The second car took off, a policeman stood in its way to stop it – the car drove over him. He's dead. The first car was a mobile bomb. The radio device which would have detonated it from a distance was dismantled.'

'You've got a big job on your hands.'

'The one I wanted. I sent you a tape recording of my TV broadcast to the nation this afternoon. Has it arrived?'

'Not yet.'

'It will do any moment. Forget vanity. I want you to see how I'm going to handle the situation. How are you doing?'

'We've got a bunch of them out here. We may be on the eve of a major battle.'

'Good luck. I must go now.'

'Take care.'

Tweed put down the phone. He stood up, hands in his pockets, staring into space. Marler thought he had never seen him stand so motionless, with such an expression on his face. It reminded him of a picture he had once seen of Bismarck. Tweed came out of his trancelike stance.

'Thank you, Arthur. Can I ask you a favour? When we cross the border into Germany could you be sure Marler's car isn't searched?'

'I'm sure Marler wouldn't be carrying anything I would disapprove of,' Beck smiled drily. 'And I'll warn the officer at the checkpoint to leave him alone. How many cars have you?'

'Just two,' Tweed replied.

Beck tore off the top sheet of his pad. He pushed it towards them. Then he rolled a pen across the table.

'Could you put down the registration numbers of your cars?'

'I can do that,' Marler told him, reaching for pad and pen.

'I'll pass those on to the checkpoint officer,' Beck told them.

'One final point, Arthur,' Tweed interjected. 'I'm assuming the same arrangement applies. You'll call me on your mobile as soon as you know Ronstadt is on the move?'

'I was going to do that anyway. Strictly between us, I have installed a new plain-clothes officer from Berne as a guest at the Euler. He'll inform me the moment he sees signs the Americans are leaving.'

'I'd like to thank you for your very thorough co-operation,' Tweed said. 'If there's what I think there is in the Black Forest you will have played a key role.'

'Nonsense.' Beck paused. 'I hope you approve, but I took it on myself to phone your old friend, Otto Kuhl-mann, chief of the Kriminalpolizei in Wiesbaden. He promised me he wouldn't get in your way, but he might just come in useful.'

'Ronstadt is not the only man who can close in a net. Thank you again. I'd better get back to the hotel. I have to brief my people.'

Ronstadt sat in the bar at the Euler with Vernon. They were the only two people in the place, except for the barman, who was a long distance from their table. Ronstadt was wearing his favourite outfit, a heavy brown leather jacket with leather trousers of the same colour, and rubber-soled shoes which made not a sound when he was moving.

'You and Brad dump all the weapons, the rest of the explosives?' Ronstadt asked.

'Sure, Chief.'

'Had to be in daylight, I guess,' Ronstadt said casually.

'No. After dark. We drove up the river. Got well out of Basle, found a quiet place. No houses. No people. Nothin' at all. Backed the car up to the river's edge. Brad handed me the stuff, I dumped it in the river.'

'You know somethin'? Go on like this and you'll make deputy.'

'Thought I was that now.'

'*Temporary* deputy – until I see how you make out. Say, Vernon, you see a big snake. Whaddya do?'

'Run like hell . . .'

'So, mebbe, Vernon, you won't make it. You cut off its head.'

'I don't get where you're comin' from.'

'Tweed. He's the head of the snake's causin' me trouble. So I made arrangements. Can't risk him messing with us where we's goin' any time now.'

'That's smart, Chief. Very smart.'

'I thought it was.' Ronstadt chuckled, an unpleasant sound. 'I thought it was . . .'

Tweed and Marler left Spiegelhof, police headquarters, for the short walk down Spiegelgasse to the Three Kings. A tram, empty except for the driver, trundled along the street they had to cross. As the rumble of its wheels disappeared the cold silence they had come to associate with Basle descended.

Marler was looking up, staring at the tops of the buildings they passed as they reached the other side. They were close now to the main entrance to the hotel. Tweed was deep in thought, his feet moving mechanically, his mind on what Buchanan had told him. He arrived at the revolving door. Suddenly Marler grabbed hold of him, shoved him forcefully into a compartment of the door which caused him to slam into it and be pushed inside. At the same moment a bullet hit the stone floor where he had been standing a millisecond before. The bullet ricocheted into space.

Glancing up at the building opposite, Marler followed him into the lobby. Tweed was waiting for him. He spoke calmly.

'What was that?'

'A bullet with your name on it.' Marler kept his voice down as the receptionist was coming towards them from behind the counter. 'I'd go after him but he's like a cat burglar. I'd say he's long gone already.'

'The Phantom?'

'No doubt about it.'

'Don't mention it to the others.'

The receptionist reached them. She was holding an addressed package. She was holding it out towards Tweed when Marler took it.

'This arrived by courier for Mr Tweed. He said the plane was late. Something about ice on the runway.'

'Thank you,' said Tweed.

'I'll take this to my room, check it carefully before I open it,' Marler said when they were inside the lift.

'Come straight to my room as soon as you can. I'll have everyone else there when you arrive. I want to ask some questions first. You're ready to leave at the drop of a hat?'

'Before the hat hits the floor.'

Tweed gave Paula some instructions when she arrived in his room first. As he was speaking she listened, then stared in disbelief.

'I want you to do the same thing with the Hotel Colombi in Freiburg that you did with the Schwarz-wälder Hof. Book rooms at the Colombi for all of us. Give them my credit card number and tell them we'll pay for any unoccupied rooms. Not sure when we'll get there.'

'What on earth for?' she wanted to know. 'Sharon is staying there.'

'I know. That's not the reason. This way we have two different bases in Freiburg. We may find it useful to flit from one to the other.'

'I'll call now . . .'

Tweed waited until everyone was settled in the room. When Paula completed her call, he used the phone to contact Keith Kent.

'Keith, like you to be here in my room to hear what's going on.'

'First of all,' he said, seated on a hard-backed chair, 'Paula, I would be interested in your impression of Sharon. You did sit facing her during our leisurely dinner.'

'She's enigmatic.'

'That doesn't tell me anything. Be more specific.'

'She's very experienced in the company of a lot of people, I'd say. But she doesn't hold the stage. I can't quite penetrate what's under that deep calm. On the other hand she can be very buoyant and great fun. I think she's tugged this way and that as to whether to stay in America or move to Britain for good. I sense she's leaning towards the latter. Sensibly, she's moving to different locations to get a perspective on her life.'

'What do you think, Bob?'

'I don't believe one word she says.'

There was a hush. Paula looked quite taken aback at his reaction. So much so, she began smoking one of her rare cigarettes.

'What do you base that on, Bob?' Tweed asked.

'I was joking. I think she's great.'

'What is it about her that makes her so attractive to men?' Tweed enquired.

'I can tell you that,' Paula replied. '*Personality*. She's a mix of the cool and the exciting. This intrigues men. They're not sure where they are with her. Outcome? They want to know her better.'

'That's pretty shrewd,' Newman agreed.

'I've got grim news for you,' Tweed said suddenly. 'It came to Marler and me via Beck and Roy Buchanan . . .'

He told them about the horror which had taken place in London. They listened in complete silence. Butler bunched a fist as though he wanted one of the opposition present to slam it into. Nield closed his eyes, then opened them, his expression one of fury.

'We've got to bust these bastards,' Butler exclaimed.

'I agree with you one hundred per cent,' Tweed assured him. 'I want you all now to watch a tape of Roy

315

Buchanan broadcasting on TV this afternoon. Marler, could you oblige?'

'Right now,' Marler said.

He inserted it into the video recorder. Picking up the remote control, he backed away, perched on the arm of Paula's chair. The red light was already glowing on the set. He pressed the button and a BBC news bulletin was showing. Scenes of carnage far worse than those seen earlier of the bombed store in Oxford Street were preceded by an unusual warning from the newsreader.

'Before we show the following pictures we would advise anyone who is squeamish not to watch. We especially suggest children should not see what follows.'

Paula gasped, wanted to close her eyes. She forced herself to go on viewing. They reminded her of scenes of the war in Vietnam. The pictures were a tangle of horribly injured victims, of stretcher after stretcher being brought out with the bodies on them showing no signs of life. Chaos and blood were everywhere. A woman staggered out of the ruined entrance. A paramedic appeared, took hold of her gently, removed her from camera range.

The scenes of carnage gave way to the reappearance of the newsreader, his voice solemn.

'There will now be a short broadcast by Superintendent Buchanan of the Metropolitan Police.'

Roy Buchanan's image appeared, a view of head and shoulders. He stared straight at the camera, his expression grim, his voice calm and determined.

'Ladies and gentlemen, the Commissioner of the Metropolitan Police has just appointed me as Head of the Anti-Terrorist Squad. I have also been given full powers to call on the help of any other unit I may deem to be necessary. We know that the atrocity you have just seen – together with the bombing of two other department stores in the capital – is not the work of the IRA. Nor is it the work of any ultra-extremist Muslim sect. I shall be working day and night to hunt down these vile murderers. I have given orders that when they are encountered by my men, if they open fire, we shall shoot to kill. Let there be no doubt about that. Thank you for giving me your attention.'

'That was pretty tough,' Newman said as Marler switched off the TV. 'Thank God. He really means it.'

'So do I,' Tweed said very quietly. 'We will exterminate these vermin.'

Marler remained behind when the others had left, after a warning from Tweed that no one should contemplate going to bed. That they must be ready to leave at a moment's notice.

'After we got back from Beck's place,' Marler said, 'and you missed death by inches, I went up to my room. I immediately phoned Windermere's room. There was no reply. I then phoned Rupert's room. Again there was no reply. So both were out.'

'You think one of them is the Phantom?'

'Don't you?'

'It could be a third person who hasn't yet appeared on the scene,' Tweed mused.

'The Phantom is a crack shot, although twice he's just missed. Once with Paula at Irongates in Kent, the second time with you tonight.'

'You don't think they could have been deliberate misses, to unnerve me? And why has it to be a man. These days there are some women who are as expert shots as men,' Tweed speculated.

'I'll get him – or her – in my sights sooner or later. I still have my Armalite.'

'By the way,' Tweed said, 'when we drive to Freiburg, which I'm convinced will be the case, we'll be staying at the Colombi to begin with. I remember it – a first-class hotel not far from the railway station and fairly close to the outskirts. We have the Schwarzwälder Hof as an alternative base. It's deep inside the old city. We may even dodge backwards and forwards. And don't be surprised if, when we do arrive at the Colombi, we see Sharon. She told me at dinner she's going there.'

'What is that woman up to? I saw her when you came through the Brasserie on your way to the bar.'

'She's trying to decide whether to leave America for ever, to settle down in England.'

Someone tapped on the door. When Marler opened it Paula walked in. Without sitting down, she stopped uncertainly.

'Is this the wrong moment for me to turn up? I can always go back to my room. I was restless. The waiting.'

'Stay,' Tweed told her. 'Sit down.' He turned to Marler. 'I was wondering why you asked about Sharon.'

'I doubt if instructions to kill you were transmitted over the phone. Which suggests to me they were given by someone inside this hotel.'

'What are you talking about?' Paula demanded. 'Instructions to kill Tweed?'

'I was going to tell you later,' Tweed said quickly. 'On our way back from seeing Beck across the road someone took a pot-shot at me. Missed by a mile.'

'A short mile,' Marler corrected.

'So why query Sharon?' Tweed asked him. 'There are other people in the hotel.'

'Who, for example?'

'Ed Osborne.'

It was in the middle of the night when Jake Ronstadt called the members of his outfit to his suite. As ordered, they were all fully dressed. Unusually he stood at the head of the table.

'Who the hell gave you permission to sit down?' he snarled when they had automatically occupied their chairs. 'Get on your feet.'

'Anyone gettin' old and tired?' he sneered as they jumped up.

'Sorry, Chief. We're OK,' said Vernon.

'You'd better be – otherwise you'll find yourself with a bullet in the head, dumped in a ditch.' His voice changed, became dangerously wheedling. 'Has everyone packed, like I said? If you ain't raise your right hand.'

No hands were raised. Ronstadt stared slowly round, his hard eyes glaring at each man. They waited, not daring to move a muscle. Ronstadt spoke again, this time in a calm voice.

'We're leaving – for Freiburg first, then the Black Forest. I've told you before. But in case you've got short memories I'm goin' to repeat myself. I'll drive the lead car. Vernon comes up behind me. When we're on the autobahn, Vernon, I'll signal where you turn off – with a wave of my arm. You go up the slip road, meet the two cars waiting, transfer the weapons into your car, then drive down to rejoin me. Is that too difficult for you?'

'Piece of cake.'

'Then ram it down your throat. The bill's paid, so why are you all hangin' around here?'

'So Denise never called you after leaving?' Tweed asked.

'No. Why would she?' Marler said. 'I'm the last person she'll want to see again. She must have concocted that whole yarn about the *Minotaur*.'

'Seems she did.'

Tweed was trying to think up things to say. In his

319

room everyone was gathered, including Keith Kent, who seemed the most placid. In the middle of the night there was an air of unspoken tension. Everyone was waiting to get on with it, knowing that nothing might happen. Paula sat in an armchair, swinging her crossed legs. She reached for her pack in her shoulder bag, then decided she didn't want a cigarette. Newman, seated on a couch, kept checking his watch. Marler was leaning against a wall. The other two who were most patient were Butler and Nield, chatting quietly to each other.

'Anyone like some more coffee?' Tweed enquired. 'Helps to keep you alert.'

No one did. Newman was thinking he could have had a nap in his room. Paula got up, went over to the windows, carefully peeked through a gap she made in the closed curtains. On the opposite bank of the Rhine a few lights gleamed in the old houses, their reflections trembling in the river. Insomniacs, she thought. They existed all over the world.

The mobile phone on the table began buzzing. Tweed forced himself not to grab. Picking it up, he was aware of six pairs of eyes watching him intently.

'Hello?'

'They're on the move. Must be close to the border.'

'Thank you.'

Beck's distinctive voice had come clearly across. Tweed put the mobile into his pocket. He spoke offhandedly, as though they were going on a day trip to a resort.

'Time to go. I suspect we have very little time left.'

In the Atlantic, well clear of the American coastline, Crag – Rear Admiral Joseph Honeywood, in command of the huge naval task force – settled into his seat in the Island of the *President*. It was night and he liked to be at control after dark. That was when you could get an unpleasant surprise. He looked at his Operations Officer.

'We're making good time. We should be on station in the English Channel less than four days from now.'

'No doubt about it, sir.'

'And so far, Bill, we've been lucky. We haven't been spotted by any other ship or a commercial airliner.'

'I have a feeling that will go on. The Brits will wake up to find us off their shores.'

'The SEALs are ready for action?'

'They are. If they have to land they'll sweep over anything that gets in their way. They're rarin' to go.'

32

Driving through Basle at night was an eerie experience, Paula was thinking. She liked the city, but in the dark the medieval buildings, illuminated only by street lanterns at intervals, had a majestic – and sinister – atmosphere. There were no trams running at this hour, the streets were deserted, the shadows deep and menacing.

She sat beside Newman, who was driving the first car. In the rear seats Tweed was alongside Keith Kent. Tweed was sitting up erect, his eyes everywhere. The adrenalin was flowing and he was very alert. He knew the layout of the city well and was on the lookout for anything unusual, which should not be there.

'We're getting close to the border,' he warned after a while.

'Marler's keeping up with us well, not too close, not far behind,' Newman commented after checking his rear-view mirror.

Tweed glanced back through the rear window. Marler

was driving the second Audi. As passengers he had Butler and Nield in the back. The seat beside him was unoccupied – for a purpose. He slowed as Newman's car lost speed, then the two cars stopped.

In the near distance was the checkpoint at the border. Paula could make out the heavy figure of Jake Ronstadt behind the wheel of a black Audi. He had his window down and appeared to be arguing with the duty officer. Another officer searched the interior of the car while three men in dark coats stood outside.

'What the hell is this all about?' Ronstadt was demanding for the third time. 'I've shown you my diplomatic passport. You have no right to stop us – let alone search the car.'

'Information received, sir,' another officer replied.

'What information might that be, buddy?'

'We are not allowed to disclose our sources. Would you mind stepping out so I can check the front?'

'I damned well would. I'm reporting this to Washington. And I'd like your name.'

'As Chief Customs Officer at this crossing point I have sole authority . . .'

He paused as another officer pulled at his sleeve. They walked a short distance from the car. They conversed briefly and the Chief Customs Officer was careful not to look to where Newman's car was waiting with Marler's, parked in the shadows. He returned to the Audi.

'If it was a large consignment we would have found it by now. You are free to proceed.'

Ronstadt started his engine. He lowered his window. The moment he had crossed the border he shouted back, 'You can stick your sole authority.'

He pressed his foot down, increasing speed as he drove onto the autobahn. Behind him three more black

Audis followed. In his own Audi, Newman commented while he waited a little longer.

'Four cars. I counted four men in each – that's sixteen. We're outnumbered.'

'That worries you?' Tweed enquired from the back.

'Not at all. We've been outnumbered more heavily before. Time to go.'

The officer waved them through. He even saluted them. Then they were on the wide autobahn. It had two lanes in both directions, separated by a metal crash barrier and hedges. They drove on through the night and there was no other traffic as Newman held back from the convoy ahead. He drove so he could always see the red lights of the rear-most vehicle. Paula was shielding a pocket torch as she examined an ADAC map she had purchased of the Schwarzwald area.

'We turn off at junction 63 to get to Freiburg,' she called out. 'It's quite a distance yet.'

'We'll get there.'

In Ronstadt's car Leo Madison, the man who had murdered Juliette Leroy in St Ursanne, sat beside Ronstadt. He kept looking back down the autobahn behind them. He was trying to decide if it was wise to speak. He decided it was.

'Every time we go round a big curve I see two white cars behind us.'

'So?'

'When you speed up, they speed up. When you go slower, they do.'

'So?'

'Reckon it could be Tweed and his mob. I've heard German drivers love overtaking.'

'That worries you, Moonhead?'

'The name is Leo Madison. They may tail us to where we're goin' and that could be a problem.'

323

'Moonhead, I expected Tweed to follow us. What do you think that crap at the checkpoint was about? Holdin' us up so Tweed could get there. A little idea of that nutter Police Chief Beck. I'm happy if that is Tweed behind us. Wait our opportunity and wipe out Tweed and his boys off the face of the earth. Any more comments floating round in that thing you call a brain?'

'Nothin' I can think of, Chief.'

'Well, we're comin' up to junction 66. That's where Vernon peels off up the slip road, collects the weapons, brings them back to us. We wait.'

A few minutes later he slowed, lowered his window, reached out an arm and made a circling gesture. He continued to slow down and then parked at the side of the autobahn, which was illegal.

Tweed had taken from his pocket a pair of night glasses. He was focusing them on the lead car of the convoy of black Audis as they swept round a curve. He grunted.

'They're slowing down a lot. More than they have previously.'

'They're testing,' Newman suggested. 'To see if we do the same thing, which we have to. Maybe Ronstadt suspects we're following him.'

'I'm sure he does,' Tweed replied. 'At least I hope so. I want to keep up the pressure on him. Keith, you saw him when you went into the Zürcher Kredit Bank. What was your impression of him?'

'Very confident, quite dynamic, impatient and with a short fuse.'

'Which is the picture I got of him when he came over to see Paula and me when we were dining at Santorini's. That short fuse may blow – when it does he's liable to make a mistake. And now the whole convoy has stopped.'

324

'So I'll park here until we see what they're up to,' Newman remarked. 'Except it's totally illegal and we'll be caught if a patrol car comes along.'

'If it does,' Tweed assured him, 'I'll ask them to use their radio transmitter to put me through to Otto Kuhlmann in Wiesbaden. That will stop them searching Marler's car ...'

'Marler wouldn't like that,' said Marler at the open window. 'I pulled up and came along to see what's happening.'

'No idea. It's possible they may be picking up some weapons. They wouldn't risk carrying them through the checkpoint.'

'Then now is the time to take them,' Marler urged.

'It is not. We shoot down unarmed men – with diplomatic passports – and we haven't a leg to stand on. Even Kuhlmann would have to arrest us.' Tweed had pressed his night glasses to his eyes after removing his spectacles as he spoke. 'The second car is moving off by itself. What's up there?'

'From my map,' said Paula, 'I'm pretty sure they're stopped just before junction 66.'

'I think you're right. The second car has disappeared up a slip road. Yes, that must be it, they're collecting a load of weapons. We'll just sit it out here until they make their next move.'

'Meantime,' Marler said, 'I'll hand you back your ironmongery.'

He gave Newman his Smith & Wesson, his holster and ammo. Then he returned to Paula her Browning and ammo. Diving his hand inside the canvas holdall slung over his shoulder, he produced two stun grenades, passed them to Newman. Taking out another grenade, he extended it to Paula.

'I don't think I need that.'

'Take it. They're not Pekinese waiting a bit further up

the autobahn. They're the most cold-blooded and professional killers we have met so far. That's better.'

He looked at Keith Kent. The money tracer was sitting relaxed as though half asleep.

'I think, Keith, you should have a Walther automatic.'

'Thank you. It's a little while since I used one of these.'

'We'd better keep you locked up safely in a cupboard somewhere, then,' Marler commented before returning to his car.

'While we're waiting,' Tweed said, 'you may be interested to hear that Sharon checked out of the hotel an hour before we left. She drove off in a Mercedes.'

'She must have made up her mind quickly to go on to Freiburg,' Paula remarked.

'She must indeed. I found that out at the last moment when I paid the bill at the Three Kings. I also heard from the receptionist that Ed Osborne also had checked out and taken off in his own car.'

'Again to Freiburg, I imagine,' said Paula. 'That town is going to be rather crowded. I meant to ask you earlier: any word from Monica about the identity of Charlie?'

'Monica did call me. Very discreetly. In words no one except me would understand she did inform me that so far she has found no trace of anyone called Charlie. She's still digging.'

Five minutes later Tweed was again gazing through his night glasses. Paula had closed the window to stop any more of the night air freezing them. Newman had kept the engine on, so the heating was beginning to warm up the interior again. Tweed lowered his glasses.

'That second car which drove off up the slip road has appeared again. All four men got out carrying suitcases. They deposited two cases in the first car and then one in each of the last two cars. They must have an armoury now.'

'So Marler was right to hand out grenades,' Newman said. 'And they're on the move again.'

He waited a short time, then drove on with Marler following behind him. Paula started checking her map again. Ahead of them the autobahn stretched away into the distance. A moon had risen, casting a milky glow over the empty countryside on either side. They had passed junction 65 when Newman reduced speed. Paula looked up, saw a faint covering of snow on the autobahn. The convoy in front of them slowed seconds later.

'Here and there are patches of ice under this snow,' Newman explained.

'I wouldn't want to skid at the speed you were going,' Paula remarked.

'It would be all right if there was ice all the way,' Newman told her. 'Then I'd know how to handle it. But they are random patches. You hit them without warning. Ronstadt has obviously come to the same conclusion. I will give him one thing – he's an expert driver.'

'He probably started out his career driving get-away cars in the States,' interjected Keith for the first time.

'Just the type,' Newman agreed. 'Then worked his way up over a pile of bodies.'

They drove on and on through the night. The black Audi convoy had slowed down. Newman guessed Ronstadt was no keener on racing across ice patches than he was. The moon was now illuminating the light covering of snow on the fields stretching away. In the rear of the car Paula was once more studying her map.

'We're just about to pass junction 65. Then it's a longish run to junction 64. When we eventually reach 63 we can drive straight into Freiburg.'

'Can I look at that map?' Tweed asked her.

327

Using the torch, he examined the map carefully. He was relying partly on his memory, but the Germans might well have changed the road layout since his previous visit. Holding on to the map, he called out to Newman.

'When we've passed junction 65, could you pull up? I need to have a brief word with Marler.'

'Will do . . .'

'We have just passed junction 65,' Paula reported a few minutes later.

'I know.'

Newman reduced speed, then pulled over and parked. Marler had stopped close behind them. Without being summoned he appeared at the window which Tweed had lowered. He smiled as he leant inside.

'So far, so good. What's the next move?'

'Look at this map.' Tweed used the torch so Marler could see clearly. 'If Ronstadt turns off at junction 63, which I think he will, we're then on route 31 leading direct to Freiburg. But here, close to the city, the road splits. Right fork leads to the Münster – close to the Schwarzwälder Hof where we have rooms booked. Left fork will take us in close to the Colombi, where we also have rooms booked. I just have a feeling that several of the cars behind Ronstadt will peel off, taking the right fork. If that happens Paula will flash her torch three times through the rear window. That means you leave us, take the right fork, follow any cars which do peel off. Wait till the occupants have booked in at the Schwarzwälder Hof, then book in yourselves.'

'Clear enough,' replied Marler. 'What are you going to do?'

'Follow Ronstadt – if he does take the left fork. You can always communicate with me at the Colombi in that eventuality.'

'I'll get back to my car.'

'And I'd better get moving,' Newman said as Tweed closed his window. 'There's continuous ice now under this snow, so hold on to your seat belts. I have to catch them up.'

Once moving, he increased speed. Now and then he could feel thinner ice crunching on his wheels. He kept up his speed. Paula was tense. Tweed, having given his instructions, leant back and closed his eyes for a brief nap. There was only one moment, as they charged forward, when the car began to skid. Newman went with the skid, hands relaxed on the wheel. He came close to the steel barrier, then straightened up, slowed.

'That's fortunate,' he remarked, 'I can see their red lights. Relax, everybody . . .'

'We're very close to junction 64,' Paula reported a while later.

'Coming up now,' Newman replied. 'There, we've passed it,' he said a few minutes later. 'So we're now heading for the vital junction 63.'

'Which isn't too far ahead,' Paula warned.

'The decisive moment,' said Tweed, who had opened his eyes.

'Be funny if Ronstadt just keeps on and on,' Newman reflected. 'We'd find ourselves heading for Mannheim.'

'Then I'd be lost,' Tweed admitted. 'All my thinking in ruins.'

'The junction beyond – 62 – also leads to Freiburg,' Paula said optimistically.

She sensed that the tension engendered by doubt was present in the car now. Newman had tightened his grip on the wheel. When she glanced back Keith Kent was leaning forward, staring ahead. Tweed, on the other hand, appeared to be the soul of relaxation, leaning back against his seat, his eyes half-closed.

'I daren't get any closer,' Newman said. 'They'd be sure we are following them.'

It was a pointless remark. Paula realized that, unusually, Newman had felt he had to say something.

'They will be sure by now,' Tweed said quietly.

'Junction 63 is coming up,' Paula said quietly.

'I *can* read the signs,' Newman snapped back at her.

A gloomy silence descended inside the car. No one spoke another word. They were staring ahead.

33

'We're really goin' to fool 'em good,' Ronstadt gloated. 'Poor old Tweed. He ain't gonna know what to do.'

'If he falls for it,' warned Leo Madison, by his side.

'Moonhead, ain't it occurred to you? I could open the door on your side and shove you out. I reckon the best you could hope for is a cracked skull.'

Madison decided it would be best not to answer back. Ronstadt had a revolver tucked down inside his belt behind the smart suit he was wearing. Madison also recalled how Ronstadt had smashed his fist into Vernon's jaw during the meeting in his suite at the Euler. Ronstadt was a very unpredictable man.

Some distance behind the black Audi convoy, Paula had heaved a sigh of relief when the cars ahead turned at junction 63 onto the road to Freiburg. She relaxed and Tweed squeezed her arm.

'It's going to work out all right.'

'I don't know how you do it. You seem to read Jake Ronstadt's mind. And I have known you do that before, with other people.'

'There's no magic about it. I just try to put myself into the shoes of the enemy. You've got a torch ready to signal to Marler when – or if – it's necessary?'

'I'm ready.'

She settled down to look at the moonlit landscape. The road they were now travelling on was narrower than the autobahn but it had a good surface. It was elevated above the surrounding white fields below them and leafless trees, like sentinels, stood at intervals on either side. It was rather like driving along a tree-lined boulevard. Then she leaned forward, peering ahead. In the mid-distance reared up a brooding white massif, a range like a huge frozen wave.

'What's the grim-looking thing in the distance?' she asked.

'That,' Tweed told her, 'is the Black Forest.'

'Looks pretty sinister.'

'In winter, after a heavy fall of snow, it can be beautiful.'

'I'll take your word for it.'

She concentrated on checking her map. They were not too far from where the road forked. When she looked ahead again the massif seemed much higher and menacing. Nearer to them she saw a wall of buildings huddled together. Above them glowed a faint halo which, she assumed, was street lights. She sat up and gazed steadily at the receding red lights of the convoy.

Then she saw the lead car disappearing to the left. Behind it three cars turned to the right. She twisted round in her seat. Marler's car was fairly close. Lifting the torch, she carefully switched it on and off three times. She thought she saw, behind the wheel, Marler's head nodding in acknowledgement.

'You predicted again what they were going to do,' she said to Tweed.

'I don't always get it right.' He leaned forward. 'When you've taken the left fork, Bob, I'll try and guide you to the Colombi. Let's just hope they haven't moved it,' he added with a touch of humour.

'Won't Ronstadt guide me there if I follow him?'

'If I'm right, yes he will. If you're getting too close call on my help. And, everyone, when we get to our rooms, unpack the very minimum of clothing. We may have to leave the hotel very quickly . . .'

They waited ten minutes parked in a dark street after Ronstadt and the three men with him had entered the Colombi. A uniformed employee took his car away. By night the dark buildings on both sides cast black shadows. In contrast, the illuminated entrance to the Colombi looked warm and inviting. Tweed checked his watch.

'Time to go inside. Let's hope Ronstadt and his thugs have gone to their rooms. If they're hungry they'll probably have to use room service . . .'

When they alighted from their car, porters took their bags. The same employee who had driven away Ronstadt's car attempted to do the same thing with their Audi. Newman intervened.

'I may have to drive off quickly soon. Please leave it where it is.'

'That would be most unusual, sir.'

'I'm an unusual man.'

Newman smiled at him. He handed him a hundred-mark note. There was no further argument. Tweed and Paula had walked inside. While Tweed was registering Paula glanced round. The hotel reeked of luxury and taste. Leaving the reception area, Tweed glanced into a lounge, stood stock-still.

'What is it?' whispered Paula as Newman joined them.

'Come in and see for yourself.'

Tweed walked in, his coat over his arm. It was like a replay of their arrival at the Three Kings. The first person he saw, leaning forward in an armchair, was Sir Guy

332

Strangeways. In another chair, facing him, with a table between them, Sharon sat with a glass in her hand. She looked up. She raised her eyebrows, then smiled invitingly.

'What an unexpected pleasure. Now you can host a dinner for me here tomorrow evening. No, it's almost 6 a.m. I should have said this evening.'

'Are you following us?' Strangeways demanded abruptly.

'You arrived together, then?'

'No, we didn't,' Sharon said quickly. 'I drove myself here in a Merc. I told Guy where I was going and he said he'd be coming too. I thought he was joking. But, as you see, here he is. Do sit down. Paula, how nice to see you. And, Bob, you have completed the party.'

'A party? At six o'clock in the morning?' Newman queried.

'Why not?' Sharon gave him an inviting smile. 'It's the serene time of the day. I love it. No one up yet in the hotel. Just the five of us. Champers, Paula?'

'Not for me, thank you.'

Sharon was holding a bottle she had taken out of a silver bucket of ice. From a side table she had picked up a fresh glass.

'You'll join me, won't you, Bob?'

'Just one glass. Might keep me awake. Or put me to sleep.'

'And, Tweed, you'll join me. Tell me, how much sleep have you had in the past twenty-four hours?'

'I had a couple of brief naps in the car on our way here.'

'I thought so. I'm sure you and I have one thing in common.' She gave him a ravishing smile as she poured him a glass. 'We are both blessed with immense stamina. I get by on four hours a night. Less, if I have to.

'More for you, Guy?' she suggested.

'No, thank you. Think I'll have to crawl up to bed soon. I did ask you a question, Tweed. Why are you following us?'

'You've just rephrased the question, Guy. And I was going to ask you just the same question. First you arrive at the Three Kings in Basle, just before I do. Now you turn up here.'

'I think I must get up to bed now.' Guy dragged himself out of his chair. 'I'm dropping. Goodnight . . .'

Tweed was mentally contrasting Guy with Sharon. The man who had just left them had had puffy eyes, a strained look, almost haggard. On the other hand Sharon looked fresh as the proverbial daisy, ready for anything. He looked at her and the green eyes glowed back.

'I got the impression Guy is very worried about something. Did you?' he asked her.

'Yes, I did. Ever since he sat down, which was quite a while ago, he's been crossing and recrossing his legs. Then he kept shifting round in his chair. I asked him point-blank. He wouldn't even give me a hint. He drank a lot of champagne and I had to order another bottle. Mind you . . .' She smiled again. 'I contributed to killing that first bottle. He's definitely got something on his mind, but won't come out with it.'

'Might depend on what it is,' Tweed mused, sipping at his glass.

'I suppose it might.' Sharon looked at Paula. 'You're awfully quiet. Hardly said a word since you sat down.'

'Sorry. Excuse my bad manners. The fact is I need some sleep. It's been a long day.' She smiled. 'And a long night. I hope you don't mind if I go up to my room.'

'Think we could all do with a bit of kip,' Newman said, standing up at the same moment as Paula. 'Look forward to seeing you later.'

'You're not going to leave me on my own, are you?' Sharon asked, gazing at Tweed.

'I'm afraid I am. I have some papers I have to go through. As Bob said, we'll see you later.'

'You're abandoning me,' she said with mock disappointment.

'Not for long. How could I?'

'Tweed,' she called out as he was leaving, 'that awful man Ed Osborne is staying here. Thought you ought to know . . .'

'The eagles gather.'

'I'd like both of you to pop along to my room with me. Just for a moment,' Tweed said as they were going upstairs. 'We have to plan for any emergency.'

Tweed unlocked the door to his room and let Paula go in first. She looked round and gave a sigh of pleasure.

'What a lovely room. Pure luxury.' She sat on his bed and bounced on it. 'If you're not careful I'm just going to drop off here.'

'Then I'll have to move all my stuff to your room. Not that I'll unpack much.'

'What do you think of Ed Osborne being here? We knew he would be coming, but he gave you details of the Schwarzwälder Hof. Not this place.'

'You heard my comment when Sharon warned me.'

'Which tells me a lot. You mentioned planning for an emergency. I took that to mean a sudden take-off. I've already decided I'll have a very quick shower, change into fresh underclothes, sleep in them. When we leave I'll be in my warm clothes, leggings and boots. I think it will be cold.'

'It will be freezing,' Newman told her.

'Paula has put her finger on the basic plan,' Tweed said, sitting in a chair. 'Ready to leave at a moment's notice. I think we'll get warning that they're on the move from Marler. There are a lot more of them at the

Schwarzwälder Hof. Here there's only Ronstadt and his three thugs.'

'So you're relying on Marler to call you?' Newman suggested.

'Yes. When he came to the car window to return your weaponry I slipped him Beck's powerful mobile phone.'

'What if Beck happened to call you?' Paula enquired.

'Then Marler would pass onto me whatever message Beck wanted to pass on. Incidentally, Ronstadt will probably leave tomorrow – that is, today – unless something happens to upset him.'

'Let's hope it does,' said Paula as she got up to leave. 'I'm not too keen on an early departure. I've got some sleep to catch up on. And I get the impression you're all falling for Sharon.'

'What man wouldn't?' Tweed said with a dry smile. 'She really is the most amazing woman.'

'Don't expect me down to breakfast. I'll have it in my room. I really couldn't stand seeing Ed Osborne at another table. He looked so grim when we left the bar at the Three Kings.' She made a face. 'As though he was expecting the heavens to fall.'

'Perhaps they will,' replied Tweed.

'Any idea where we're going when we head into the Black Forest?' she asked as she reached the door.

'In Kurt Schwarz's little black notebook, which I have with me, he mentioned Höllental. Which, as you know, is German for Hell's Valley.'

'You're so good for my morale. Give my love to Marler if he does call . . .'

Earlier, after turning down the right fork, Marler had found it easy to follow the three black Audis. Not that the route was easy. They soon plunged into a one-way system which twisted and turned. It wasn't long before

Marler realized they had entered the Altstadt – the Old City of Freiburg, built centuries ago.

Ancient stone buildings lined either side of the narrow streets. The lighting, from old street lanterns, was dim but adequate. They kept moving into shadows, then briefly into an illuminated area. The streets became cobbled, the car rocked as Marler kept down to a slow pace, imitating the red lights of the three cars ahead. There was hardly any other traffic, which was a blessing, but cars were parked everywhere, which was a curse.

Suddenly he caught sight of the moonlit towering spire of the Münster. Nield, sitting beside him, stared fixedly ahead.

'I reckon we must be nearly there. I think they're parking in that big open space by the Münster.'

'I think so too,' Marler agreed.

'So we wait until they've pushed off to the hotel.'

'Seems sensible. We'll give them time to register, get up to their rooms. If possible, I'd like both of you to keep under cover. It probably means going straight up to your rooms while I register, then having something to eat in the rooms.'

'Suits me,' said Butler.

'Good strategy, I'd say,' Nield agreed. 'What will you do?'

'Eat in the restaurant. I think those thugs will do the same. I want to memorize their faces.'

'Not an enjoyable pastime, I'd imagine,' commented Nield.

Having parked their cars, all twelve occupants walked out of the Münsterplatz and down a side street. Marler waited a little longer, then drove his car into the square and chose a place to park some distance from the three black Audis. He checked his watch, waited a minute or two longer, then they left the car, carrying their bags and walking down the side street.

It was very narrow, cobbled and black as pitch. Emerging at the other end they saw to their left the bright lights of the hotel. They entered, were met by a wave of warmth as they opened the door. Marler made straight for the reception desk.

'I'm sorry, but we are rather late,' he said to the man behind the counter. 'We have bookings.' He gave their names. 'My two friends are very tired. Could they go straight up to their rooms while I register?'

'Yes, sir. Here are their keys. Now, if you will register . . .'

'I'd like something to eat,' Marler told the receptionist. 'Any chance that the restaurant is still open?'

'Of course. You go through there. I can take your case to your room.'

'Thank you. I'll keep my holdall.'

The restaurant was large and inviting. It was constructed almost entirely of pinewood. It had panelled walls of pine, here and there were square pillars of pine, the woodblock floor was pine. They have an awful lot of timber in the Black Forest, Marler thought. On one side of the restaurant were banquette booths, each large enough to seat six people. He checked the menu, ordered one substantial dish when the waiter came.

He was alone in the spacious restaurant, but not for long. He was drinking a glass of wine, eating bread, when twelve tough-looking men trooped in. After looking round, a tall thin man ushered them into the booths. Several carried black anoraks and most wore thick woollen sweaters and heavy dark trousers.

Without appearing to do so, he kept an eye on them as he hurried through his meal. Next to the tall thin man sat a smaller man who was also not carrying much weight. Marler caught the small man staring at him. As soon as he looked up the man looked away, started talking to the thug who seemed to be the boss.

338

'Vernon,' he said quietly. 'That guy over in the corner with the smart clothes. I've seen him before.'

'And where would that be, Bernie?'

'Once when Jake put me on watch duty, checking out the Three Kings Hotel. Jake had given me a description of the girl with Tweed. Seem to recall her name was Paula Grey.'

'So what? Get to it.'

'I saw the Grey girl comin' out with another guy – and with the guy over there. My bet is he's here to spy on us.'

'You're sure?'

Bernie looked across at Marler again. He looked away quickly. Marler had glanced at him again. Bernie was hungry. He stuffed bread in his mouth.'

'Don't do that,' Vernon snapped. 'I asked were you sure.'

'I'm certain.'

When he had finished his meal Marler called out to the waiter. He raised his voice so it carried.

'Is it much colder outside? I feel like a breath of fresh air before I go to bed.'

'It is very cold,' the waiter replied.

'I still feel like a short walk.' He scribbled on the bill given to him by the waiter. 'Put the meal on my room number.'

With the holdall slung over his shoulder, he walked out of the restaurant into the lobby. Climbing a curving staircase he soon located his room. He looked round for a hiding place. Then he explored the bathroom. He put the holdall inside a linen bin, roughed up some towels, shoved them on top, replaced the lid. He left his coat in a cupboard. Marler could stand a lot of cold weather and a coat restricted his movements.

Returning downstairs, he walked through the restaurant. He had earlier spotted another door which led

339

to the outside world. He closed the door after stepping into a narrow street, little more than an alley. In the restaurant he had left, Vernon put his face close to his subordinate's.

'Bernie, go after him. Waste him. Not too close to the hotel.'

'Not my job, Vernon. I'm a printer.'

'Bernie, listen. Listen good. When you joined this outfit I remember Jake sent you to Philadelphia to eliminate a certain guy. It was a test. Jake likes all his people to handle a gun when it comes to it. You killed the guy in Philadelphia. You got a gun on you now.'

'I know. Do I get more bucks for doin' this?'

'That we can discuss later. Get after him.'

When he had closed the restaurant door behind him Marler looked up at a street sign, which was illuminated. *Munzgasse.* The alley was cobbled – and deserted. He started walking along it to get an idea of his surroundings. Knowledge which might come in useful later. It was very cold, very silent.

Near the end of the long alley he paused. To his left there was a café, Wirschaft. It was closed, as everywhere else would be now. He had heard footsteps behind him. Slow, cautious footsteps. Whoever he was, the damned fool had metal studs in the soles of his shoes. When he paused he no longer heard the footsteps. He was careful not to look back.

He walked out of the alley and stared ahead in surprise. Ahead was the last thing he had expected to see in the Old City. A weird complex of very modern concrete houses were stepped steeply up the side of a hill. They appeared to be detached residences and were the sort of structures he'd have expected to find in America.

340

The complex – with houses on either side – was divided into two sections by a long flight of wide concrete steps. Apart from those at street level, you had to climb the steps to reach the houses, which were on different levels. Behind them, higher still, loomed dense tree-clad slopes. He imagined this was the verge of the Black Forest. He could hear the footsteps behind him again, moving more rapidly.

He began climbing the steps quickly. The footsteps hurried now. Suddenly turning round, he looked down. It was the small thin man, wearing an anorak. Marler was almost at the top level. In his right hand his tail carried a gun. Marler smiled.

'What's all this about?'

'We kinda don't like spies.'

'What makes you think I am a spy?'

'Saw you leavin' the Three Kings in Basle. With your friend, Paula Grey.'

'You're not threatening me?' said Marler, still smiling.

'I'm kinda goin' to kill you.'

Marler stared down behind the gunman. It was the oldest trick in the world. He smiled again as though he hadn't a care in the universe.

'I like to know who's pointing a gun at me. You got a name?'

'Bernie Warner. Guess you might as well know the name of the last guy you'll ever see in this world.'

Marler was still staring fixedly behind Bernie. The thug was beginning to notice this. Also the fact that Marler kept smiling bothered him. You don't keep smiling when you're expecting a bullet in the chest. Marler nodded his head.

'Take him, Mike,' he called out.

Bernie swung round, saw there was no one behind him, turned back to shoot. In the two seconds it had taken him to check his rear Marler jumped on to the top step, dived sideways behind a concrete pillar. Crouched down, he found himself hemmed in by a collection of large, filled rubbish sacks with a sheaf of folded spares under his knees. Obviously when it became daylight the dustcart was due.

Jumping up the last few steps, Bernie stopped, swivelled the muzzle of his gun to where Marler crouched. A shot rang out. A red spot like an Eastern caste mark appeared on his forehead. Still gripping the Walther automatic in his hand, Marler watched Bernie collapse backwards, sprawling down the top steps.

Standing up, he walked down a couple of steps, checked the neck pulse. Nothing. Marler then became very active. He took one of the large spare sacks, walked down the two steps to where Bernie's head rested. He eased the head inside the sack first, then manoeuvred the shoulders inside. He had trouble getting the arms in but he managed it. Then he lifted the sack carefully and the rest of the corpse slithered in, leaving space at the top.

'Lucky he was a small man,' Marler said to himself.

He used a handkerchief to pick up Bernie's Beretta pistol, which still had his fingerprints on it, then dropped it into the sack. He next went back to the piled sacks, opened one, took out rubbish, stuffed it inside Bernie's sack. Fastening it, he heaved it over his shoulders, dumped it with the other sacks awaiting collection. His last precaution was to use his handerchief to remove the few spots of blood on the steps.

For the third time he glanced quickly round the concrete villas. No sign of lights, of life. It would be daylight soon. If anyone had heard the shot they'd probably thought it was a car backfiring.

He hurried down the steps. At the bottom he turned left and soon saw a main highway. He guessed that would be the route they'd take when they left Freiburg. Then he saw what he was looking for – a street drain.

Screwing up the blood-stained handkerchief, he pushed it down into the drain. He had once bought it while in Berlin, as one of a set. There was no way it could be traced back to him.

Turning back, he walked down Munzgasse to the hotel. He entered by the door leading into the restaurant. Five of the thugs were still seated in their booth – with the thin man Marler had picked out as the boss. Then he recalled Keith Kent's description of the man with Ronstadt in the Zürcher Kredit Bank. A tall thin man with a hard, thin bony face. The description fitted. And Newman had identified him as Vernon Kolkowski. Vernon had two empty steins in front of him and was halfway through a third. He was glowering when Marler walked in. His expression changed to one of disbelief when he saw Marler.

'Goodnight,' said Marler as he passed close to their table. 'Or, rather, good morning.'

Vernon's glower returned. He said nothing as Marler walked on, went up the curving staircase to his room. As soon as he was inside, the door relocked, Marler sat on his bed. He took from his pocket the small mobile, pressed numbers without consulting the piece of paper Tweed had provided with the number of the Colombi. When the night operator came on he asked to be put through to Tweed.

'Marler here. There were twelve little black men. Now there are eleven. And I'm coming to the Colombi – to attach another tracking gizmo to Ronstadt's Audi. Earlier in Basle he had a Citroën.'

'Thank you for keeping me informed . . .'

Tweed, still up, making notes on a pad, knew what Marler had meant. The twelve men in black Audis had now been reduced to eleven.

343

34

The repercussions of Marler's encounter with Bernie Warner were far more widespread than he could ever have anticipated. Jake Ronstadt, unable to sleep in his luxurious bedroom at the Colombi, was still up long after a grey and gloomy dawn light had spread over Freiburg. He sat in a chair, wearing an oriental dressing gown with dragons rampant. He was trying to make up his mind whether to move on to Höllental that day, or whether to wait for twenty-four hours.

On the one hand he was very short of time. On the other he knew his troops were fatigued, and by no means at their fighting best. The short, barrel-chested figure wedged in the armchair was also not in good shape. The fact that he had been drinking generous slugs of the precious bourbon he kept in a hip flask had not helped.

He'd had a shock earlier when, hidden in the bar, he'd seen Tweed, Newman and Paula Grey sitting with Sharon and Sir Guy. Where were Tweed's other men? He'd expected they would all head for the Schwarz-wälder Hof. They appeared to have split into two forces, which worried him.

He was helping himself to another slug of bourbon when his phone rang. He clambered out of his chair, picked up the instrument.

'Yeah?'

'It's Vernon, Chief. We have a problem.'

'That I could do without. What problem? Spit it out.'

'Bernie has gone missin' – we've looked everywhere and he's just gone . . .'

'*I don't believe you!*' Ronstadt yelled down the phone.

'He has to be with you. Goddamn it, he's the printer. I need him as a double-check.'

'I don't get that.'

'You're not supposed to. What the hell are you talkin' about?' he raved. 'Maybe you'll get around to tellin' me what's goin' on.'

'Give me a chance, Chief. We're eatin' in the restaurant here. Bernie recognized one of Tweed's men. Saw him comin' out of the Three Kings place. I thought it was a good moment to cut down the opposition. This guy goes for a walk in the night, I send Bernie after him. The guy comes back! About half an hour later. Bernie never comes back.'

'You shouldn't have sent Bernie, you friggin' idiot.'

'He was the one who recognized him.'

'You said you'd looked everywhere. What in hell does that mean?' Ronstadt snarled.

'Six of us went out. I went myself. Brad nearly got knocked down by a dustcart collectin' rubbish.'

'Pity you weren't knocked down.' Ronstadt took a deep breath to get himself under control. 'Here's what you all do for today. Nothin' at all. Get it? You stay in your rooms and wait there for me to call.'

'OK, Chief. We need the rest.'

'Stick your rest. Why you had to send the printer on a job like that I don't know. Bernie was important. A damn sight more important than you!' he shouted, then slammed down the phone.

He went back to his armchair, slumped into it. He had a lot to think about. Should he try and contact Charlie? No! Charlie would crucify him. He had a deadline to keep and, in his fury, he had thrown away twenty-four hours. Unusually for Ronstadt, he wasn't sure what to do. His mind whirled. Should he ask Charlie to find a substitute for Bernie? No! Even if he risked Charlie's wrath there wasn't time. He reached for his hip flask, then left it in his hip pocket.

He'd have a bath, get dressed, then go down for breakfast. He might get an inkling of what Tweed was up to. Then he had a bright idea. They'd leave for Höllental in the middle of the night. The decision taken, he felt better. He decided a shower might help to clear his brain. He had the mother of all headaches.

Paula woke, felt her normal alert self. She checked the time. It was only 9.30 a.m. Maybe they would still be serving breakfast in the dining room. She disliked room service. An American habit. Showering and dressing quickly, she went down and paused at the entrance. They were still serving breakfast.

Ed Osborne, big in a thick white polo-necked sweater and grey slacks, sat at a table by himself from where he could survey the whole room. At a remote corner table Sharon also sat by herself, eating buttered toast with one hand, marking up a file with the other. That woman never stops working, Paula thought. Osborne saw her, looked at her with a forbidding expression, then bent his head over a newspaper.

At another table for four Tweed sat with Newman. He caught her eye, gestured for her to join them. She sat down so she was facing the distant Sharon.

'When I came in,' Tweed said, 'I went over to her and suggested she'd probably sooner be on her own at breakfast. She thanked me for my intuition and consideration.'

'She's a slave-driver,' said Newman, 'the slave being herself. We didn't expect you down so early. You got some sleep?'

'I crashed out. It may not have been for long but I feel I've had the best sleep for days.' She looked up as a waiter stood by her. 'I'll have coffee, a glass of orange juice, and also croissants. Nothing else, thank you.' She looked at Tweed. 'Any idea of what we're doing today?'

'None at all. I'm waiting for Marler to press the button. Look who's just arrived.'

She stared at the entrance. Jake Ronstadt was standing there as she had, scanning the restaurant. She was staring because of the way he was dressed. Granted it was breakfast time, so she wouldn't have expected guests to dress up. But Ronstadt was wearing a brown leather jacket, heavy brown leather trousers and thick-soled shoes. Over his arm he carried a black overcoat and his left hand clutched a baseball cap.

'Looks as though he could be leaving,' Paula whispered. 'Oh, Lord, I think he's coming over to us.'

Before he started moving towards their table Sharon had glanced up, then immediately looked down at her file. Osborne, also, had seen his arrival. He gave the newcomer one bleak stare, then resumed reading his newspaper.

'Hi, folks,' Ronstadt greeted them. 'What a big surprise. You're a long way from Goodfellows back in London,' he said addressing Paula. He held out his large hand and she felt compelled to shake it. 'Say, you've got quite a grip there.'

'It comes in useful on occasion,' she replied, staring straight into his hard eyes.

'I guess it does.' He chuckled, a deep rumble which seemed to originate deep down in his chest. 'Fending off unwanted admirers. I guess there must be quite a few of 'em.' He turned his attention to Tweed. 'You sure get around.'

'So do you,' Tweed replied bluntly. 'Where exactly have you come from to get here?'

'I was in Basle. Nice peaceful city. Nothin' ever

347

happens there.' He paused, as though expecting a reaction. 'Now I'm tourin' Germany. Kinda restin' up. Got a big job in London when I get back there.'

'What kind of a job is that?' Newman rapped out.

'Settlin' in new staff. We're enlarging the Embassy. London is becomin' the key city in the Western world.'

'London could do without the bombs,' Paula said, lifting her voice. 'And the hideous casualties caused by mindless terrorists.'

Out of the corner of her eye she saw both Sharon and Osborne look up, startled by her vehemence.

'You're sure right there,' Ronstadt agreed equably. 'Think I've disturbed you folks enough. Have a nice day.'

He walked off to an isolated table. On the way he called out in a rough manner.

'Waiter! Over here! I'm hungry.'

'Aggressive, callous bastard,' Paula hissed quietly, her hand gripping the napkin in her lap to regain self-control.

'Oh, he was deliberately being provocative,' Tweed said calmly. 'I liked your reference to bombs and terrorists, Paula. He didn't linger after that. I don't think he was very happy about the whole restaurant hearing you.'

'Did he hurt your hand when he shook it?' Newman enquired. 'I saw he exerted all his strength.'

'No, he didn't. My grip is as strong as his. My aerobics. And I wanted to test his strength. I might come up against him later on my own.'

'Don't,' Newman warned, keeping his voice down. 'He's probably packing a gun at this moment.'

'And I'm packing my Browning,' Paula retorted. 'It does look as though he's leaving after breakfast, doesn't it?'

'No,' said Tweed.

'What makes you say that?' she demanded.

'The fact that he was putting on a demonstration for our benefit.'

'What kind of a demonstration?'

'Rather an obvious ploy. To give us the impression that he is leaving shortly. Hence his clothes, his overcoat and baseball cap. If he was on his way he'd attempt to conceal it. I think he's had enough of us. And something Marler phoned me about will, I'm sure, have upset Mr Jake Ronstadt. Thrown him off balance. Tell you later.'

'So we're here a bit longer?'

'At least for the rest of the day would be my guess. I see Sharon is leaving. She's gone now.' He drank more coffee. A short while later he stared. 'Well, look who's arrived.'

Paula and Newman stared across the dining room. Standing in the entrance, looking round the room, dressed in a dove-grey two-piece suit, was Denise Chatel. She was clutching a large handbag. After swiftly checking out who was having breakfast she vanished.

35

Newman was getting up from the table when Tweed glanced across at Ronstadt. It seemed obvious he hadn't seen Denise. Crouched over a mobile phone, he had his head down, concentrating on his conversation.

'I'm going after her,' said Newman.

'Good idea,' said Tweed.

He doubted whether Newman had heard him. Without appearing to hurry, he was moving at speed out of the restaurant. He found no trace of Sharon outside. She must have gone straight up to her room. He saw Denise at the *garderobe*, collecting her coat. He went over in time to help her on with it. She nearly jumped out of her skin

349

until she saw who it was. She moved towards the exit and Newman walked alongside her.

'Someone in the restaurant you didn't like the look of?' he asked cheerfully.

'Yes.'

'Ronstadt? Osborne?'

'I don't want to talk about it.'

'But you do want breakfast. We can find a café outside. Plenty of them in Freiburg.'

'I'm ravenous, Bob.'

They were already outside in the street. She was becoming more confident about him, he sensed. They turned left and, walking fast, she almost slipped on a stretch of ice. He grasped hold of her, saved her from falling.

'Loop you arm through mine,' he said firmly.

She did so. She was trembling, and not with the cold. She was wearing a thick overcoat with a high collar. He smiled at her as they continued walking.

'People will start talking if they see us like this.'

'That's not funny.'

'Just a joke.'

'Bob.' She looked at him. 'You haven't got a coat and it's freezing. Should we go back so you can get one?' she suggested without any enthusiasm.

'The cold doesn't worry me. It's the great heat – with humidity – which I find trying.'

He was telling the truth. In this respect he was like Tweed, who also could stand any amount of cold, but he had to push himself hard in hot, humid weather. They arrived outside a large café-cum-restaurant. Denise tugged at his arm.

'Let's check out this place. I want to get you inside into some warmth.'

It was an old place, with huge dark wooden beams across the ceiling. There were several couples inside, dressed like locals. Denise nodded, guided him inside, made for a remote table near the back. He helped her off with her coat and felt the warmth on his face and bare hands. They sat facing each other.

'When did you last eat?' he asked, picking up the menu.

'I had a snack yesterday afternoon in my room at the Three Kings.'

'Nothing since? I see. How about a whopping great omelette?'

'Sounds wonderful. Mushroom, if they've got it. Otherwise plain would do fine. And a lot of coffee, with milk.'

The waitress, with a checked blouse and a dark skirt, appeared. He ordered a large omelette for Denise, a small one for himself. He had already had breakfast but he thought it would make her feel more comfortable if he ate with her. He didn't look at her. Instead he looked round the restaurant.

'Is Alec with you?' she asked suddenly.

'Alec?'

'Marler.'

'Of course. I was dreaming. He's in the city, but he's some way off. I'm afraid you'll have to put up with me.'

'I'm sorry, Bob. I didn't mean it like that. I feel perfectly comfortable with you.'

'Thank you. Good . . .'

He said no more until they were served. Then he waited until she had eaten every scrap of her huge omelette, plus quite a lot of bread, drinking her milky coffee between bites. Her face had been ashen, but now her high colour had returned. She leant back in her chair, laid a hand on her tummy.

'Not very elegant, but I do feel better.'

'You drove here from Basle?'

'Yes, I did. It was very tiring. When I appeared in the

restaurant I registered, had my bag taken up to a room, was given my key.'

She produced it from her handbag. Holding it, she let him read the number, then dropped it back into her handbag. He asked her if she'd mind if he smoked one cigarette.

'Not if you give me one too. Thank you. Did Alec tell you what I'd told him? About my parents in the States?'

'Yes, he did.'

'You probably wonder what I've been doing. First I disappear, then I reappear.'

'Tell me only if you want to.'

'I didn't tell Marler. I kept it as a secret from everyone. I felt I didn't know *who* I could trust. I recently hired another top private investigator in Virginia to check out my parents' so-called accident at that lonely bridge. A man called Walt Banker. He's visited that retired sheriff, Jim Briscoe, the man who took me to the site of the tragedy, then was retired quickly. Banker told me Briscoe has changed his story, says it was an accident. Banker was sure he was lying. Somehow he checked his balance at the local bank. Recently he paid in fifty thousand dollars. My investigator said it had to be a bribe paid to Briscoe, which is why he now says it was an accident.'

'Did this Banker go back to see Briscoe to ask him about this big sum of money?'

'Yes, he said he did. Briscoe hit the roof. Said it was a legacy from an uncle. Banker asked for the uncle's name. Briscoe flew into a rage, threw him out. A couple of days later Banker was nearly killed. A car tried to run him down. Banker got the registration number of the car, checked it out.' She paused. 'He found it had been hired. In Washington.'

'Interesting. Very. And what are you going to do now? Go back to the hotel?'

'I'm scared, Bob. What do I tell Sharon? After I left the Three Kings I took a room in a small hotel so I could phone the investigator safely. She'll go stark raving mad if I tell her. I'll be fired and I'll never get another job. She pays me very well.'

'Why wouldn't you get another job? There must be plenty available in Washington for someone with your experience.'

'Because it will be passed down the grapevine. I'll be blacklisted. That's how it works in Washington.'

'Just exactly how does it work in Washington?' Newman asked.

'Employers at Sharon's top level form a kind of club. They tell each other about their employees. You get blacklisted, and every door is closed to you.'

'Really. And Sharon would blow the whistle on you?'

'I know she would.'

'Then here's what you tell her.' Newman drank more coffee while he worked it out, checking to make sure it was watertight. 'You went out for a walk in the evening – to freshen up for more work. You were followed by a tall thin man with a thin bony face. Can you remember that?'

'Yes, he doesn't sound very nice.'

'He isn't. He exists. Sharon may well have caught sight of him back at the Embassy in London. The tall thin man was very close to you – he wore a black overcoat – when a cruising police car approached. You crossed the street, hurried back to the hotel. You were just going inside when you saw the same man coming towards you from the opposite direction. You rushed up to your room, packed, asked the doorman to bring your car. Then you drove off, stayed for a few hours at the small hotel in Basle, the one where you did stay. When you'd recovered you drove to the Colombi. Have you got that?'

'Every word. I was imagining it happening while you were talking. Sharon may start questioning me. She's like that.'

'Just stick to the same story. Don't embroider. No more details. If necessary blow your top, tell her you were scared out of your wits. Tell her you're still thinking of phoning the police in Basle to report the incident.'

'It might work,' Denise said.

'It will work. Now go back to the Colombi on your own. When you arrive ask for Sharon's room number. Find her at once.'

'I'm very grateful to you, Bob . . .'

'Just go. Now.'

When he was alone Newman drank more coffee. He decided that he would try and contact Marler. The intense cold hit him when he left the café. Walking a short distance, he found a smart-looking men's clothier. Going inside, he bought a German coat, a pair of gloves. Resuming his walk, he passed locals muffled up, treading warily on the slippery pavements. Overhead a low grey bank of cloud pressed down on the city like a lid. He stopped to study a big map of Freiburg, located Konvikstrasse near the Münster.

Threading his way through a network of alleys, he was guided by the looming spire of the Münster. More people were about as he entered Münsterplatz. Hurrying, to get out of the cold, a few bumped into him. Apologizing, they hastened on. Then he saw Marler. Newman siffened. Locals pushed past Marler, who was walking slowly. Behind him a hatless man in a black coat was only three people away from Marler's back.

Newman himself began hurrying, bumping into people. Then he stopped at the edge of the crowd. Marler had also stopped, glancing over his shoulder. The hatless man in a black coat had turned away, was hustling off towards the edge of the square. Newman saw him enter a narrow alley, stop, then he turned round and waited as though observing Marler.

Newman had had a better look at him in profile. Tall, thin with a hard bony face. It was the man he had described to Denise. Vernon Kolkowski, the man Keith Kent had seen with Ronstadt inside the Zürcher Kredit in Basle. Kent's description fitted perfectly. Newman joined Marler.

'You had company.'

'Mornin' to you, Bob,' Marler drawled. 'And I knew I had company. He's standing in an alley leading to the Schwarzwälder Hof, watching me – while I watch something else.'

'Which is?'

'Look across the square. Three black Audis parked close together. Four of Ronstadt's men getting into one car.'

'They're on the move . . .'

'Are they? Where are the rest of them? Eight more men – seven, now. I had an arument with one of them early this morning. He won't be arguing with anyone else ever again. There they go, driving off.'

'Did they have luggage?'

'Yes, each man carried a bag.'

'Then we'd better break all records getting to the Colombi so we can warn Tweed. Won't take us long to get there.'

'My idea too!'

In his room at the Colombi Jake Ronstadt was sprawled along an expensively upholstered couch. He had his back against one arm, his body and legs stretched out. He hadn't bothered to take off his boots, which rested on a

355

decorated cushion. His mobile phone had started buzzing.

'Yeah?'

'Vernon here. It worked like a dream.'

'Get your head screwed on, Vernon. I do like specifics.'

'Your plan. The guy who went out early this morning – and Bernie follows him – was eating a late breakfast. I sent out four of my guys with bags through the restaurant. The guy leaves the rest of his breakfast, follows my four to their Audi. Another guy – one of them – joins him. They stand in the square, watch the Audi take off, then they move like hell away from the square. Could they be comin' to your place?'

'Of course they are, Brainless.'

'So I tells the six still here to pack and we all move off with Brad in the Audi that's just left?'

'Brainless, you stay exactly where you are until you hear from me. Are you listenin' with both your thick ears?' Ronstadt snarled.

'Sure, Chief.'

'When I say you stays there you all stays in your rooms. Got it?'

'Sure, Chief.'

'Miracles sometimes happen. Brad and his three men don't go to the base. They waits at the point I tells you about earlier.'

'Brad knows. I marked the place on a map, the place you described to me. Brad said looks like they's gonna have to drive up a bloody mountain,' Vernon warned.

'That's his problem. They got food and drink? They's gonna have to wait a long time. Till after dark. Till a coupla white Audis follow me along that road into Höllental. Did Brad get the crowbars?'

'Sure, Chief. Sent him out early this mornin' and he finds a car spares shop. He buys three crowbars, has 'em well wrapped, and he locks them in the Audi. He said it sounds like a long wait and a lot of hard work diggin' out boulders. If there are any.'

'There are. I noticed them last time I visited the base when I flew over earlier in the year. Can't start an avalanche without a bit of work. Go back to your room, Brainless.'

'That's where I am now.'

'Get some sleep, if you want to. Keep the phone close to your thick ear. Get the kitchen there to make up food packs for all of you. With drink,' Ronstadt demanded.

'Sure, Chief.'

'Another miracle. You musta eaten a lotta fish. Good for the brain. Eat a whole lot more . . .'

Ronstadt cut the connection. He stretched out a bit further on the couch. This was an unusual experience. Enjoying a bit of comfort. He grinned savagely and said the words aloud.

'Good place for you to end your career, Tweed. In the dark of the Black Forest.'

36

'No! Definitely not!' said Tweed.

Ten minutes earlier he had listened in silence while Newman and Marler told him what they had seen close to the Münster. In his room, when they had arrived, were also Paula and Keith Kent. Newman let Marler speak first. Then he reported what Denise Chatel had told him when they'd breakfasted together in the café further into Freiburg. Tweed stood as he listened, close to a window with hands clasped behind his back, his eyes fixed on whichever man was speaking. It was after Newman made a suggestion that Tweed spoke so emphatically.

'So,' Newman had remarked, 'we think the best thing

is to leave here now, follow that Audi – I'm sure we can catch them up on the main route into Höllental.'

'What's your objective?' Newman persisted in response to Tweed's vehement rejection. 'Or perhaps I should say objection? They have made a fatal mistake. They've split their forces. We can destroy them piecemeal.'

'My main objective is to destroy their base.' Tweed took from his pocket an envelope, extracted the two fake British banknotes they had obtained in St Ursanne. 'I'm convinced the Americans have devised a deadly plan to destabilize Britain.'

'I don't see their significance,' said Paula.

'Oh, you will, you will. Marler, you've just told me about how you dealt with Bernie Warner, whoever he was. Did you notice whether the tips of his fingers were dirty?'

'Yes, I did. At the time I didn't think anything of it. They were stained black.'

'Printing ink,' said Tweed. 'You probably exterminated one of Ronstadt's key men.' His voice took on a grimmer note. 'But we must destroy that base. And the only man who'll lead us to it is Ronstadt. So we have to wait until he leaves here on his way to Höllental. Have you a good supply of explosives, Marler?'

'Enough to blow half Freiburg sky high.'

'Good.'

'What Bob is worried about,' Marler explained, 'is that the Audi which has left with four men inside could be setting up an ambush.'

'I'm sure it is,' Tweed agreed equably. 'I'm sure you can deal with that, Marler, while we keep after Ronstadt.'

'They may be using something like bazookas,' Paula warned. 'You know what the Americans are – they think anything big is better, whether it's a battleship or a weapon operated by one man.'

'We do have smoke bombs, a lot of them,' Marler reminded her. 'A man using a bazooka has to see his

358

target. Smoke bombs land all round him. He's in a fog. Target disappears. I'll give you a few more.'

'Another point,' Newman pressed, 'is how can we be sure we'll know when Ronstadt is leaving?'

'I've attended to that,' Tweed told him. 'I phoned Kuhlmann, head of the Federal Kriminalpolizei in Wiesbaden, as you know. Also a close friend. He has phoned the manager here, saying he is tracking terrorists. He's asked the manager to inform me of any sign that Ronstadt is leaving.'

'Point covered, then.'

'Reverting to that intriguing story Denise Chatel told you: if it's true, wouldn't it be strange if the key to the momentous events we're caught up in lies in the car accident, so called, which killed both her parents in Virginia?'

'It would be very strange,' Newman agreed. 'But I don't see how.'

'It's just a glimmer of an idea which flashed into my mind as I listened to you. And we still don't know who the mysterious Charlie is. Charlie's identity is possibly the real key.'

A little later Tweed told Marler to go back to the Schwarzwälder Hof and to keep him informed. He then looked round at the others and said he wanted a private meeting with someone, so would they mind leaving him until he phoned them in their rooms? As soon as he was alone he picked up the phone and asked Guy Strangeways to come and see him for a chat. While he waited Tweed took out a recording device, tested it to make sure it was in working order.

'Guy, do sit down. Would you like some coffee?'

'No, thank you. Drank too much of it already at breakfast.'

'You don't look your normal self, you know.'

Strangeways had seated himself in an armchair, slumped against the back. Tweed sat in a chair opposite him with a small table between them. His guest showed every sign of nervous exhaustion. He kept pulling at his moustache, staring at Tweed. When he did speak his voice almost quivered.

'What is this all about?'

'It's about you. You've got something on your mind and it is tearing you to pieces. We've known each other a long time, off and on, so maybe you can help me.'

'God knows, I'm the one who needs help.' He paused, then it all came tumbling out. 'I've besmirched the family name. That must sound pretty old-fashioned.'

'Not to me, it doesn't. What happened?'

'I took a gamble in business in the States and I was short of money. Only for a while but my competitors were closing in on me. Tweed, to cut a long story short, I accepted a bribe from the Americans of half a million dollars.'

'Anyone operating in the States can get caught up in the corrupt atmosphere that prevails over there. You must have promised something in return for the bribe.'

'The Yanks are planning on converting Britain into a colony of America,' he burst out. His voice grew stronger. 'We will become a state of their bloody Union. Hawaii was the fiftieth state. We would become the fifty-first state. The condition of the bribe was that if you refused to become Governor – they were very keen for you to accept – then I'd assume the post. If you accepted I'd get another big post running Britain.' He stood up, began marching round the room as he talked. 'I feel better now I've told you. Ironically, I didn't need the half a million. I tried to give it back. It's still in a special account I had set up in London.'

'What happened when you attempted to return the half a million?'

'They showed me a photo – taken secretly – of my opening their executive case with the money inside. They said they'd send the photo, and the story, to tabloids in Britain and to top newspapers in New York. My reputation would be ruined.'

'Guy, who handed you the money?'

'That vile creature Jake Ronstadt. A man I wouldn't have inside Irongates. In the photo he's smirking. I'm going to return the money anyway. I had put a codicil in my will that it was to go to a charity.' His voice had become vibrant. 'Now I'm going to return it and damn the consequences.'

'How will you do that?'

'I've asked Sharon if she knows the private address of the Secretary of the Treasury in Washington. She does. I didn't give her any idea what I wanted it for.'

'But by accepting the money you were able to gain information as to what they intended,' Tweed said quietly.

'That's true.'

'So that's why you accepted the supposed bribe. Guy, we have to defeat them, even at the eleventh hour. I have a recording machine here. I want us to start the conversation all over again. You answer my questions, explain that you accepted the so-called bribe to find out what they were really up to. So you could tell me. If you do this it will help me enormously.'

'It will?'

'Enormously. Let's start now . . .'

Tweed put the same kind of questions, Guy answered them as Tweed had suggested. The answers came in a strong clear voice. Watching him, Tweed was startled by the transformation which had come over Guy Strangeways.

He looked years younger, totally alert, his blue eyes fiery. When they had finished Tweed switched off his small recorder.

'Are you expecting a firefight with the enemy?' Guy asked suddenly.

'It could be on the cards.'

'Got as many men as they have?'

'No. We are outnumbered, but that doesn't worry us.'

'Take me with you, to help even things up.'

'Can I think about that?' Tweed suggested.

'Don't think I'm up to it, do you? I am armed.'

Guy slid a Smith & Wesson .38 revolver out of a shoulder holster under his jacket, the weapon favoured by Newman. He began unloading the gun, placing six bullets on the small table.

'Why are you carrying that?' Tweed asked quietly.

'Like to be able to look after myself in a tight corner. See that picture of a man over there? That's the target.'

Guy loaded and raised the revolver, aiming at the picture. Tweed watched him closely. Guy held the revolver in one hand, pulled the trigger six times in rapid succession. The gun was steady as a rock. No sign of even a hint of a quiver. The demonstration impressed Tweed far more than he'd expected. Guy talked while he reloaded the weapon, returned it to his holster.

'I did manage to cope in the Gulf War. As you know, I was a general. Part of the sweeping left hook which raced across the desert to cut off the whole of Saddam's Presidential Guard. Then the damn Yanks stopped us. In another twenty-four hours we'd have destroyed Saddam for ever.'

'I know,' said Tweed. 'I'd like first to get in touch with one of my team. Then could I phone you in your room?'

'Of course. Incidentally, when you speak to your chap stress I take orders from him. I serve as a simple foot soldier. Won't make any suggestions unless I'm specifically asked for them.'

'I'll tell him. Going back briefly to that silly business about the money. Did you tell Sharon?'

'Good God, no! Thought I'd made that clear. Wouldn't dream of it. I've told no one except you, and I'll keep it that way. Just before I leave you alone, there is another problem.'

'Which is?'

'The usual one. Rupert. He's traipsing round with that swine, Basil. Windermere is a bad influence on him.' He smiled grimly. 'And probably Rupert is equally a bad influence on Basil.'

'You don't mean they're here?'

'They are. Both have a room in this hotel. They were passengers when I drove here from Basle. Found myself between the devil and the deep blue sea. Didn't want them with me. Didn't want to leave them behind. Thought it best to keep an eye on them. At this moment they're in the bar downstairs, of course. Saw them a few minutes before I went back up to my room in time to take your phone call.'

'You'll have to leave them on their own if you should come with us – if we're going anywhere.'

'Trouble is Basil has hired a car here in Freiburg. So they're mobile. But there are more important things than those two. I'd better go now. I'll wait for your phone call . . .'

Alone in his room, Tweed called Monica on Beck's mobile phone. He could tell from her voice the moment she answered that she was excited.

'Tweed, is this line safe?'

'Yes, it is. You have news?'

'Roy Buchanan called me, wanted to speak to you.

363

When I said you weren't available he gave some data to pass on. No more bombs have exploded. You know why?'

'I will if you tell me.'

'Well—'

'Monica, could you hold on? Something I have to check. Back in a moment . . .'

Tweed had started calling Monica as soon as Guy had left the room. He had vaguely been aware of some kind of commotion outside in the corridor. Running to the door, he opened it. Paula stood there. Her expression was strange. He went into the corridor. To his right stood Osborne, smoking a fresh cigar.

'Hi there, Tweed. Time we had that drink in the bar.'

Osborne seemed the jovial hail-fellow-well-met type he had been when he had visited Tweed in his office at Park Crescent. He waved his cigar in greeting.

'What is it, Paula?' Tweed asked, irritated.

'I was coming along to your room when I heard an argument. Two voices. One was Sir Guy's. He was shouting, sounded furious. I couldn't see who the other person was. The argument sounded vicious. I was a little way round a corner, so I couldn't see anything. When I got here I saw Sir Guy disappearing. Mr Osborne was standing where he is now . . .'

'The name is *Ed*,' Osborne called out amiably. 'OK, Paula?'

'The name is Miss Grey,' she shot back. 'Did you see who was in the corridor with Sir Guy Strangeways?'

'Nope. I just came outta my room. What's the problem?'

'There isn't one,' said Tweed. 'Paula, come in. I'm talking to somebody.'

He locked the door when they were both inside, ran back to the phone he'd left on a table. He explained briefly to Paula over his shoulder.

'I have Monica holding on. Be with you soon . . .

'Monica. Sorry about that. Turned out to be nothing. Now I can give you my full attention.'

'Well, Buchanan is using to the full his new powers. He's ringed the American Embassy in Grosvenor Square with a large team of plain-clothes officers, all armed. When anyone comes out they're followed – on foot if they're walking, in a car if they drive away. Since he employed these tactics no more bombs, as I told you earlier.'

'Any protests from the Americans?'

'You bet. Buchanan happened to be there in a car with a team when Morgenstern came out, was driven off in a limo. Buchanan followed him. Morgenstern stopped his limo, demanded to know what was going on. Buchanan explained they'd had a tip-off that terrorists were going to bomb the Embassy, so he was providing protection.'

'Clever. Significant that the bombings have stopped.'

'Earlier someone had placed a bomb – a big one – inside a key telephone exchange. The Bomb Squad found it, defused it.'

'Any other developments?'

'I was just going to tell you. An FBI team flew in, offered their services. Buchanan said he didn't need an alien force to help. They didn't like that at all. The situation appears to be under control. For the moment.'

'Thank you, Monica. Make a note of this hotel's name and my room number. I may not be here long. And I'll give you the number of my mobile phone . . .'

He gave her the data, thanked her again, ended the call, turned to look at Paula. She was sitting down, listened intently as he asked the question.

'Something very weird went on in that corridor a few minutes ago. I even thought I heard the sounds of a

365

struggle. Were you able to identify the second voice – the voice of the person arguing with Guy?'

'No. It was a voice I haven't heard before. Strident. Using filthy language.'

'Voice of a man, a woman?'

'Sorry, Tweed, but I couldn't tell. I thought I caught the tone of a very American accent, but I could be wrong. I was still a distance along the other corridor, which muffled things a lot.'

'But you could hear Sir Guy's voice?'

'Definitely. His is so distinctive. I thought I heard him shout, "Don't you damned well talk to me like that." But again I'm not sure. When I turned the corner he was just disappearing round a corner in the distance. Ed Osborne wa standing outside his room.'

'How long do you think he'd been there?'

'No idea. It looked as though he'd just come out of his room. His cigar had been trimmed and was alight.'

'I don't like it.' Tweed stirred in the arm chair he had sat in. 'Something very weird is going on, as I said a few minutes ago.'

Paula, sitting in an armchair opposite him, the one Guy had occupied, reached out and felt the coffee pot on the table. She reached for a clean cup and saucer.

'This coffee feels fresh. Drink some. It will help you to get the brain racing.'

She watched while he drank slowly. He was staring at nothing, as though his mind was miles away. He put the cup down and spoke slowly.

'Guy was with me before he left this room. He's offered to join us as a reinforcement. He knows roughly what they're up to and thinks they should be stopped. Incidentally, regarding what happened in the corridor you used the word "vicious". Were you referring to Guy?'

'No, to whoever he was arguing with. I've just had a

thought. Osborne was in the corridor. Could he have been the person Guy was having a verbal battle with?'

'Wouldn't you have recognized his voice?'

'Not necessarily. I've never heard Osborne in a towering rage.'

'Voices do change according to the mood a person is in.'

'You said Guy was going to join us. Is that a good idea?'

'I came to the conclusion he would be an asset. But if he does come he'll have to travel in Marler's Audi. There's space for a fourth person there. I must phone Marler, put the idea to him. If he doesn't agree, Guy doesn't come.'

Tweed took the mobile out of his pocket. He called the other hotel, explained the position to Marler vaguely, not using Guy's name. Then he put the phone on the table.

'Marler's phoning me back from an outside phone. We'll have to wait.'

They waited ten minutes. During that time they didn't speak a word to each other. Paula deliberately kept silent. Tweed was frowning, had a look of intense concentration. When the phone rang he explained the idea in detail, emphasizing it was up to Marler whether he agreed. When he broke the connection he smiled at Paula.

'Marler agrees we take Guy. It was Guy's reference to his being treated as a foot soldier which convinced him. And Guy knows something about war. Which is what I foresee we'll be engaged in during our trip to the Black Forest. All-out war.'

'Any chance of a quick lunch downstairs?' Paula suggested. 'I had a good breakfast but I'm hungry again. Must be the cold.'

'We'll go down now.'

It was when they arrived in the lobby, bustling with staff, all moving about in a chaotic state and apparently to no purpose, that they received a dreadful shock. The chief receptionist ran up to Tweed. His hands were trembling.

'Mr Tweed, Sir Guy Strangeways has been shot. He's dead. He went out for a walk and left his gloves on the counter. I ran out and saw him fall. I heard the shot.'

37

Paula stood very still, hardly able to take in the news. Tweed also froze, his expression blank. But not for long. He spoke quietly to the receptionist to calm him down.

'Did you see anyone, or anything, else while you were outside?'

'No one. I thought I saw the rear of a brown Opel disappearing round a corner. But I can't be sure about that.'

'Where is the body?'

'With the help of some of the staff I put it in that room over there. The one with the closed door.'

'Thank you,' Tweed said as Newman appeared.

He heard Paula telling Newman what had happened as he walked towards the closed door. He had his hand on the handle when Rupert arrived, grabbing his arm.

'You can't go in there,' Rupert growled.

'Don't ever take hold of me again!'

Tweed heaved his shoulder against Rupert. The impact sent Rupert staggering back. He recovered and was advancing again on Tweed when Newman grasped hold of Rupert from behind, twisting up his arm.

'You're hurting me,' Rupert snarled.

'Make any more wrong moves and I'll break your bloody arm.'

Tweed had opened the door and walked into a sitting room. Over a couch a sheet had been drawn. He lifted it, looked down at the body laid on its back. Guy, eyes closed, looked very peaceful, except for one blemish. In the centre of his forehead was a ragged hole with congealed blood where the bullet had gone in. He replaced the sheet, left the room, closed the door, walked over to the receptionist.

'How long ago did this happen?'

'I suppose it must have been at least half an hour ago, sir.'

Tweed turned to Paula. He guided her away from the staff milling round in the lobby. He spoke to her in a quiet corner.

'Could it really have been half an hour?'

'Easily – or longer. After we heard Sir Guy arguing with someone in the corridor you took a while drinking coffee and thinking. Then you called Marler,' she went on, keeping her voice low, 'and we had to wait for him to call us back. Afterwards, when he did call back, you spent quite a bit of time explaining things to him about Sir Guy's offer to come with us. Time can pass more quickly than we realize. Now I come to reckon it up, it could have been well over half an hour before we came down to get some lunch.'

'What's happening now?'

Paula turned round and saw men in white coats and trousers come in carrying a stretcher. Rupert guided them to the room where his father lay. Tweed strode forward with Paula at his heels until he reached Rupert.

'What's going on?' Tweed demanded.

'I called them after consulting the receptionist. They're taking him to the airport just outside Freiburg, if you must know.'

369

'The airport? Why, in Heaven's name?'

'Because – ' Rupert's manner became sarcastic – 'at airports they have planes. I've hired a private aircraft to fly him straight home. I know that's what he would have wanted.'

'You must be mad. Your father was murdered. There'll have to be an autopsy here.'

'I'm not having foreign doctors cutting up my father's body. In case you haven't grasped it, I'm his next of kin. It's nothing to do with you.'

'It has a lot to do with the German police.'

'Oh, I fixed that. I phoned Chief Inspector Kuhlmann at Wiesbaden. I told him you agreed the body should be flown straight back to Britain.'

'You told him *what*?' Tweed was in one of his rare rages. 'How dare you use my name without my permission? And what exactly did Kuhlmann say?'

'Something about in view of the present situation he'd make an exception and waive the normal formalities. Reluctantly, I believe he said – providing he received a full report from London.'

'And where is this private aircraft flying your father to?'

'Heathrow. Kuhlmann also agreed that under the circumstances he'd phone the airport controller here to authorize the flight. Some such bull.' Rupert adopted a sneering tone. 'Don't know why you're fussing like an old woman. You were supposed to be a friend of my father's.'

'You're flying home with the body?'

'Glory, no. Think I want to put myself through that? Because I don't – and won't.'

Newman made a move to grab hold of Rupert. Paula grasped his sleeve, held him back, whispered something. While all this was going on the stretcher-bearers were carrying the body outside to a van waiting at the kerb.

'I've a good mind to call Kuhlmann, tell him the truth, and make him reverse his decision,' Tweed rasped. 'Let's get just one thing clear. If you ever use my name again without coming to me first I'll have you arrested and charged with deception of the authorities.'

'Do what you bloody well like!'

'You mind your filthy mouth.' Newman snapped. 'Or I'll close it for you.'

'Toodle-pip. I have to go with the van to the airport.'

'I'm going to tell the driver he's acting illegally,' Tweed said in a cold voice.

'Wait a minute,' Paula said urgently, again keeping her voice low. 'You don't want to get involved. Haven't you enough on your mind? Far more important things to attend to?'

'You're right, of course.' Tweed was suddenly calm. 'And now look what we've got on our doorstep. I think I'll have a word with him.'

Basil Windermere, sporting a cashmere overcoat, had appeared at the entrance. He walked in, stared round at the air of chaos. Tweed went up to him.

'I say,' said Basil, 'what's the party in aid of? All the staff standing round. And didn't I see Rupert getting into the front seat of a van? Having fun, are we?'

'Hardly,' Tweed replied. 'Rupert's father has just been murdered. Shot down in cold blood in the street outside.'

'You don't say. Of course the old boy was getting on a bit. But to go like that. Not cricket.'

'Where have you been?' Tweed asked through gritted teeth.

'Doing the Grand Tour of Freiburg. Parked by an expensive fashion shop, watched some nifty fillies going in. And a few older ones. Must be rolling in it.'

'I heard you'd hired a car. Is it outside?'

'Think so. Unless the hotel attendant chappie has taken it to the garage.'

'Show me. What's the make?'

'An Opel. Nothing to top up the image.'

'Let's have a look now.' Tweed beckoned to the chief receptionist. They walked outside. The Opel was still there, it's colour blue. 'Was this the car you saw disappearing?' Tweed asked the receptionist.

'I do not really know, sir. It all happened so quickly.'

'You said a brown Opel,' Tweed reminded him. 'This is blue.'

'I only saw it for a second, sir. I was really looking at the body.'

'Anyone mind telling me what this is in aid of?' Basil demanded.

Tweed looked straight into the pallid eyes of Basil Windermere. He could detect no sign of any kind of human feeling, no reaction at all to the news Windermere had just heard. He went on staring into the eyes while he answered.

'We're looking for a serial murderer.'

Then he turned away and joined Paula and Newman. He led them up to his room and sat down in a chair, telling them to make themselves at home. He took Beck's mobile from his pocket.

'What does it all mean?' Newman asked. 'Was it the Phantom?'

'I'm sure it was. Guy had a bullet dead centre in his forehead. Wasn't that the case with Kurt Schwarz?'

'Yes, it was.'

'Why would they kill Guy?' Paula asked.

'I think it was triggered off by the argument you and I heard outside in the corridor. I think that after a while in his room Guy decided to go out for a walk to calm down. By that time arrangements had been made to kill him. Someone moved very fast.' As he spoke he was pressing numbers on the mobile.

'Marler? You recognize my voice? Good. The extra asset we thought we'd have with us is no longer available.'

'Understood,' Marler acknowledged.

'I had to be careful,' Tweed remarked, 'since I was phoning him at the Schwarzwälder Hof. Now I'm going to try and get hold of Roy Buchanan. I can remember his mobile number.'

'Why Buchanan?' Paula asked.

'Listen and you'll see – if I get him . . .'

Buchanan responded very quickly and Tweed explained that Sir Guy Strangeways had just been murdered, most probably by the Phantom. He told him of the arrangement to fly the body to Heathrow, asked if he could arrange to have the private plane met, then for an autopsy to be performed.

'When they've taken the bullet out of Guy,' Tweed continued, 'I suggest it's compared with the one which killed our Prime Minister, the one which killed a man found dead off Regent Street, the one which killed the German, Keller, and the one which killed a French Minister . . .'

Tweed listened for a few minutes, replied briefly, listened again and then thanked Buchanan before he broke the connection.

'Any news from Roy?' Paula enquired.

'Yes. He was on his way to Heathrow. They had an anonymous call that a bomb has been placed aboard a plane bound for the Western hemisphere. That covers a lot of territory. Umpteen planes are grounded. Chaos at Heathrow. A fresh ploy to destabilize us. Roy is going to wait to meet the plane flying in Guy's body. I think that tells you all we said to each other.'

'I forgot to mention it earlier,' Newman said. 'Just before we came up here I noticed someone come back into the hotel from outside. It was Ed Osborne.'

'Interesting,' commented Tweed. 'Now let's go down and see if we can get a late lunch. I think zero hour is very close.'

When they entered the dining room waiters were clearing away the empty tables. But the maître d' told Tweed that of course they could have lunch. The only other guest in the room as they made their way to their table was Sharon.

She raised a hand, waved to them, then returned to checking a file. A waiter brought her a fresh pot of coffee, removed an old one. Paula sighed after they had ordered.

'That woman never stops working. She has a pile of files on a chair.'

'She's dedicated,' said Tweed.

'I wonder if she's heard about Guy.'

'Paula, if she has, she has. If she hasn't she'll hear sooner or later.'

'You're in a hurry, aren't you?'

'Yes. It will be dark soon. It would be anyway at this time of the year, but with this heavy overcast it will come quicker.'

Like Paula, Tweed was eating quickly during gaps in their conversation.

'Which means?' she asked quietly.

'I think Ronstadt will be leaving any minute. I'm surprised I haven't heard from Marler. I'd expect activity over where he's staying.'

'We've finished dessert. We could skip coffee.'

'I think we should.'

Newman looked up as someone appeared at the entrance to the restaurant. A tall smooth-faced man wearing a good suit. He glanced across at Sharon. She was so absorbed in her file she didn't see him beckon briefly to Newman.

'Excuse me,' said Newman. 'Back in a minute.'

The tall man had disappeared. Newman found him waiting at the entrance to the bar. Inside Basil Windermere sat with his back to the entrance, nursing a glass. The tall man moved a few feet along the wall as Newman approached him with a smile.

'Well, if it isn't Chuck Venacki. Last seen with a car parked outside Park Crescent, watching the place.'

'And then Bob Newman rams me up the rear in his four-wheel drive. You pulled that job pretty smartly.'

'What is it, Venacki?'

'You can call me Chuck. Tell Tweed to go to his room now. I do mean now.'

'Why?'

'He'll find out why very quickly. You're short of time.'

'Can you tell me why?'

'Make with the feet, Newman, for God's sake.'

Newman walked back into the restaurant. He sat down, pushed his dessert dish away. While he did this he leant close to Tweed.

'I suggest you go to your room immediately. It could be urgent.'

'I'll come with you, if that's all right,' Paula said.

'Yes, come with me.'

'I'm going to my room,' Newman said. 'So you know where to get me.'

Tweed, with Paula by his side, strolled out of the restaurant. He looked across at Sharon, but she was so absorbed in working on her file she didn't notice them.

'That woman,' Paula remarked on their way up, 'has extraordinary powers of concentration.'

'A real brainbox,' he agreed.

They were inside his room, the door relocked, when she asked a question. Perched on the arm of a chair, she was wearing her outdoors outfit, complete with leggings and a strong pair of boots which would grip firmly on rough ground.

'I wonder who that man was, the one Bob went out to talk to? He seemed to know him.'

'Maybe an old contact from his days as an active journalist.'

'You don't really believe that.'

'Frankly, at the moment I don't know what to believe.'

'And why, I wonder, was it so important that you came up here?'

'No idea. I just do what I'm told – when it's Bob who tells me.'

A minute or two later the phone rang. 'Maybe it was this. We'll soon know. Yes,' he said, 'who is it?'

'Ronstadt left a few minutes ago. With his bag. He checked out.'

'You'd sooner not give me a name?'

'Right on the button. Good luck.'

Tweed put the phone down. He spoke as he went to a cupboard to fetch his packed bag.

'We're on our way. Whoever phoned had a smooth American voice. And I have to call the others.'

Paula was already on her way to the door, heading for her room. She stopped as Tweed's mobile started buzzing. He snatched it out of his pocket.

'Yes. Who's calling?'

'Me.' Marler's voice. 'Activity here. Drive over. Tell Bob to park at the edge of the Münsterplatz. He knows where ...'

'That was Marler,' Tweed said and Paula left the room.

Tweed picked up the phone after dumping his bag

close to his feet. He called Newman and Keith Kent. His message was the same to both of them.

'Now! Meet you with your bag outside the hotel. On our way to the car. I've kept the bill up to date, so paying won't take a moment.'

38

It seemed almost night as they drove away from the Colombi. In the white Audi they occupied the same positions as they had when driving from Basle. Newman was behind the wheel with Paula beside him, a map open on her lap. In the rear Tweed sat with Keith Kent. The traffic was light amid the gloom and soon Newman was approaching the Münsterplatz. He slowed down, dimmed his lights, stopped. Out of nowhere Marler appeared. He spoke quickly but concisely through Newman's lowered window.

'You got here just in time, I reckon. Ronstadt's black Audi has just left. Four men inside, including nice Jake, who's driving. The two Audis parked here also left, with seven men inside them. They're in front, with Ronstadt following. Bob, haven't you turned on the gizmo I bought in Geneva? The tracking device.'

'No, I forgot. I've switched it on now.'

'How does it work?' Tweed asked, leaning forward. 'I hadn't even noticed it.'

Below the dashboard, Marler had earlier attached, with magnetic grips, a circular screen about six inches in diameter. Illuminated now, the glow showed it was divided by thin lines into the points of the compass. A round red light, about the size of a British five-pence piece, was moving very slowly in an easterly direction.

'That red light,' Marler explained, 'is Ronstadt. Earlier,

Bob and I slipped back to where the Colombi parks cars. The signal-sending device was still on the roof of his car. It's about as big as one of those buttons you see on camelhair coats. The signal travels up to a satellite which instantly returns it to your receiver, which you're looking at. To mine also. Luckily the device is black, so it merges with the colour of Ronstadt's car. Got it?'

'Just assume we do,' pleaded Paula. 'No more technicalities.'

'He can't move all that fast,' Marler went on. 'Heard a forecast. There's been another heavy fall of snow in the Black Forest. Before we move off I'm Father Christmas.' He hitched up a long canvas holdall, started handing weapons through the window.

'One machine-pistol with ammo.'

'I'll take that,' said Paula. 'I've practised with them a lot recently down at the mansion in Surrey.'

'Walther 7.65mm automatics with spare mags.'

'I'll take one of those,' said Tweed, his voice grim. 'I remarked earlier we must exterminate this vermin.'

Keith Kent accepted a Walther as Marler went on producing more.

'Grenades, smoke bombs . . .'

'Some for me,' called out Paula.

She stuffed them carefully inside her shoulder bag. She had already loaded the machine-pistol, laying it at her feet, the muzzle pointed at the door. Marler emptied his holdall, then said:

'Tweed, do you agree I drive ahead, Bob follows? Then if there's an ambush, which I think there will be – remember one Audi left hours ago – I'll deal with it. Bob drives on to maintain contact with Ronstadt and his convoy. If they reach their base wait until I catch you up. Four men went ahead earlier, there are seven with Ronstadt, which makes eleven thugs. You'd be outgunned.'

'You might have trouble finding us,' Newman warned.

'No, I won't. I'm attaching another gizmo to your roof. It will show a blue light on my screen so I'll find you. That is if all this lot works. Modern technology. Dicey business.'

'I agree your strategy,' said Tweed.

'Then I'm off to the killing ground, as they say. The Black Forest.'

Marler reached up. Paula heard the magnetic clamps of the gizmo attach to the roof of their car. Marler ran off to where his white Audi was parked. Nield was already waiting in the front passenger seat. Butler sat hunched in the rear. Then Marler ran back to Newman's car.

'I forgot,' he told Newman through the window which had been lowered again. 'When that red light starts flashing you're almost on top of Ronstadt. Now I really must get moving . . .'

'Paula,' said Tweed, 'sometimes Marler does have a grisly way of putting things.'

'You're referring to his use of the phrase "killing ground",' she replied. 'I don't care. I was thinking of poor Guy. I want to send the lot of them to where he's gone.'

They left Freiburg behind more quickly than Paula had expected. Soon they were driving over thick snow. As darkness fell the moon had risen, casting its vaporous glow over the lonely countryside. They entered a world of steep rolling hills covered with dense masses of fir trees, marshalled trunk to trunk like an invading army about to overwhelm them. Their branches and foliage, holding the snow, glittered like Christmas trees in the moonlight.

'You see now,' Tweed said to Paula, 'why I said it can be very beautiful. Are you listening to me?'

She was staring at the red light on the glowing screen. Her expression was almost brooding as though her thoughts were miles away. She shook her head, looked at Tweed.

'Sorry, I didn't catch what you said.'

'Doesn't matter. What were you pondering?'

'A lot of things. For one, why didn't the manager of the Colombi warn us Ronstadt had checked out? Especially after Kuhlmann had spoken to him.'

'Could be he was away from the hotel at the time. Or, if he was there, he might not have wanted to report the movements of one guest to another. If that was the case, I don't blame him. He has the reputation of the hotel to think of.'

'I was also wondering about the three thugs who travelled with Ronstadt. We never saw them while we were there.'

'He probably confined them to their rooms.'

'I do remember what you said now.' She looked out of the window. 'It is beautiful – but also sinister. And we haven't seen any traffic since we started out. Except for Marler's rear lights in the distance.'

'Something's coming towards us now in the opposite direction,' Newman remarked.

'What on earth is it, Bob?'

'Giant snowplough, clearing the snow. You have to give it to the Germans. They don't waste any time keeping the highways clear.'

'It's the first one we've seen,' she objected.

'Not surprising. It's out of season. Tourists – the skiing type – don't expect snow here as late as this. It's a really huge machine.'

'Bob, slow down,' Tweed ordered.

'Marler didn't.'

'I said slow down until we've passed it. Ronstadt is capable of any trickery.'

Tweed had lowered his window. He had his Walther in his hand. Paula automatically picked up the machine-pistol, laid it on her lap. The machine came closer, Newman had obeyed Tweed's command to slow down. Paula took a firmer grip on her weapon. The snowplough was moving very slowly and now the driver was visible. He appeared to be operating his machine innocently. Newman slowed down even more, cruising across the snow.

'Can you see anyone else other than the driver?' Tweed asked.

'Not from where I'm sitting,' Newman replied.

Paula gently pushed Tweed back against his seat. She elevated her machine-pistol, aiming it through the open window. It had been so warm in the car before the window was lowered she had begun to feel sleepy. Now, with the ice-cold air pouring in, she was totally alert.

The rumble of the big snowplough was very loud as it came on, much closer, spewing great quantities of snow off the highway. Just before it drew level the driver took off his peaked cap, waved it to them, then proceeded past them as Paula swiftly dropped her weapon out of sight. She let out her breath.

'Now we can relax.'

'No, we can't,' Tweed warned. 'Somewhere ahead I anticipate a major attack. So stay at the ready.'

Newman increased speed – the gap between his and Marler's car had grown. Tweed closed the window and Paula started gazing out. Here and there she saw an isolated house made of wood, standing well back from the road, with welcoming lights. The houses had very steep roofs, presumably to slough off an accumulation of heavy snow.

In the distance was a sweeping panorama of far-off

summits, white with snow, of deep valleys inside which she saw tiny colonies of houses huddled at the bottom. One panorama succeeded another and in the moonlight it looked like paradise.

'It's so peaceful,' she commented.

'It is, so far,' Tweed warned.

'The red light is growing fainter,' called out Newman. 'Same direction, but for some reason Ronstadt has speeded up.'

'So has Marler,' Keith Kent said, speaking for the first time.

'I'm doing the same,' Newman replied as he accelerated.

'We're getting close to the Höllental,' Paula announced after checking her map with the aid of her torch. 'Very close, I'd say.'

A few minutes later they entered a vast gorge. On both sides steep rugged slopes closed in on the highway. Paula felt a return of a sense of tension. The slopes, almost vertical in places, seemed to hem in the car. And now their height hid the moon, still shining on the upper slopes, but plunging the gorge into deepest shadow. No more cosy little houses with their welcoming lights. Just the dark remote gorge, cutting off all contact with the outside world.

'I wonder how Marler's getting on?' Newman speculated. 'For some reason he's slowed down again.'

'Keep a close eye on the heights,' Marler said to Nield.

'I am doing just that.'

'If they're up there they have to have found somewhere they could drive up. I don't think they'd go in for any mountaineering if they could help it. In any case they'd have to park the car on the highway.'

'Why are we going so slowly?' Butler called out from the back.

'So we can see if they have turned off,' Marler told him.

He had his lights on full beam, so he could look as far ahead as possible. Glancing up, he detected enormous snow-covered boulders poised high above them. Not a sight he welcomed. He checked his screen. The red light, which was Ronstadt's car, was fainter, telling him the American had increased his speed considerably. Why?

He leaned forward, staring at the precipitous slope to his left. Could he be wrong? He drove on, still staring hard. Then he saw it wasn't his imagination. Ahead, climbing up the slope to his left, he made out the double tracks of a car's wheels, deep ruts in the otherwise virgin snow. He increased his speed.

'Hold on to your seat belts. We're going up that slope. That's where they are. Lord knows how high above us.'

Butler held his breath as Marler swung the car at speed – skidding as his rear wheels swung round. He rammed his foot down and began climbing what turned out to be a curving gulley with high banks of snow on either side. The snow tyres gripped the hard-frozen ground as he plunged higher still.

Perched on the heights way above where the gulley left the highway, Brad, squat and ugly, but powerful, had earlier watched the highway far below through his night glasses. He had seen Ronstadt's convoy of three black Audis pass, heading deeper into the Höllental. Brad was in charge of the unit of four men, given the task of destroying Tweed and his team.

'Dan,' he called out to a big man with a down-curving

moustache, 'you've got an automatic rifle. Climb that tall tree over there. Do it now – before the bastards arrive.'

'Buster,' he shouted to a fat man with a face like a slab of stone, 'you've got your machine-pistol. Get down behind that boulder so's you can cover the exit from the gulley. Just in case.'

'And you, Bruce,' he shouted again, 'you got your boulder ready to go down with mine?'

Bruce, heavily built with a scarred forehead, like Brad stood at the edge of the ridge with a steep rolling slope below, but further along. He held a crowbar he'd used to lever the rock loose. Now he only had to heave on the crowbar inserted under it to send it down at murderous speed onto the highway.

Brad was standing behind an enormous snow-covered boulder. It had taken all his considerable strength to lever it out so now it was poised on the brink. He stood with his crowbar shoved well underneath it. Like Bruce, he had only to exert enough pressure to send it flying into space. He called out again to Bruce.

'T'ain't just the boulders which will kill Tweed's cars and everyone inside them. When the boulders go down they'll start an avalanche. Slope below us is unstable . . .'

When Marler suddenly swung off the highway up the gulley at speed he had no way of knowing he had averted – at least temporarily – their doom.

About to lever the boulders, Brad was taken by surprise at Marler's unexpected and swift manoeuvre. Earlier he had used his glasses to check who was in Marler's car. No sign of the girl Ronstadt had described to him, no sign of Tweed, also described to him. He decided to take the car out anyway – until the last second.

'*Bruce!*' he screamed. 'Not yet! They're in the gulley, comin' up.' He switched his attention to the man with the machine-pistol behind a boulder. 'Buster! They's drivin' up the gulley. Blast the car to hell soon as it appears . . .'

Marler was making steady progress, swinging the wheel quickly as one curve succeeded another and blotted out any view of the top. The snow tyres saved him, kept the car moving up and up and up. It was still deep in the gulley with the high snow-covered banks on both sides.

'Damned gulley goes on for ever,' Butler called out.

'It has to end somewhere,' Marler called back.

He had just spoken when the car swung round another curve and he saw, beyond a very steep stretch of track, moonlight glowing at the top.

On the highway Newman, worried that the red circle on the screen which was Ronstadt's car was fading, had accelerated. He was now moving at speed as Paula looked up at the steep slope on her left. High up along the rim in the near distance she saw boulders perched – boulders which had been there probably since prehistoric times.

'We're catching up with Ronstadt,' Newman told them. 'The red light is stronger. Can't see any sign of Marler's rear lights. Don't understand that.'

'Just keep moving,' Tweed urged.

'What do you think I'm doing!'

Near the top of the gulley Marler braked at the foot of the last steep stretch. He left the engine running. No profit in finding themselves without transport out here in the middle of nowhere. His mind was racing as he tried to put himself inside the head of the enemy – what he would have done had he been in his position. He decided quickly.

'This is where we get out. I don't like what might be waiting for us at the top.'

'We scatter,' said Nield.

'That's right.'

'I'll climb the left bank,' said Butler, already opening the door.

'Pete, you and I'll take the right bank. Don't peer over the top too quickly . . .'

The verbal exchange had taken only seconds. Marler carried his Armalite in his left hand, a Walther automatic in his right. Butler started climbing the left bank, digging his feet into the snow. His right hand was gripping a Walther. Cautiously, he peered over the top, blinked in sheer astonishment.

He was only feet away from Brad, who was standing with both hands gripping the crowbar, his eyes on the second white Audi approaching at high speed. He had no fewer than three pistols shoved down inside the belt round his anorak. A flicker of movement caught his eye. He turned to his left, saw Butler, did all the wrong things. He let go of the crowbar, desperately tried to haul out one of the pistols from his belt.

Butler shot him three times. Blood spurted, a pool of it staining Brad's anorak. He staggered to the side of the huge boulder, grabbed at it for support, slipped, fell forward, began sliding down the slope. Grabbing at the boulder had upset its delicate stability. It began to roll down, gathering momentum. Brad had fallen in its path. It rolled over him. By the moonlight Butler saw one large arc of the boulder had turned red, was smeared with parts of the body it had crushed. It thundered on down towards the highway.

*

Inside their Audi, Paula saw the massive boulder roaring down. She calculated it would hit the highway just ahead of them – or hit them.

'*Brake!*' she screamed.

Newman reacted, not knowing why. He brought the car to an emergency stop. In the back Tweed and Kent had braced themselves but they were thrown forward against their seat belts, which saved them. The boulder hit the highway, bounced, seemed to pass across their windscreen. It continued its passage of tremendous velocity across the highway, dived down into a gulch, clear of the other lane.

'Thank you,' said Newman.

'Any time,' said Paula.

He began moving forward at speed. Paula peered out of the window again, gasped. Ahead of them another huge boulder was starting to come down. For a moment she was stupefied, unable to speak. Then she screamed again.

'*Speed!* As fast as you can!'

Newman pressed his foot through the floor. The Audi took off as though flying, sending up bursts of powdered snow. Paula, hands clammy, gripped together, watched the projectile coming. She also saw that the whole slope now was on the move, a tidal wave of snow and rock descending. The second boulder had triggered an avalanche. She prayed, which she rarely did. Newman was fighting to keep the car on the road.

Looking back, she saw the boulder hit the highway behind them. Like its predecessor, it bounced, then tore across the other lane and disappeared. The avalance had now landed on their lane of the highway, quietened down suddenly, leaving the lane in the opposite direction comparatively clear.

'You'd better take over the bloody wheel,' Newman told Paula amiably.

'We must be getting close to Ronstadt,' Tweed's calm voice called out. 'The red light is very strong now . . .'

Bruce, the man with the scarred forehead, had levered down the second boulder and immediately snatched a pistol from his belt. He had heard Butler's three shots. He could see no sign of Brad, but he could see two men crouched in the snow on his side of the gulley. He raised the pistol, gripped it in both hands. There was another shot. Marler had had the cross-hairs of his Armalite aimed, had fired. A red disc appeared on his forehead in the middle of the scar. He stood quite still for a moment, his arms falling, letting go of the pistol, then he fell over backwards, staring sightlessly at the moonlit sky.

'Be careful,' Marler warned. 'There are two more of them somewhere.'

'I thought I saw movement in the forest. I'm going to fan out,' Nield replied in a whisper.

'Good idea.'

Marler began crawling along a dip in the ground towards where the gulley they had driven up ended. Nield moved in a different direction, crouching low and running in spurts from boulder to boulder. He'd noticed one of the tall trees had dropped some snow. Why this tree?

In a roundabout way he approached closer, went into the forest. The particular tree which had caught his attention had a thick trunk with small lower branches which provided a natural ladder for anyone who wanted to climb high. He found his own tree trunk, not too close, not too far away from the tree attracting his curiosity. He saw Marler beginning to get exposed in the open. Three huge clots of snow fell from the tall tree.

Now he was sure, and with Marler in the open he had to act at once. He studied the tree, took a grenade from his pocket, lobbed it about fifteen feet up through a gap in the snow-covered foliage. The grenade denotated, Nield thought he heard a muffled scream. Then the body fell, Dan catapulting from branch to branch until he hit the ground and lay still. His rifle came down a second later.

At almost the same moment Buster stood up from behind his large boulder, swivelling his weapon for a quick burst. Marler shot him twice. Buster sagged to the snow, on top of his gun.

'That's four of them,' Nield called out. 'I've found their car.'

'Lose it,' Marler ordered.

'Both of you get down into the gulley near our car, then.'

Nield had found the car easily. He had simply followed the twin tracks of wheel marks in the snow. Ronstadt's thugs had parked it out of sight behind a large copse of frosted shrubbery. Above it loomed a large tree.

Nield found a deep dip in the ground behind one of the boulders strewn everywhere. He stood in the dip, took out a grenade, lobbed it carefully so it would land under the car's petrol tank and dropped behind the boulder. He heard the grenade detonate. Then there was a roar. The petrol tank had blown. A spectacular shaft of flames soared up. Snow on the tree melted instantly. He peered over the boulder. The black Audi was a total wreck, looked as though it had been through a car crusher. He walked down the gulley and Marler was behind the wheel of the white Audi with Butler in the back. Nield sat again in the front passenger seat and Marler revved up to take it to the top, turn it round and drive back down the gulley.

'Funny,' Butler said, 'we could all be dead by now.'

'Not really,' Marler replied, 'not when the Americans are such amateurs when it comes to tactics.'

39

'We're in danger of losing Marler,' Newman warned, 'moving at this speed.'

'We'll have to risk that,' Tweed replied from the back of the car. 'The man we mustn't lose is Ronstadt. If the Americans are planning what I suspect they are, then they'll win. Britain will be plunged into turmoil – from which it may not recover.'

'There are four of us, eleven of them,' Newman persisted. 'The odds are lethal.'

'Keep going,' Tweed ordered. 'What I can't understand is that we've passed the Höllental. The base has to be somewhere else. Kurt Schwarz missed something. At least, I think he did.' He took out the little black notebook they had found behind the loose brick when Irina had been rescued in Basle. 'Paula, let me borrow your torch.'

'What's worrying you?' she asked.

'Kurt wrote down Höllental on one page, then that was followed by a blank page. I don't understand it.'

'The explanation could be very simple,' said Paula, handing him her torch. 'I've done it myself. Turned over two pages without realizing it, leaving one page blank.'

'I hope you're right. Let me check what's on the following page. I see. Just one word. *Schluchsee.* Sounds like a lake.'

'Give me back my torch. I want to check the map.'

She studied the map, looked quickly at the screen with the red light showing Ronstadt's convoy ahead of them. She watched the light for a few minutes. Then she spoke rapidly.

'We were moving south-east through the Höllental.

Now we're heading east towards Titisee, which has a smaller lake and is a famous resort. But soon there's a big junction which turns us southwest and soon runs alongside Lake Titisee . . .'

'Which we don't want,' Tweed protested.

'If you'd just let me finish,' Paula snapped. 'There is a Schluchsee, a much bigger lake, and it looks remote. After passing Lake Titisee we come to another junction on the way to Feldberg.'

'Highest point in the Black Forest,' said Tweed. 'About four thousand five hundred feet high. Sorry,' he concluded.

'I can do without any more interruptions until I've finished. At the junction we turn left and then we're heading due southeast – straight for Schluchsee.'

'If the blue light on Marler's screen which is us vanishes, he will never follow such a complicated route,' Newman objected.

'We'll have to take that risk,' Tweed repeated.

'I don't like it. I should slow down, give Marler time to catch up with us,' Newman insisted.

'I'm not going to keep giving the same order,' Tweed told him. 'Your job is to keep Ronstadt in sight. That's a direct order.'

'Might be a good idea if we all calmed down a bit,' Keith Kent suggested.

'You're right,' Tweed agreed. 'Tension will get us nowhere.'

'So,' said Paula, 'let's all relax – including you, Tweed.'

'We're losing Tweed,' said Marler, driving his Audi at speed. 'The blue light is fading. We'll just have to go faster.'

'And end up going off the road,' Nield warned.

'I don't think so,' Marler drawled. 'I used to be a racing driver.'

'But this isn't Le Mans,' Nield remarked as Marler accelerated even more. 'Strange that we've left the Höllental behind. I thought that's where their base was. And you're not flying a plane, Marler.'

'And there could be ice under this snow,' called out Butler, which was the first time Nield could recall him ever showing nervousness.

'I'm not going to let Tweed down,' Marler informed them. 'Did you,' he began, changing the subject, 'notice that amazing complex of buildings in the Höllental – the Hofgut Sternen?'

'Wouldn't have minded stopping there for a bite to eat,' Butler remarked. 'Place was enormous and a blaze of lights.'

'I was surprised to see a number of parked cars,' Nield replied. 'And I caught sight of people eating in a pretty good-looking restaurant.'

'Germans,' Marler said, 'coming from not too far away. The cars had skis attached to their roofs. A few hoping to take advantage of the falls of snow.'

There was silence for a while. Marler refused to moderate his speed. To their left a dense forest of firs stretched endlessly up a slope. Still no other traffic on the road. Thank heavens for small mercies, Nield thought.

'Tweed's blue light is growing stronger,' Marler said suddenly. 'We're catching him up. Half a mo' – he's changed direction. He's going due southwest now.'

'We're coming up to a junction,' Nield told him.

Like Paula, he had a map open on his lap. He had been studying it with a small torch. He stared fixedly ahead for signs of a turn.

'Newman's now heading for the Feldberg,' he

announced. 'That is the highest point in the whole of the Black Forest.'

'Deeper snow up there,' Butler commented, half to himself.

'Slow down, for God's sake,' Nield pleaded.

Marler, content now that he was much closer to the other Audi, reduced his breakneck pace. Nield leaned forward even more, stretching his seat belt.

'Turn here. We're on our way to Titisee.'

Marler obeyed his instructions. He pressed his foot down again. A short while later on their right they had glimpses of Lake Titisee, gleaming in the moonlight and utterly deserted. Close to the far shore Nield caught sight of colonies of holiday cabins. Marler checked the blue light again.

'Now Newman's turned due southeast,' he remarked.

'He's not heading for the Feldberg,' Nield reported after checking his map. 'There's another junction ahead. He appears to be heading instead for a big lake, Schluchsee. I wonder why?'

'Still no sign of Marler,' Newman commented to Paula.

'The red light which is Ronstadt flashed once,' she warned. 'So we must be closing on him.'

'Drop back a bit, then,' Tweed ordered. 'But don't lose him.'

'I've got it – do two things at once,' Newman cracked back at him.

But he did slow down. Everyone in the car noticed that now they had begun to descend and kept on doing so. Paula checked her map again.

'Soon the road zigzags a lot,' she warned.

'Well, I have slowed down,' Newman reassured her.

'Good job you did.'

As she spoke Newman was guiding the car round a

steep bend and then immediately afterwards he was swinging round another. By his side Paula was staring through the windscreen, hoping to catch sight of the mysterious lake. The atmosphere inside the car was now far more relaxed, Tweed was thinking. Which he welcomed. Lord knew what was facing them ahead, if they were able to track Ronstadt to his base.

'I can see something now.'

As Paula spoke Newman stopped the car. The red light on his screen was flashing madly. He had almost overtaken Ronstadt's convoy. Paula raised a small pair of high-powered night binoculars she'd had looped round her neck. She thought she had never seen anywhere so lonely and forbidding.

They were still high up and she was looking down on a small section of the long lake way below. She felt she might have been in a remote region of Canada. The moon kept fading as transparent drifts of cloud crossed beneath it. The lake was still as death and black as pitch. Its surface was so unruffled it gave her the impression it was covered with ice. The opposite shore was banked by steep hills choked with fir forest.

'See anything?' Tweed asked.

'Nothing. No sign of life, of human habitation. Just nothing.'

'Very promising.'

'Marler has caught us up,' Newman called out, unable to conceal his relief.

'I'm getting out of the car for a closer look,' said Paula.

She had got out, closed the door quietly, when she found Marler standing beside her. A few yards behind Newman's Audi, Marler's was parked, lights dimmed, as were Newman's.

'Well, I gather Ronstadt's base wasn't in the Höllental,' Marler remarked.

'No, it wasn't,' Paula replied. 'Tweed has an idea it has to be somewhere near here. That weird lake down there is called Schluchsee.'

'Tweed is sure the base is in this area,' Tweed called out through a window he had lowered. 'Kurt Schwarz has a reference to this place in his little book. I missed the significance of the name – a blank page followed his note on the Höllental.'

'Let's get closer,' Paula suggested to Marler. 'I think there's a track beyond the verge.'

Newman had switched off his engine. They had been so close to Ronstadt he'd felt it was a wise precaution. The enemy could have had the same idea and switched off their engines to listen. Walking a few paces along the track, Paula was struck by the incredible silence which added to the sinister atmosphere of this place out in the wilds. She sensed they were waiting for something terrible to happen.

For a short time she welcomed the bitter night air, well below zero. It was a pleasant contrast to the fetid air which had built up inside the car. She'd left her gloves in the car so she could manipulate the binoculars more easily and already her face and hands were beginning to feel frozen.

'Marler, I should have asked first what happened when you vanished off the highway. Are Nield and Kent OK?'

'In the pink. We had a bit of a dust-up. Four down, eleven in front to go. Tell you about it later.'

Moving a short distance down the track gave her a far more panoramic view, no longer obscured by a copse of firs at the roadside. The lake was wide but seemed immensely long – far longer than Lake Titisee which she had caught sight of earlier. She scanned it through her binoculars. Still no sign of a single building, or even a landing stage. The silence, lack of movement, the absence

395

of even a small wooden house with lights in it was getting to her.

'Lake surface looks as solid as slate,' Marler commented. 'A perfect setting for a horror film. Subhuman giants with huge axes creeping out of the woods.'

'Stop it,' Paula protested. 'I have a vivid imagination. I'll be seeing them now.'

'Any data?' asked Tweed behind her after getting quietly out of the car.

'Not a damned thing. Look for yourself.'

'No thanks. I can see with my own eyes. As desolate a spot as I've seen for a long time. We'd better get back in the car. The red light has stopped flashing. Ronstadt's on the move.'

40

'We're nearly there, Moonhead,' Ronstadt said to the man beside him.

Ronstadt was behind the wheel of the third Audi, following the two cars ahead of him as they bumped over the wide track round the tip of the lake. The moon had temporarily been blotted out by a dark cloud and the cars had their headlights full on. He suddenly let out a belly laugh of pure pleasure.

'What is it?' asked Leo Madison.

'Moonhead, it's turnin' out great. No sign of Tweed and his miserable crew. Brad and his boys must have made hash browns of them back in Höllental. With ketchup for the blood.' He laughed again, a raucous sound. 'Think of the avalanche hittin' those two white Audis. Think of what the people inside look like now. Hope that Paula Grey was with 'em. It's great.'

'Funny Brad and his boys haven't caught up with us,' Madison commented.

'Takes time to cook a dish like that.' He laughed again. 'I like it. Cookin' a dish like that. The dish is Paula Grey.'

'I just hope you're right.'

'You know your problem, Moonhead?'

'I guess you're gonna tell me.'

'You ain't got no sense of humour. Better roll up your sleeves, feller. Lot of work to do.'

'What kinda work?'

'Loading cartons – heavy ones – on to three trucks. I guess Bernhard Yorcke will have loaded one truck ready for the go. Makes four truckloads. What's in 'em will destroy Britain.'

'Who is this Bernhard Yorcke?'

'Came from Luxembourg years ago. He's a printer. Moved on to Switzerland as a youngster. Stayed there ever since. Just where he shoulda gone, being a printer. Swiss, I'll give 'em that, are best printers in the world.' He peered up through the windscreen. 'Nearly there. Trouble with Bernhard Yorcke is he can be a very nasty piece of work.'

Coming from Ronstadt, Madison wondered what on earth this Yorcke could be like.

'What's he print?' he asked.

'See when we gets there, won't you?'

'There is a base,' Paula said, 'and that has to be it.'

'I agree,' said Tweed.

They had driven down and down from the point where Paula had surveyed Schluchsee through her binoculars. Newman's car had progressed first, with Marler's following close behind. The red light on Newman's screen had glowed so strongly he had driven at a slow pace. Gradually the red glow had dimmed. Newman had had his lights dimmed when he'd stopped suddenly for two reasons. They were now on the level and he'd caught sight of an open stretch of road running next to the lake. They parked the cars on the left-hand verge, under cover of a copse of trees. Then they had cautiously walked into the open.

To their right was a shoulder-high wall between the road and the lake. All seven of them had kept out of sight behind the wall, peering over it. Paula had perched her elbows on top of the wall and stared through her binoculars. Immediately opposite them on the far side of the lake was the base.

A very large and old two-storey building stood on top of a bluff at the lake's edge. It had huge and very steep gables, was built of wood as far as she could see. It appeared to be a cross between a farmhouse and a private residence. It had been masked from her previous survey, much higher up, by the fir forest which extended forward almost to the brink of the bluff. Tweed had borrowed Marler's binoculars and now Newman spoke urgently.

'Tweed, loan me those glasses for a minute.'

'Take mine,' said Paula and handed them to him.

Newman swiftly focused them. His target was not the house. He was aiming them at the string of red lights from the three black Audis retreating round the tip of the lake. As he spoke he followed them through the lenses.

'They're driving along a wide track which leads round the end of the lake. That's where we'll follow them when they've reached their base. I can drive along that track without lights.'

'And with luck,' Tweed commented, 'driving in white

398

Audis they won't see us coming. We'll merge with the snow.'

'Is that why you asked me to get white cars?' Marler enquired.

'Yes. I'd heard about the first snowfall. It struck me white cars would be less visible, which might come in useful.'

'It will,' agreed Newman, still staring through the binoculars. 'We'll just hope the moon stays the way it is now. Not too strong but with a bit of light. They've reached the end of the track, turning away from the lake. Now they're half-hidden so the track must lead up through a gulley.'

'Which will help us too,' Marler remarked.

Paula was standing with her arms folded, trying to keep in a bit of warmth. The well below zero temperature was gradually penetrating the extra clothing she was wearing. Her head was perched on the wall top as she crouched to keep hidden.

'It reminds me of that house in *Psycho*,' she said. 'It has a flight of railed steps leading up to the front door. The main difference is that large ramp to the right. Frightening.'

'It's just a house,' said Newman.

'That ramp is interesting,' Tweed observed, his binoculars still trained on the house, 'because it would be possible for two cars to drive down it at the same moment – or a very large truck.'

'Why would they want trucks?' Kent asked.

'To transport what I think they've produced inside that building. If I'm right, it's far more deadly than bombs. That edifice beyond the top of the ramp looks like a huge garage. I'd swear the door is modern – unlike everything else about the place.'

Paula was staring round the shores of the lake in the

ghostly light. The moon came out from behind a cloud briefly and she saw she was right.

'There are sandy beaches here and there along the edges of the lake. But I can't see any sign of holiday chalets.'

'They all go to Titisee in the season.' Tweed told her. 'The convoy has almost arrived.'

'The track forks three ways when it gets close to the house,' Newman reported. 'One route up to the bottom of the flight of steps, another proceeds on to the foot of that ramp. The third leads to somewhere behind the house – and that's the route they are taking. Time to go?'

'Let's wait a little longer,' Tweed suggested. 'Give them time to settle in.'

'No lights at all in the place,' Paula pointed out.

'There are several,' Tweed corrected her. 'Difficult to see because they're low down – must be a basement. I think there are curtains drawn across them.'

'You mean there's someone there already?' Paula asked.

'I'm sure there is. In the basement. Now, I wonder? Yes, it might well be in the basement – if it's big enough.'

'What might?'

'What we've come to destroy.'

'Which is?'

'A fortune,' replied Tweed, and he smiled. 'Time to find out.'

The moon obliged. It cast no more than a half-glow as Newman, in the lead, turned off the road and down onto the track. Behind him Marler's Audi followed. They drove without lights and Newman, having studied the track, found he could see where he was going without difficulty.

400

'What were you and Tweed discussing with Marler before we left?' Paula, seated beside Newman again, asked him.

'We were planning tactics for the assault,' Tweed answered her from the rear of the car. 'We had several options.'

'Which did you choose?' she asked.

'I was just going to tell you when you spoke. It's important you know as much as the rest of us. Bob, do you want to start putting Paula in the picture?'

'There are seven of us,' Newman began. 'We thought there'd be eleven of the enemy but that light in the basement Tweed spotted means there will be at least twelve of them. At least,' he repeated. 'The obvious point of attack is to follow their cars round the back. Maybe a bit too obvious, wouldn't you agree?'

'Yes, I would,' replied Paula. 'I'd have thought we have to split up a bit – so we have the place surrounded.'

'Which is exactly what we decided,' said Newman. 'Keith, I'd like you to get out when we reach the house, so you can creep up that staircase to the main front door. I don't think this will happen, but they may all come out there. Marler gave you an extra Walther – you may not have time to reload. Shoot them down as they emerge.'

'I think I can manage that,' Kent said easily. 'Tweed must have told you I'm what they call a shooter back home. Belong to a club.'

'What about the rest of us?' Paula pressed.

'Marler and Butler take up the best positions they can find at the back of the house. Tweed and Nield follow Keith when we drop him off, then they go further along to take up positions on the ramp side of the house.'

'What about you?'

'I've got a roving commission. I'll be circling the house – as reinforcement wherever I'm needed.'

'You've left someone out,' Paula said coolly. 'Me.'

'No, I haven't. You'll come with me.'

'As protection?' she asked not so coolly.

'Of course not. As backup – for me.'

'The essence of our strategy,' Tweed intervened, 'is to entice them out of the house. By now they'll be getting to know its layout. We haven't the faintest idea of that. So we bring them out to us.'

'And how exactly do we do that?' Paula wanted to know.

'You've noticed lights are starting to come on inside the house. So we—'

'Shows overconfidence,' Newman interrupted. 'That's helpful.'

'I was going to tell Paula that Bob will throw grenades inside the house through the windows. That will shake them up, bring some of them outside where we'll be waiting for them.'

'That's clever,' Paula replied.

'We'll soon be there,' Newman warned.

The track had now entered the gulley, which was steep and wide. Newman felt relieved. There was no sign so far that the thugs inside had noticed their approach. He reached the top of the gulley and then the point where the track forked in three directions.

'They may not hear our cars coming,' said Paula. 'As you know, I have acute hearing, and I can hear machines whirring inside the place.'

'This is where Keith and Tweed drop off,' said Newman. 'In the rear-view mirror I can see Nield leaving Marler's car ready to join you.'

'Keith,' Newman called out, 'I suggest you crouch against the wall of the house – between the front door and the ramp. Less of a target.'

'I'm going to do just that,' Kent replied.

Both Tweed and Kent were careful not to slam their doors as they left the car. Tweed had his Walther in his right hand, spare magazines in his left. The moonlight did not reach the outside of the house and the two men disappeared like wraiths. As Newman drove on at a slow pace Paula bent down, picked up her machine-pistol.

'We'll make a good team,' said Newman.

'If you say so,' she snapped, still annoyed.

They were moving along the track which ran past the side of the large house. In the distance Paula could just make out the silhouettes of three parked black Audis. All of them were turned round for a swift getaway. They were crawling past the side of the house when she called out.

'Stop!'

'Why?'

'Stop! Damn you! There's a side door at the top of a flight of steps. I'm getting out. No bloody argument.'

Newman sighed, stopped. It was no use arguing with Paula once she'd made up her mind. And she had a point. They hadn't expected a side entrance. She opened the door, smiled at him, slipped out, closed the door. He drove on with Marler following him with only Butler in his car now.

The first thing that occurred to Paula as she stood for a moment, adjusting to the huge drop in temperature, was the extent of the flight leading up to a closed door. At least a dozen steps. Her eyes were becoming accustomed to the pitch darkness and she saw the ground was littered with boulders.

She crouched behind one, then decided crouching would restrict her movements. It would all happen so quickly if some of the thugs did emerge from the side door. She found a flat-topped rock in the shadows. She checked behind her, listening for the sound of someone prowling. Maybe they had posted sentries outside. No one had thought of that. Satisfied with the heavy silence, she perched on the rock, putting spare mags in her lap. Then she elevated the machine-pistol until the muzzle was aimed at the platform outside the door. She lowered it swiftly, repeated the exercise.

'This is a damned quiet forest,' she said to herself. 'No bird song. No sign of night birds.'

She had removed the glove from her right hand – her trigger hand. It would freeze but she'd have to put up with that. She kept flexing the finger round the trigger.

'Come on, you swine,' she said under her breath. 'Your lot has killed enough people with the bombs in London . . .'

More lights had come on in the house, Newman observed as he began circling the building. He had another reason for choosing his role. He wanted to check that everyone was in as safe a position as possible. He saw Paula sitting erect on her rock and he sighed. He was going to go to her to say something, decided not to. Paula had come a long way, knew what she was doing. He recalled how she'd dealt with Hank Waltz in the Eagle Street warehouse in London's East End.

He went in the opposite direction to the rear of the house. He found Marler behind a tree, his Armalite at the ready. Beyond was Butler, crouched behind a shrub. Both were watching yet another exit – this door level with the ground. He continued walking round the far side of the house.

Nield peered out from behind a small wooden hut. He waved his Walther at Newman. Further on, closer to the ramp and under its slope, Tweed stood waiting, unconcerned, staring upwards. He didn't even look as Newman passed him and reached the front.

As he'd suggested, Keith was beyond the top of the staircase leading to the massive front door. He was crouched with his back to the wall of the house. He must have heard Newman. He suddenly swung round, Walther aimed. Then he lowered it. Time, he decided, to wake up the thugs inside, to throw a few grenades through the lighted windows.

When the three black Audis arrived at the parking place, Ronstadt was first out of his car. As he hurried towards the door at the back of the house he was accompanied by three men – Leo Madison, Chuck Venacki and Vernon Kolkowski. They had all travelled in his car.

'Moonhead,' he warned, 'you've seen a few tough guys in your time, but prepare yourself for Bernhard Yorcke . . .'

'Guess I've seen all the tough guys,' Madison said dismissively.

'You keep your big mouth shut. I hadn't finished. Yorcke is about five foot three tall. He's a gnome – and a hunchback, and strong as an ox. He gets very nasty if you says the wrong thing. Admire his work. Tell him what a great guy he is.'

'OK. If you say so.'

Ronstadt pressed the door bell three times slowly, then twice, then three times again.

They waited. Madison shuffled his feet. Behind him the other three thugs stood back. Ronstadt liked men to observe the courtesies where he was concerned. Which meant he led the way and the others followed like hired lackeys.

'Where the hell is he?' snapped Madison. 'Friggin' cold stuck out here.'

He had just spoken when they heard the door being unlocked from the inside. When it opened a strong light shone from the large room inside. Madison sucked in his breath. Standing crouched in the doorway was the ugliest, most evil-looking man he'd ever seen.

Bernhard Yorcke had a high forehead and lank, greasy dark hair. His nose was hooked and the dark eyes which stared out strangely were black and menacing. Below the nose a wide, thin-lipped mouth was twisted at an odd angle, which gave the impression he was smiling permanently in a sneering way. A most unpleasant smile. Clean-shaven, his long face tapered to a pointed chin which increased his gnomelike look. His fingertips were black. They would always be black – with printer's ink.

'You are late,' he said nastily.

'Sorry 'bout that,' Ronstadt replied, smiling. 'Difficult drivin' conditions. A lot of snow and ice.'

'You're still late. You had better come inside with your men. There will be no food for them. I cannot waste my valuable time looking after strange visitors.'

Yorcke spoke English slowly, with great precision, emphasizing syllables. His voice was high-pitched, which added to the sinister aura of his personality. He stood to one side as Ronstadt's thugs filed in, then locked the door with his left hand. In his right hand he held a long black iron bar which terminated at one end in a sharp point. At the top a small bar extended at right-angles. It gave Madison the feeling of a vicious dagger.

'You are wondering what I am holding in my hand,' Yorcke said to Madison. This horrible guy misses nothing, thought Madison, who had been glancing at the bar. 'It is an instrument of my trade.'

'Bernhard is the greatest printer in the whole world,' boomed Ronstadt. 'He gives you a date and the work is finished by that date.'

'Everything is ready now, Ronstadt,' Yorcke confirmed. 'I have even printed a greater quantity. It is running on the machines now. For that, of course, I expect a bigger fee.'

As he spoke he advanced very close to Ronstadt. The spiked bar was raised to his chest level as though about to strike. He stared hard at Ronstadt, who answered quickly, trying not to look at the nearness of the spike.

'You'll get a big extra fee. And I won't pay you in what you've produced.'

'Don't do that,' purred Yorcke. 'Life can be short.'

'It was a joke,' Ronstadt assured him hastily. 'Can we start loading the trucks?'

'One truck is already loaded. The driver is waiting to leave.'

'Tell him to get moving, please.'

His men were exploring different rooms as Yorcke went to an old-fashioned phone attached to the wall. He used a turn-handle to ring the bell in the garage.

'Dave, take the truck to its destination. Yes, now.'

Newman, with a holdall he had borrowed from Marler, was starting his tour of the house. He grabbed a grenade from the holdall, hurled it with great force through an illuminated window. Glass cracked as the missile landed somewhere inside. It detonated. The window shattered, scattering glass all over the snow outside. Newman had already moved on, hurled another grenade. He continued throwing the grenades almost nonstop as he ran.

Below the wide ramp Tweed was crouched against the wall, Walther in his hand. He suddenly heard the sound of a powerful engine starting. Looking up, he saw the huge door of the garage elevating swiftly, automatically. A large white Mercedes truck roared out, sped down the ramp. He aimed his gun, fired. A useless shot. The driver inside his cab was way past him, had swung the vehicle round at the bottom, accelerated, headed for the track and thundered down it. Nield was by his side.

'We've lost it. I fired but hit nothing. Where could it be going?'

'Tell you in a minute . . .'

He watched the truck rushing along the track. In no time at all it reached the road, swung left, heading back the way they had come. Then it was gone.

'Freiburg for starters would be my guess,' said Tweed. 'There may be a way of stopping it later.'

Newman dashed past them. He was running round the house, hurling more grenades from the holdall slung over his shoulder. He aimed one well clear of Kent, crouched by the front wall at the top of the steps. There was a fresh detonation. More glass sprayed the outside, none of it coming near Tweed and Nield. He didn't stop running.

Half a minute earlier, the door at the top of the steps at the side of the house where Paula waited, was thrown open. Three thugs rushed out, down the steps, firing at random. Paula elevated her machine-pistol. She fired one long burst, lowering the weapon. The thugs on the steps tumbled over each other, fell in a heap, very still. She was reloading, expecting more, when Newman rushed round the corner, took in the situation at a glance.

'Great work. Don't go inside!'

He ran on. Paula waited. No one else emerged. She laid her machine-pistol on the ground. It would be difficult to manipulate inside the confines of the house. Holding her Walther gripped in both hands, she walked to the foot of the steps. Slowly she began to climb them, threading her way between the strewn corpses. Then she disappeared inside.

At the rear of the house Marler waited well back at the edge of the trees, holding his Armalite. Butler was standing nearby, crouched low behind some wild shrubbery.

'Keep your eyes on that door,' Marler called out.

'They're doing that.'

When the assault came it was in an unexpected way – and from an unexpected direction. Without warning –

they had heard, had seen, no sign of activity – a hail of smoke bombs arrived from inside the shattered windows. Marler and Butler were lost in a dense, choking fog.

The door opened quietly. Ronstadt led the way out, followed by Leo Madison, Chuck Venacki and Vernon Kolkowski. They had guns in their hands but they did not fire them. Instead they ran for Ronstadt's Audi, now parked in front and facing the track. Ronstadt opened the driver's door quietly, sat behind the wheel as he was joined by Chuck at his side with Madison and Vernon in the back. He started the engine, accelerated.

Marler, coughing, emerged from the smoke. He saw Newman appear round the side of the house. Ronstadt drove the car straight at him. Newman jumped clear just in time. Then the car had gone, vanishing down the gulley.

Newman clambered to his feet, realized he had sprained his ankle. He stared at the flat-topped rock where Paula had been sitting. He looked quickly up at the open door at the top of the steps, beyond the piled bodies.

'Marler!' he shouted. 'Paula's gone inside. Up those steps. For God's sake go after her.'

'On my way.'

When Paula reached the open doorway she paused, listened, then peered inside. She was looking up and down a lighted corridor. Deserted. She frowned. She could hear a strange noise. Clatter ... clatter ... clatter ...

It went on and on and was coming from an open door further down the corridor to her right. As she walked down the corridor the noise became louder and louder. A slablike door was open, pushed back against

409

the wall. As she came closer she saw it was made of solid steel. She peered round it and suppressed a gasp of surprise. She was looking down into a vast basement which must run under the entire house.

She understood the noise now. The basement was occupied by an array of machines working like mad. Illumination came from fluorescent tubes suspended from the ceiling. Beyond the door a flight of concrete steps led down into the basement, with a metal rail on one side. She scanned the area as far as she could. No sign of anyone. Step by step she began to descend the flight. The noise of the clattering machines was hellish, trapped inside the basement.

Walking down stealthily, she caught glimpses of the battery of machines. At one end large reels of paper were being fed in. They became perfectly flat sheets as the first machine carried them along. Then they passed under a series of huge revolving rollers. They emerged, still flat, but now printed with what, at first, she thought were outsize postage stamps. A moment later she realized they were banknotes, row upon row of them. They continued their journey until they reached a series of very large metal plates which jumped up and down, slicing them.

She had almost reached the bottom step when she slipped on some spilt oil. Her legs collapsed under her as she grabbed for the rail. The hand was still holding the Walther and she bruised herself, dropping the gun. Picking herself up, she flexed her hands and legs. No damage – she always fell limply. But where was the Walther?

The light was bright enough for her to see clearly but there was no sign of the weapon. It must have slid under one of the machines. She swore. Shaking her head to clear her mind, she began walking towards where the printing process started. Near the end was a concrete platform, elevated about a foot high. She assumed it was an observation platform so a printer could check to make sure everything was functioning properly.

Suddenly she sensed a presence behind her. She swung round and let out a gasp of fear. The most hideous man she had ever seen was close to her. A gnome with a hunchback, his evil face twisted in a leer of anticipation of a pleasure to come. In his right hand, raised high, he held a ferocious-looking black spike.

'I am Bernhard Yorcke,' he called out above the noise of the machinery. 'The greatest printer in the world. You have come to sabotage my beautiful work.'

'I think your work is the most beautiful I've ever seen,' she said quickly.

'No, you don't. You have been sent to destroy it. So I will destroy you.'

'You're a genius,' she babbled.

'I am the greatest genius of them all,' he said, coming closer.

'That's why I came here. To see your wonderful work.'

'You lie,' he snarled. 'You came to destroy. Instead, I am going to destroy you.'

She knew he was going to drive the dreadful spike into her face. As she backed away her right hand was feeling desperately inside her shoulder bag. Her fall had pushed it behind her back. She missed the special pocket sewn in which held her Browning. Her hand plunged deep, felt a canister of hair spray. He was very close to her as she brought out the spray, aimed it, her own eyes closed, ejected the spray.

'You foul whore.'

She opened her eyes, then realized the spray had only hit his left eye. His right eye stared into hers as he lifted the spike higher to jab it forward. Backing away from him she had come up against the wall. There was nowhere to go, to escape.

Marler came bounding down the steps like a rocket, Armalite in his right hand. He hadn't been able to shoot from the top for fear of hitting Paula. He saw the oil on the step which had brought down Paula, leapt over it.

'You ugly deformed little bastard!' he shouted.

The insult had the effect he had prayed for. Yorcke, about to jab the spike forward, turned round. Marler used the barrel of his Armalite like a club, smashing it across Yorcke's forehead. Yorcke staggered back, still clutching the spike. He felt his legs press against the concrete platform. With incredible agility he jumped up on to the platform to give himself extra height. He was waving the spike when the Armalite hammered into him again, catching him across the hooked nose.

He lost his balance, fell backwards on to the moving machine. Sprawled on the paper, he was carried along to the rollers. They had a safety device, jumping up when something large hit them. The large object was Yorcke's head. The roller came crashing down and Marler turned Paula away so she couldn't see. Yorcke let out a ghastly scream, heard clearly above the noise of the machinery. His shoulders reached the roller which jumped up again, then down. There was no further scream and the rest of his body swept under as the immensely heavy roller crashed down again. The paper was stained with a spreading pool of blood. Marler spoke quickly.

'Don't look.'

He heard someone call down from the top of the steps. Newman stood there with Tweed. Newman, followed by Tweed, hobbled down the steps, stopped when Marler warned him about the oil. Marler, his arm round Paula, guided her to Newman.

'Take her to the car. Stay with her.'

'You've hurt your foot,' Paula observed. 'I'll tend to it in the car. I've got a first-aid kit. Let's go. Take your time.'

Tweed stared at the printed sheets still proceeding along the battery of machines. Then he looked at Marler.

'British twenty-pound notes, ten-pound notes and fivers. It was Lenin who said, "If you want to destroy a country debauch the currency." Something like that. It's quite fiendish. The Americans were going to flood Britain with forged banknotes. We'd lose all faith in the pound. Then the Americans would persuade the population to switch to dollars. Then they would have taken us over.'

He looked up. At the top of the staircase Kent, Butler and Nield were gazing down. He shouted up to them.

'The three of you move as a unit. Check every room in this house. Make sure no one else is here. If it's all clear come back and tell me. But be careful.'

'I imagine you'd like all this to be wiped out?' Marler suggested.

'As soon as possible. Trouble is, the ceiling's concrete.'

'I think not.'

Marler climbed a ladder perched against a wall. Reaching up, he tapped at the ceiling. Looking down he shook his head.

'Not concrete at all. Some kind of polystyrene – to match the concrete floor. Above it will be wood flooring. And wood burns. I need to go back to my car for extra supplies. Don't go round the end of this battery of machines. Something very unpleasant will be there.'

When Marler had gone Tweed started to walk to the end of the conveyor belt of machines. He had a Walther in his right hand. Seeing what the last machine had spewed out onto the floor he skirted the remains of Bernhard Yorcke. His stomach churned. He walked on, past large packed bales piled to the ceiling, reaching a very wide door which was open. Beyond the door steps led up to a lighted area. He found himself inside the huge garage with the automatic door at the front still open.

It was freezing cold. He saw a switch on the wall, pressed it. The automatic door lowered swiftly. More fluorescent tubes lit the interior of the garage and three more white Mercedes trucks stood parked, replicas of the truck he had seen driven away. He looked inside the open backs. Empty. He went back down the steps into the machine room.

Inside a drawer he found a collection of knives. Selecting one, he bent down to rip open one of several bales on the floor. He stared at its contents – stack after stack of British twenty-pound notes, each neatly held together with an elastic band. He heard footsteps running down the steps from the house. Kent was in the forefront with Nield and Butler behind him.

'Come and look at this,' Tweed called out. 'But when you reach the end look at the wall.'

'All's clear,' Nield reported. 'No one else in the house.'

'Oh, my God . . .' gasped Kent. 'What is it?'

He had overlooked Tweed's advice. Now he was staring at what had seeped out of the last machine onto the floor.

'Don't ask,' Tweed snapped. 'I told you not to look. Instead, come and look at this.'

Kent came round the corner, bent down. He extracted a stack of the banknotes, took off the elastic band. His expression was grim.

'More forgeries. I don't need to use my eyeglass. They are very good, but once you know what to look for you can see at once they're fakes.'

'So once the knowledge spread like wildfire every bank teller, every shopkeeper, every shopper in Britain would know they were holding useless money?'

'That's how it would work,' Kent agreed. 'Then panic.'

Picking up the knife Tweed had used, he ripped open another bale. This one was brimful of stacks of fivers. He opened a stack, glanced quickly at several banknotes, shook his head.

'Again, at first glance they're the real thing, but they're not.'

Kent ripped open several more bales. He found stacks of ten-pound notes, fifty-pound notes. Tweed then led him up the steps into the garage. He pointed at one of the trucks.

'How much of the faked currency do you reckon that could contain?'

'Millions and millions,' Kent replied. 'It's a big truck. It would contain enough – if distributed – to start a run on the pound.'

'Worse than I thought. Much worse. One loaded truck got away.'

They returned to the machine room as Marler appeared, lugging a very heavy holdall. He dumped it on the floor, well clear of the spreading reddish pool. He glanced round the huge basement.

'I imagine you'd like me to lose this lot?'

'Yes. And the whole house. Can it be done?'

'Without difficulty. I've got thermite bombs which will turn the place into an inferno. Plus high explosive – just to make a professional job of it. If you've finished here, I suggest you leave me to it. Everyone returns to the Audis, then drive down to the end of the gulley. I'd appreciate it if you'd wait for me to arrive.'

'How does it work?'

'With this.' Marler took a small black object smaller than a matchbox from his pocket. It had a shallow depression on one side.

'I press that,' he explained, 'and the world blows up. It works rather like the gizmo you press when you drive home, pause at the end of your drive, press your gizmo. Hey Presto! The garage door lifts automatically. Based on a radio signal with a code. Same thing here. I've laced the rooms in the house with thermite and high-explosive bombs. All have a signal receiver. The whole shooting match goes up when I press this gizmo.'

'Put it away in your pocket,' Kent suggested. 'We don't want an accident.'

'Then clear off now and leave me to it,' Marler repeated.

With their two Audis parked beyond the bottom of the gulley, they waited. They had a clear view of the strange house perched on its bluff. Also they were close to the road running alongside the lake. They seemed to wait for ever but, by Tweed's watch, it was only five minutes later when they heard two dull explosions.

'It's started,' said Paula. 'Oh, Lord, where's Marler?'

'Hasn't started yet,' Tweed assured her. 'And here comes Marler like a rocket.'

When he reached the two cars Marler was out of breath. He stood still for a moment. Then he took the small black object he had shown them from his pocket. He looked at Tweed.

'Ready for the fireworks?'

'We are.'

Marler pressed the device. They all stared fixedly at the weird house. They had left all the lights on. Paula could make out the broken windows. There was a sim-ultaneous roar blasting out across the forest – accompanied by a searing sheet of fire. At first flames shot out of the windows, then the house began to come apart. The garage elevated. A truck rocketed into the air, on fire. It shot forward in an arc, descended into the lake. Flames fizzled, the truck sank. Within seconds there was an even more deafening roar. The house came apart. The front section elevated, was lifted bodily forward like the removal of a stage façade. It fell forward, dived off the bluff, landed in the lake. For a moment it floated, burning, a bizarre sight. Then it sank below the surface with a sinister sizzle. It created a small tidal wave which rushed forward, hit a long beach, sent up high a cloud of spray which settled.

'Those are banknotes,' shouted Paula.

She snatched up the binoculars she had focused on the house before Marler arrived. Above the crumbling side and rear walls of the house was a snowstorm. In her lenses she could see she was right. They were banknotes. Then a sheet of flame soared up, consumed the snow-storm. A strange large object was carried forward by the shockwave. She caught it in her binoculars. It was a huge section of a printing machine with a slab of concrete attached to its base. It dropped into the lake with a tremendous splash, sank instantly without trace. The flames, which had become an inferno had reached the nearest trees, setting them on fire.

'The forest is burning,' cried out Paula.

'Won't get far – not when they're saturated with snow,' Tweed remarked.

Slowly the wall of flames became less ferocious, suddenly no more than a series of flickers. They could see now that the house had vanished, reduced to a pile of ashes. The crackle of the flames had been loud as the wood burned but now there was a deathly silence. It was as though the *Psycho*-like house had never existed.

'We'll get moving,' Tweed decided. 'Back to Freiburg.'

41

The black Audi was driven at speed through Höllental. Ronstadt was behind the wheel with Chuck Venacki by his side. In the back Madison sat with Kolkowski. No one had spoken since their wild departure from the base at Schluchsee. They had sensed that their driver was in a very bad mood.

'We'll put those guys under ground for good later,' Ronstadt said suddenly. 'The main thing is one truckload is on the way. Should just meet the deadline. That will mess up the British currency real good. There's millions aboard it.'

'Where are we goin' to now?' Madison called out.

'Listen, fellers. Moonhead wants to know where we's goin' now. Maybe I'll tell 'im. Moonhead, we're on our way back to Freiburg. When we gets there you three guys have dinner. I'll book my room again.'

'We're stayin' there for the night?' Madison enquired.

'Sure. That's why I just booked one room. Friggin' idiot. I need the room so I can contact Charlie. For that I needs privacy. I likes to let Charlie know where we are in the game.'

'Say, where is this Charlie?' Madison went on. 'Washington? No. I got it. Charlie's in the London Embassy.'

'You keep on with that guessin' game and I'll put a bullet in your head.'

Ronstadt stared at Madison in his rear-view mirror. He gave him a look of pure venom, then increased speed. When they arrived at the Colombi everything went according to plan. Ronstadt collared the receptionist while his three men marched into the dining room. They were halfway through their meal before Ronstadt joined them. Madison noticed Ronstadt was ashen-faced.

'Charlie give you a hard time?' he enquired.

'All of you finish your food quick as you can. We have to get on the road again fast. You can fill your bellies at the Petite France in Strasbourg.'

'Petite France?' Madison queried. 'Is that a hotel?'

'No, Moonhead, it's a district of Strasbourg. We'll stay at the Hôtel Regent. Now, shut your mouth – or I'll shut it for you.'

Ronstadt's impatience to get going was so obviously mounting that they all stopped eating. Before getting up Ronstadt piled meat between two pieces of bread, making himself a sandwich which he wrapped in a napkin.

'I've got to go to the men's room,' said Venacki.

'Hurry it up. Car's waiting outside.'

The two white Audis raced through Höllental at a speed Paula was hardly able to believe. She kept glancing at the speedometer. Tweed was driving the first Audi. He had insisted on taking over when they left Schluchsee. He had pointed out that Newman must rest his damaged ankle.

Paula had used ointment on the ankle, then wrapped it in a bandage before they started out. Tweed enquired how bad it was.

'Not too bad,' Paula told him. 'With the ointment I've used the swelling will have gone away in three or four hours – maybe less. But he can't drive yet. I could.'

'I'll drive,' Tweed said firmly. 'I have the stamina.'

He now had Paula beside him with Newman and Kent in the back. Behind them Marler drove his Audi, again with Nield next to him and Butler in the back. He'd almost had trouble keeping up with Tweed.

419

'We're really moving,' Paula ventured as they were passing through Höllental.

'Don't worry,' Tweed assured her. 'That snowplough we saw has cleared this lane of snow. I'm anxious to get to Freiburg, back to the Colombi as soon as possible. There may be a message for me.'

'Who from?'

'Monica, of course.'

'I suppose we botched it back at Schluchsee,' Paula mused. 'We let one truck get away.'

'Oh, come off it,' Newman called out. 'Ronstadt started out with twelve men when he left Basle. Now he's down to four, including himself.'

'And,' Tweed pointed out, 'we have destroyed a fortune in forged banknotes, plus the machines for producing more, plus the base. When we reach the Colombi I'll try again to reach Roy Buchanan to deal with that single truck.'

'You tried earlier a way back,' Paula reminded him. 'You made no contact.'

'I think the Feldberg was in the way.'

'Why Buchanan when Otto Kuhlmann would do everything he can to help?'

'Because I think Otto would find himself in an impossible position politically. I'm convinced that truck is on its way to one of the American airbases in Germany. I think they have a transport plane lined up to take the truck aboard, then fly it to one of their bases in East Anglia. There should just be time for Roy to stop the truck – providing we keep moving. I have a feeling we're now desperately short of time.'

'Incidentally,' Newman said, 'those two small explosions we heard before the house went into the sky were Marler throwing a grenade under each of the two remaining black Audis. He aimed them under the petrol tanks. Told me while we were watching the fireworks.'

420

'We'll get a meal at the Colombi,' Tweed announced. 'An army marches on its stomach, as Napoleon once said.'

'Then what do we do?' Paula asked.

'No idea. That's why I hope there'll be a message at the Colombi.'

When the two cars were parked outside the hotel Tweed succeeded in contacting Buchanan on Beck's mobile. He explained the problem tersely. Buchanan listened without saying a word until Tweed finished: 'I do think, Roy, it's important to locate that truck.'

'Tweed, it's not important, it's absolutely vital. If the forged money is as good as you say it is we must do everything we can to stop it getting into circulation.'

'I just hope you have time.'

'I have. By chance I'm in Norwich. I'm going to use all the power I've been given to ring every possible American airbase. You said you thought it might well come aboard a C47 transport. That needs a long runway, which cuts down the number of airbases I have to think of. I'm getting on it now.'

Tweed and Newman, with Paula, were the first to enter the lobby. The receptionist leaned over the counter.

'Mr Newman, I have a message for you. In case you came back.'

Newman looked surprised. He took the sealed envelope. Tweed was about to head for the dining room when the receptionist called out again.

'I also have a message for you, sir.'

Tweed took the sealed envelope, put it in his pocket. Then he questioned the receptionist, phrasing his words carefully.

'A close friend of mine might still be in the hotel. A

Sharon Mandeville. You probably saw us together in the lounge.'

'Yes, sir, I did. Ms Mandeville checked out a good few hours ago. She drove off with her secretary, Ms Denise Chatel.'

'Did she leave a forwarding address?'

'No, sir, I'm afraid she didn't. We've had a bit of activity this evening – and now you turn up.'

'Mind if I ask who else has been here? It couldn't be my old friend, Jake Ronstadt?'

'I'm only here temporarily, sir.' The receptionist lowered his voice. 'Yes, Mr Ronstadt was here with three other men. They had dinner and then left.'

'Thank you. So I've missed him. Can't be helped . . .'

They left their coats, followed Tweed and Paula into the dining room. There were only two couples having dinner. Waiters made up a large table and they settled down to study the menu. When they had ordered, Tweed took out the envelope, opened it. The wording, like his name on the front of the envelope, was in ill-formed block letters.

REGENT HOTEL, PETITE FRANCE, STRASBOURG.

Newman had at the same time opened his envelope. He frowned as he reading the wording, written with a pen in a strange script.

Hôtel Regent, Petite France, Strasbourg.

'What on earth can this mean?' he asked, handing the letter to Tweed. 'And I most certainly don't recognize the handwriting.'

'I'd say you weren't meant to,' Tweed commented after scrutinizing the communication. 'It's educated, but awkward handwriting. My guess is it was written quickly by a right-handed man – using his left hand. Now look at my message.'

'This is incredible,' Newman exclaimed. 'What does it mean?'

'The version you're looking at was probably written by a less-educated man. Also, notice the different way the hotels are named. I've stayed there. I know in France it's called Hôtel Regent. Which again suggests a well-educated person.'

'Is someone going to let me in on the secret?' Paula pleaded.

They both handed her their letters. She studied them, took her time. Then she looked up.

'This is crazy. Same address, but apparently provided by two quite different people. Why?'

'It's a mystery,' Tweed agreed. 'And here's our meal. I'd like everyone to get on with it. I'm sure we're very short of time.'

'I know,' said Paula, 'gobble it down even though we haven't eaten for hours. Then we all get indigestion.'

'No need to do that,' Tweed assured her.

Marler finished first. Like Tweed and Paula he drank only water, avoiding wine. They didn't believe in touching alcohol when it came to driving.

'I told you about our brief confrontation with those four thugs in Höllental,' he began. 'I also mentioned the landslide. I was worried that when I drove to the bottom of the gulch that the exit would be blocked. Luckily, the landslide which covered the highway had not reached the right-hand lane. So we just drove straight off.'

Soon afterwards Tweed summoned the waiter, paid the bill. He pushed his chair back, anxious to leave.

'Just a moment,' Paula said. 'It would be nice to know where we're going.'

'To Strasbourg, of course.'

'It could be a trap,' Newman warned.

'I agree. Only way to find out is to get there. As I mentioned earlier, I once stayed at the Hôtel Regent. It's a very good hotel.'

'I'll take over the driving,' Paula offered.

'Thank you. But I'm just waking up,' said Tweed, 'so I'll go on driving.'

'And I'll continue behind the wheel,' Marler chimed in.

'Oh, well,' Paula sighed. 'Strasbourg here we come.'

Paula was certain she would never forget the headlong drive up the autobahn heading for Strasbourg. They were all seated as they had been during the drive from Schluchsee. She was next to Tweed, with Newman and Kent in the back. She had her map in her lap and referred to it frequently with the aid of her torch.

There was no longer any trace of snow and the moon glowed down brightly. Ahead she could see nothing but the endless stretch of the autobahn going on for ever. Tweed kept overtaking huge trucks lumbering along. One moment they saw red lights, the next, so it seemed to Paula, they had whipped past the vehicle. Hedges on the central reservation whipped past in a blur. She glanced at Tweed.

He was sitting quite still, his hands on the wheel relaxed as he continued staring into the distance. Her next glance was at the speedometer. Oh, my God! she thought. But of course there was no speed limit on German autobahns. There was also no speed limit for Tweed as the Audi devoured the miles.

'Are we trying to break some record?' Newman called out.

'We have so little time left,' Tweed replied.

As if Newman's comment and his own reply had

424

alerted him he pressed his foot down even further. Paula suppressed a gasp. She thanked Heaven they had left the snow behind long ago. Red pinpoint lights appeared in the distance. Another truck. Then Tweed was overtaking. The juggernaut whizzed past, was gone. Paula realized she was pressing her feet hard against the floor, that the palms of her hands were damp. Surreptitiously, she wiped them on her trousers.

'We're getting there,' said Tweed cheerfully.

'I'd already gathered that,' she replied.

In the second Audi, some distance behind them, Marler kept up his speed. Once he glanced at his speed-ometer. He raised his eyebrows.

'You know something,' he said to Nield next to him, 'this is North Pole or bust. In other words, Tweed has really got the bit between his teeth.'

'Oh, is that what is happening,' Nield answered, suddenly aware that he was sitting very tensely.

'I think he's in a bit of a hurry to get to Strasbourg,' Marler remarked.

'And I think he believes he's flying Concorde.'

Paula was studying her map again. She looked up as something flashed past. She cleared her throat to warn Tweed she was going to say something. He glanced at her.

'Comfortable?' he enquired.

'Oh, very. Would you mind if I suggested you slowed down just a bit?'

'We've got to get there.'

'I know. But we're approaching junction 54. That's where we'll turn off the autobahn and head for Kehl.'

'But we just passed junction 55,' Tweed objected.

'Yes, we did. And at the rate we're moving we'll overshoot 54.'

'Not a chance.'

They overtook a convoy of three huge trucks. Paula

425

looked up at the roof. It had been like watching a video on fast-forward. They had to be very close to 54 now. Then she realized Tweed was slowing – at least they were not travelling quite at supersonic speed any more.

'We have to be extremely close to it now,' she warned.

'I'm sure we are.'

She glanced at him again. For the first time she realized that mixed with his sense of anxiety about time was a sense of pure enjoyment. He felt he was achieving something. Which, she supposed, he was – if they got there in one piece.

'We're nearly at junction 54,' she said. 'And before you slap me down may I remind you I am the navigator?'

'Best in the world, I'd say.'

'Flattery will get you nowhere!'

Tweed had reduced his speed a lot. Turning off the autobahn at the junction he proceeded at a more sedate pace. Paula checked her map again.

'Soon we'll cross a bridge over the Rhine. After that we're in Strasbourg in no time.'

'Look for the spire of the cathedral,' Tweed suggested. 'It is immensely high. From the top on a clear day you can see the Vosges Mountains and the Black Forest, and they're a long way off.'

'What's Strasbourg like?'

'The centre, crowded round the cathedral, is a labyrinth of streets and alleyways. The buildings are as old as the hills. They're crammed together and their rooftops are all different heights, a lot of them lopsided and odd-looking. The best part is where we're going – Petite France.'

'And what do you expect when we reach the Hôtel Regent?'

426

'Something unpleasant, but we're getting used to that.'

42

Paula almost purred with delight as Tweed, deep inside Strasbourg, drove across an old bridge lined with elegant iron railings and she saw the Hôtel Regent. A large old four-square building, it was illuminated with tinted floodlights. She stared down beyond the railings at its reflection in the water under the bridge.

'We seem to have crossed a lot of bridges to get here.'

'The waterways are an essential part of Strasbourg,' Tweed explained. 'It's a very complex system and eventually you can sail in boats which take you on to the Rhine. Pleasure boats operate a lot in the season. I'm just hoping the hotel has rooms for all of us. The European so-called Parliament is here and when in session European MPs with fat expenses grab all the best accommodation.'

Paula glowed as they walked into a very modern and palatial reception area. The floor was paved with light green marble and the sides of the reception counter were also faced with marble. Round white pillars supported a high ceiling where the illumination was provided by recessed spotlights.

'We'd like rooms for seven people if that's possible,' Tweed said to the woman behind the curved counter. She was attractive, very fashionably dressed and had an air of authority. 'We have driven a long way,' Tweed added.

'No problem,' the woman said with a welcoming smile. 'We can give you all very nice rooms. If you could register, sir.'

Tweed dealt with the formalities, then looked at the woman as he returned her smile.

'If the porters could take our coats, some of us would like to go straight to the bar.'

'Certainly. Let me show you the way.'

Paula and Tweed were followed by Newman and Kent. Tweed heard Marler say the rest of them would like to go straight up to their rooms. Like the reception hall, the bar was modern but tasteful. In the manner of certain high-class cocktail bars it had comfortable arm-chairs upholstered in purple.

Tweed smiled to himself as they walked into the bar. By herself, seated in one of a series of banquettes facing each other, was Sharon Mandeville.

Marler was on his way upstairs to his room when a woman rounded a corner and started to descend. Denise Chatel. She looked harassed and had a briefcase tucked under her arm. She stopped dead when she saw him.

'Hello, Denise,' he greeted her. 'You'll think I'm fol-lowing you.'

'Are you?' she snapped.

Then she hurried past him down the stairs. Her expression was bleak and completely lacking in warmth. Marler shrugged.

'I think,' Nield whispered, 'she's gone off you . . .'

In the bar Tweed walked straight over to Sharon. She looked up and gave him a smile of extreme pleasure. Putting down her file, she stood up so he could hug her.

'Just when I was getting so bored with all this work you walk in, so now I can look forward to a really entertaining evening.'

'Rather a late evening,' he said sitting down facing her.

'Oh, the night is young. Who knows? We may be here at dawn.'

'This is Keith Kent,' Tweed introduced. 'Keith, Sharon Mandeville.'

'How nice to meet such a competent-looking man for a change. I am wondering what you do for a living.'

'I'm a banker.'

'A moneyman. Well, they say money makes the world go round.'

'Except,' Tweed said, 'at times the lust for money, when satisfied, is sometimes succeeded by the lust for power.'

'Tweed, you are a cynic.' She laughed. 'A dyed-in-the-wool cynic.'

'Or maybe a realist.'

'Paula.' Sharon focused her attention on her. 'I'm so glad you're here. Otherwise I'd feel outgunned. Why don't we go shopping together? There are some marvellous shops here if you know where to go.'

'I doubt if my bank balance would come up to yours,' Paula said with a smile.

'Nonsense. It would be a change to have some female company. I'm drinking champagne. I'll order another bottle.'

'Not for me,' Tweed said hastily.

'There's Paula and Keith. May I call you Keith? Good. And now, Bob, I noticed you were hobbling. You've been in the wars?'

'Slipped on a flight of stone steps in Freiburg. It's nothing.'

Sharon waved to a waiter. She ordered two more bottles of Dom Perignon. Then she leaned towards Tweed, speaking quietly.

'Talking about company, have you seen who is at the bar?'

Tweed turned round. At the bar, which had a pale yellow front, two men were perched on bar stools, their backs to the room. Rupert and Basil Windermere. He looked back at Sharon.

'What are they doing here?'

'Lord knows. They're a nuisance. Both of them, separately, have pestered me. I gave them a very cold shoulder. I can't imagine why they turned up here – unless they followed me on the autobahn. But why would they do that?'

'Your guess is as good as mine.'

'Then, to cap it all, you haven't noticed who is at a corner table by himself over there. That boor, Ed Osborne.'

Tweed again twisted round on his banquette. At that moment Ed Osborne looked up, caught his eye, stood up and lumbered over to their table between the facing banquettes. He slapped Tweed on the back, grinning, slurring his speech.

'Hi, feller! Great to see you again. You folks mind if I join you? Guess it's OK.'

As he sat down next to Tweed he looked across at Sharon and winked. She ignored him and started chatting with Newman. Osborne had a glass of Scotch in his right hand. Waves of the drink were drifting into Tweed's nostrils.

'What brings you all, as I believe they say in our Deep South, to this part of the world?'

'What brings *you* here?' Sharon asked sharply, her expression cold.

'Good question. Very good question,' Osborne mumbled. 'Guess I can give you a good answer. Had a hard time in Washington, then in London. So I'm takin' a few days off. Kinda holiday – just roamin' around, roamin' where the spirit takes me.'

430

'Then I hope you're enjoying yourself,' Sharon replied, her manner still cold.

'What gets me,' Osborne went on, 'is how we all keeps turnin' up in the same places. First there was Basle, then Freiburg and now, believe it or not, Strasbourg. I reckon it's a case of who is following who?'

There was a silence. Sharon busied herself pouring champagne into glasses. Paula shook her head, thanked her. Kent leaned forward, his voice crisp.

'Maybe if we started with leaving London we'd know what is going on. Would you agree, Sharon?'

'Sorry, Keith, but you've fogged me.'

'Well, take myself. I travelled to Basle to check a bank account. Then I moved on to Freiburg because a man called Jake Ronstadt was going there.'

'A horrible man,' Sharon exclaimed. 'No manners at all.'

'I agree with you,' Paula joined in. 'He kills people – like all those victims in Britain when bombs went off in department stores. Random massacres.'

'I can't believe that, Paula,' Sharon flared up indignantly. 'You will have gathered Ronstadt is not a man I want anything to do with from what I said earlier, but the idea that he could in any way be involved with those horrific outrages is absurd. Damn it, he has a big job at the American Embassy in London.'

'What sort of job?' Paula asked.

'I'm sorry, but I have no idea.' Sharon had calmed down. 'At the Embassy we function in watertight compartments. It's the new Ambassador's idea. Something to do with security, as far as I can gather.'

'So he wouldn't be running the Executive Action Department, then?' Newman suggested. 'The EAD for short.'

'I've never heard of it.' Sharon sipped champagne,

431

frowned. 'If it exists it sounds like a section directly controlled by the Ambassador – to ensure his decisions are carried out. He's more corporate than diplomatic, came after resigning as president of a big oil company.'

'Ruthless people,' Osborne commented, 'bosses of big oil outfits. Get up to a lot of skulduggery. Stuff the public never hears about. Washington shouldn't bring big business into diplomacy.'

'He – the Ambassador – has always been perfectly charming to me,' said Sharon. She looked up as Denise Chatel appeared, holding a file. 'Not now, Denise. Can't you see I've got company?'

'You said it was important,' Denise began.

'Well, it will have to wait. I don't get much chance of relaxation for a change. We'll deal with it later. Understand?'

Denise, looking humiliated, started leaving. On her way out she was passing close to the bar. Rupert's hand came out, wrapped itself round her waist.

'Let go of me.'

'You all play hard to get. Think I don't know that by now?' he sneered.

Newman stood up, walked over, still hobbling slightly. Reaching the bar, he laid a hand on Rupert's shoulder. He was smiling when he spoke.

'Lady doesn't want your attentions, Rupert. Doesn't like being touched by you.'

'And I'm fussy about who touches me. So kindly remove your hand from my shoulder. I never hit cripples,' he sneered viciously.

'Very wise of you.'

Newman removed his hand. In a blur of movement he bunched his fist, slammed it into Rupert's jaw. Rupert came off his stool, just managed to grab the edge of the bar to stop himself sprawling on the floor. Denise had gone as he lifted his hand, felt his jaw, glaring at Newman.

'I'll get you for this. That's a promise.'

'I say, chaps,' Basil broke in, 'we do have an audience. Best to preserve our dignity in such situations, don't you think?'

'Couldn't agree more,' said Newman, and he returned to his banquette seat.

'They really are a most unpleasant couple,' Sharon commented. She looked at Newman. 'I like a man who can take care of himself.'

'You know something,' Tweed said, speaking for the first time, 'I've done a lot of driving. I feel like stretching the limbs. I think a little walk might do us good, freshen us up.'

'Good idea,' said Newman. He looked at Sharon. 'I hope that you won't think us rude.'

'Not at all. When you get back I'll be here going through my work. Must make up for lost time. Then you can come in and rescue me and we'll kill the rest of the champagne.'

Tweed was helping Paula on with her coat in the lobby while Kent and Newman collected theirs from reception. Marler appeared, already attired in his coat. Tweed told him what they proposed doing.

'I've just come back from checking where they park guests' cars. Ronstadt's black Audi is there.'

'I thought Ronstadt and his thugs might be hidden away inside this hotel,' Tweed remarked as they wandered outside. 'It is high time they were taken off the face of the planet.'

'Setting yourself up as bait?' Marler suggested.

'I'm worried about the passage of time. I want us to

be able to stop having to think about Ronstadt and his lethal tricks. And look who we have here.'

Butler and Nield, muffled in coats, stood just out of sight of the hotel entrance. Marler told them to follow a little way behind them.

'Ronstadt and Co. are probably going to put in an appearance,' he warned.

'Can't wait,' said Butler.

Paula slipped her hand inside her shoulder bag, withdrew her Browning .32 automatic, slipped her hand under her coat. Again the arctic air hit them after the cosy warmth of the interior of the Hôtel Regent.

They walked past a waterway and Paula paused to peer down over a steep wall. The water was about fifteen feet below here. She glanced back, saw a flight of steps leading down to a small landing stage. A small open launch was tied up to the foot of the steps. She thought she saw movement, then decided it was her imagination. They walked on, trailed by Marler with Nield and Butler.

'You really have to see this part of Strasbourg by night – this way you appreciate its beauty, its strange character,' Tweed said.

'Strange is the word,' Paula agreed, huddled in her coat.

Their footsteps were the only sounds in the dark of the night. No traffic anywhere. No people at this hour. Paula was fascinated by the architecture. Hulking ancient buildings leant out over cobbled streets. She saw that many of them had pointy gables, that the roofline went up and down and in the walls was embedded a crisscross of old wooden beams. Most of the buildings were four storeys high with an endless variety of tiny dormer windows in the ski-slope roofs above, dormers perched so precariously they seemed to be on the verge of sliding down into the streets below. One grotesque old house was so crowded with dormers on its roof and looked like Gothic gone mad. She was reminded of a scene from Grimm's *Fairy Tales* – with the emphasis on grim.

'It gets claustrophobic,' she said, 'with the narrow streets and the buildings looming over us.'

'It's unique, as far as I know,' said Tweed.

They had followed a complex route, turning into different streets at almost each corner. Always, to their right, the stone wall rose above the pavement and, beyond it, another waterway. She was beginning to feel lost.

'I hope someone knows the way back,' she remarked.

'I do,' replied Tweed.

'A stranger would need a map.'

'I've got one in my head from the last time I was here. And I noticed in the hotel they have another kind of map – one showing the network of waterways for people hiring boats.'

Paula was disturbed by the areas of dark shadow where the moonlight couldn't penetrate. At intervals there were street lamps and then more shadows. She kept looking back and always Marler and his two friends were a short distance behind them. Marler waved at her encouragingly. She waved back, then stopped.

'We've actually walking in a circle to take us back to the hotel,' Tweed told her.

'I can hear a strange noise. Water rushing.'

'That is the sluice, which is quite spectacular. Heaven help anyone who takes the wrong turning on the waterways and finds himself being carried down it. They do have notices on the walls warning sailors. And we're nearly at Pont St-Martin. That's the bridge nearest the sluice. We might take a look at it.'

Tweed had started walking again and the sound of water rushing at immense speed grew louder. Paula stopped again.

'What is it now?' Tweed asked gently.

'I can hear a different sound. Chug-chug. Like the motor of a launch.'

'You're right. And it's coming closer. *Don't* look over that wall,' he warned.

'I'd take his advice,' said Kent. 'Stay where you are now.'

They had all stopped. Paula looked back. Marler held up a hand to keep her where she was. She watched him as he conferred with Butler and Nield briefly. Perplexed, she watched as Butler took a beret from his pocket. He placed it at the end of his Walther. He was standing by the wall.

Paula took her Browning from under her coat as the chug-chug grew nearer and nearer. Keeping his head well clear of the far edge of the wall, Butler eased the beret forward until it perched over the brink. There was a shattering rattle of machine-pistol fire. The beret was shredded, disappeared. Marler, dipping his hand into the holdall slung over his shoulder, took out one of his remaining grenades.

Butler had taken off his scarf. He wrapped it round his Walther. He had twisted the scarf so in the gloom it looked almost like a man's head. Again he eased his weapon close to the edge, then a few inches over the brink. A fresh murderous rattle from a machine-pistol ripped the scarf to bits. It was a long burst and when it stopped Paula guessed the unseen weapon needed reloading.

Immediately Marler looked over the top of the wall, dropped the grenade. Ignoring Tweed's warning, Paula was peering along the waterway. Illuminated by a street lamp she saw the small launch she had seen much earlier, tied to a landing stage. In the launch stood Ronstadt, fiddling desperately with the machine-pistol. With him was a moon-faced man and a third man with a

436

hard bony face. She saw Marler's grenade dropping and jerked her head back. The detonation, although muffled by the walls, still sounded very loud in the silence of the night. Looking back over the wall Paula saw the half-wrecked launch racing towards her. Moonface had been at the controls and had kept the engine running. Now it proceeded along the waterway without any human guidance. Tweed, Newman and Kent were also gazing at it as the launch passed below them. Three crumpled bodies lay in it, motionless.

'It's taking in water,' said Tweed. 'And it's near the sluice.'

They watched, hypnotized, as it entered the narrow sluice of churning, foaming water. The launch slid downwards, toppled over sideways, casting its cargo into the maelstrom. In seconds the corpses had disappeared, swallowed up by the wild water.

'I hope no one has unpacked,' Tweed said as they approached the entrance to the Hôtel Regent.

No one had. Tweed was walking quickly as they reached the hotel. He paused for a moment while they were still outside.

'We're leaving immediately,' he told them. 'We're driving now to Paris, then on to London. Get your bags and we meet in the lobby. I'll pay for the rooms.'

Paula waited with him while he explained to the receptionist he had received an urgent message. If anyone wanted to contact him would she please tell them they were on their way to Paris, that they might stay a few hours at the Ritz before going on to London.

He was walking along the first-floor corridor when they heard voices behind a closed door as Newman joined them. Tweed put a finger to his lips and they stopped to listen. Denise's voice was clear and very loud.

'I won't take any more from you. You were a horrible person back at the Embassy . . .'

'Don't you dare talk to me like that, you friggin' little traitor,' an unrecognizable voice shouted and roared. 'You've had enough money out of the Embassy funds to put Versace on your rotten little back.'

'You're always pestering me!' Denise screamed back. 'Back at the Embassy I avoided you whenever I could.'

'I'll kill you if you say any more. I'll push you out of a high window, watch you fall, hit the street with a splash of blood!'

'No you won't,' Denise shrieked back. 'From now on I'll take good care there's always a witness with me!'

'A witness! What are you insinuating, you ignorant wretch? You think the organization can't do without you? Who are you, anyway? A small-time adventuress!'

Tweed started walking swiftly towards his room with Paula and Newman. No one said anything until he reached it.

'They were having quite a party, weren't they?' Tweed remarked.

43

Tweed again insisted on driving and Paula was beside him as navigator, a new section of map open on her lap. In the back Newman sat with Keith Kent. Behind them followed Marler, with Nield and Butler as passengers. If Paula had expected Tweed to take it easy along the autoroute to Paris she was soon disillusioned.

He rapidly built up speed until Strasbourg was just a distant memory. Newman leaned down against his seat belt, removed his bandage, felt his ankle, flexed it this way and that. Kent asked him how it was. Newman replied it was OK.

'Tweed,' he called out, 'my ankle is normal now. I can take over the wheel whenever you want me to.'

'Maybe later.'

'Maybe never,' Paula said under her breath. She looked at Tweed. 'I was surprised at the twists and turns of our conversation with Sharon and Ed Osborne in the bar. You came out with some pretty blunt remarks,' she continued, glancing over her shoulder.

'They did so at my suggestion,' Tweed informed her. 'I had a few words with Bob and Keith at the reception counter. They reacted splendidly. And you, Paula, caught on quick and added your own loaded comments. You sensed the rhythm of how things were going very skilfully.'

'Did you learn something from that conversation, then?'

'Let's say I found it intriguing.'

'I thought Sharon held her own very well, bearing in mind that Osborne was present. Who knows how much power that man wields,' Paula said thoughtfully.

'That's what all this spilt blood and upheaval is about,' Tweed told her. 'Power. It's all about power, which can intoxicate people.'

'The only thing you said during the conversation referred to power,' Paula recalled. 'Apart from that you kept absolutely quiet.'

'I was listening, watching.'

'Why,' she asked, 'did you leave details of where we're going at the Hôtel Regent reception? Not like you.'

'So that anyone who wants to follow us knows where to head for. We might as well flush out as many of them as we can.'

'So Paris may not be safe.'

'Nowhere is safe now.'

'You're really stepping on the gas,' she said.

'I'm convinced we're almost fatally short of time.'

Rear Admiral Honeywood, known throughout the naval service as Crag, settled himself into his chair on the control deck of the immense aircraft carrier, the *President*. The vast array of escorts were way ahead of their bow, way behind their stern and spread out to port and starboard.

'We'll be on station in the English Channel, I reckon, about two days from now,' he remarked to his Operations Officer.

'That would be my estimate.'

'And so far,' Crag reflected, 'we haven't been seen by anyone.'

'Correct, sir. No submarines have been detected by sonar. We have seen not a single ship which might have reported our presence. And no commercial airliner has passed over the task force.'

'Let's hope it continues that way. The Pentagon is counting on our surprise arrival on their doorstep to stun the Brits out of their skulls.'

'Maybe it's time to report our situation back to the Chairman of the Joint Chiefs of Staff. He gets restless if he isn't kept regularly in the picture.'

'Old Stone-Face does just that. Send him another report. Include that worn-out phrase "proceeding according to plan". He'll like that.'

'Can't this buggy move any faster?' Osborne demanded.

'The chauffeur is doing very well. We're going at high speed now,' replied Sharon acidly.

She was sitting in the back of the stretch limo with

Osborne by her side. In the front Denise Chatel sat next to the chauffeur, her head down as she studied a file open on her lap. The limo streaked along the autoroute to Paris.

'Guess I could drive the jalopy faster myself,' Osborne grumbled.

'I don't know why you had to come with me as a passenger,' Sharon retorted.

'Simple, lady. Your limo was just leavin' when I needed to. I want to reach the Ritz before Tweed does, to be waitin' for him.'

'Well, I would appreciate it if you would leave the driver to do his job – which he's doing very well.'

'We gotta keep movin', baby.'

'And please do not call me baby. I really have no idea what your position is at the Embassy.'

'Call me an expediter. Hi, Denise,' he called out, 'how is the world goin' with you?'

Denise Chatel kept her head bent over her file. She made no reply. With one hand she shut the half-open section of the glass partition dividing the front of the limo from the rear. Osborne shrugged, waved both large hands in a gesture of resignation.

'If I'm not being nosy,' said Paula, 'why are we going to Paris?'

'I want to see René Lasalle, head of the DST. I think face to face, as opposed to talking on the phone, René may tell me more about the father of Denise.'

'Her father who was killed with his wife in a car crash somewhere in Virginia a year or so ago?'

'That's right – Jean Chatel. Sent over officially as an attaché, but really a member of the French Secret Service.'

'Why are you so interested in him?' she asked as Tweed overtook a convoy of three large trucks.

441

'Because he was sent to find out what the Americans were up to – and especially because Jean Chatel and his wife died in a car accident at exactly the same bridge where years before Sharon's parents died in a car accident.'

'I don't see the connection.'

'Neither do I,' admitted Tweed. 'But I have a feeling there is a connection – and that it might be the key to what is going on now. I'm hoping René will be able to give me more information.'

'Does he know you're coming?'

'Yes. I called him briefly on Beck's mobile from my room when I went to collect my case before we left the Hôtel Regent.'

'We're getting low on petrol,' Paula warned.

'Yes, I had noticed. And I think I see the lights of an all-night service station ahead. While we're filling up I want to call Roy Buchanan.'

'I'll deal with the petrol,' Newman called out.

'I can do that myself,' said Kent. 'I feel like stretching my legs, making myself useful.'

'You've been of invaluable help already, Keith,' Tweed assured him. 'But if you feel like that you can tank us up. Here we are.'

While Kent was filling up the tank Tweed used the mobile to try to contact Buchanan. He was lucky. The familiar voice, taut and grim, answered immediately.

'Who is this?'

'It's Tweed. Roy, if you can, I'd like you to do something for me. I'm going to see Jefferson Morgenstern when I get back to London. Have you any evidence that the Americans were behind the bombings in London?'

'Yes. A security video in the Oxford Street outrage survived the blast. We have a very clear picture of the man who planted that bomb. A very tall thin man with a hard bony face . . .'

442

'A very tall thin man with a hard bony face,' Tweed repeated, looking back at Newman.

'Vernon Kolkowski,' Newman said promptly.

'We know – knew – him,' Tweed reported to Buchanan 'He's dead as the proverbial doornail. Name of Vernon Kolkowski. I'll spell that ... Got it? Good. He was probably based at the American Embassy while I was still in London.'

'He was. We secretly photographed him when he re-entered the Embassy. Couldn't do a thing about it. They all carried those diplomatic passports.'

'What I'd like you to do is to compile a file of evidence – including what you've told me, with pics. I'd like as fat a file as possible to show Morgenstern when I get back.'

'Consider it done. No more bombings. Our drastic security precautions are working. Touch wood,' he added. 'When will you be back?'

'At a guess, within the next twenty-four hours.'

'The file will be waiting for you.'

The connection was broken and Tweed sank back with relief. He smiled as Paula asked the question he'd been expecting.

'Why do you want to talk to Morgenstern?'

'I said quite a while ago that I was convinced that the Americans are operating at two different levels, in watertight compartments. Sharon confirmed that. I don't think the diplomatic side has any idea of what the Executive Action Department lot have been up to, the crimes they've committed. And Morgenstern is greatly respected not only globally but also inside the States. To the American public Morgenstern *is* Washington.'

He glanced in his rear-view mirror. Marler's Audi was parked behind them while Butler filled up its tank. Kent reappeared out of a large café attached to the petrol station. Paula lowered her window as he handed her two large paper bags. He leaned into the car.

'Mineral water in one bag, fresh croissants in the other. Most of the customers sitting inside are truckers. Their vehicles are parked out at the back. In France bakeries work through the night to produce fresh croissants. The French insist on them, as you may know. In the morning housewives make a trip to the nearest source of supply. Must have fresh croissants for breakfast.'

'Keith, you're an angel,' Paula purred.

She leant out of the window, kissed him on the cheek. At that moment Marler strolled up to Tweed's window. He was stretching his arms.

'Got a moment?' he asked.

'A few minutes only. Think I'll get out and flex my muscles . . .'

Paula was drinking water out of the bottle. When she'd quenched her thirst she wiped the neck of the bottle with a clean handkerchief. Then she handed the bottle to Newman.

'Excuse my unladylike manners. When you've had a drink I'll pass you some croissants. Don't forget Keith,' she went on as Kent got back in beside Newman.

'While I was marooned back at the Schwarzwälder Hof in Freiburg,' Marler began, 'I went out, found a public phone, called Alf.'

'Alf?'

'Alf Rudge. Top man in that cockney mob I once mentioned to you. In my spare time, for several weeks I've been training them as a reserve. Tough lot. All cab drivers. Took them out into the wilds of the Chiltern Hills. Seven of them, including Alf. Set up a makeshift shooting range in the middle of nowhere. Trained them with handguns, grenades, and machine-pistols. Three of them already knew their stuff – veterans of the Gulf War. They're all pretty much crack shots now.'

'Could come in very useful,' Tweed mused. 'The Americans have unlimited manpower. How can they afford the time if they're cab drivers?'

'Easy. They all own their cabs. Alf has one or two Americans as friends, but like the rest of his mob he does not like the Yanks. Can I tell you quickly a story about Alf?'

'In five minutes – at the outside – we must head for Paris again.'

They were walking about, working their legs in the glare of lights. Nield, a grenade concealed in one hand, his Walther in the other, was outside, watching the highway.

'Alf,' Marler explained, 'flew to LA for a change. One night he's out for a walk when three thugs approach him, demand his money. He takes out his wallet, shows them it has only a single one-hundred-dollar bill. Tells them he has more back where he's staying nearby. If they promise not to harm him they can have all the money. Leads them back to the rundown hotel where he's staying, up to his room. The chief thug has a gun barrel pressed into his neck, the other two stay downstairs in case police appear. Alf says if the chief thug takes the gun off his neck he'll tell him where to get the money. The thug obliges, Alf tells him to open a heavy drawer. The thug does so, Alf jams his hand inside, ramming the drawer shut. Alf slams him one on the jaw, the thug collapses, semiconscious. Alf calls down to the others. They arrive, Alf uses the chief thug's gun to hammer their heads. He topples all three down the stairs, out into the street. Sleazy owner turns up, Alf pays his bill, tells him he's going to Malibu. Packs his case, flags down a cab, goes to the airport, catches the first flight home.'

'Alf can take care of himself,' Tweed commented. 'I

445

see Butler, like Kent, has taken a bag of goodies to your car. Now, we get moving. Fast.'

'Shove your ruddy foot down,' snarled Rupert. 'This car's moving like a snail.'

'Some snail, my dear chap,' replied Basil, behind the wheel. 'I'm driving right on the speed limit.'

'To hell with the speed limit. I wanna get to Paris.'

'That's where we're going, dear boy.'

'Don't you "dear boy" me. We're the same flaming age. Thirty-two. In case you've forgotten,' he sneered.

'I had not forgotten. Exceed the speed limit and a patrol car nabs us. We end up in the Santé Prison in Paris. Heard of what it's like inside there, have we? They shove you inside and throw away the key.'

'I'll take over the wheel. Stop the car,' Rupert raged.

'Not sure that would be a frightfully good idea. Not after how much you consumed in the bar at the Hôtel Regent. What's all this hurry to reach Paris?'

'I wanna drink.'

'I think you want to have a go at Newman. Not a good idea. He can look after himself in a mean way.'

'Not interested in Newman. A has-been fifth-rate reporter. I wanna drink. Couldn't get one to bring with me at that crazy bar. Closing as early as that.'

'It was the middle of the night,' Basil pointed out.

'What's that got to do with it? I should have brought a bottle.'

'Well, I fear you didn't – because you couldn't. You did drink five times as much as me.'

'You were counting, were you?' Rupert sneered once more. 'Just the kind of thing you would do.' He waved his hand about. 'I know you won't mind if I say you're one lousy driver.'

'We're getting closer to Paris now. Why don't you have a nap?'

'Don't wanna a nap. Wanna a drink.'

'While I think of it, Rupert. You phoned your late father's lawyer from the Colombi in Freiburg,' said Basil in a perfectly sober voice. 'You told me he'd agreed to advance you some money. I'm desperately short of that commodity. I could do with a loan very urgently. I'm sure you could spare ten thousand pounds.'

'I suspect we're not too far from Paris,' said Tweed.

'You're right,' Paula agreed. 'We'll soon be seeing the outskirts. Why? Are you getting tired?'

'No, just impatient. I have a feeling we should get back to London as fast as we can, that time is running out.'

'I've just remembered something important,' Newman called out from the back. 'Back at Schluchsee, when I was nearly knocked down by Ronstadt when he was fleeing in his car. There were *four* men in that car. But when Marler dropped his grenade into the launch in Strasbourg there were only *three* men in it. One is still missing.'

'Maybe the Phantom,' Paula joked. 'He seems to live a charmed life.'

'You could be right,' Newman replied seriously. 'So far as we know he's still on the loose.'

'If he isn't dead,' Tweed remarked. 'I hope he appears sooner or later. He has to be wiped out – the number of people he's killed up to now.'

'When you've finished your business in Paris how do we get home?' Newman enquired.

'It all depends on which is the quickest way back,' Tweed answered. 'It could be by Eurostar or flying back from Charles de Gaulle airport. Lasalle will know the answer.'

'It's beginning to get light,' said Paula. 'With a bit of luck we'll reach the Ritz before the horrendous rush hour starts in Paris.'

A faint glow of light was rising in the east. Gradually it spread across the cultivated fields on either side of the autoroute. The clear sky was a pallid blue. There was a promise of a fine day on the way.

'A bit different from the Black Forest,' Paula said cheerfully.

'The weather forecast predicted a brighter fresh day for this area,' Tweed recalled. 'Makes a change. And I was just wondering how Howard is coping. He's had to run the whole show himself under very difficult circumstances ...'

Many hours earlier – it was midafternoon of the previous day – Howard had decided he must drive down to the Bunker to see for himself how they were getting on. It was a gloriously sunny day but Howard had to force himself to make the trip. He'd had hardly any sleep for the past forty-eight hours and was concentrating as best he could behind the wheel of the car.

By himself, he had passed through the village of Parham. He had given a brief thought to calling at Irongates on Sir Guy Strangeways, but had decided he'd better keep going while he was still awake.

His eyes kept wanting to close and he nearly missed the turn-off from the road south of Ashford to Ivychurch. Now all his concentration was called for as he negotiated the narrow, twisting lanes. Half the time, the spiky hedges, waiting for spring to come into leaf, blotted out his view of what lay beyond the next bend.

'I'm driving a lethal weapon,' he said aloud. 'I must look out for other people.'

Normally he would have been alerted by the *beat-beat* of a helicopter approaching. In his exhausted state he assumed it was a traffic-checking machine. He drove very slowly as he approached the automatic farm gate which would be operated by Mrs Carson. He could still hear the chopper when Mrs Carson ran out into the yard and gestured to him furiously to drive on inside a large barn with its door open. He did so. Getting out of the car, he nearly stumbled. As soon as he was outside Mrs Carson slammed the barn door shut.

'Get inside the house. Quick!' she shouted.

Once he was inside she shut the door immediately. He slumped into an armchair. He knew that if he wasn't careful he'd fall fast asleep.

'Black coffee, please,' he mumbled. 'A litre of it.'

'That chopper circling above us,' she said. 'It hasn't got any kind of markings. You should have waited further up the road.'

'Sorry. Could I have that coffee, please?'

Inside the helicopter the co-pilot held a powerful camera, aiming it down at the farmhouse. As the machine circled he took pictures from every angle. His tone was exultant when he spoke.

'Gene, we've just located the Brits' secret communications centre. I've gotten some great pictures.'

'That's great, Lou. What about the exact location?'

'I've marked that clearly on my detailed map of Romney Marsh. Guess we should get promotion for this.'

'What about those hedges surrounding the perimeter?'

'They're just hedges. I've got all we need.'

449

'OK, Lou. Then it's back to base. The pics and the map can be sent back to Washington. Guess they could go right up to the Chairman of the Joint Chiefs of Staff.'

44

'René Lasalle is out,' Tweed said as he put down the phone in his bedroom at the Ritz. 'He left a message that he'd call as soon as he returns.'

'This is a lovely room,' Paula enthused, 'with a wonderful view out over the Place Vendôme. It looks marvellous – especially as the day is so glorious.'

Tweed joined her, gazed at the famous column erected to Napoleon in the centre of the many-sided square. The superb architecture of the stone buildings enclosing the *place* had been cleaned. He had always thought this was the most magnificent square in the whole of Paris.'

'You'll never guess why René had to rush off,' he remarked.

'Tell me, then.'

'A bomb has exploded in a big department store. Quite a few casualties.'

'You mean the Americans are now turning their attentions to France? More work by the Executive Action Department?'

'No, I don't think so for a minute. The deputy of René's to whom I spoke said it's the work of Algerian extremists. The world is in a wild state.'

'So the Cold War is over and now we have an equally sinister Hot War? Worse, in a way, because it's so difficult to locate the fanatical killers.'

'I want to phone Monica later, maybe have a word

with Howard. Meantime I feel like a full English break-fast. What about you?'

'I've got a void in my tummy. Full English will do me.'

Emerging from the lift at ground-floor level Newman, who had joined them, rubbed his hands in anticipation. He looked around as they walked to the dining room.

'You know something? I've learned to enjoy luxury. I even think I've earned it – when I think of some of the hovels I tried to sleep in overseas as a foreign correspondent.'

'The pack has followed us,' Paula whispered to Tweed.

Running down the stairs, with surprising agility for so big a man, was Ed Osborne. At the same moment, as they approached the entrance to the restaurant, Rupert came out with Basil Windermere. As they reached the couple Rupert had paused. He bowed with mock cour-tesy to Paula.

'We've beaten you to it. Early bird catches the worm.'

'I've no intention of trying to catch you,' she replied tartly.

'One in the eye for you, Rupert,' Basil commented.

Rupert gave Paula a venomous look. As the two men strolled on Newman caught Tweed's arm to get him to pause. No one else was about and he could hear what the two men were saying.

'I'm off out to get something from my car,' Basil said.

'And I,' Rupert said in a loud voice, glancing over his shoulder, 'am going to get a shower. It's fun to have company in a shower,' he went on, staring at Paula. 'Maybe you'd consider joining me sometime soon.'

As they continued strolling away Paula flushed. She gritted her teeth. Had Rupert been close enough she'd have slapped his face. Newman took her arm, guided her into the restaurant, followed by Tweed.

'No point in exchanging more insults with such trash,' he advised her. 'And surprise, surprise, look who is here.'

Sharon sat at a large table by herself, breaking a croissant between her elegant hands. She waved to them, an invitation to share her table. Tweed walked to her table, waited for Paula and Newman to join him.

'Paula, do sit by me,' Sharon suggested. 'Gentlemen, choose your seats.'

'I thought you were going to say choose your weapons,' Newman joked.

'Are you following me, Bob?' Sharon enquired as Newman sat down. 'If so, I take that as a great compliment. Or maybe, Tweed, you are the one who is pursuing me?'

'That's right,' Tweed replied, glancing at the menu, 'divine inspiration told us you'd be staying here.'

'Is there anywhere else to stay in Paris?' she retorted.

'Mind if I join you folks?' a deep American voice rumbled. Ed Osborne had a hand on the back of an empty chair facing Tweed. 'Guess we're gettin' to be a family – the way we keep meetin' up.'

'You're welcome, of course, Ed,' Sharon replied unenthusiastically.

'Great. I'm a sociable guy. Like company. What are you guys havin' for breakfast?' he enquired.

'We're having the full English,' Tweed told him. 'Here's the waiter.'

'Guess I'll go along with that,' Osborne agreed.

After they had ordered Sharon concentrated her attention on Paula. Putting a shielding hand to her face, she raised her eyebrows and glanced to her left at Osborne, as much as to say 'Here we go again.' Instead she said something else.

'When I've finished breakfast I'm off to the hairdresser. They have a good one here.'

Paula looked at Sharon's blonde waves, sweeping down gracefully to her shoulders.

'You look as though you've just come from the hair-dresser,' she remarked.

'That's the nicest thing anyone's said to me for a while.' Sharon extended a hand across the table, clasped Paula's. 'Thank you. Tweed, why are you in Paris?' she asked suddenly.

'I'm investigating the probable murder of Denise Chatel's father and mother at a lonely bridge in the state of Virginia.'

Osborne spilt coffee from the cup he was holding on his napkin. A waiter hurried forward, checked to make sure no coffee had stained his smart beige suit. Presenting him with a fresh napkin the waiter took away the spoilt one.

Paula was stunned by Tweed's unusual candour. She stiffened but managed to avoid a startled expression.

'Murder?' Sharon looked puzzled. 'I thought they died in a road accident.'

'You got something wrong there, brother,' said Osborne. 'It *was* an accident, according to the official report.'

'I have a witness who says otherwise,' Tweed told him.

'A witness?' Osborne was incredulous. 'Who is this so-called witness?'

'I don't think I can reveal a name at this stage.'

'This is Paris, France, not Virginia,' Osborne protested.

'The long arm of retribution sometimes stretches across continents.'

'I'm stupefied,' said Sharon. 'Stupefied and shaken. If you're right, does Denise know about this?'

'By the way, where is Denise?' Tweed enquired, evading a direct answer.

'In her room here. Working. She had a very early breakfast.'

'Talkin' about breakfast, here it comes, praise the Lord,' said Osborne. 'Everybody here probably thinks with my weight I'd be better off with just grapefruit. Fact is, I'm in good shape. Keep myself in good shape at the gym. Slam at punchbags, lift weights. All that stuff.'

'You must have good reflexes, then,' Newman suggested.

'He has,' Paula confirmed. 'I saw him coming downstairs this morning like a ten-year-old.'

'In a hurry for my breakfast,' said Osborne, and he chuckled.

'I have to go upstairs to make a phone call,' Tweed announced after finishing his meal.

He glanced round the restaurant. Marler, as instructed, sat at a table by himself some distance away. At another table, again as instructed by Tweed, Butler and Nield sat at their own table. No point in identifying all his people to anyone in the restaurant who might be interested.

'I hope you'll excuse me,' Tweed said to Sharon.

'Of course. I'm just going to have another cup of coffee and then I'll be working too.'

As Tweed left the restaurant Marler stood up, strolled casually after him. En route to the lift with Newman, Tweed felt like a breath of fresh air. As Paula, following behind them, had said earlier, it was a glorious day.

Walking the full length of the wide corridor Tweed approached the main exit leading out onto the Place Vendôme. He reached the door and no one else was about. He stepped forward into the open and was forcefully jerked backwards by Marler. A bullet struck the exact point where he'd been a second earlier. The bullet ricocheted out into the *place*. The uniformed doorman on duty outside ran up to him.

'Something wrong, sir?'

'Caught my foot on a stone someone must have kicked into the entrance.'

'I thought I heard a noise.'

'Car backfiring.'

Marler had run out into the *place*. The doorman saw nothing of what he was doing as he was talking inside to Tweed. Marler was circling the empty *place*, a Walther in his hand. He had it pointed upwards along the rim of the mansard rooftops opposite. He didn't expect to be fired at – he was a moving target. His reaction was a warning to the invisible marksman who had aimed to kill Tweed. Again from a rooftop, as had been the case in Basle.

Inside the reception hall Tweed was viewing the potentially lethal incident calmly and philosophically. Which was not the case with either Paula or Newman. She kept her voice down but didn't mince her words.

'You must be crazy to walk out of that door by yourself. It was only due to Marler that you weren't killed. What were you thinking of?'

'Paula's right,' Newman agreed. 'What the hell were you thinking about – taking a risk like that?'

'Yes, you are both right,' Tweed responded. 'I was thinking about something that happened at breakfast – or rather something that didn't happen. I'll express my gratitude to Marler when I see him.'

'It means,' Newman pointed out grimly, 'that the Phantom tracked you to this hotel.'

'It means just that,' Tweed agreed.

Earlier, en route to the lift, before he had decided to sample some fresh air, Tweed had paused to take a good look at the patio beyond some windows. He had recalled

455

this was where, in summer, society women gathered for tea and an exchange of the latest scandal. Osborne had passed them on his way out from the restaurant, hurrying to the exit.

Now it was Paula who paused. She was examining the contents of a glass showcase displaying *objets d'art* sold by a famous shop in the rue St-Honoré. The prices were sky high.

'Some valuable stuff there,' Tweed commented.

'You're far more valuable than anything in that showcase,' she reprimanded him. 'In future you don't go out unless Bob and I are with you.'

'Well, you know I always do as I'm told,' he replied with a smile.

'I'm not joking,' she snapped. 'I want you to promise us.'

'I promise. Now I'm going up to my room to make a phone call.'

He had just spoken when Osborne came in through the front entrance. The American was breathless, waited a moment before he could talk.

'Hi, folks. Just been for a quick jog. Told you I kept in shape. Don't tell on me – I've just committed a crime.'

'What was that?' Newman asked.

'Fed a parking meter. It was way over the top. Parked my car in a side street just off the rue St-Honoré last night. No space left in the Ritz garage. See you.'

Paula watched him run nimbly up the stairs he had earlier descended on his way to breakfast. He took the steps two at a time.

'He's recovered quickly from his jog,' Paula observed.

Tweed had gone up in the lift by himself. Paula had paused again to take another look at the showcase. A diamond clasp shaped like the wings of a bird was fascinating her. Newman had waited with her. Marler returned through the front entrance and strolled up to them.

'Like a word. Up those few steps is a small lounge. No one in it.'

'Find anything?' Newman asked when they were settled on a couch.

'I found the bullet intended for Tweed. Here it is.'

He took from his pocket an old tobacco tin with the lid fixed on. Paula stared at it. Then she remembered the time when Marler had smoked a pipe before he switched to king-size cigarettes. He removed the lid. Inside the tin rested an ugly-looking bullet.

'Evidence of a sort,' Marler commented.

'Any sign of the assassin?' Paula asked.

'No. At first I assumed he'd fired from a rooftop. After I hauled Tweed inside I was out there like a rabbit. I scanned the entire square. Then I realized even a cat burglar could never have scaled those roofs. And no window was open. Had one been pulled shut I was out there so fast I'd have noticed it.'

'Then where did he shoot from?' Newman enquired.

'Had to be from ground level, from behind a corner. A bit further along to your right, as you leave the entrance here, there's a large arcade. It was deserted. We had a very late breakfast. All the workers are in their offices. The ladies who shop are still in front of their mirrors, applying make-up and Lord knows what else.'

'You're a cynic, Marler,' Paula teased him.

'I'm wrong, then?'

'No, you're right. I was just amused at your perception about the habits of some women. Comes from experience, I suppose.'

'Where else?' Marler replied.

*

Flight BA 9999, bound for New York, was well out over the Atlantic. It was temporarily flying an unusual course to avoid turbulence. The captain had handed over control to his co-pilot for a few minutes to refresh himself. He was gazing down through a window.

At thirty-five thousand feet there was a sea of endless cloud below them, masking any sight of the ocean far below. The forecast had been for a continuous overcast all the way to their destination, many hours away. Captain Stuart Henderson was sucking a sweet provided by his chief stewardess, Linda. On a shelf, securely wedged in, was his video camera. Henderson had promised his wife that he'd try to get a series of shots of the approach to New York. Linda had agreed to operate the camera. Not that Henderson thought they'd have any luck – not at this time of the year. The overcast would stay with them all the way to JFK.

Henderson glanced at his watch. Time to take over from the co-pilot – he'd had his break. He took one final look down, stiffened, stared in sheer disbelief.

'Give me the video camera, Linda,' he called out. 'Quick.'

Below there was an enormous break in the clouds. Below that he saw a gigantic aircraft carrier. Spread out well beyond it to port and starboard were escorts of heavy cruisers. While Linda patiently held the camera Henderson used a pair of high-powered binoculars. He could just make out it was flying the Stars and Stripes. Guided-missile cruisers were protecting the carrier. Midway between the two destroyers sailed on a parallel course.

'Linda, take these, give me the camera. There's a ruddy great American task force down there. At a guess it's heading straight for Britain.'

He was operating the camera as he spoke. He swivelled it at different angles, trying to take in the whole of the vast battle fleet. Then the overcast reappeared, blotted out everything. Henderson stood motionless for a minute, his index finger tapping the side of the camera he was no longer operating.

'Frank,' he said to the co-pilot, 'have you heard anything about a major American task force heading for British waters?'

'No.'

'Neither have I,' said Linda. 'And I read the newspapers from page to page. Nothing on the radio. Nothing on TV.'

'I think I'm going to send a detailed and urgent radio signal to the Ministry of Defence,' Henderson decided.

45

Tweed first attempted to call Monica, using Beck's mobile. He had to give up eventually – the line was constantly engaged. Instead he called Roy Buchanan, reaching the Chief Inspector immediately.

'Tweed!' Buchanan sounded triumphant. 'The bullet matches.'

'Pardon?'

His mind had been elsewhere, replaying the breakfast conversation in the Ritz dining room when Osborne had joined the party.

'The bullet!' Buchanan repeated. 'Remember? You called me from Freiburg, told me to have the plane carrying the body of Sir Guy Strangeways met here. I personally was on the spot when the machine landed at Heathrow. I had a top doctor standing by, had the body rushed to him. He performed the autopsy, dug out the bullet which killed Strangeways. I had it compared with the bullet which assassinated our Prime Minister. Both bullets matched up perfectly. Which means the Phantom shot both the PM and Strangeways.'

'He has a lot to answer for . . .'

'Haven't finished yet. I've sent the Strangeways bullet to René Lasalle in Paris by courier. He'll have it by now. So he can compare it with the bullet which assassinated the French Minister.'

'Very good work, Roy.'

'More yet. I had patrol cars waiting in secret just outside all American airbases in East Anglia. One of them grabbed the big white truck flown in from Germany. Also its driver. You know what was inside that truck?'

'Money.'

'Enough brilliantly forged British banknotes to cause a financial panic here if they'd been distributed. I've got them under heavy guard. Have sent specimens to the Bank of England. They are in a state of shock.'

'This is wonderful news, Roy. Congratulations.'

'We've beaten the so-and-sos,' Buchanan said jubilantly, a man Tweed had never before known to show emotion.

'Hold on, Roy,' he warned. 'I think the monster crisis is yet to come. How about the bombings?'

'None since I surrounded the American Embassy with plain-clothes men.'

'Thank Heaven for that. Just don't relax your efforts one inch.'

Tweed had just put down the phone when it started ringing. He picked it up quickly.

'Hello, who is it?'

'René. I'm back. Could you come now to rue . . .' Lasalle paused. 'Is this phone safe?'

'Yes. I'm on a hacker-proof mobile.'

'Then could you come now to rue des Saussaies? I have news for you.'

'Can you dig out your file on Jean Chatel?'

'It will be waiting for you, my friend.'

'I'm on my way. Oh, can I bring Paula and Newman with me?'

'They will be most welcome.'

Tweed kept his word. He phoned Paula and Newman, asked them to come to his room immediately.

Very few people know about – or notice – rue des Saussaies, the headquarters of the *Direction de la Surveillance du Territoire*. In other words, French counterespionage. A short narrow street almost opposite the Elysée Palace, it is passed by without so much as a glance by tourists. The entrance to the nondescript building is halfway along on the left, approached from the Elysée end. Newman stopped the car at the entrance and Tweed showed the guard his passport. The guard waved them inside.

'M. Lasalle is expecting you, sir.'

Newman parked the car in the small cobbled courtyard at the end of a short stone tunnel. An officer in plain clothes led them inside and up an old stone staircase to an office on the first floor. Lasalle rose from behind an old wooden desk to greet his guests.

'Coffee?' he suggested.

'It would help,' Tweed agreed.

René Lasalle, in his fifties, was small and slim and sported a neat moustache. He was dressed in a dark business suit and he pulled out a chair for Paula, then returned to sit behind his desk. A shabby green file was the only object on its surface apart from a telephone.

'The bullet arrived from Chief Inspector Buchanan some time ago,' he began. 'I'm sure you know which bullet I'm referring to.'

'I know very well,' Tweed assured him.

461

'We have had time,' Lasalle explained in his excellent English, 'to compare it meticulously with the bullet extracted from our late French Minister. It is a perfect match.'

'Then it's the Phantom again.'

'I would like your permission to send this bullet to my colleague in the German police at Wiesbaden, Otto Kuhlmann. For comparison with the bullet extracted from the body of Keller, also assassinated, as you know.'

'Send it by all means,' Tweed urged. 'Is that the file on Jean Chatel?'

'It is. I would ask you to treat its contents with confidentiality. In fact, officially you have never seen it. The Secret Service is very prickly about its documentation. Rightly so, you might agree.'

'Of course.' Tweed read the first few paragraphs, typed in French, then began to comment. 'This states that the real purpose of Jean Chatel's assignment to Washington is illumination. Specifically, is it true the Americans are preparing a plan which would change the geopolitical balance in Europe? Important that this includes the state of Great Britain . . .' Tweed went on reading.

'It was just over a year ago roughly when Chatel went to Washington, wasn't it?' asked Newman.

'No. Twenty months ago. But it was just over a year ago when he and his wife were murdered in the fake car accident in Virginia.'

'Murdered? You have evidence?' Newman queried.

'Let Tweed read on. You will see then.'

'This,' said Tweed, 'is a summary of a report sent to Paris by Chatel fifteen months ago. Chatel has reported he is followed everywhere by a team of American agents. He fears for his life, but asks to be allowed to continue his investigation.'

'It's getting grimmer,' commented Paula.

'It gets even grimmer,' Lasalle told her.

'The next report from Chatel,' Tweed went on, 'states that there is a highly detailed plan for the Americans to occupy Great Britain by subterfuge, employing every ruthless technique which will help to bring this objective about.'

'Why didn't you warn us?' Newman demanded.

'I wished to do just that,' Lasalle said bitterly. 'But it was argued by my superior that we had no concrete evidence, no documentation. He said the British would simply think it was a device by the French government to drive a wedge between Britain and the United States. I protested vigorously. The issue went up to the President in the Elysée. He agreed with my superior's decision.'

'Here we come to it,' said Tweed. 'Chatel reported that the momentous operation had been devised and was being directed by an individual called Charlie . . .'

'My God,' exclaimed Paula.

'Let me go on,' said Tweed. 'Chatel reported that he had made all efforts to identify the individual, Charlie, but so far had had no success. He ends by saying he thinks he is very close to locating Charlie.' Tweed looked up at Lasalle. 'How recent was this final report?'

'One week before he was killed in the so-called road accident.'

'Would it be possible, René, for me to have a copy of this final report? If so, I suggest you do so in a way which eliminates the printed reference to your department at the top of this sheet?'

'You ask a lot.' Lasalle paused, clasped his hands, stared up at the ceiling. 'But you deserve a lot,' he decided eventually. 'Considering we did not warn you earlier. Ah, at long last, we have coffee.' He spoke in French to the officer who carried a tray. 'Have you had to fly to Brazil to get the beans? Just put it down on my desk and leave us alone.'

463

He picked up his phone and spoke rapidly in French. Almost at once when he had ended the call an attractive girl came in, took the sheet he had extracted from the file handed back to him by Tweed. Then he poured coffee, handing the first cup to Paula.

'I have it on my conscience that I did not contact you to warn you. We have worked so well together in the past it seemed to me I was guilty of a kind of betrayal.'

'Nonsense,' replied Tweed, after sipping coffee, 'and it is very possible your President was right. Our late Prime Minister was not strong on international politics. He might well have thought it was all more French trickery to undermine our relationship with the Americans.'

'I comfort myself with the fact that I did report to you that a horde of strange Americans were infiltrating Britain by air and by Eurostar.'

'Also, René, the photos you sent enabled us to identify some of the most villainous types – most of whom are now dead.'

'Dead?' Lasalle's grey eyes twinkled as he glanced at Newman and Paula. 'I expect you have all been very busy.'

'There has been a certain amount of activity,' Newman replied.

The four of them chatted for a few minutes about times when they had cooperated during a crisis. The attractive girl came back, handed several sheets to Lasalle, who thanked her. Lasalle took the original sheet, carefully inserted it back inside his file. He then folded three other sheets, inserted them into a thick white envelope which he handed to Tweed.

'There are three excellent photocopies of the vital page. You are most welcome.'

The phone rang. Lasalle answered, listened, took a pad from a drawer, scribbled on it. At one stage Tweed heard him asking the caller to spell a name. He then ended the call.

'Tweed, this information may – or may not – be of interest to you. A Mlle Sharon Mandeville left the Ritz a while ago to catch a flight back to London. Shortly afterwards, in another car, a M. Osborne also left to catch the same flight. A M. Basil Windermere with a M. Rupert Strangeways left earlier to board the Eurostar for London.'

'Yes, the information is useful,' Tweed replied. 'May I ask, how do you know this?'

'Because I had one of my men staying as a guest at the Ritz to see what was going on. The information does not involve the staff of the Ritz in any way.'

'Thank you, René, for everything. We had better get back to the Ritz ourselves now. Would you know the quickest way we can get back to London?'

'Yes.' Lasalle checked his watch. 'You have two to three hours. The next Eurostar will get you back to London most quickly.'

In the lobby of the Ritz Tweed quietly gave Newman some instructions.

'Please contact Marler, Nield and Butler. Also Keith Kent, of course. Tell them to be ready to leave with us in precisely ninety minutes from now. And book seven first-class seats on Eurostar through the concierge. Also we shall need two hotel cars to take us to the Gare du Nord, where we board Eurostar. Finally, hand in to the nearest relevant car-hire outfits the two Audis we drove here in. Now, I'm going to my room to make a phone call.'

'Can I come with you?' Paula asked. 'I'm ready to leave now.'

'Yes, you can.'

Once inside his room Tweed hurried to the desk, sat down, used Beck's mobile to call Monica. Paula wandered over to the window to take a last look at the Place Vendôme.

'Tweed!' Monica sounded so relieved. 'I've been trying to call you but the hotel operator said you were out.'

'I was. What is it?'

'I've got a whole load of data for you, on all the profiles I've been working on. Birth certificates sent to me by courier from the States. giving most of the profiles' full names, et cetera. Are you ready?'

'Hold on just a moment.' Tweed called out to Paula, 'Get me the pad out of the zipped-up pocket in my suitcase.'

She found the pad, ran with it, placed it in front of him on the desk. Then she returned to the window.

'Fire away, Monica.'

Tweed began scribbling away, using sheet after sheet, keeping all the data on each name on a separate sheet. When Monica had come to the end he stared at one sheet, then closed the pad.

'Howard wants to speak to you very urgently. He's here now,' Monica said quickly.

'Tweed, when are you going to be back at Park Crescent? It's vital you arrive here within hours. A monster crisis has arisen. Defeat is staring us in the face. A hideous defeat.'

There was no element of panic in Howard's voice. He sounded to be in command of himself. But, underneath, Tweed detected a terrible anxiety.

'Tell me about it,' he said quietly.

'Not over the phone.'

'This line is safe. Perfectly safe.'

'No phone line is safe. I can't risk going into any detail. I have to wait until I see you. When will that be?'

'Today. Definitely. At a guess, midafternoon.'

'I can't wait to see you.'

When the connection was broken Tweed decided he wouldn't mention what Howard had said. What was the point in unsettling his team, even causing an atmosphere of alarm? He swung round in his chair.

'I now know who Charlie is,' he told Paula.

'Who?'

'I'm not saying yet. Before you accuse me of being cryptic, it's unlikely you'll meet Charlie, but you might have trouble keeping a blank expression, behaving normally. I think I'd like us to get to Gare du Nord early.'

Settling himself once again in his chair on the control level of the *President*, Crag opened the signal which had just arrived from the Pentagon. It was a long signal and was accompanied by a map. As he finished reading it once he sat up straighter, his mouth tightened. He looked at his Operations Officer.

'Bill, we have to hit the Brits.'

'What?'

'Not with missiles, Bill. This is a job for the SEALs.'

'What's their objective, sir?'

'A main and secret communications centre. Situation between a funny little place called Dungeness and another one called Hythe. The actual area of attack is Romney Marsh. It's almost on the coast – there are smooth sandy beaches the SEALs can land on, then they move a short distance inland, locate the installation, destroy it.'

'Won't it cause an international crisis?'

'The Chairman usually knows what he's doing and this operation has top sanction. The map is good – pinpoints the exact location of this communications centre. Contact the Mission Controller aboard the vessel carrying the SEALs. I reckon the attack ought to go in at midnight tomorrow. Get the Commander's opinion – after he's received this signal and the map. Have a look at it yourself first.'

'So this is going to be more than a demonstration of power?'

'Kind of looks that way.'

46

Arriving at Park Crescent, Tweed first ran up the stairs to his own office with Paula and Newman. Monica beamed with relief when she saw him. She pointed to his desk.

'The fat envelope came in from Roy Buchanan.'

'Good.' Tweed opened it, glanced quickly at its contents. 'Now, Monica, try and get Jefferson Morgenstern on the line.'

'I'm sorry. That's one thing I forgot to tell you. Morgenstern wants to see you. He must have called me eight times.'

'Tell him I'm now available to meet him within the hour. At any place of his choosing. Now I have to go up and see Howard.'

He left his office, ran up the stairs, followed by Paula and Newman, who waited outside Howard's office. Tweed walked straight in. Howard, as always impeccably dressed, was seated behind his desk. He showed signs of strain but his voice was firm.

'Am I glad to see you,' he greeted Tweed, standing up to shake his hand. 'Do sit down.'

'I have Paula and Bob outside. Could they join us?'

'I think they'd better.'

When everyone was seated Howard clasped his hands on top of his desk. He leaned forward.

'Briefly, a vast American task force is approaching our shores. No warning from Washington that it was on its way here. We'd never have known until the bastards showed up – except for the captain of a BA jet flying to New York. He saw it through a break in the clouds, even took video pictures of the damned thing, which was smart of him. The pics were flown back here on the next flight from New York. See for yourselves.'

Howard pushed forward a number of large colour prints across his desk. Tweed was surprised at their clarity. He looked at Howard.

'How high up was the aircraft?'

'I spoke to the captain myself over the phone. He was flying at thirty-five thousand feet. Apparently photography is his hobby. Told me he'd spent a mint on his camera. As soon as he'd taken his pics he sent a signal to the Ministry of Defence. A high-ranking pal of mine contacted me. The originals are with the MoD. Those are copies.'

'Amazing detail. What's that microscope you've got on your desk?'

'The most advanced version in the world. Loaned to me by my naval pal. Use it.'

Newman reached for the microscope. Under its lens he studied a warship sailing to port of the aircraft carrier. Then he whistled quietly.

'I'd say there are a load of SEALs aboard that ship. And they appear to be exercising for a landing. They're lowering small motorized amphibious landing craft over the side.'

'That's what my naval friend said,' Howard confirmed. 'Sinister, don't you think?'

'Any idea of their course, of when this battle group arrives?' asked Tweed.

'The captain of the aircraft told me that, as far as he could tell, it is headed straight for Britain. Time of arrival? The naval people tell me that, if it continues on course, they estimate the task force should appear in the English Channel after dark. Tomorrow.'

'Engagement possibly imminent.'

'Tweed . . .' Howard paused, appeared embarrassed. 'I have to tell you I made a real botch-up. I was tired out, hadn't slept for forty-eight hours – but I wouldn't take that as an excuse from a subordinate. I was driving down to the Bunker in daylight, middle of the afternoon. I was vaguely aware of a chopper hanging around. Took no notice. Drove straight into the courtyard of the Bunker. Mrs Carson tore me off a real strip. Deservedly so. The damned machine then circled over the complex for several minutes, flew off. Mrs Carson said the helicopter had no markings. I'm sorry, very sorry. Let the side down in a big way.'

'Don't be sorry.' Tweed smiled. 'No one is infallible. I have made some pretty stupid mistakes myself in the past. Do you mind if I leave now? I had a lot to do anyway, but after what you've told me I must move like Concorde.'

'I feel better now you're back.'

'I'll keep you fully informed about developments. Everything is going to happen very quickly now.'

He was on his way when Howard jumped up, followed him to the door. Howard almost whispered.

'One more very important point. The PM is anxious to see you as soon as possible.' He smiled ruefully. 'I think he regards me as second best.'

'Nonsense . . .'

Returning to his office, Tweed found an impatient Monica waiting for him. She waved a bit of paper.

'Jefferson Morgenstern says he'll see you at his office in the Embassy. He'll wait for you. Any time this afternoon.'

'Good. Now I want you to get me Sharon Mandeville on the phone. She's probably at the Embassy.'

Paula was behind her desk, Newman had settled himself in an armchair, Tweed was just about to seat himself in his own chair when the door opened. Marler walked in, an unlit king-size in his right hand.

'Sorry to barge in but I have someone downstairs I think you'd like to meet. Alf Rudge, boss of my cab-driver mob.'

'Ask him to come up now.'

When the door opened again everyone stared at the figure Marler ushered in. Alf Rudge was at least six feet tall, in his fifties, with a burly figure. In his hand he held one of the old-fashioned caps many cabbies used to wear. His blue eyes scanned the room quickly.

'Pleased to meet you, Alf,' Tweed said, extending a hand. 'I am Tweed. Make yourself at home. Try that armchair.'

'Hold that call for the moment,' he called across to Monica.

Tweed then introduced Alf to everyone in the room. Alf got up, shook hands with them. He struck Paula as being rather shy – or reserved – as his large paw squeezed hers. The big man then sat down in the arm-chair again, looked across the desk.

'I've 'eard a lot about you, Mr Tweed. No one except an idiot tries any monkey business with you.'

His cockney accent was very pronounced. Tweed immediately warmed to Alf. The salt of the earth, he thought. The backbone of England which really counted.

'Anything we can do to 'elp,' Alf went on, 'we'll do. Marler 'ere has knocked 'ell out of us in his trainin' out in the country.' He looked over his shoulder at Paula and Monica. 'Excuse me, ladies.'

'We may need you as reinforcements at a moment's

471

notice,' Tweed told him. 'Tomorrow at the latest, I would guess. How can we have your people close at hand?'

'Easy, Mr Tweed. I've got my mobile and the boys 'ave got theirs. Tell you what, if you agree – from this evening I'll have all of 'em patrolling the streets near here. They won't pick up no customers. Don't think they should be parked – make 'em obvious.'

'They'll patrol throughout the night – without sleep?'

'Won't worry 'em one little bit. They can always park for forty winks if they feels they needs it. Shall I lay it on?'

'Yes, please, Alf. Keep in touch with Marler. And thank you for offering to help us.'

'It's nothin', Mr Tweed,' Alf said, embarrassed as he stood up to leave. He turned at the door. 'If this means we 'ave a go at the Yanks the boys will love it . . .'

Marler returned almost immediately after escorting Alf to the front door. He looked round.

'Well, what's the verdict?'

'If all Alf's friends are like Alf,' Tweed said, 'then we have the equivalent of a very tough army platoon at our disposal.'

'They're all like Alf,' Marler declared.

'I really took to him,' Paula enthused. 'I was touched by his shyness, but I detected underneath it a man who would never let us down, however desperate the situation.'

'I'm on the side of Alf,' Newman agreed.

'But what about weapons?' Tweed queried.

'You know me,' Marler said, leaning against a wall, 'I break all the regulations. For training purposes I had a whole armoury of weapons sent up from the Surrey mansion a few weeks ago. Alf and his mob are armed to the teeth. Including bazookas.'

'You trained them to use bazookas?' asked Tweed.

'Yes. And they really know how to use them.

472

Especially the three who were in the Gulf War. Alf will have thought of weapons. His boys will be carrying them secreted inside their cabs. Now, I'll love you and leave you. Things to do.'

'Make that call, please, Monica,' Tweed requested when Marler had gone.

'*Tweed!*' Sharon's soft voice purred with delight over the phone. 'You're back in London? Wonderful. You have neglected me, you know. You can't deny it.'

'I wouldn't even try, Sharon. Good to know you are safely back. If possible, I'd like to come and see you this afternoon. The answer is yes? Splendid. Oh, do you mind if I bring Newman and Paula with me? You'd love to see them. Sometime this afternoon, then.'

As he put his coat on he gave Monica an instruction.

'Please inform Howard where I'm going. Tell him Paula and Bob are coming with me. Then Howard won't worry.'

'Who do we see first?' Paula asked.

They were sitting in the back of the car Newman was driving towards Grosvenor Square. The good weather was lasting. It was a brilliantly sunny afternoon with not a cloud in a duck-egg blue sky. The air was fresh and pedestrians were walking briskly as though enjoying the return of the sun.

'The sequence is important,' Tweed said. 'First we see Morgenstern. Afterwards we call in on Sharon.'

'So you can ask her out to dinner,' she teased.

'I thought I came first,' Newman called out. 'Am I supposed to stand in line?'

'We'll see,' Tweed replied.

'And you are clutching that package of evidence from Buchanan as though the fate of the world depended on it,' Paula commented.

'Maybe it does,' Tweed told her.

'What's inside it?'

'Among other things, photos of the dead Umbrella Men who tried to kill me in Basle near Market-platz. With their names.'

'How on earth did you get hold of them?'

'Reliable Arthur Beck again. He omitted to mention it, but he sent the material to Roy Buchanan at New Scotland Yard. The two men met at an international police conference a few months ago. Roy told me they got on very well together.'

'I can spot some of them already,' Newman reported as they neared Grosvenor Square.

'Some of who?' Paula wanted to know.

'Buchanan's plain-clothes sleuths. Stationed to keep a close eye on who comes and goes from the American Embassy. I think he's told some of them to make their presence obvious – to act as a deterrent. Roy Buchanan really never, under any circumstances, misses a trick.'

For Tweed, as they mounted the steps and walked inside the spacious entrance hall, it was like a replay of a film he had seen before. The girl who had treated him so offhandedly on his previous visit was behind the reception desk. But this time when he gave his name her attitude was very different. Standing up, she gave him a beaming smile.

'Mr Tweed, Mr Morgenstern is waiting to see you. His suite of offices is on the first floor. Here is the number,' she said, handing him a plastic disc. 'And could you please take this card? There are a lot of guards about who may stop you. If you show them this they will let you straight through.'

'Thank you,' said Tweed.

He led the way to the elevator, pressed the button. The door opened and inside he pressed the first floor button. The elevator ascended, the doors opened and they stepped out into the wide corridor. Tweed stopped, smiled.

Denise Chatel had been walking towards the elevator. For once, Paula noticed, she was not carrying a file. More than that, she was stylishly dressed in riding kit, complete with jodhpurs and gleaming riding boots.

She gave them a great big smile. Coming forward she hugged Paula, kissed Tweed on the cheek and then gave Newman the same attention. To Tweed she seemed a different woman. Her attitude was buoyant and cheerful and warm. What could have happened?

'How do you like my outfit?' Denise asked.

She swivelled round in a circle. Her brunette hair swung over her shoulders. Her face was pink and full of life.

'Very fetching,' said Paula.

'The picture of happiness,' said Tweed.

'You look just terrific,' Newman told her. 'What have you been up to?'

'I've just come back from a ride in Hyde Park. It's a wonderful day. I even managed a gallop, which may be illegal, but I just didn't care. I was on top of the world.'

'Hence your high spirits,' Tweed remarked.

'You've hit the nail on the head,' Denise responded.

'And what else?'

'Why?' She hesitated. 'Nothing else.'

'You'll excuse us. We've come to keep an appointment.'

'What was all that about?' Paula asked as they proceeded along the corridor.

'No idea.'

A tall, smooth-faced man came out of a room, closed the door behind him. Dressed in a smart blue pin-stripe suit, he strode confidently towards them. Then he stopped, gave a broad grin.

'Chuck Venacki,' greeted Newman. 'The great survivor. How do you do it?'

'Do what?' Venacki asked amiably.

'Survive. The catastrophe at Schluchsee.'

'Where's that?' Venacki enquired, still amiable. 'Sounds as though it could be Austria, Switzerland, Germany?'

'Give the man the money,' Newman went on. 'Even though he didn't get it until his third try. Come off it, Venacki. You remember when we last met.'

'Sure I do. Outside Park Crescent a hundred years ago. When you rammed the Lincoln Continental with your four-wheel drive.'

'Nice try. At Schluchsee Ronstadt drove his car straight at me. Four men inside that car. You were sitting with Ronstadt in the front. Ronstadt, by the way, is dead, but you survive.'

'Guess you mistook me for someone else, wherever this dramatic car incident took place. Now, I have to get going.' He looked at Paula, then at Tweed. 'Enjoy yourselves. We try to make visitors feel at home here.'

'And that,' said Tweed quietly, 'sounded like the voice of the anonymous American who phoned me in my room at the Colombi. The call which told me Ronstadt had left.'

'I don't get it,' Paula commented. 'He seemed nice enough.'

'And this,' Tweed said in the same quiet voice, pointing to a door they were passing, 'is where Sharon lives. We'll come back later. The critical interview is the one with Morgenstern.'

47

'Do come in. Good to see you. I've had fresh coffee delivered. The receptionist told me you were here.'

In response to Tweed's knock Jefferson Morgenstern himself opened the door, ushered them inside. He locked the door, then gazed at his visitors with a smile. Tweed introduced Paula as his assistant and confidante. Morgenstern smiled even more broadly as Tweed turned to Newman.

'No introduction necessary here, Tweed. Bob Newman once interviewed me. And I don't give many interviews.' He shook Newman's hand warmly. 'You're looking great and maybe a bit tougher. Experience does that to us all – if we have the fibre. Come and sit down. I'll serve coffee.'

Paula had been studying Morgenstern closely. He was shorter than she had imagined, but his figure in a grey Savile Row suit was well padded. She had the impression of a man of great intelligence who enjoyed the good things of life – especially wine and food. His hair, neatly brushed, was greying and he emanated an aura of supreme self-confidence and dynamic energy – of power.

His large desk was a genuine antique, Chippendale, she thought. On it was a silver engraved tray with a silver coffee service. Three comfortable upright chairs were arranged in front of the desk and Morgenstern dragged his swivel chair round to join them. Not a man to flaunt his importance.

'You were looking at my coffee service,' he said to Paula after she had seated herself, which made her realize this man didn't miss a thing. 'When I was a poor

477

student in Europe I was once invited to a mansion where they had such a service. I decided then,' he continued as he poured coffee, 'that one day I'd have one like it.' He smiled. 'It was a long journey before I was able to purchase one.'

His face was long, Paula noted. His nose was long, his features strong, and beneath his American accent she detected a trace of some European accent. When he had served coffee he sat down near Paula, drank half the contents of his cup, folded his arms.

'Tweed, I've been giving a lot of thought to what you said to me when we last met. At the time I was dismissive. Since then I have given your accusations more thought. I admit I'm a troubled man.' He looked at Paula, then at Newman. 'May I take it that anything we talk about today will be in complete confidence?'

'Quite definitely. These two are my right and left arm. I said recently I'd trust them with my life. That I had done.'

'Good enough for me. The weak link in what you said is a complete lack of evidence.'

'That is what I have brought with me. Overwhelming evidence. In photographs and documents. Some of it was supplied by Arthur Beck, Chief of Swiss Federal Police. I can supply you with his number in Berne if you want it later. While in Basle recently four of the men attached to this Embassy tried to murder me – along with Paula and Bob. Instead, they were killed. They all carried American diplomatic passports. Here is a photograph of the dead killers, supplied to me by Beck. Their names are on the back. And here are photocopies of the passports they carried. Beck has the originals.'

Morgenstern studied the photo of the dead Umbrella Men. He looked at the back, where their names were given. Placing it on his desk, he looked at the photo-

478

copies of the passports. His mouth tightened. He placed them on his desk.

'There's worse to come,' Tweed warned. 'There's a clear video picture of the man who left the bomb in the Oxford Street department store.'

'His name is Vernon Kolkowski,' Newman said quietly. 'He also had a diplomatic passport. Once, in New York, the police chief told me he was a professional who had murdered at least six men. They could never indict him. No witness dared testify. If one was willing to testify he'd been found dead in a side street.'

'Then,' Tweed continued, 'we rescued a poor woman who was being tortured by another American with a diplomatic passport. Name of Rick Sherman. He's dead too.'

'Could you pause?' Morgenstern requested. He took from his pocket a leather-bound notebook. 'I'd like to note down some of these names. What was that last one?'

'Rick Sherman.'

'Thank you. And Vernon someone. I'd like the surname.'

Newman spelt it out carefully. Morgenstern wrote it down in his notebook. Then he looked again at the video print of the man who had planted the bomb in the Oxford Street department store.

'As far as I can gather,' Tweed went on, 'I know you are handling the diplomatic side of this huge operation. But there is another secret section inside this Embassy called the Executive Action Department. That is staffed by what I would call the gangster level – and all the members have been given diplomatic passports.'

'How can I phrase this?' Morgenstern wondered aloud. 'While you were away I made certain enquiries here. I had the impression certain people evaded giving me answers to my questions.'

'Have you heard of the Executive Action Department?'

'No.'

'I'm certain it's located in this building. That it is responsible for the outrages. Individual murders and wholesale bombings.'

'I am good at assessing character, Tweed. I am sure you would not ever invent such horrific stories.'

'Is there any way you could check the names of everyone who has been issued with a diplomatic passport over, say, the past seven weeks?'

'I was thinking of that. Yes, there is. But first I must refresh your cups.'

Paula glanced round the large room while Morgenstern manipulated the silver coffee pot. The room was furnished in expensive but restrained taste. Heavy floor-to-ceiling curtains flanked the windows, curtains with a Regency stripe. The wall-to-wall carpet was a pale mushroom colour. The few pieces of other furniture were also antiques. The room had a restful atmosphere. On another desk the Stars and Stripes was suspended from a bronze column.

'I'm going to ask the Ambassador's personal assistant for the record of all diplomatic passports issued recently,' said Morgenstern.

'Mrs Pendleton,' he said on the phone, 'I require urgently the list of all personnel working here issued with diplomatic passports over the past seven weeks.'

Mrs Pendleton had a loud raucous American voice. Tweed could hear her end of the conversation clearly.

'Well, the list exists, but I can't supply it to you without the consent of the Ambassador.'

'Ask him now, then.'

'I can't. He is out.'

'Mrs Pendleton, do you recognize my voice?'

'Of course, sir.'

'Then kindly remember you are talking to the Secretary of State.'

'I do know that, sir.'

'Then I expect you to deliver the list to me within two minutes.'

'Some people,' Morgenstern smiled briefly, 'who have held down a job for years develop delusions of grandeur.'

Paula was struck by the brief smile. Since Tweed had started to produce his evidence a change had come over Morgenstern. Instead of his earlier amiability his expression had become one of gravity. He's taking this very seriously, she thought.

There was a tap on the door, Morgenstern called out to come in. A plump self-important looking woman in her late fifties entered. She was holding a green leather-bound ledger which she placed on the desk.

'I'm afraid I need a receipt before I release that ledger,' she said, producing a small pad.

'Really?' Morgenstern stared at her. 'Have you a short memory? If so, something could be done about that. Only minutes ago I reminded you I am Secretary of State.'

'I suppose I could make an exception.'

'Mrs Pendleton. Do you see the handle of that door you opened to come in here?'

'Yes, sir.'

'Go over it, take hold of it. That's right. Now turn it to the left.'

'I'm sorry, sir, if . . .'

'Now you keep hold of the handle. Pull the door open towards you. I see you've managed it. Now, walk into the corridor and close the door quietly behind you. It's not too difficult.'

Tweed smiled to himself. It was notorious that Morgenstern had an acid side to his nature. He couldn't suffer fools gladly.

'Now, we can do our homework,' said Morgenstern. 'Excuse me if I go and sit behind my desk for a moment.'

Taking his chair back to its original position, he sifted through the photos and documents he had quickly arranged in a pile before Mrs Pendleton arrived, so she couldn't see anything. Taking out his notebook, he then opened the ledger. He had perched it on an inkstand so his visitors could not see its pages.

Using a pen as a pointer, he began to check the names provided by Tweed with the list inside the ledger. It took a while but often he stabbed at a name in the ledger with his pen. His expression became grimmer. When he had closed the ledger he sat staring at Tweed. Then he hauled his chair back to join his visitors.

'I have decided,' he said.

'What is your decision?' Tweed enquired.

'Can you leave with me all the items you have given me?'

'Certainly.'

'I have a Gulfstream jet standing by permanently at Heathrow. I like to be mobile. Soon after you have left me I shall drive to Heathrow, board the jet, and fly immediately to Washington. If you want to contact me, call this number.' He took a pad from a drawer, wrote on it, handed it to Tweed. 'I shall inform all my aides that if you call you are to be put through to me – even if I'm at the White House.'

'Sharon Mandeville next,' Tweed said when they had left Jefferson's lair. 'Might as well tie the lot up at once.'

'Do come in.' Sharon, like Jefferson, had opened the

door herself to welcome them inside. 'What a pleasure to see you all again.'

She kissed Tweed on the cheek, shook hands with Paula and Newman. Then she escorted them across the spacious room towards a desk which was even larger than Jefferson's. As they followed her Paula glanced round the room. It was very expensively furnished – money had been no object – but unlike Jefferson's office, it was very modern.

Sharon's enormous desk was made of gleaming white wood, all the chairs were upholstered in white leather, the carpet was white and scattered across it were tiger-skin rugs. The coffee service on a tray on her desk was almost surreal in design. And the rims of the cups were six-sided, which made them very difficult to drink out of without the contents ending up in your lap.

Three chairs were arranged in front of the desk. Behind it was a high-backed chair which reminded Paula of a throne. Sharon gave Tweed a ravishing smile.

'Do sit down, all of you, please. Coffee for everyone?'

'Not for me,' said Tweed as he sat down.

'Me too neither, thank you,' said Newman.

'I'll also pass,' said Paula.

Sharon was wearing a navy blue trouser suit which suggested the high-powered businesswoman. Newman thought she had never looked more attractive. She was pouring herself a cup.

'Excuse me, but I need an ocean of caffeine to keep me going.' She sat in the chair behind the desk. 'Well, Tweed, I suppose we can say we have completed the Grand Tour of Europe.'

'Something like that.'

'Oh, come –' she gazed at him over the rim of her cup – 'no call to be so serious. It isn't the end of the world.'

'Isn't it?'

Sharon's nails were painted blood-red, a varnish which Paula hated. She had a high collar, buttoned up to her neck. She went on gazing at Tweed, as though assessing his mood. He had taken off his glasses and was cleaning them on his handkerchief. He put the glasses on again.

'Now you get a clearer view of beauty,' Newman joked.

'I have a clearer view of a lot of things now,' Tweed replied.

'So why have you come to see me?' Sharon asked in her soft voice. 'How can I help you?'

'You can confirm certain information I have received.'

'You sound just like a policeman.'

'I was once a policeman,' Tweed told her. 'A century ago.'

'He was the youngest superintendent at Scotland Yard,' Paula explained. 'His speciality was Homicide.'

'What information are you referring to?' Sharon asked.

She was still her calm self. She was leaning back upright in her chair. Her half-closed eyes, glowing greenly, were fixed on Tweed.

'I have here a certain document.' Tweed took a thick envelope out of his breast pocket, extracted a sheet. 'This is a copy of your birth certificate.'

'Really? Isn't this rather personal? How, I wonder, were you able to obtain it?'

'By perfectly legal means. Such certificates are in the public domain, as you must know.'

'Oh, come on, Tweed.' She smiled, still leaning against the back of her upright chair, her body very erect. 'All the way across the Atlantic?'

'Precisely. All the way across the Atlantic.' Tweed

unfolded the sheet of paper. 'You were born in Washington, DC. You are forty-two years old.'

'Not very gallant of you, to broadcast my age.'

'On this copy of the certificate it gives your full names. Sharon Charlotte Anderson.'

'So?' Her eyes were almost closed now. 'Where does this lead us to?'

'*Charlotte*. Sometimes abbreviated to Charlie. Even with a woman. You are Charlie.'

Paula had difficulty suppressing a gasp. She glanced at Newman. He looked stunned. She switched her glance to Tweed, sitting next to her. He looked very relaxed. Still holding the document, he was gazing back at Sharon.

'Charlie,' he said, 'we know masterminded the gigantic operation under way to absorb Britain into America as the fifty-first state. Do you deny you are Charlie?'

'*Damn you!* Nosy, insignificant little man. Friggin' two-bit so-called detective!' Sharon was standing up now, leaning over her desk as though about to leap at Tweed. 'You don't know what the bloody hell you're talking about!'

She continued screaming at the top of her voice, uttering a foul stream of obscene abuse. Her voice had completely changed. Her lung power was awesome. Suddenly she grabbed the certificate out of his hands, tore it to shreds, threw the pieces over her visitors.

'I do have other copies of that birth certificate,' Tweed informed her quietly.

'Much good they will do you. You can't prove any of this friggin' nonsense you've been spouting at me. How dare you?' she yelled.

'Imminent events will prove me right.'

'Imminent events,' she screamed, 'will see you out of a job, you friggin' nobody. You'll be lucky to stay alive.'

'Is that a threat?' Tweed asked quietly. 'The kind of order you gave to Jake Ronstadt? Because he is no longer available.'

'What do you mean by that?' she raged.

'Jake Ronstadt is dead.'

'Dead?'

'He tried to kill me in Strasbourg – under your orders, I'm sure. One of my people dropped a grenade into the launch Ronstadt was guiding along a waterway. Result? Ronstadt and the two men with him vanished when the launch sailed on into a wild sluice.'

'Tweed, you are a very inventive man,' she spat at him.

'Then there was Rick Sherman. He was torturing the wife of Kurt Schwarz – again on your orders, I'm certain. He's dead – with a knife through his throat.'

'You're lying, Tweed,' she said in a deep voice full of hate. 'You always lie.'

'I'm sure, when it is checked, that it will be found you organized the recruitment of this large gang of thugs from the back streets of New York. You must have sanctioned the issue of diplomatic passports to an army of killers. There has to be a record of who did that.'

'You're crazy,' she went on screaming. 'Stark raving mad. That is something which will be proved. Do you hear me? Do you hear me? *Do you hear me?*'

'I can hardly avoid hearing you, Sharon.' Tweed stood up. 'I suggest this interview is over, that it is time for us to leave.'

She picked up a cup, threw it at him. Tweed ducked. The cup hit the white wall on the far side of the room, broke into a dozen pieces. Tweed led the way to the door, opened it, stood aside as Paula and Newman walked into the corridor, then walked out himself, closing the door with never a backward glance.

'I'm breathless,' said Paula.

'I'm staggered,' said Newman.

'And you, Bob, once described her as a demure English lady,' Tweed recalled as they headed for the elevator.

'Is Sharon really Charlie?' asked Paula.

Tweed hadn't the opportunity to reply. Walking briskly towards them was a familiar figure, a large man. Paula never ceased to be surprised that big heavyweight men often had small feet and moved with such agility.

'Hi, folks,' called out Ed Osborne. 'Great to see you paying us a visit. That's what I call real friendly.'

'Do excuse us, Ed,' responded Tweed, 'we're late for an urgent appointment. See you sometime.'

'Sure thing.'

'We have to keep moving,' Tweed warned as they approached the lift. 'Howard said the PM wants to see me. So, Bob, drop me off at Downing Street before you go on to Park Crescent.'

'We'll drop you off – then wait for you,' Newman said firmly.

When they stepped out of the lift on the ground floor the receptionist rose to her feet and called out to them, 'Have a nice day.'

48

Arriving back at Park Crescent from Downing Street, Tweed dashed upstairs to his office. Besides Monica in her usual post behind her desk Marler was waiting for him. Paula and Newman came in, sat down.

'I've just come back from a record-breaking trip to the Bunker,' Marler said.

'What sent you down there?' Tweed asked from behind his desk.

'Howard had briefed me after you'd rushed off to the American Embassy. Told me about the American task force, what Newman had observed from the pics about the SEALs and their exercises. He also told me about his own trip, how a chopper circled above the complex. I have a suggestion.'

'Fire away.'

'Howard told me that everything that mattered here is now down at the Bunker. I reckon one of the prime targets of that task force will be the Bunker. So I went down there to check out the defences. They seem OK to me.'

'Good. What is your suggestion?'

'I think we ought to send Alf's mob down there. I can contact Alf.'

'I agree. They won't travel in convoy, I hope?'

'No. Alf has his head screwed on. Also, if they drive down just after dark no one will spot them.'

'I agree. Monica, phone Mrs Carson and warn her seven men with their cabs will be descending on her. You can explain to her about Alf's mob.' He looked at Marler. 'They'll have to find somewhere to hide all those cabs – so they won't be seen from the air.'

'Alf will think of that himself. He does have all his marbles.'

'One more thing.' Tweed opened a drawer. 'Give him this map, otherwise he'll never find the place.'

'I was about to ask you.' Marler looked out of the window after taking the map. 'Talk of the devil. Alf's cab is parked on the main street. I think he's stopped to light a fag. I can tell him now if I move. See you all later. Things to do.'

'Blow!' said Tweed. 'One thing I forgot to tell him. When I've finished, Monica, phone this data to Mrs Carson. Tell her to warn Alf and his mob as soon as they arrive. I've warned everyone else down there, including Cord.'

'Warn him about what?' Paula enquired.

'When Marler was supervising the construction of the Bunker he found there were a number of very deep shafts in the grounds. He guessed, as they looked so ancient, they were ventilation shafts. They're like vertical tunnels which lead down to horizontal tunnels the smugglers used in the old days. Marler had metal gratings put over the top of each shaft so nobody would ever fall down one. They already had ancient grilles over them but they were crumbling with the passage of time, so he had them renewed. I worry he might have missed one.'

'I'll make it all one call to Mrs Carson,' Monica promised.

'So you're sure Sharon is Charlie?' Paula remarked. 'If we've time to relax for five minutes.'

'We not only have the time – we need it.'

'Were you suspicious of her earlier?' Paula suggested.

'Yes, up to a point. Who was always on the spot when attempts were made to kill us? In Basle? In Freiburg? In Strasbourg? Sharon Mandeville. Someone had to be instructing Ronstadt and his thugs.'

'Monica,' Paula went on, turning in her chair, 'while building up your profiles did you ever fill in those long strange gaps in Ed Osborne's life?'

'No, I was never able to fill one of them. A mystery man.'

Paula turned back to Tweed. 'I noticed that Sharon never admitted she was Charlie. And Osborne was always on the spot. In Basle. In Freiburg. In Strasbourg.'

'You are a very observant lady,' Tweed told her.

'And I was also struck,' she said, 'by Chuck Venacki,

489

the smooth-faced man we met in the corridor. He was so much more polished, spoke very well, an educated man who was very well dressed.'

'A lot of Americans are,' Newman said. 'We've been meeting the dregs of American society. We do have the same type over here.'

'Are you sure,' she pressed him, 'that you saw him in that car by the side of Ronstadt at Schluchsee?'

'I am sure. I know I was jumping for my life out of the way but I saw him clearly. Don't ask me who the other two were.'

'It's weird,' she said. 'And when do we all go down to Romney Marsh?'

'That reminds me,' said Tweed. 'I have to phone a friend of mine at the MoD. What he tells me will answer your question.'

Paula got up to stretch her legs. She gazed out of the window. Marler was still talking to Alf. As she watched he got into the cab as though he were a passenger. Alf had not got his light on. Not available for taking fares.

'Philip,' Tweed began, using Beck's mobile, 'Howard has told me about—'

'Hold it, please,' a cultured voice interrupted. 'Is this a safe line?'

'Absolutely. I'm on a hacker-proof mobile, advanced Swiss version. Can I go on? Good. Philip, I need to know the progress of that American task force – how close it is.'

'You're talking to the right chap, Tweed. I'm in charge of monitoring it. It's still heading straight for us. We estimate it will be well inside the English Channel late tomorrow night. I can keep you informed of its progress, if that would help.'

'It would be a life-saver. A plan I'm working on depends on my knowing their timetable. If I'm not here

490

could you give the latest news to Monica? You know how reliable she is.'

'Think I'd trust Monica before I trusted you,' Philip joked. 'I'll keep you in close touch with developments. Let's have a drink when this is all over.'

'Time you paid for your round. Bye . . .'

'There's something else,' Newman remarked.

'And I thought we'd got enough on our plate,' Paula chided him.

'We mustn't forget the Phantom is still on the loose,' Newman warned.

'Oh, he'll turn up again,' Tweed assured him. 'Maybe next time he will make a fatal mistake. I wonder who's paying him.'

'Sharon?' Paula suggested.

'Possibly.'

'So when is zero hour? I imagine you know, after talking to your old chum, Philip.'

'At a guess I'd say between 2200 hours and midnight. So it will be dark, which worries me.'

At that moment Marler returned. He gave Paula a little salute and took up his favourite position. Leaning against a wall he looked at Tweed.

'Alf is all clued up. He's gone off to meet his pals one by one. He'll brief them. He's going to photocopy that map in some small all-night shop he knows about. Alf knows where to get anything done.'

'I'm glad you came back so quickly, Marler. A friend of mine at the MoD has warned me that task force will arrive after dark tomorrow. That's when I think they will launch their attack on the Bunker. The dark will make it difficult to see them coming.'

'Problem solved. I'll go back to my office now to call down to the mansion in deep and darkest Surrey. They have a collection of mobile hand-operated searchlights.

And a goodly number of star shells would come in handy. I'll talk to the one man who knows where the Bunker is, tell him to load up a van immediately, to drive it himself through the night to the Bunker.'

'You're a genius,' said Tweed.

'Oh, I know. But it's nice to have it confirmed. See you.'

'Why didn't I think of that?' Tweed asked when Marler had gone.

'Because you're not a genius,' said Paula. 'Incidentally, I'm not going to ask you what you discussed with the PM. Out of bounds. But what was your objective during our visit to those people at the American Embassy?'

'To destabilize them, the way they're trying to destabilize us. It worked better than I'd hoped. Morgenstern is the kingpin.' He looked at his watch. 'By now he should be airborne in his Gulfstream jet, heading for Washington.'

'You certainly destabilized Sharon.'

'A trifle dramatic, wasn't it? I'd wondered what lay under her deep calm at all times. Now we know. A volcano. And I managed to trigger it off. A real eruption.'

'What do you imagine she's doing now? Checking out the first flight back to the States in the morning?'

'Maybe. And maybe not.'

In her white office at the Embassy Sharon Mandeville was her normal cool self. Leaning back in her tall chair she was on the phone to Washington.

'Hi there, Senator, this is Sharon. How goes it?'

'Great. Just great, honey. You'll be needed back here soon to start your campaign. All the posters are printed for the billboards. You look a winner on them. You will be. I'm banking on it.'

'I'm very grateful to you, Grant. I hope you know that.'

'Hell with that. I'm looking forward to retiring, to putting you in my place. Don't forget this is a big state, a key state when it comes later to the nomination for a presidential candidate. A whole load of electoral college votes in your pocket.'

'I've got to get there first, Grant. To become a senator as a springboard for the big one.'

'You'll walk it. Both elections. For senator. For presidential candidate. Lord knows you've made enough speeches so far. And everywhere you spoke the crowds went wild. I know it hasn't hit the press or TV yet, but that's the way we want it. You come out as the big surprise. Is this phone OK?'

'Totally OK.'

'Got a bit of great news. Keep it quiet. Your nearest rival for senator is withdrawing from the race.'

'He is? How the hell did that happen?'

'Wise old me made it happen. Had him investigated. He's taken bribes from the Chinese. Needed a whole load of dough and Beijing coughed up. Needed that dough to try and keep his companies afloat. He's still bankrupt. Nobody knows, but I got hold of documents. Went to have a chat with my old enemy at that palatial house of his. Told him to announce his withdrawal – for reasons of health – or I'd send the documents to CNN and the *New York Times*. He's making his announcement tomorrow.'

'You're wicked. That's blackmail.'

'Aren't you glad I'm on your side? You know what?'

'Do tell, Grant.'

'I'm looking forward one day to telling my grandchildren how I propelled the first woman in history into the White House.'

'Thank you, Grant.'

'With your money and my know-how you're home and dry.'

'Thank you again, Grant.'

'When can I expect you to reach Washington?'

'Soon, very soon now. I'll let you know when I'm flying over, give you my ETA.'

'I'll be there to meet you. With flowers.'

'Anybody ever tell you that you're a great guy? I'm telling you now.' She paused. 'I've some unfinished business to attend to.'

'Goodnight, Madame President.'

Crag had sat immobile in his chair as the task force headed at speed for its objective. A few minutes later an aide appeared, crossed the deck, saluted, handed the Rear Admiral an envelope.

'New maps, sir. Just transmitted to us from Washington.'

'Thank you.'

The aide saluted again, left the deck. Crag opened the envelope, extracted several maps. An attached signal explained the aerial photos the aide had called maps had been taken by a helicopter flying over the vital section of the Kent coast. Crag reached for a powerful magnifying glass resting on his work table.

He grunted as he studied the photos carefully. Then he looked up. He handed the photos to his Operations Officer.

'Bill, I guess we ought to rush these over to the SEALs commander. Seems to me the operation will be a piece of cake. They land on a flat beach of pebbles just east of some place called New Romney. Then they strike inland over territory as flat as a pancake. Only a short distance to that communications HQ.'

'I'm worried, sir, that the Brits may know we're

coming. That commercial airliner which flew above us just when there was the only break so far in the overcast.'

'I wouldn't worry.' Crag stretched his long arms, suppressed a yawn. 'Passengers on those flights soon get tired of looking out of the windows. They'd either be tired or drunk – or both. And it was at pretty high altitude. We estimated thirty-five thousand feet.'

'I'd better report to the Chairman that we've received the signal and the maps.'

'Aerial photos, Bill. Hold on sending a report. Let's first get the reaction of the SEALs' commander aboard the warship he's travelling on.'

Crag sat thinking. In his mind he was checking over the sections of the task force he'd contacted recently. Some admirals in his position, he knew, had a written list they ticked off. Crag carried the list in his head.

Fifteen minutes later – ten of which had been taken up lowering the fast boat over the side which had taken the data and its racing to the warship – his Operations Officer returned with a signal in his hand.

'May I read this to you, sir? I emphasize I'm using the words used by the SEALs' commander.'

'Let's hear it, Bill.'

'"To hell and high water in fifteen minutes." That must mean the time he estimates to complete the whole operation.'

'It must.' Crag allowed himself one of his rare smiles. 'I always thought that commander was a top gun.'

49

It was the middle of the night. Tweed was asleep in his office. Monica had hauled out his camp bed from a cupboard, had then made it up for him. Tireless, she watched over him from behind her desk. The door opened and Marler walked in. Monica put a finger to her lips.

'Progress to report, Marler?' enquired Tweed.

He had lifted his head off the pillow, was now sitting up in his dressing gown, with the vivid Oriental design. Marler hesitated, worried that he had woken Tweed.

'Well?' prodded Tweed, who had put his glasses on. 'I'm only taking catnaps. I like to be kept informed.'

'Progress, yes,' Marler replied. 'First, the van from the Surrey mansion reached the Bunker two hours ago. They now have a large collection of searchlights and star shells. I gather Alf and his mob have been practising with them.'

'So Alf is down there already?'

'He's been down there with his chums for at least three hours.'

'I find that very satisfactory,' said Tweed, stretching himself higher up. He checked his watch. 'I was going to wake up now, anyway. As you know, I have an alarm clock in my head. Monica, get me Philip at the MoD. I'd like a word with him.'

Tying the belt round his dressing gown, he padded over to his desk. He smiled grimly as he addressed Marler.

'At times likes this the essential thing is to stay calm. Did I detect a note of subdued excitement in your voice?'

'You might have done,' Marler admitted.

'Wait until I've taken this call and then go to your office and bed down on your couch.'

'Don't feel sleepy.'

'Irrelevant. We all need a little sleep to keep us on our toes.'

'If you insist,' grumbled Marler.

'I'm giving you a direct order.'

He picked up the phone as Monica gestured to him madly. He was still using Beck's mobile. He asked Monica to tell Philip he'd call him back immediately, which he did.

'Tweed here. Yes, Philip, again on a very safe line. What news?'

'The task force continues to head straight for the English Channel. We've sent special high-flying planes out with the latest radar. So the Yanks don't catch on, as soon as the planes have located its present position they fly back here.'

'Time of arrival in the Channel?'

'No change. Between 2200 hours and midnight tonight. They are getting pretty close.'

'No rumours of their presence?'

'None that have reached me. And any would. I'll go on keeping you in touch. Or tell Monica. Do you ever sleep?'

'I've just had forty winks.'

'Some people have all the luck.'

Tweed pushed the mobile across his desk. He was wide awake and looked very fresh. He spoke to Marler.

'I've been thinking – probably in my sleep. I do that. Before you get some kip – which you must do – could you call Paula, Newman, Nield and Butler from your office? Tell them we leave from here ten o'clock sharp in the morning – to drive down to the Bunker. At that time the traffic may be quieter, as far as it ever is quieter.'

'I'll do that right away.' Marler smiled. 'I'm going to

be so popular, waking them up in the middle of the night.'

'I wouldn't worry. As soon as you've called they'll swear at you, then they'll fall fast asleep again. They've had a really exhausting time of it recently. So have you, Marler, so don't forget my order.'

'There's one thing I've forgotten,' he said when Marler had gone. 'Food. Down at the Bunker.'

'Two cooks went with the staff when they moved down there from here,' Monica informed him. 'I hope you don't mind, but it occurred to me the arrival of Alf and his men might strain the situation to the limit. I phoned the mansion. Their best cook, Mrs Payne, travelled to the Bunker in the truck when the driver took the star shells and searchlights. She makes giant shepherd's pies. She's taken ingredients and cooking utensils with her.'

'You're an angel. Shepherds pie? You're making my mouth water.'

'I can probably get you one now. There's a place that stays open all night not far from here.'

'Wait until I've had a shower and got dressed,' he said, collecting his clothes.

'For when you drive down there your warm coat's on that hanger. I got it out for you. It will be chilly on the coast – after dark it could be freezing.'

'Again, you're an angel. Shepherd's pie.'

Tweed had a dreamy look at he left his office.

When Tweed returned, fully dressed, he had a shock. Sitting at her desk was Paula, also fully dressed, wearing the same outfit, complete with leggings and boots, she'd worn in the Black Forest. Her jacket hung from the back of her chair. She gave him a great big smile.

'Good morning, Tweed. You're up early.'

'So are you. And you look fresh as a daisy, a very fresh daisy. Couldn't you sleep after Marler called you?'

'I was awake when he did call. Have you forgotten? I'm like you. I can get by with a few hours' sleep. Monica's gone out to fetch the goodies. I told her I'd look after the phone while she was gone. Trust Monica to know probably the only food shop round here open all night.'

She had just finished speaking when the door opened and Monica walked in carrying a tray. Arranged on it were two large plastic cartons with covers. She placed the tray end on, so one end was in front of Tweed's chair, the other facing it.

'Now how did I know, Paula, you'd be here? Fancy shepherd's pie?'

'I'm so hungry,' Paula told her, 'I could devour it. I hadn't the patience to make myself something at the flat.'

'Bring your chair over this side,' Monica ordered.

She waited until they were settled, facing each other across the desk. Then she bent forward.

'Have to do this properly like they do in posh restaurants,' she announced.

Monica grasped the covers of each carton, paused, then with a flourish she removed the covers. Tweed realized he was famished as an appetizing aroma drifted into the room.

'Thank you, waiter,' said Paula.

'There'll be a pot of tea shortly. Don't wait for it – your food will get cold.'

'I have things to tell you,' Tweed said between mouthfuls.

He told her about his conversations with Philip at the MoD, about the arrival of Alf's mob at the Bunker, about the delivery of the searchlights and star shells. They were still eating when Howard came into the room, a rather dishevelled Howard. His shirt collar was open at the

499

neck, his hair was only roughly brushed, his jaw whiskery.

'Excuse my appearance. I fell asleep for hours in my office. Pardon me, Tweed.' Taking a spoon, he scooped up a helping of shepherd's pie. 'That's very good. Why don't I get service like this?'

'Make passionate love to Monica,' Paula suggested.

'I'll get it for him anyway,' Monica said hastily.

'Howard,' said Tweed, 'we drive down at ten o'clock on the dot this morning. I'll keep you in touch as far as I can.'

'Please do that. I'll be thinking of you all.' He put his hand on Paula's shoulder, squeezed it. 'You take care of yourself.'

'I don't think I'm too bad at doing that. But thank you for the thought.'

'I'm going off now to make myself respectable. Good luck to you all.'

He left quickly. Paula had the impression he was on the verge of getting emotional. As they finished their meal Monica was working away at her desk. She was checking the profiles again.

'Sharon Charlotte Mandeville,' she called out suddenly. 'Charlotte. I suppose she couldn't be Charlie.'

'Tweed thinks she is,' Paula replied. 'I'm not one hundred per cent certain.'

At precisely 10 a.m. two cars drove away from Park Crescent. In the lead car Paula was behind the wheel with Tweed by her side. In the back Newman relaxed, legs crossed as he gazed out of the window.

Behind them Marler drove the second car. Next to him sat Nield and in the back Butler sat very upright, scanning the traffic, looking frequently back through the rear window to see if there was any sign they were being followed. There wasn't.

'Thank you for letting me take the wheel,' Paula said as they left London behind.

'I thought it was your turn,' Tweed replied. 'And I know that you love driving. You realize you're humming a tune?'

'I know. It's such a lovely day. Not a cloud in the sky and the air is so crisp and fresh.'

'It will be a different atmosphere after dark,' Newman commented. 'Might be a bit too fresh for you, Paula.'

'Now don't you get fresh with her,' Tweed joked. 'I think she's safer with you in the back.'

'So she's safe with you in the front?'

'So far she is. I'm not making any promises about later.'

Tweed continued keeping up a bantering conversation. He knew that they wouldn't be able to avoid the growing tension once they had reached the Bunker. For as long as possible he wanted to create a holiday mood. The atmosphere changed when they were driving slowly through Parham.

'Sir Guy's village,' Paula recalled. 'And the poor chap will never again see Irongates. What guts – the way he offered his help when we were going on to the Black Forest. You know something? I could strangle the Phantom with my bare hands. And slowly.'

'He was a remarkable man,' agreed Tweed, 'both in his military career and in business. I share your sentiments, Paula.'

There was a brooding silence in the car as they continued on their way, south through Ashford, then the turn-off from the highway to Ivychurch. Paula had slowed down, was driving carefully as she negotiated the twists and turns of the narrow lanes.

She was approaching the farmhouse where the Bunker was located when she suddenly stopped, staring to her left. Tweed and Newman looked in the same direction.

'What is it?' Tweed asked.

'I think I saw something. Back in a minute.'

Before Tweed could protest she had jumped out of the car and plunged along a track leading to a large copse of evergreen trees, a rare sight on Romney Marsh. Newman dived out to follow her, his Smith & Wesson in his hand.

'What the hell are you doing?' he hissed as he caught up with her.

'I thought the sun flashed off something. Look.' She stopped. 'See where Alf parked all his cabs? That was clever. They can't be seen from the air.'

Newman stared. The cabs were arranged laager fashion, left in a small circle. All were sheltered from observation from the air under great evergreen spreading branches.

'No flies on Alf,' he said.

'I think he's a very astute man. Better get back to the car or Tweed will fret.'

Once inside the car, they told Tweed what they had found. He was intrigued. He agreed that Alf knew exactly what he was doing in any given situation. Paula lowered her window, switched off the engine. She had repeated this performance several times after leaving Parham behind.

'Why do you keep doing this?' Tweed enquired.

'Listening. For any sign of a chopper. Not a whisper. So we can drive on. We're nearly there.'

'I know,' Tweed said quietly.

She was crawling as the farmhouse came into view. Deliberately to give Mrs Carson time to observe them, then to open the automatic gate.

Tweed stared hard at the frmhouse. He kept his expression neutral to conceal his reaction. He spoke to himself without letting anyone hear a word.

'The battlefield.'

50

Paula was amazed by the complexity and the global reach of the communications system which had been created. Mrs Carson was taking her on a conducted tour. They had reached the underground rabbit warren of offices by first descending into the cellar beneath the farmhouse.

'We enter through here,' Mrs Carson explained.

She opened a slablike steel door and they entered a long tunnel. The concrete roof above them was arched, illumination was by a series of fluorescent tubes suspended from above. She opened one door and Paula peered inside. A large number of men in shirtsleeves sat behind computers and radio terminals. All wore earphones and most were scribbling like mad on yellow pads.

'Coded messages coming through from all over the world,' Mrs C. explained.

'I didn't see any masts with aerials when we arrived,' Paula commented.

'Wait till we get back upstairs. Alf and Marler have redesigned the whole reception before you got down to see us. Staggering what those two men – with helpers – achieved. This is the decoding room.'

She opened another door further along the corridor. Inside there were more men in shirtsleeves. They were working at desks with codebooks open while they deciphered messages, writing on more yellow pads.

Paula noticed that in both rooms no one had looked up when they stood in the doorways, such was the concentration on the work.

Mrs C. led Paula into another tunnel, running at right angles to the main one. Opening another door they peered inside a vast canteen. Paula recognized Mrs Payne, wearing whites and preparing large quantities of food. Guiding Paula further down the tunnel, Mrs C. opened yet another door. Beyond was a large, very clean and modern washroom.

'I think you've seen enough to give you the general idea,' Mrs C. decided. 'If you stay down here too long and you're not used to it you get a feeling of claustrophobia. And the rattle of the teleprinters gets on your nerves.'

'How can Mrs Payne possibly cope on her own?'

'She won't have to. Other cooks on the staff come on duty shortly. She was preparing lunch for you and the people who drove down in your two cars.'

'And all this converted out of what was once a major smugglers' haunt, ages ago.'

'Yes. And the main tunnel extended to close to the sea. They must have worked like madmen with the most primitive of tools.'

'Imagine the number of casks of brandy which must have travelled along these tunnels at one time.'

'Makes me feel tiddly just to think of it,' said Mrs C. leading them back into the farmhouse's cellar. 'Now I've shown you the system I can get back to reassembling my machine-pistol. I dismantled it this morning to clean it.'

'Machine-pistol?' Paula queried as they mounted the steps and arrived back in the farmhouse.

'Yes. Tweed phoned me earlier to warn me what's coming. It will be all hands to the pumps. I was trained by that nice man, Sarge, at the mansion in Surrey. Wonder why they call him Sarge?'

'He was a sergeant at one time, SAS I believe.'

Tweed sat drinking tea by himself at the large old wooden table in the living room. He put down his cup when they arrived.

'Well, Paula, what do you think?'

'They have much more space down there than in the second building they normally occupy in Park Crescent. Would it be an idea to keep them down here?'

'We're considering just that – if we survive tonight.'

'Of course we will,' scoffed Mrs C. 'We'll blow hell out of them.'

Paula stared at Mrs C. Plump-figured, her apple-cheeked face was smiling. She was actually looking forward to what was coming.

'I'll go now,' she said.

'Put your coat on,' called out Mrs C., disappearing into another room. 'It's pretty nippy out there.'

She must have eyes in the back of her head, Paula thought. She was slipping on her coat as she went out into the farmyard. Newman, standing at the entrance to a narrow passage between two old barns, beckoned to her. She followed him, emerged at the other end into the open. She gazed around. As on her previous visit, she thought she had never seen bleaker terrain.

To the south, until the ground belonging to the farm terminated at a hedge, the land was almost completely flat, covered with miserable tufts of grass. Like a desert, she said to herself. A chill wind, freezing her face, made her glad she'd taken Mrs C.'s advice.

'This way,' said Newman.

He was leading her to a copse of very tall leafless deciduous trees. Thick, black, skeletal branches extended out way above her. Marler was standing next to a large thigh-high wooden box which had a pyramid of thick wires over it. From the tip of the pyramid a pulley was attached. A cable, extended high up, was looped over two heavy branches, then its remaining length dropped to the ground. Marler was wearing motoring gloves.

'What on earth is all this?' Paula asked.

'Observation point. One of Alf's Gulf War veterans said we needed one. And that box he's standing by is like one of those cat's cradles window cleaners are suspended from to clean the windows of high buildings. Care for a ride up?'

'On my own? Who made the box?'

'Alf, with the help of Marler and some of Alf's men. When this place was built the builders left behind a workhouse complete with tools in one of those barns. And you won't be on your own. I'm coming up with you.'

Newman had a powerful pair of binoculars slung around his neck. From the pocket of his weather-proof jacket he produced Beck's mobile, loaned to him by Tweed. Marler had his own mobile suspended from his neck.

'Communication,' said Newman. 'All aboard.'

He helped her climb inside the cradle, then joined her. There was plenty of room for both of them. She heard Marler shout to one of Alf's men to come and give a hand. Hypnotized, she watched the two men, both with gloved hands, haul on the wire cable. She gripped the side of the cradle with both hands as it began its ascent. It moved upwards faster than she had anticipated, swayed a little. She gritted her teeth, refused to look down. Newman put an arm round her waist.

'Safe as houses.'

'I'll have to take your word for that.'

She experienced an unexpected change of mood as the ascent continued. As a vast panorama of Romney Marsh spread out she experienced a sense of exhilaration. They were very high up when their cradle stopped moving. She stared at a large wooden platform, constructed of wooden planks, situated between heavy branches.

'Time to disembark,' said Newman. 'Don't look down.'

He helped her to leave the cradle. Then she was standing on the platform. Her nervousness disappeared as she gazed into the distance.

'You can see far out into the Channel.'

'That's the idea. Like to use my binoculars? I'll hold on to you,' he said, clasping her round the waist.

'I can see a ship sailing up the Channel.' She focused the binoculars. 'I can read its name. The *Mexicali*. This is wonderful.'

'Get the idea?'

'We'll see them coming. No, it will be dark.'

'So we use night glasses. And we have communication.' He took out Beck's mobile. 'Marler, they're here.'

'*What?* Where!'

'Just joking.'

'Bob, don't do that again. I was about to raise a general alarm.'

'Sorry. That was stupid of me.' He looked at Paula. 'At least it proves the communication works. Time to go down.'

When they had climbed back into the cradle Newman called Marler on the mobile. The two men waiting on the ground released the wire cable from a large iron hook driven deep into the ground they had wrapped the end round. As it descended Paula noticed a thin black cable attached to the tree trunk. She pointed to it.

'What is that?'

'The cable from the underground complex up to a camouflaged aerial at the top of this tree. We had a normal thirty-foot mast sticking up out of the ground, thought it was too prominent, so we substituted that.'

'Clever.'

The cradle landed gently and Paula stepped out with Newman. She was surprised to realize her legs felt stiff. With tension, she assumed. They next showed her how to operate one of the compact mobile searchlights which manoeuvred easily on thick rubber tyres. At Newman's suggestion she aimed it at the copse of evergreens concealing the taxi cabs. She switched it on, was startled by the intensity of the device even in daylight. The evergreens glowed in the glare. She switched if off quickly. Mrs C. appeared.

'I've slowed down lunch,' she called out. 'You're busy. Tweed said he'd like you to join him. He's way over by the perimeter.'

It was quite a walk over the open ground but Paula welcomed it. A chance to stretch her legs, get them moving. Tweed stood, hands in his coat pockets, waiting for them.

'See anything wrong with this hedge?' he asked her.

'No,' she replied, after studying it. 'Just a very prickly hedge.'

'Very prickly,' he told her. 'We've entwined coils of barbed wire inside the whole length of hedge round the perimeter. The wire was painted the same colour as the twigs. Anyone trying to get through it will be ripped to pieces.'

'Diabolical,' she said.

'We're playing for keeps,' Tweed said grimly. 'Time for lunch, I'm sure. Let's get moving. I'm hungry again.'

The afternoon dragged by on sluggish legs. Waiting was always the worst part. Weapons had been distributed. Everyone was issued with a large shoulder-slung canvas holdall, packed with deadly material.

'I'll take a machine-pistol and extra ammo,' Paula said at one point to Newman.

'You've got your Browning and loads in the holdall.'

'Have you lost your memory, Bob? I used a machine-pistol back at Schluchsee to take out three thugs emerging from a side door of that *Psycho* house.'

Paula was given her machine-pistol. Unloading it, she went outside to practise, to get the feel of it again. In the late afternoon it was still a brilliantly sunny day. Tweed and Newman joined her, strolled across the flatlands.

Without warning a low-flying light aircraft appeared from the direction of the Channel. It swooped low over them, circled as Tweed looked up. Marler came running out, gripping his Armalite. The plane flew off inland, vanished.

'You think it was them?' Newman asked.

'I'm sure it was,' Tweed replied. 'Lucky you weren't up the tree, Marler, and that the mobile searchlights are hidden in a barn. So it won't help them – the fact that the passenger had a camera. I suggest we keep under cover inside the farmhouse.'

Night came suddenly like a black menace. Inside the farmhouse Mrs C. served supper at six o'clock. To her disappointment they ate only half of what was on their plates, except for Paula, who was famished again. By now they had all been issued with mobile phones which would be worn slung from their necks. The mobiles had special amplifiers, so everyone would hear what was said no matter how much noise was generated by weapon fire. The amplifiers had been designed by the boffins in the basement at Park Crescent weeks before.

'Don't forget,' Newman warned, 'that the whole perimeter is split up into sectors A, B, C, D, E, F and G.'

'That's the third time you've told us that,' Paula complained.

'I want you to remember it,' Newman told her.

'We ought to have had music to see us through the evening,' said Marler.

'What would you have suggested?' enquired Newman.

'The end of the *1812 Overture*. The crash of the guns.'

'I don't think that's funny,' snapped Paula.

'Wasn't meant to be,' Marler rapped back.

Tweed again checked his watch. He pursed his lips, glanced at everyone round the table.

'That's the fifth time you've checked the time,' said Paula.

'Who's counting?' Newman snapped back.

'I am.'

'It's nine o'clock,' Tweed said in a bored voice.

He had just spoken when Mike, one of Alf's Gulf War veterans, got up from the table. He put on a short sheepskin coat. His night glasses were slung round his neck.

'Time I went up that tree. It is the observation point. Come and haul me up to heaven.'

Newman and Marler stood up, accompanied Mike outside. Paula, on edge, frowned.

'He'll freeze to death up that tree. It's too early.

'Never too early,' said Alf, who rarely spoke. 'And he'll be all right. Once trained for three months in the Arctic.'

'I could put the radio on,' Mrs C. said brightly. 'That is, if anyone wants it on.'

No one wanted the radio. The silence was oppressive. But the radio squawking away would be even more irksome. Tweed again checked his watch. Paula bit her lip to stop herself protesting. With Tweed it was not nerves – he was probably the coolest person sitting at the table. But he knew how time could suddenly flash by.

Paula got up, went outside. The moon was high and brilliant she was thankful to see. They would need its pallid light to detect signs of movement. She took a deep

510

breath, almost felt giddy. The temperature had dropped below zero. She hurried inside again.

'What is it like out there?' Tweed asked casually. 'I know I could find out for myself, but why should both of us freeze?' he asked humorously.

'It's godawful cold. But the moon is up and casting plenty of light.'

'Couldn't be better. Just what I ordered from the weather man.'

'Any more coffee for anyone?' asked Mrs C.

'Have some, Paula,' Newman urged. 'Keep you alert.'

'For your information, *Mr* Newman, I have never felt more alert.'

'Suit yourself.'

'That's exactly what I propose to do. Thank you, Mrs Carson, but I've had enough for now.'

'It's fairly near ten o'clock,' Tweed announced, after checking his watch. 'Bob, could you describe again – for everyone's benefit – the small advanced landing craft your American friend showed you when you visited that naval base in the States six months ago?'

'Very hush-hush,' Newman began. 'Had to sign a document that under no circumstances would I publish anything. These vessels, for use by the SEALs, are about the size of a small country bus – but they have no roof. They're amphibious, very stable on water. But also when they reach land huge wheels like snow tyres project underneath the craft. Driver just pulls a lever. On land they can move at about forty miles an hour.'

'How many occupants?' asked Tweed.

'Maximum of ten SEALs per craft. Three doors on either side – so they can get out fast. On land the powerful engine makes a gentle purring sound.'

'We have to call them something,' Tweed said. He gazed into space. 'Got it. Something that's at home in water and on land. Crabs. That's what we'll call them.' He pressed a button on his mobile. 'Tweed here. If the enemy has landing craft we're going to call them crabs.'

'What's that?' Mike's voice queried. 'Got it. Crabs. Like the name, matey.'

He came back on the line less than five minutes later. A cool voice. Everyone had switched on their mobiles.

'They're coming now. Enormous ruddy fleet. Stretches back miles down the Channel. Wait a minute.' At the table they all sat upright in silence. 'Now I can just make out a ruddy great aircraft carrier, big as a football pitch. Hang on, one warship well ahead is turning this way, belting towards the coast at a rate of knots. Hang on a mo.' Round the table they seemed to wait forever this time. A crackle on the mobiles. 'Looks like they're coming for us now. Lowering crabs over the side Hang on.'

'How many crabs?' asked Tweed.

'Three in the sea now. I think that's it. Three crabs coming.'

'I suggest we all take up battle positions now,' said Tweed. 'Do not forget my earlier order. No one opens fire until – or unless – they start shooting at us, or try to break through the wired hedge. I want to be able to say later they opened hostilities first.'

'Matey, another crab lowered,' Mike warned. 'Following the first three heading for the shore now. Fast.'

'That's forty men,' Tweed said coldly. 'We're outnumbered. So the first shot they fire, we all open up. When we see a target.'

'Matey, another crab lowered over the side. Now following the others.'

'Fifty men, then,' Tweed said. 'Same instruction as before . . .'

512

51

Paula was first outside. She had slipped on her warm coat earlier while Mike was still talking. She wore surgical gloves. They'd keep out a bit of the cold, but she needed flexible fingers to press triggers. Over one shoulder hung her shoulder bag with her Browning inside, over the other was looped the heavy canvas holdall. She'd grabbed her machine-pistol and extra ammo off a couch.

Mrs C. followed her. She had the same equipment. She caught up with Paula and chuckled, brandishing her weapon.

'Used this to shoot rabbits. They were overrunning us. Men are bigger than rabbits. We're both Sector A.'

'Centre of the hedge where they'll probably attack,' Paula replied drily. 'Some kind of a compliment, I suppose.'

'I'll be with you,' said Newman as he joined them. 'Paula, you take A. You took your searchlight out there earlier?'

'Of course.'

They walked quickly across the flat earth, but refrained from running. With what they were carrying that could be fatal. Paula had lost her edginess. She was now cool, determined, alert. In the moonlight they could see the distant hedge they were advancing towards clearly. It had a blurred look at night, more like a wall. Paula revelled in the ice-cold air. It had become stuffy inside the farmhouse.

To their left and right shadowy silhouettes of men moving quickly were ahead of them. Alf's mob were swift on their feet. Hunched forward with the weights they were carrying, they reminded Paula of the opening scene in *Silas Marner*. There a shadowy figure moving through the night had been laden down.

'Rabbits,' said Newman, who had heard Mrs C.'s earlier remark. 'That means rabbit holes, risk of twisted ankles. We'd better be careful.'

'No need,' Mrs C. replied, moving quickly. 'They're all in that southeast corner – and beyond the hedge.'

Tweed was the only man who had not joined the relentless march to the southern hedge. After putting on his coat, he had gone out and climbed a wooden staircase Mrs C. had shown him. It was attached to the side of the farmhouse and led to a platform at the top. Standing on it, he could see clearly over the top of the roof. It did not give him the panoramic view from the observation post, but it did provide an uninterrupted view over the hedge and Romney Marsh beyond. He focused his night glasses on the hedge.

'Matey, four crabs landed on beach. Crossing it. Heading inland at speed towards us. Crab number five now beaching . . .'

'Everyone,' said Tweed into the mobile slung close to his mouth, 'get into position as soon as you can. You heard the latest report. Keep your heads down.'

Tweed, who normally mistrusted mobiles, thought the communication system was excellent. Everyone could hear him. Everyone could hear the reports from the observation post. Knowledge was power. Could make all the difference to the outcome.

'Matey, four crabs approaching. Number five coming up behind. Fast.'

Tweed refocused his glasses to see a low ridge on the marsh. Within a minute he saw four of the strange vehicles poking their snouts over the ridge. They came over it. They were advancing towards Sectors A. B and

C. A frontal attack. Just like the Americans. Get up and go.

'Matey, count ten men in each crab. Number five a weirdo. Seems only to have the driver. No other men aboard it.'

Tweed frowned. He could see No. 5 now. Heading for the centre of the hedge. The first four crabs stopped suddenly. About one hundred feet from the hedge. Large men, uniformed, wearing helmets, jumped out from the four stationary crabs, spreading out, weapons gripped in their hands. No. 5 continued advancing, stopped no more than thirty feet from the hedge. What the devil was its purpose?

'Everyone in position?' Tweed asked into his mobile.

'Yes ... Yes ... Yes ...'

The stream of replies continued. Paula's voice first, Mrs C.'s next, then a jumble as confirmations overlaid each other. Tweed was satisfied that everyone was where they should be. He spoke into his mobile.

'They've left their crabs. Forty men advancing. Objective appears to be Sectors A, B and C. Close in on those sectors.'

Any moment now, he thought. Would the invaders open fire? Or would they try to keep advancing through the hedge? He couldn't guess this one.

Sharon was driving the limo at manic speed. She had just left Ashford behind. She accelerated. The speedometer climbed. By her side Denise Chatel was petrified. She crouched back in her seat. Sharon sat very erect.

'Where are we going?' Denise asked.

'To check that a key installation has been destroyed.'

'What key installation?'

'Shut your stupid mouth.'

515

'But where are we going?' Denise repeated.

'If you want to gab, we'll gab. For starters, how did you get hold of that file I found you reading?'

'You sent me to fetch you a file. I must have picked up the wrong one.'

'Crap.'

'It was all about the investigation into my father's death in a so-called car crash in Virginia.'

'It was a red file.'

'I found it on your desk.'

'You're lying. Most of my files are green. The one I sent you to get was on my desk. You poked your nose into my filing cabinet. I'd forgotten to lock it. That red file was in front of the cabinet.'

'I don't know what you're talking about. And I did read some of that file, which reported doubts as to whether the so-called car crash was an accident.'

'You shut your mouth! If I didn't need both hands for the wheel I'd slap your idiotic face. And,' Sharon sneered, 'you've no idea how stupid you look in that riding outfit.'

'You wouldn't give me time to change. Look out!'

Sharon had swung off the highway where a signpost pointed to Ivychurch. Before leaving she had attached to the dashboard a map showing the route to the Bunker, a map radioed to her from Washington. Instead of a main road, she was now driving along a winding lane at speed. Denise had called out because as they rounded a bend a single light rushed towards them. The motor-cyclist was only moving at thirty miles an hour. Before Sharon could brake the limo swept past, its side brushing the motorcycle. The machine toppled over, hurling the rider into a ditch. Denise just had time to stare back – to see the inert body in the ditch, the machine on its side, its wheels still revolving futilely.

516

'We may have killed him,' Denise gasped.

'Killed who?'

'That motorcyclist you hit.'

'What motorcyclist are you talking about? Must be your imagination. I haven't seen anyone.'

'You're dangerous.'

'Don't talk to me like that,' Sharon responded, her voice and her expression now very calm.

The eerie silence of the night on the Romney Marsh was broken only by a single eerie sound. The purring of the engines which had not been turned off, the engines of the motionless crabs. To Paula it sounded like the purring of some monstrous and evil cat. She was crouched down, as were all the others. She had no idea what was happening and the tension was growing.

It was broken by one powerful shout of one word. She thought the American accent was Texan.

'Barrage!'

The night came apart. A thunderous fusillade of gunfire coming from automatic weapons shot at the same moment caused her to press her head into the earth. The commander of the invading SEALs was a Texan. He was also not a man to take any chances – even though there was no sign of life from the invisible installation. It was the American way – equivalent to the battleships far out at sea which had once bombarded the Vietnam jungle, killing no one.

The fusillade had been aimed at the middle of the fields beyond the farmhouse. The rain of bullets spurted up tufts of grass, pellets of soil. The barrage, deafening, continued for a short time, then stopped as abruptly as it had started. The SEALs were reloading.

From his platform Tweed observed all this, realized

that there had been no casualties among his own troops, who were too far forward. He spoke quickly into his mobile.

'Shoot any target you can see.'

Marler, stationed in Sector C, to Paula's right, aimed his Armalite. A heavily built SEAL, confident he could take on anybody, swaggered forward as he reloaded his automatic rifle. Marler's bullet hit him dead centre in the chest. The SEAL stopped, let out a strangled yell, dropped, lay still.

Alf aimed his automatic rifle at two SEALs standing too close together. He fired twice. Both men sank to the ground. Then a fresh fusillade was let loose, aimed at the same area as its predecessor. More grass tufts, more soil jumped into the air. Tweed spoke again.

'Wait till they've stopped . . .'

The Texan commander, who believed in barrages, as opposed to any individual shooting, waited for his men to reload. One six-foot SEAL had had enough. The guys should be breaking through the friggin' hedge. He had reloaded quickly. Now he ran forward, plunged into and across the hedge. His body fell onto the hedge, onto the concealed barbed wire. He screamed, then stopped moving.

Mrs C., close to Paula, saw an even taller, heavier SEAL rushing forward. He'd realized he could use the prone body as a bridge. Mrs C. hissed at Paula.

'Use your searchlight. Quick.'

A second SEAL followed the first, with the same idea in mind – they had a bridge. Paula swivelled the light, aimed it just above the prone body, now dripping blood. The incredibly powerful glare shone at the moment the first SEAL was treading on the body, standing upright. Mrs C. let rip with her machine-pistol. The SEAL remained upright briefly, his arms shot up, releasing his

518

weapon, which curved in an arc, landing on the far side of the hedge. Mrs C. continued blasting, bullets thudded into the second SEAL. The first SEAL toppled over backwards as the SEAL behind him staggered, moved a few steps as though drunk, then sagged to the ground.

'Barrage!' roared the Texan.

'Cease fire for a moment,' Tweed ordered.

'Barrage!' shouted the Texan.

This new fusillade came closer, but it was still a dozen yards beyond where the defenders lay still. Three more SEALs, who had ignored their commander's order, rushed forward, guns blazing, to use the prone body as a bridge. Mrs C.'s machine-pistol chattered as they ran into the glare of Paula's searchlight. All three fell beyond the hedge, tumbling on top of each other.

On his platform, Tweed was intrigued by the motionless crab – No. 5. Then it struck him what it might contain. He spoke.

'Marler, bomb that forward crab. Everybody flatten yourselves.'

Paula glanced to her right as Marler glanced at her. While he felt in his holdall for a grenade with his right hand he saluted her with his left hand, grinning. She nodded her head, acknowledging. Then she wriggled herself a couple of yards closer to Mrs C. She was moving away from the glaring searchlight, an obvious target.

She glanced sideways again at Marler, realizing he'd had something in his left hand when he'd saluted. It was a wide-mouthed short-barrelled pistol. She had forgotten the star shells.

As the fresh fusillade died away Butler and Nield, both holding machine-pistols, suddenly stood up. Marler waited. Beyond the hedge four SEALs, not too far apart, were reloading. Nield and Butler opened fire, swinging their weapons slightly. All of the four SEALs dropped, lay still. Marler watched Butler and Nield as they kissed the earth, waited. This was the moment.

Marler jumped to his feet. His right arm, holding the grenade, swung in a high arc, then he flattened himself. In the glare of Paula's searchlight Tweed saw, from his platform, the grenade land inside crab No. 5. A second later Paula's searchlight went out, hit by a SEAL's bullet.

Synchronizing with the flight of the grenade, Marler began firing star shells, his body still flat with the earth. White, and then green bursts, illuminated the scene from high up. The grenade detonated. The world went wild. The crab burst as a tremendous explosion echoed across the marsh. Tweed saw between ten and fifteen SEALs hurled into the air, thrown sideways over the marsh. Where the crab had been was a deep hole. The star shell illumination was blotted out by the flash of the explosion.

As Tweed had guessed, No. 5 had been filled with explosives intended for the destruction of the complex. More star shells burst high above the marsh, green, red and white. They showed Tweed a scene of utter devastation. Bodies lay everywhere. A few injured SEALs staggered, limped towards the two crabs still intact, their engines still purring, the only sound in a sudden deathly hush.

Tweed, who had been counting enemy casualties as far as he was able to, estimated more than half the enemy's attack force had been wiped out. Men were carrying injured comrades towards the remaining two undamaged crabs. There were no more shouts from the Texan commander – if he was still alive. Tweed watched for a few minutes longer. There was no more sign of aggression on the part of the SEALs. Those who had survived were concentrating on limping, hobbling, dragging themselves to board one of the intact crabs. Other SEALs, who had taken no punishment, were carrying their injured and dead comrades to the second intact crab.

'Cease fire,' Tweed ordered. 'Marler, shout at the top of your voice the two words I just uttered.'

'*Cease fire!*' Marler bellowed.

His words galvanized the mood of the enemy. The SEALs moved more quickly, more confidently. Two came up to the hedge, began wrestling free the prone SEAL impaled on the wire. Paula turned her head away. When she looked again the body had gone but that part of the hedge was tainted a dark red colour.

The next sound she heard was an increase in the purring noise of the crabs' engines. From his platform Tweed saw the two crabs turn round, start to move away, circumnavigating the enormous hole left when crab No. 5 had blown up. Tweed still waited to be sure. The crabs disappeared beyond the slight ridge.

'Matey, they're going home, heading for the beach and then their mother ship.'

'Everyone return to base – with your equipment,' Tweed ordered.

Tweed, Paula and Newman stood on their own in the open air a little distance from the farmhouse. Everyone else had gone down into the washroom under the farmhouse. Mrs C. was the last to leave.

'Well at least the staff stayed under ground, as they were ordered to. Think I'll go down and reassure them. They must have felt and heard the explosion when that ammunition dump inside the crab went up.'

'Good idea,' said Tweed.

'I think I'd sooner stay out here in the fresh air for a bit,' Paula said.

'Me too,' Newman agreed.

'Sensible,' said Tweed. 'After a period of tension –

mental and physical – it helps to have a period of relaxation. Doing nothing, saying nothing.'

They stood quietly. No one spoke. A couple of times Paula walked a few paces backwards and forwards to stretch her stiff legs. For once she welcomed the dead silence of Romney Marsh. It was peace. Then her mouth tightened.

'I can hear a car coming at speed. Not more, please.'

A black stretch limo, with Sharon behind the wheel, braked with an emergency stop, inches from the closed gate. Newman sighed, ran to the farmhouse, reached inside the front door, pressed the switch which opened the gate. He ran back outside. Sharon was turning the car, ended up with it pointing back to London. Then she alighted, walked towards them.

She was wearing a mink coat and slung from her right shoulder was the largest white leather handbag Paula had ever seen. It was like a huge envelope. Paula blinked as Denise followed her. She was still clad in riding kit. Most peculiar. Her knee-length boots gleamed in the moonlight. To Paula, the silence suddenly seemed menacing as Sharon continued walking towards them. She stopped about fifteen feet from them.

'What brings you down here, Charlie?' Tweed began.

'*Charlie!*' gasped Denise.

'Yes, Charlie,' replied Sharon, moving a few paces, putting space between herself and Denise. 'My middle name's Charlotte, as Tweed was clever enough – and foolish enough – to discover. Don't you reach for that gun, Newman,' she snapped.

As she spoke, Sharon's right hand emerged from her handbag holding a Magnum revolver. Paula gazed at the large weapon, surprised that Sharon's small hand could level it so easily. She swivelled it in an arc between Tweed, Paula and Newman, covering them all.

'Spread out your hands,' she screamed suddenly.

'Well away from your bodies – or I'll shoot you in the stomachs. You'll take a long painful time to die. Such a long-painful time . . .'

They spread their hands, stretched them outwards. To Paula the end of the Magnum's muzzle looked like the mouth of a cannon.

'The report in that red file said my father was killed on the orders of Charlie,' Denise screeched.

Sharon slipped closer to Denise. With a movement almost too quick to follow she slashed at Denise's face with the barrel of her gun. Denise moved her head quickly. The barrel barely scraped her but she slipped on a smooth stone, toppled backwards, saved her head striking the ground with her hands. Then she sat there, her right leg turned at an awkward angle.

'I've twisted my leg,' she yelped, rubbing her boot with one hand.

'Stay down there,' Sharon snarled. 'A twisted leg won't kill you. I will.'

The Magnum had instantly been swivelled back to cover the trio with outstretched hands. She's quick, too damned quick for me to haul out my Smith & Wesson, Newman thought. Before I grabbed the butt all three of us would be dead. Sharon knew exactly what she was doing. She stood too far away to be rushed, but near enough to shoot them all.

'I'll ask you again, Charlie,' Tweed said quietly. 'What brought you down here?'

'To make sure your bloody stupid communications centre has been destroyed.'

'It hasn't. The Americans who tried it are on their way back to their task force ship, those who survived.'

'You're lying! You always lie! Damn your soul to hell, Tweed,' she went on screaming with fury. 'You always lie, you friggin' little nobody! You're trying to trick me. Me! Of all people!'

Newman simply gazed at her in disbelief. An extraordinary transformation had taken place. Her face was so contorted with insane rage she was hardly recognizable. Jekyll had become Hyde. She suddenly moved sideways on to a small elevated piece of ground. It gave her greater command of the situation. Denise, moaning, still sitting, was rubbing her hand over the boot on her twisted leg.

'You said, Charlie,' Tweed remarked, 'a moment ago, "Me! Of all people!" Where do you think you're going? As President in the Oval Office?' he suggested sarcastically.

'That's exactly where I'm going, you not-so-clever little nobody! You think I'm going to let any of you stop me? You'll all be dead and buried while I'm starting my campaign to be senator. I won't let any of you get in my way! Hear me! I won't!'

Her face was still hideously contorted, still hardly recognizable. She kept swivelling the Magnum to cover them. She was breathing deeply now, working herself up to press the trigger.

'You killed my dear father,' Denise bleated.

'Sure I gave the order to waste your late father. Another friggin' nobody who was getting in my way. Nobody gets in my way and survives!'

Paula had dropped her eyes briefly. The mound Sharon stood on had a rusty grating like a drain cover. She raised her eyes quickly. Tweed had glanced at Denise's right hand. It was levering something from inside her boot.

'Can't we compromise in some way, Sharon?' he suggested.

'So it's gone back to Sharon now, has it? You're trembling in your shoes, aren't you, Tweed! And with good reason!'

Distracted by her venom for Tweed, Sharon had

forgotten Denise for the moment. Jerking her hand out of the boot, Denise aimed, fired the .22 Beretta at random. The bullet hit Sharon in the thigh. She gasped, dropped the Magnum, clutched her side. The weight of the weapon, added to Sharon's, caused the grating to crumble. The ground gave way under her. She started falling into the pit the grating had covered. She screamed like an animal in terror. Marler came running out from the farmhouse at that moment.

Only her head and shoulders were visible. Her hands clawed desperately at the edges, digging into the soil. She screamed again.

'Help me! *Help me!* HELP . . .'

The earth she was clutching at with both hands crumbled. Blonde hair vanished. There was a hellish scream, which faded quickly. Like a dying echo. Huge quantities of earth gave way, plunged downwards.

'Any chance she's alive?' Tweed asked.

'No chance at all,' Marler replied. 'It's an eighty-foot drop down those old ventilation shafts. And the builders sealed all of them up at the bottom with two feet of concrete.'

'Plus all that earth going down. There must have been over a ton of it.'

'At least.'

'Bob,' Tweed requested, 'take that Beretta from Denise. Clean off her fingerprints, then throw it down the hole. The Magnum went with her.'

'There are spare new steel gratings in the workshop,' Marler said. 'Alf will help me to cover up that hole. It's dangerous.'

'And, Bob,' Tweed went on as Newman, holding the Beretta with a handkerchief, tossed it down, 'maybe you'd take Denise to see a doctor.'

'Won't be necessary,' Denise intervened, standing up straight. 'I just pretended my leg was twisted. Easier for me to get my hands on the Beretta. I brought it to kill her, but she was driving so fast.'

'Then maybe you'd take her back to her Belgravia flat, Bob.' Tweed turned to Denise. 'This never happened. You've never been here. You went straight home on your own from the Embassy.'

Epilogue

It was early morning in London. Some time after dawn the sky was once more a cloudless blue. Very little traffic at that early hour. This time Marler, with Butler and Nield, had taken the lead car, had gone on ahead.

Newman, behind the wheel, slowed to a crawl as he approached the entrance to Park Crescent. Tweed was beside him, with Paula in the back. Newman turned the corner into Park Crescent, driving at no miles per hour. He continued crawling forward. The left-hand side of the windscreen was blurred with mist. The shot pierced the glass, the windscreen crackled. The passenger by his side slumped.

Stopping the car, Newman jumped out. A second rifle shot rang out. Paula, crouched down a few seconds earlier, had left the car, followed by the man who had crouched beside her. They were just in time to see the figure perched on the roof above their entrance rear up, as though subjected to a high-voltage electric charge. Then the figure plunged down vertically, landing on the steps leading up.

'Not on my doorstep,' said Tweed, running forward with Paula.

Newman had got there first. He waited for them. The body of a man wearing a balaclava lay very still. Newman bent down, checked the neck pulse, shook his head. He then took hold of the balaclava, gently pulled it back to reveal the face.

Rupert Strangeways stared up at them, the eyes open, the mouth twisted. Paula had the grisly impression he was sneering at them. Newman stepped back as Marler, who had raced round the Crescent, arrived.

'And I thought it was Basil,' said Paula. 'The Phantom.'

'Good shot,' said Newman.

Marler's bullet, fired from his Armalite, had made a smudged red hole in Rupert's forehead. George, their doorkeeper and guard, came out of the front door. He stared down.

'My Gawd, who is that?'

'A phantom,' said Tweed. 'Cover it with a sheet. We don't want passers-by gawking.' He ran upstairs, with Paula at his heels. 'I must phone Roy Buchanan at once, ask him to send an ambulance.'

Inside his office he stared at the empty desk on his left. The cover was still on Monica's computer, her chair pushed under her desk.

'Where is Monica?'

Paula picked up a hastily scribbled note. It was an apology from Monica. Despite her allergy to shellfish, she'd indulged in a shrimp cocktail for supper. It had upset her and she wouldn't be in for the day.

'I'll call Buchanan, explain the position,' she said. 'And I'll sit at Monica's desk, look after the phone today.'

A few minutes later Newman and Marler came in. Newman sat down while he explained.

'Marler and I think it best to leave the car you travelled up in where it is until Buchanan arrives. Then he can see the dummy Tweed for himself. Rupert's bullet would have hit you in your head – if you'd been sitting beside me. The bullet penetrated the dummy and is lodged in the padded head rest I reinforced.'

They had created the dummy to look like Tweed before leaving the Bunker. Mrs C. had helped – supplying pillows to pad out a jacket she had borrowed from one of the staff. The upper part of the top pillow had been squeezed into the size of a head. Marler had provided a pair of horn-rimmed glasses with plain lenses he'd used in the past for disguise. Mrs C. had used safety pins to attach the glasses to where Tweed's eyes would have been. As a final precaution, Newman had carried Mrs C.'s hair spray. He had stopped the car a short distance before they reached Park Crescent, had used the hair spray on the dummy's side of the windscreen to blur the image.

'Well, it worked,' said Marler. 'And we were right in thinking the Phantom would be waiting for Tweed's arrival here. Now, I'm going up to my office.'

'Now, I'll make us all some coffee,' said Paula.

Buchanan, with Sergeant Warden, his wooden-faced assistant, was standing in Tweed's office fifteen minutes later. Looking out of the window, Paula saw two men carrying a stretcher with the body covered with a sheet. They hoisted it inside an ambulance.

Buchanan listened without interruption while Tweed and Newman explained what had happened. They kept their statements terse and made no reference to either Sharon or Denise.

'Marler is waiting in his office upstairs,' Tweed went on, 'so you can take a statement from him.'

'I prefer it that way,' Buchanan agreed. 'Having a separate interview with him. I have only one question. Who fired first?'

'Rupert Strangeways did,' Newman confirmed. 'Marler will tell you he was crouched with his Armalite behind his parked car. It was only when he saw the muzzle flash from Strangeways' shot that he located where he was.'

'Glad you left the Tweed dummy in the other car,' Buchanan said. 'Before we go and have a word with Marler we'll take a look at that, then leave a couple of policemen on guard. We'll get moving.' He paused by the door before opening it. 'Tweed, you'd like to know, I'm sure, that bullet I sent by courier to René Lasalle not only matches the bullet which killed our late PM, it also matches the bullet which killed that German, Heinz Keller. Otto Kuhlmann, your friend and the police chief from Wiesbaden, happened to be visiting Lasalle. He brought the Keller bullet. That also matches. Rupert Strangeways was not only a hired hit man – he was also a mass-murderer.'

'It's dreadful,' Paula said when the policeman had gone, 'when we realize Rupert also murdered his own father in Freiburg.'

'As cold and greedy as they come,' replied Tweed. 'Doubtless he hoped to inherit his father's fortune. I have a feeling he would have done no such thing when the will is read. Changing the subject, I think Denise will keep quiet.'

'She promised me she would off her own bat when we left her at that flat in Belgravia,' said Paula.

She was referring to the fact that they had driven back from the Bunker in three cars. Wearing gloves – to avoid fingerprints – Newman had driven the stretch limo, with Denise by his side. In the car following him, Tweed was behind the wheel with Paula and Newman as passengers. Behind them, Marler had driven the third car, which contained Butler and Nield.

There had been no one about when Newman dropped off Denise at her Belgravia flat. He had then driven the limo to Mayfair and, unseen, had parked it in a mews. He had then transferred to the car with the dummy while Tweed and Paula had crouched low in the rear.

Howard then stormed into the office, his normal self. Wearing a grey Chester Barrie suit, he was freshly shaved, pink-faced and with neatly brushed hair. He assumed his favourite position, sitting in an armchair, one leg perched over an arm.

530

'Sensational news from Washington. Morgenstern has resigned as Secretary of State. His action has hit the States like a thunderbolt. He's holding a press conference later today.'

'That's due to Tweed's final interview with him,' Paula said.

'Really?' Howard stared at her before going on. 'And thank you, Tweed, for calling me on your mobile on your way back here in the car. Just afterwards Philip, your naval pal at the MoD, phoned me. That American task force has left the Channel, is steaming back at a rate of knots towards the States. Another sensation. A rumour is circulating the US that a SEALs landing exercise went horribly wrong. Dummy ammunition should have been issued. SEALs were divided into two forces, one attack, one defence. But the ammo issued was the real thing, due to some cock-up. SEALs have twenty-five dead. Combined with Morgenstern's action, all hell has broken loose.' Howard jumped up. 'Must go. Tweed, we will have lunch at my club.'

Paula had answered the phone just before Howard finished. She waited until he had left, her expression bleak.

'Tweed, you have visitors downstairs. Ed Osborne and Chuck Venacki. What shall I do?'

Newman reached inside his jacket. He was grabbing his Smith & Wesson.

'Don't do that, Bob,' said Tweed. 'Paula, ask them to come up.'

Ed Osborne entered, quietly and smiling. Behind him Chuck Venacki was also smiling. Tweed stood up, shook their hands, invited them to sit down.

'Everyone here,' he began as he sat down, 'must treat what they listen to as top secret for ever. Meet Ed Osborne who, as far as he could, kept me informed about what Ronstadt was up to.'

531

'My mother was English,' Ed said, his manner now pleasant. 'So I always had a soft spot for this country, totally disagreed with their plan. But the man you should thank is Chuck Venacki, my confidant. He put his life on the line, travelling round with Jake Ronstadt, keeping me in touch when he could.'

'We have you both to thank,' said Tweed.

'That's nice. I can't linger. Felt I just had to come over to see you. Washington is in a state of chaos. The Ambassador here has been recalled – he'll be replaced. And I'm resigning as Deputy Director of the CIA. There's a new director at Langley. Old friend of Cord Dillon's. Guess who's going to get my job.' He stood up. 'Great to see you all survived.' He went round, shook everyone by the hand. 'Take care. I'm off with Chuck.'

'I'm staggered,' Paula said when they had gone. 'But I suspected you had someone on the inside. Incidentally, who was the Phantom's paymaster?'

'Paymistress. Sharon, I'm sure. She must have disguised her voice, phoned Rupert about the targets. She'd guard her identity.'

'And I've wondered about a coincidence. Sharon's parents were killed in a car crash. Years later poor Denise's parents are killed in a car crash on the same bridge.'

'I'm sure Sharon gave orders for Denise's father to be murdered by staging a fake collision on that same old bridge in Virginia. The bridge would linger in her memory as a place where accidents did happen. Never prove it, of course.'

'Another thing,' Paula went on. 'Monica struggled like mad to fill in those mysterious gaps in Ed Osborne's life. She never could find out where Osborne was when he seemed to disappear off the face of the earth for longish periods. Where on earth was he during those long disappearances?'

'That,' said Tweed, 'is something I'd decided to apol-

532

ogize for to Monica. During those gaps he was working for me, so any record was carefully erased. So, that's it. Although I do have one more problem.'

'What's that?' enquired Newman.

'Paula,' Tweed pleaded, 'can you think of some way I can decently avoid that lunch with Howard? I can't stand the food at his club. And I can't stand the other members – they sit there like waxworks.'